# Wintersong

ALSO BY S. JAE-JONES

*Shadowsong*

# Wintersong

## S. JAE-JONES

WEDNESDAY BOOKS
NEW YORK

WINTERSONG. Copyright © 2017 by S. Jae-Jones. All rights reserved. Printed in the United States of America. For information, address St. Martin's Press, 175 Fifth Avenue, New York, N.Y. 10010.

www.wednesdaybooks.com
www.stmartins.com

Hand-lettering and title page art courtesy of the author

Designed by Anna Gorovoy

The Library of Congress has cataloged the hardcover edition as follows:

Names: Jae-Jones, S. author
Title: Wintersong / S. Jae-Jones.
Description: First edition. | New York : Thomas Dunne Books,
    St Martin's Press, 2016.
Identifiers: LCCN 2016013865 | ISBN 9781250079213 (hardcover) |
    ISBN 9781466892040 (ebook)
Subjects: LCSH: Imaginary places—Fiction. | GSAFD: Fantasy fiction |
    Adventure fiction
Classification: LCC PS3610.A35694 W56 2016 | DDC 813/.6—dc23
LC record available at https://lccn.loc.gov/2016013865

ISBN 978-1-250-15736-2 (trade paperback)

Our books may be purchased in bulk for promotional, educational, or business use. Please contact your local bookseller or the Macmillan Corporate and Premium Sales Department at 1-800-221-7945, extension 5442, or by email at MacmillanSpecialMarkets@macmillan.com.

First Wednesday Books Edition: February 2018

10  9  8  7  6  5  4

For 할머니,
for being the best fairy-tale grandmother
of all time
사랑해.

# ACKNOWLEDGMENTS

When my editor first asked me if I wanted to include acknowledgments in my book, I immediately said, "Sure! Absolutely!" without necessarily thinking just what an impossible task that would be. In many ways, writing acknowledgments was a lot harder than writing the whole of *Wintersong*. Who do I include? What if I forget to include someone? WHAT IF I INADVERTENTLY OFFEND SOMEONE POWERFUL WITH THE ABILITY TO MAKE OR BREAK MY BOOK? So, in order to cover my bases, I am hereby issuing a blanket statement of gratitude to anyone and everyone who has read, worked on, touched, or even looked at my book: Thank you so, so very much. Your help and support mean so much more than you could ever know.

I've never been particularly good with thanks, either giving or receiving, but I would be remiss if I didn't single out those who have been my most staunch and stalwart champions, starting with the person who asked if I wanted to write these acknowledgments in the first place.

To my editor, Jennifer Letwack, who was my first and best champion in-house, the person who saw potential in this strange in-between manuscript and stuck with it through category changes and other unexpected turns in this crazy roller-coaster ride we call publishing. Thanks for not (letting me know just how much you were) panicking when I turned in a draft with an entirely different ending or a completely different prologue than expected, or any other time I've come back to you with "But how about . . . ?" Many thanks as well to Karen Masnica and Brittani Hilles for being early enthusiasts of *Wintersong* (and fellow fans of *Labyrinth*), to Danielle Fiorella for the amazing cover (and letting me have input!), to Anna Gorovoy for the beautiful design (and letting me contribute my own artwork!), and to Melanie Sanders for guiding the book through production.

To Katelyn Detweiler, my agent and partner-in-arms, my tireless advocate and adviser, a super-talented writer in her own right. You were the absolute first person to take a chance on me, and you never flinched or let your belief in *Wintersong* flag, even when the industry didn't know what to do with us. Here's to many more books in our future! Also to Jill Grinberg, Cheryl Pientka, Denise St. Pierre, and everyone at Jill Grinberg Literary Management, thank you so much for all your support.

To my writer friends Marie Lu, Renee Ahdieh, and Roshani Chokshi, thank you so much for the advice, the cocktails, and the commiseration, for letting me kvetch and pull my hair out over email and in person, and for being my emotional bedrock throughout this entire journey. Thanks also to Kate Elliott and Charlie N. Holmberg for your kind words about *Wintersong;* yours were the first words of praise outside my friends, family, and paid sycophants (I kid, I kid), and I am extremely grateful for them.

Every writer needs a support network to keep them sane, so shout-out to Sarah Lemon, Beth Revis, Carrie Ryan, all my co-contributors at Pub(lishing) Crawl, and my fellow Swankys—but especial kudos to Kelly Van Sant and Vicki Lame for being there for me every day on Google Hangouts and talking me off whatever ledge I've wandered close to. My friends in New York, LA, and North Carolina, all the places I've called home, thank you, thank you, thank you.

Last but not least, my eternal love and gratitude to my family. To Sue Mi, Michael, and Taylor Jones for supporting and believing in the black sheep of the SoCal Jones clan; to my Halmeoni for her unconditional love and prayers; and of course, to Bear. Who knows, maybe one day you'll be able to make good on your promise to your colleagues to quit and become a poker-playing kept man should *Wintersong* become successful. Let's keep dreaming.

# Overture

**O**nce there was a little girl who played her music for a little boy in the wood. She was small and dark, he was tall and fair, and the two of them made a fancy pair as they danced together, dancing to the music the little girl heard in her head.

Her grandmother had told her to beware the wolves that prowled in the wood, but the little girl knew the little boy was not dangerous, even if he was the king of the goblins.

*Will you marry me, Elisabeth?* the little boy asked, and the little girl did not wonder at how he knew her name.

*Oh,* she replied, *but I am too young to marry.*

*Then I will wait,* the little boy said. *I will wait as long as you remember.*

And the little girl laughed as she danced with the Goblin King, the little boy who was always just a little older, a little out of reach.

As the seasons turned and the years passed, the little girl grew older but the Goblin King remained the same. She washed the dishes, cleaned the floors, brushed her sister's hair, yet still ran to the forest to meet her old friend in the grove. Their games were different now, truth and forfeit and challenges and dares.

*Will you marry me, Elisabeth?* the little boy asked, and the little girl did not yet understand his question was not part of a game.

*Oh,* she replied, *but you have not yet won my hand.*

*Then I will win,* the little boy said. *I will win until you surrender.*

And the little girl laughed as she played against the Goblin King, losing every hand and every round.

Winter turned to spring, spring to summer, summer into autumn, autumn back into winter, but each turning of the year grew harder and harder as the little girl grew up while the Goblin King remained the same. She washed the dishes, cleaned the floors, brushed her sister's hair, soothed her brother's fears, hid her father's purse, counted the coins, and no longer went into the woods to see her old friend.

*Will you marry me, Elisabeth?* the Goblin King asked.

But the little girl did not reply.

# Part I

## THE GOBLIN MARKET

*We must not look at goblin men,*
*We must not buy their fruits:*
*Who knows upon what soil they fed*
*Their hungry, thirsty roots?*

—CHRISTINA ROSSETTI,
*Goblin Market*

## BEWARE THE
## GOBLIN MEN

**b**eware the goblin men," Constanze said. "And the wares they sell."

I jumped when my grandmother's shadow swept across my notes, scattering my thoughts and foolscap along with it. I scrambled to cover my music, shame shaking my hands, but Constanze hadn't been addressing me. She stood perched on the threshold, scowling at my sister, Käthe, who primped and preened before the mirror in our bedroom—the only mirror in our entire inn.

"Listen well, Katharina." Constanze pointed a gnarled finger at my sister's reflection. "Vanity invites temptation, and is the sign of a weak will."

Käthe ignored her, pinching her cheeks and fluffing her curls. "Liesl," she said, reaching for a hat on the dressing table. "Could you come help me with this?"

I put my notes back into their little lockbox. "It's a market,

Käthe, not a ball. We're just going to pick up Josef's bows from Herr Kassl's."

"Liesl," Käthe whined. "Please."

Constanze harrumphed and thumped the floor with her cane, but my sister and I paid her no heed. We were used to our grandmother's dour and direful pronouncements.

I sighed. "All right." I hid the lockbox beneath our bed and rose to help pin the hat to Käthe's hair.

The hat was a towering confection of silk and feathers, a ridiculous affectation, especially in our little provincial village. But my sister was also ridiculous, so she and the hat were well matched.

"Ouch!" Käthe said as I accidentally jabbed her with a hatpin. "Watch where you stick that thing."

"Learn to dress yourself, then." I smoothed down my sister's curls and settled her shawl so that it covered her bare shoulders. The waist of her gown was gathered high beneath her bosom, the simple lines of her dress showing every curve of her figure. It was, Käthe claimed, the latest fashion in Paris, but my sister seemed scandalously unclothed to my eyes.

"Tut." Käthe preened before her reflection. "You're just jealous."

I winced. Käthe was the beauty of our family, with sunshine hair, summer-blue eyes, apple-blossom cheeks, and a buxom figure. At seventeen, she already looked like a woman full-grown, with a small waist and generous hips that her new dress showed off to great advantage. I was nearly two years older but still looked like a child: small, thin, and sallow. *The little hobgoblin,* Papa called me. *Fey,* was Constanze's pronouncement. Only Josef ever called me beautiful. *Not pretty,* my brother would say. *Beautiful.*

"Yes, I'm jealous," I said. "Now, are we going to the market or not?"

"In a bit." Käthe rummaged through her box of trinkets. "What do you think, Liesl?" she asked, holding up a few lengths of ribbon. "Red or blue?"

"Does it matter?"

She sighed. "I suppose not. None of the village boys will care anymore, now that I'm to be married." She glumly plucked at the trim on her gown. "Hans isn't the sort for fun or finery."

My lips tightened. "Hans is a good man."

"A good man, and *boring*," Käthe said. "Did you see him at the dance the other night? He never, *not once*, asked me to take a turn with him. He just stood in the corner and glared disapprovingly."

It was because Käthe had been flirting shamelessly with a handful of Austrian soldiers en route to Munich to oust the French. *Pretty girl*, they coaxed her in their funny Austrian accents, *Come give us a kiss!*

"A wanton woman is ripened fruit," Constanze intoned, "begging to be plucked by the Goblin King."

A frisson of unease ran up my spine. Our grandmother liked to scare us with tales of goblins and other creatures that lived in the woods beyond our village, but Käthe, Josef, and I hadn't taken her stories seriously since we were children. At eighteen, I was too old for my grandmother's fairy tales, yet I cherished the guilty thrill that ran through me whenever the Goblin King was mentioned. Despite everything, I still believed in the Goblin King. I still wanted to believe in the Goblin King.

"Oh, go squawk at someone else, you old crow." Käthe pouted. "Why must you always be pecking at me?"

"Mark my words." Constanze glared at my sister from beneath layers of yellowed lace and faded ruffles, her dark brown eyes the only sharp things in her wizened face. "You watch yourself, Katharina, lest the goblins come take you for your licentious ways."

"Enough, Constanze," I said. "Leave Käthe alone and let us go on our way. We must be back before Master Antonius arrives."

"Yes, Heaven forbid we miss our precious little Josef's audition for the famous violin maestro," my sister muttered.

"Käthe!"

"I know, I know." She sighed. "Stop worrying, Liesl. He'll be fine. You're worse than a hen with a fox at the door."

"He won't be fine if he doesn't have any bows to play with." I turned to leave. "Come, or I'll be going without you."

"Wait." Käthe grabbed my hand. "Would you let me do a little something with your hair? You have such gorgeous locks; it's a shame you plait them out of the way. I could—"

"A wren is still a wren, even in a peacock's feathers." I shook her off. "Don't waste your time. It's not like Hans—anyone—would notice anyway."

My sister flinched at the mention of her betrothed's name. "Fine," she said shortly, then strode past me without another word.

"Ka—" I began, but Constanze stopped me before I could follow.

"You take care of your sister, girlie," she warned. "You watch over her."

"Don't I always?" I snapped. It had always been up to me—me and Mother—to hold the family together. Mother looked after the inn that was our house and livelihood; I looked after the members who made it home.

"Do you?" My grandmother fixed her dark eyes on my face. "Josef isn't the only one who needs looking after, you know."

I frowned. "What do you mean?"

"You forget what day it is."

Sometimes it was easier to humor Constanze than to ignore her. I sighed. "What day is it?"

"The day the old year dies."

Another shiver up my spine. My grandmother still kept to the old laws and the old calendar, and this last night of autumn was when the old year died and the barrier between worlds was thin. When the denizens of the Underground walked the world above during the days of winter, before the year began again in the spring.

"The last night of the year," Constanze said. "Now the days of winter begin and the Goblin King rides abroad, searching for his bride."

I turned my face away. Once I would have remembered without any prompting. Once I would have joined my grandmother in pouring salt along every windowsill, every threshold, every entrance as a precaution against these wildling nights. Once, once, once. But I could no longer afford the luxury of my indulgent imaginings. It was time, as the apostle Paul said to the Corinthians, to put aside childish things.

"I don't have time for this." I pushed Constanze aside. "Let me pass."

Sorrow pushed the lines of my grandmother's face into even deeper grooves, sorrow and loneliness, her hunched shoulders bowing with the weight of her beliefs. She bore those beliefs alone now. None of us kept faith with *Der Erlkönig* anymore; none save Josef.

"Liesl!" Käthe shouted from downstairs. "Can I borrow your red cloak?"

"Mind how you choose, girl," Constanze told me. "Josef is not part of the game. When *Der Erlkönig* plays, he plays for keeps."

Her words stopped me short. "What are you talking about?" I asked. "What game?"

"You tell me." Constanze's expression was grave. "The wishes we make in the dark have consequences, and the Lord of Mischief will call their reckoning."

Her words prickled against my mind. I minded how Mother warned us of Constanze's aged and feeble wits, but my grandmother had never seemed more lucid or more earnest, and despite myself, a thread of fear began to wind about my throat.

"Is that a yes?" Käthe called. "Because I'm taking it if so!"

I groaned. "No, you may not!" I said, leaning over the stair rail. "I'll be right there, I promise!"

"Promises, eh?" Constanze cackled. "You make so many, but how many of them can you keep?"

"What—" I began, but when I turned to face her, my grandmother was gone.

Downstairs, Käthe had taken my red cloak off its peg, but I plucked it from her hands and settled it about my own shoulders. The last time Hans had brought us gifts from his father's fabric goods store—before his proposal to Käthe, before everything between us changed—he had given us a beautiful bolt of heavy wool. *For the family,* he'd said, but everyone had known the gift was for me. The bolt of wool was a deep blood-red, perfectly suited to my darker coloring and warming to my sallow complexion. Mother and Constanze had made me a winter cloak from the cloth, and Käthe made no secret of how much she coveted it.

We passed our father playing dreamy old airs on his violin in the main hall. I looked around for our guests, but the room was empty, the hearth cold and the coals dead. Papa still wore his clothes from the night before, and the whiff of stale beer lingered about him like mist.

"Where's Mother?" Käthe asked.

Mother was nowhere to be seen, which was probably why Papa felt bold enough to play out here in the main hall, where anyone might hear him. The violin was a sore point between our parents; money was tight, and Mother would rather Papa play his instrument for hire than pleasure. But perhaps Master Antonius's imminent arrival had loosened Mother's purse strings as well as her heartstrings. The renowned virtuoso was to stop at our inn on his way from Vienna to Munich in order to audition my little brother.

"Likely taking a nap," I ventured. "We were up before dawn, scrubbing out the rooms for Master Antonius."

Our father was a violinist nonpareil, who had once played with the finest court musicians in Salzburg. It was in Salzburg, Papa would boast, where he had had the privilege of playing with Mozart, one of the late, great composer's concertos. *Genius like that,* Papa said, *comes only once in a lifetime. Once in two lifetimes. But sometimes,* he would continue, giving Josef a sly glance, *lightning does strike twice.*

Josef was not among the gathered guests. My little brother was shy of strangers, so he was likely hiding at the Goblin Grove, practicing until his fingers bled. My heart ached to join him, even as my fingertips twinged with sympathetic pain.

"Good, I won't be missed," Käthe said cheerfully. My sister often found any excuse to skip out on her chores. "Let's go."

Outside, the air was brisk. The day was uncommonly cold, even for late autumn. The light was sparse, weak and wavering, as though seen through curtains or a veil. A faint mist wrapped the trees along the path into town, wraithing their spindly branches into spectral limbs. *The last night of the year.* On a day like this, I could believe the barriers between worlds were thin indeed.

The path that led into town was pitted and rutted with carriage tracks and spotted with horse dung. Käthe and I took care to keep to the edges, where the short, dead grass helped prevent the damp from seeping into our boots.

"Ugh." Käthe stepped around another dung puddle. "I wish we could afford a carriage."

"If only our wishes had power," I said.

"Then I'd be the most powerful person in the world," Käthe remarked, "for I have wishes aplenty. I wish we were rich. I wish we could afford whatever we wanted. Just imagine, Liesl: what if, what if, what if."

I smiled. As little girls, Käthe and I were fond of *What if* games. While my sister's imagination did not encompass the uncanny, as mine and Josef's did, she had an extraordinary capacity for pretend nonetheless.

"What if, indeed?" I asked softly.

"Let's play," she said. "The Ideal Imaginary World. You first, Liesl."

"All right." I thought of Hans, then pushed him aside. "Josef would be a famous musician."

Käthe made a face. "It's always about Josef with you. Don't you have any dreams of your own?"

I did. They were locked up in a box, safe and sound beneath the bed we shared, never to be seen, never to be heard.

"Fine," I said. "You go, then, Käthe. Your Ideal Imaginary World."

She laughed, a bright, bell-like sound, the only musical thing about my sister. "I am a princess."

"Naturally."

Käthe shot me a look. "I am a princess, and you are a queen. Happy now?"

I waved her on.

"I am a princess," she continued. "Papa is the Prince-Bishop's *Kapellmeister*, and we all live in Salzburg."

Käthe and I had been born in Salzburg, when Papa was still a court musician and Mother a singer in a troupe, before poverty chased us to the backwoods of Bavaria.

"Mother is the toast of the city for her beauty and her voice, and Josef is Master Antonius's prize pupil."

"Studying in Salzburg?" I asked. "Not Vienna?"

"In Vienna, then," Käthe amended. "Oh yes, Vienna." Her blue eyes sparkled as she spun out her fantasy for us. "We would travel to visit him, of course. Perhaps we'll see him perform in the great cities of Paris, Mannheim, and Munich, maybe even London! We shall have a grand house in each city, trimmed with gold and marble and mahogany wood. We'll wear gowns made in the most luxurious silks and brocades, a different color for every day of the week. Invitations to the fanciest balls and parties and operas and plays shall flood our post every morning, and a bevy of swains will storm the barricades for our favor. The greatest artists and musicians would consider us their intimate acquaintances, and we would dance and feast all night long on cake and pie and schnitzel and—"

"Chocolate torte," I added. It was my favorite.

"Chocolate torte," Käthe agreed. "We would have the finest coaches and the handsomest horses and"—she squeaked as she slipped in a mud puddle—"never walk on foot through unpaved roads to market again."

I laughed, and helped her regain her footing. "Parties, balls, glittering society. Is that what princesses do? What of queens? What of me?"

"You?" Käthe fell silent for a moment. "No. Queens are destined for greatness."

"Greatness?" I mused. "A poor, plain little thing like me?"

"You have something much more enduring than beauty," she said severely.

"And what is that?"

"Grace," she said simply. "Grace, and talent."

I laughed. "So what is to be my destiny?"

She cut me a sidelong glance. "To be a composer of great renown."

A chill wind blew through me, freezing me to the marrow. It was as though my sister had reached into my breast and wrenched out my heart, still beating, with her fist. I had jotted down small snatches of melody here and there, scribbling little ditties instead of hymns into the corners of my Sunday chapbook, intending to gather them into sonatas and concertos, romances and symphonies someday. My hopes and dreams, so tattered and tender, had been sheltered by secrecy for so long that I could not bear to bring them to light.

"Liesl?" Käthe tugged at my sleeve. "Liesl, are you all right?"

"How—" I said hoarsely. "How did you . . ."

She squirmed. "I found your box of compositions beneath our bed one day. I swear I didn't mean any harm," she added quickly. "But I was looking for a button I'd dropped, and . . ." Her voice trailed off at the look upon my face.

My hands were shaking. How dare she? How dare she open my most private thoughts and expose them to her prying eyes?

"Liesl?" Käthe looked worried. "What's wrong?"

I did not answer. I could not answer, not when my sister would never understand just how she had trespassed against me. Käthe had not a modicum of musical ability, nearly a mortal sin in a family such as ours. I turned and marched down the path to market.

"What did I say?" My sister hurried to catch up with me. "I thought you'd be pleased. Now that Josef's going away, I thought Papa might—I mean, we all know you have just as much talent as—"

"Stop it." The words cracked in the autumn air, snapping beneath the coldness of my voice. "Stop it, Käthe."

Her cheeks reddened as though she had been slapped. "I don't understand you," she said.

"What don't you understand?"

"Why you hide behind Josef."

"What does Sepperl have to do with anything?"

Käthe narrowed her eyes. "For you? Everything. I bet you never kept your music secret from our little brother."

I paused. "He's different."

"Of course he's different." Käthe threw up her hands in exasperation. "Precious Josef, delicate Josef, talented Josef. He has music and madness and magic in his blood, something poor, ordinary, tone-deaf Katharina does not understand, could never understand."

I opened my mouth to protest, then shut it again. "Sepperl needs me," I said softly. It was true. Our brother was fragile, in more than just bones and blood.

"*I* need you," she said, and her voice was quiet. Hurt.

Constanze's words returned to me. *Josef isn't the only one who needs looking after.*

"You don't need me." I shook my head. "You have Hans now."

Käthe stiffened. Her lips went white, her nostrils flared. "If that's what you think," she said in a low voice, "then you're even crueler than I thought."

Cruel? What did my sister know of cruelty? The world had shown her considerably more favor than it had ever shown me. Her prospects were happy, her future certain. She would marry the most eligible man in the village while I became the unwanted sister, the discarded one. And I . . . I had Josef, but not for long. When my little brother left, he would take the last of my childhood with him: our revels in the woods, our stories of kobolds and *Hödekin* dancing in the moonlight, our games of music and make-believe. When he was gone, all that would remain to me was music—music and the Goblin King.

"Be grateful for what you have," I snapped back. "Youth, beauty, and, very soon, a husband who will make you happy."

"Happy?" Käthe's eyes flashed. "Do you honestly think Hans will make me happy? Dull, boring Hans, whose mind is as limited as the borders of the stupid, provincial village in which he grew up? Stolid, dependable Hans, who would keep me rooted to the inn with a deed in my hand and a baby in my lap?"

I was stunned. Hans was an old friend of the family, and while he and Käthe had not been close as children—as Hans and I had been—I had not known until this moment just how little my sister loved him. "Käthe," I said. "Why—"

"Why did I agree to marry him? Why haven't I said anything before now?"

I nodded.

"I did." Tears welled up in her eyes. "Over and over. But you never listened. This morning, when I said he was boring, you told me he was a good man." She turned her face away. "You never hear a word I say, Liesl. You're too busy listening to Josef instead."

*Mind how you choose.* Guilt clotted my throat.

"Oh, Käthe," I whispered. "You could have said no."

"Could I?" she scoffed. "Would you or Mother have let me? What choice did I have but to accept his hand?"

Her accusation gutted me, made me complicit in my own resentment. I had been so sure that this was the way of the world that I hadn't questioned it. Handsome Hans and beautiful Käthe—of course they were meant to be together.

"You have choices," I repeated uncertainly. "More than I ever will."

"Choices, ha." Käthe's laugh was raw. "Well, Liesl, you made your choice about Josef a long time ago. You can't fault me for making mine about Hans."

The rest of our walk to the market continued without another word.

## COME BUY,
## COME BUY

*ome buy, come buy!*

In the town square, the market stalls were laden with goods, their sellers hawking their wares at the top of their lungs. *Fresh bread! Fresh milk! Goat cheese! Warm wool, the softest wool you've ever felt!* Some vendors rang bells, some rattled wooden clappers, and still others beat an erratic *rat-a-tat-tat* on a homemade drum, all in an effort to bring custom to their tables. As we drew nearer, Käthe began to brighten.

I never did understand the prospect of spending coin for pleasure, but my sister loved to shop. She ran her fingers lovingly over the fabrics on sale: silks and velvets and satins imported from England, Italy, and even the Far East. She buried her nose in bouquets of dried lavender and rosemary, and closed her eyes as she savored the tart taste of mustard on the doughy pretzel she had bought. Such sensuous enjoyment.

I trailed behind, lingering over wreaths of dried flowers and ribbons, thinking I might buy one as a wedding gift for my sister—or an apology. Käthe loved beautiful things; no, more than loved—reveled in them. I noted how the sour-lipped matrons and stern-browed elders of the town gave my sister dark looks, as though her thorough delight in small luxuries was something obscene, something dirty. One man in particular, a tall, pale, elegant shade of a man, watched her with an intensity that would have ignited me, had he but glanced my way.

*Come buy, come buy!*

A group of fruit-sellers on the fringes of the market called in high, clear voices that carried over the din of the crowd. Their silvery, chime-like tones tingled the ear, drawing me close, almost against my will. It was late in the season for fresh fruit, and I marked the unusual color and texture of their offerings: round, luscious, tempting.

"Ooh, Liesl!" Käthe pointed, our earlier argument forgotten. "Peaches!"

The fruit-sellers beckoned us with fluid gestures, holding their wares in their hands, and the tantalizing scent of ripe fruit wafted past. My mouth watered, but I turned away, pulling Käthe with me. I had no coin to spare.

A few weeks ago, I had sent for a few of Josef's bows to be re-haired and repaired by an *archetier* before my brother's audition with Master Antonius. I had hoarded, scrimped, and saved what I could, for repairs did not come cheap.

But now the fruit-sellers had caught sight of us and our longing glances. "Come, lovely ladies!" they sang. "Come, sweet darlings. Come buy, come buy!" One of them tapped out a rhythm on the wooden planks that served as their table, while the others took up a melody. "Damsons and apricots, peaches and blackberries, taste them and try!"

Without thinking, I began to sing with them, a wordless *ooh-oo* searching for harmony and counterpoint in their music. Thirds, fifths, diminished sevenths, I played with the chords beneath my breath. Together, the fruit-sellers and I wove a shimmering web of sound, haunting, strange, and a little wild.

The vendors suddenly focused their eyes on me, their features sharpening, their smiles lengthening. The hairs on the back of my neck stood on end and I let the melody drop. The touch of their eyes was a tickle on my skin, but behind me I could sense the gaze of an unseen other, as palpable as a hand caressing my nape. I glanced over my shoulder.

The tall, pale, elegant stranger.

His features were shadowed by a hood, but beneath the cloak, his clothes were fine. I noted the glint of gold and silver thread on green velvet brocade. Seeing my inquisitive expression, the stranger stirred and folded his cloak about him, but not before I caught a glimpse of dun-colored leather breeches outlining the slim shape of his hips. I turned my face away, my blush heating the air about me. He seemed familiar, somehow.

"*Brava, brava!*" the fruit-sellers cried once they had finished their song. "Clever maiden in red, come take your reward!"

They waved their hands over the fruits on display, their fingers long and slim. For a moment, it seemed as though there were too many joints in their fingers, and I felt the brush of something uncanny. But that moment passed, and the merchants picked up a peach, offering it to me with open hands.

The fruit's perfume was thick on the chill autumn air, but beneath the cloying smell was the tang of something rotten, something putrid. I recoiled, and it seemed to me these sellers' appearances had changed. Their skin had taken on a greenish tinge, the tips of their teeth were pointed and sharp, and instead of fingernails, they seemed to have claws.

*Beware the goblin men, and the wares they sell.*

Käthe reached for the peach with both hands. "Oh yes, please!"

I grabbed my sister's shawl and yanked her back.

"The maiden knows what she wants," said one of the vendors. He grinned at Käthe, but it was more leer than smile. His lips seemed stretched a little too far, his yellowed teeth sharp. "Full of passions, full of desire. Easily spent, easily satiated."

Spooked, I turned to Käthe. "Let's go," I said. "We shouldn't tarry. We need to stop by Herr Kassl's before heading home."

Käthe's eyes remained fixed on the array of fruit laid before her. She looked sick, her brows furrowed, her bosom heaving, her cheeks flushed, her eyes bright and feverish. She looked sick, or . . . *excited*. A feeling of wrongness settled over me, wrongness and fear, even as a hint of her excitement roused my own limbs.

"Let's go," I repeated. Käthe's eyes were dull and glassy. "Anna Katharina Magdalena Ingeborg Vogler!" I snapped. "We are leaving."

"Perhaps another time then, dearie," sneered the fruit-seller. I gathered my sister close, draping one arm protectively about her shoulders. "She'll be back," he said. "Girls like her can never put off temptation for long. Both are . . . ripe for the plucking."

I walked away, pushing Käthe ahead of me. Out of the corner of my eye, I glimpsed the tall, elegant stranger again. From beneath his hood, I sensed him watching us. Watching. Considering. Judging. One of the fruit-sellers tugged at the stranger's cloak, and the man bent his head to listen, but I felt his gaze upon us. Upon me.

"Beware."

I stopped in my tracks. It was another one of the fruit-sellers, a smallish man with frizzy hair like a thistle cloud and a pinched face. He wasn't more than the size of a child, although his expression was old, older than Constanze, older than the forest itself.

"That one," the merchant said, pointing to Käthe, whose head lolled against my shoulder, "burns like kindling. All flash, and no real heat. But you," he said. "You smolder, mistress. There is a fire burning within you, but it is a slow burn. It shimmers with heat, waiting only for a breath to fan it to life. Most curious." A slow grin spread over his mouth. "Most curious, indeed."

The merchant vanished. I blinked, but he never returned, leaving me to wonder if I had dreamed the encounter. I shook my head, tightened my grip on Käthe's arm, and marched toward Herr Kassl's shop, determined to forget these strange goblin men and their fruits: so tantalizing, so sweet, and so very far out of reach.


Käthe shook me off as we drew away from the fruit-sellers. "I'm not a child what needs looking after, you know," she snapped.

I tightened my lips, biting back my sharp retort. "Fine."

I held out a small purse. "Go find Johannes the brewer and tell him—"

"I know what I'm doing, Liesl," she said, snatching the purse from my hand. "I'm not completely helpless."

And with that she flounced away from me, disappearing into the hustle and bustle of the crowd.

With some misgiving, I turned and found my way to Herr Kassl's. We had no bow-maker or luthier in our little village, but Herr Kassl knew all the best craftsmen in Munich. During his long acquaintance with our family, Herr Kassl had seen many valuable instruments pass through his shop, and therefore made it his business to maintain contact with those in the trade. He was an old friend of Papa's, insofar as a pawnbroker could be a friend.

Once I had finished conducting business with Herr Kassl, I went in search of my sister. Käthe was easy to find, even in this sea of faces in the square. Her smiles were the broadest, her blue eyes the brightest, her pink cheeks the rosiest. Even her hair beneath that ridiculous hat shone like a bird of golden plumage. All I had to do was follow the path traced by the eyes of the onlookers in the village, those admiring, appreciative glances that led me straight to my sister at the center.

For a moment, I watched her bargain and haggle with the sellers. Käthe was like an actress on the stage, all heightened emotion and intense passion, her gestures affected, her smiles calculated. She fluttered and flirted outrageously, carefully oblivious to the stares she drew like moths to the flame. Both men and women traced the lines of her body, the curve of her cheek, the pout of her lip.

Looking at Käthe, it was difficult to forget just how sinful our bodies were, just how prone we were to wickedness. *Born unto trouble, as the sparks fly upward,* or so saith Job. Clothed in clinging fabrics, with every line of her body exposed, every gasp of pleasure unconcealed, everything about Käthe suggested voluptuousness.

With a start, I realized I was looking at a woman—a woman and not a child. Käthe knew of the power her body wielded over others, and that knowledge had replaced her innocence. My sister had crossed the threshold from girl to woman without me, and I felt abandoned. Betrayed. I watched a young man fawn over my sister as she perused his booth, and a lump rose in my throat, resentment so bitter I nearly choked on it.

What I wouldn't have given to be the object of someone's desire, just for one moment. What I wouldn't have given to taste that fruit, that heady sweetness, of being wanted. I wanted. I wanted what Käthe took for granted. I wanted wantonness.

"Might I interest the young lady in red in a few curious trinkets?"

Startled from my reverie, I looked up to see the tall, elegant stranger once more.

"No, thank you, sir." I shook my head. "I have no money to spare."

The stranger stepped closer. In his gloved hands he held a flute, beautifully carved and polished to a high shine. Up close, I could see the gleam of his eyes from beneath the hood.

"No? Well, then, if you won't buy my wares, would you accept a gift?"

"A—a gift?" I was hot and uncomfortable beneath his scrutiny. He looked at me as no one had before, as though

I were more than the sum of my eyes, my nose, my lips, my hair, and my wretched plainness. He looked as though he saw me entire, as though he *knew* me. But did I know him? His presence scratched at my mind, like a half-remembered song. "What for?"

"Do I need a reason?" His voice was neither deep nor high, but there was a quality to it that spoke of dark woods and dry winter nights. "Perhaps I just wanted to make a young woman's day a little bit brighter. The nights grow long and cold, after all."

"Oh no, sir," I said again. "My grandmother warned me against the wolves that prowl in the woods."

The stranger laughed, and I caught a glimpse of sharp, white teeth. I shivered.

"Your grandmother is wise," he said. "I'm sure she also told you to avoid the goblin men. Or perhaps she told you we were one and the same."

I did not answer.

"You are clever. I do not offer this gift to you out of the goodness of my heart, but out of a selfish need to see what you might do with it."

"What do you mean?"

"There is music in your soul. A wild and untamed sort of music that speaks to me. It defies all the rules and laws you humans set upon it. It grows from inside you, and I have a wish to set that music free."

He had heard me sing with the fruit-sellers. *A wild, untamed sort of music.* I'd heard those words before, from Papa. Then, it had seemed like an insult. My musical education had been rudimentary at best; of us all, Papa had taken the most time and care with Josef, making sure my brother understood the theory and history of music, its building blocks and foundations. I had always listened in on the edges of those lessons, taking whatever notes I could, applying them slipshod to my own compositions.

But this elegant stranger cast no judgment on my lack of formal structure, my lack of learning. I took his words and planted them deep inside.

"For you, Elisabeth." He offered me the flute again. This time I took it. Despite the cold air, the instrument was warm, and felt almost like skin beneath my hands.

It was only after the stranger disappeared that I realized he had called me by my given name.

*Elisabeth.*

How could he have possibly known?

I held the flute in my hands, admiring its build, running my fingers over its rich grain and smooth finish. A persistent thought niggled at the back of my mind, a sense I had lost or forgotten something, but it hovered on the edges of memory, a word on the tip of my tongue.

*Käthe.*

A jolt of fear stirred my sluggish thoughts. Käthe, where was Käthe? In the milling crowd, there was no sign of my sister's ridiculous confectionary hat, nor an echo of her chiming laugh. A deep sense of dread overcame me, along with the troubling feeling that I had been tricked.

Why had that tall, elegant stranger offered me a gift? Was it truly out of selfish curiosity for *my* sake, or just another ploy to distract me while the goblin men stole my sister away?

I thrust the flute into my satchel and picked up the hems of my skirts, ignoring the scandalized glances of the town fussbudgets and the hooting calls of village ne'er-do-wells. I ran through the market in a blind panic, calling Käthe's name.

Reason warred with faith. I was too old to indulge in the stories of my childhood, but I could not deny the strangeness of my encounter with the fruit-sellers. With the tall, elegant stranger.

They were the goblin men.

There were no goblin men.

*Come buy, come buy!*

The spectral voices of the merchants were faint and thin on the breeze, more memory than sound. I followed that thread of music, hearing its eerie melodies not with my ears, but with another part of me, unseen and unnoticed. The music reached into my heart and tugged, pulling me along like a puppet on its strings.

I knew where my sister had gone. Terror seized me, along with the unquestioned certainty that *something bad will happen* if I did not reach her in time. I had promised to keep my sister safe.

*Come buy, come buy!*

The voices were softer now, distant and hollow, fading into silence with a ghostly whisper. I reached the edges of the market, but the fruit-sellers were no longer there. There were no stalls, no tables, no tents, no fruit, nothing to suggest they had ever been there. Nothing save Käthe's lonely form in the mist, her flimsy dress fluttering about her like one of the White Ladies of Frau Perchta, like a figure from one of Constanze's fairy tales. Perhaps I had reached my sister in time. Perhaps there was nothing to fear.

"Käthe!" I cried, running to embrace her.

She turned around. My sister's lips glistened—red, sticky, and sweet—her pout swollen as though she had just been thoroughly kissed.

In her hands was a half-eaten peach, its juice dripping down her fingers like rivulets of blood.

## SHE IS FOR THE
## GOBLIN KING NOW

äthe did not speak to me on our walk home. I was nursing a foul mood myself: my irritation with my sister, the unsettling encounter with the fruit-sellers, the shivery longing the tall, elegant stranger had stirred in me—all swirled together into a maelstrom of confusion. A misty quality shrouded my memories of the market, and I could not be certain if it hadn't all been a dream.

Yet nestled in my satchel was the stranger's gift. The flute jostled against my leg with every step, as real as Josef's bows in my hand. I wondered why the stranger had gifted the flute to me. I was a mediocre flautist at best; the thin, ghostly sounds I could produce on the instrument were more strange than sweet. I wondered how I would explain its existence to Mother. I wondered how I could explain it to myself.

"Liesl."

To my surprise, it was Josef who greeted us at the door.

He peered at us from around the posts, hovering uncomfortably on the threshold.

"What is it, Sepp?" I asked gently. I knew my brother was nervous about his upcoming audition, what it would cost him to show his face to so many strangers. Like me, my brother hid in the shadows; unlike me, he preferred it there.

"Master Antonius," he whispered, "is here."

"What?" I dropped my satchel. "So soon?" We hadn't expected the old violin master until the evening.

He nodded. A wary expression crossed his face, his pale features pinched with worry. "He made good time over the Alps. Didn't want to get caught out by an early snowstorm."

"He needn't have worried," Käthe said. Both Josef and I turned to look at her in surprise. Our sister was gazing into the distance, her eyes a glassy glaze. "The king still sleeps, waiting. The days of winter have not yet begun."

My pulse beat hard. "Who's sleeping? Who's waiting?"

But she said no more, and merely walked past Josef into the inn.

My brother and I exchanged a glance. "Is she all right?" he asked.

I bit my lip, remembering how the goblin fruit had stained her lips and chin with something like blood. Then I shook my head. "She's fine. Where is Master Antonius now?"

"Upstairs, taking a nap," Josef said. "Mother told us not to disturb him."

"And Papa?"

Josef slid his gaze from mine. "I don't know."

I closed my eyes. Of all the moments for Papa to disappear. The old violin virtuoso had been a friend of Papa's from the Prince-Bishop's court. Both Master Antonius and Papa had left those days behind them, but one had traveled further than the other. One had just finished a post as a visiting resident at the court of the Austrian emperor, while the other found solace at the bottom of a beer barrel every night.

"Well." I opened my eyes and forced my lips into a smile. I handed Josef his newly repaired bows and gathered an arm about his shoulders. "Let's get ready to put on a show, shall we?"

The kitchen was a flurry of baking, boiling, broiling. "Good, you're back," Mother said shortly. She nodded at a bowl on the counter. "The meat is spiced, so start trimming the lengths." She stood over a large vat of boiling water, stirring a batch of sausages.

I put on an apron and immediately began measuring the sausage casing to twist and tie into individual links. Käthe was nowhere to be seen, so I sent Josef to go look for her.

"Have you seen your father?" Mother asked.

I dared not look at her face. Mother was an extraordinarily lovely woman, her figure still slim and youthful, her hair still bright, her skin still fair. In the half-light of dusk and dawn, in the in-between hours, in the golden edge of a candle flame, one could see how she had been renowned throughout Salzburg not only for her beautiful voice, but for her beautiful face as well. But time had graven lines at the corners of her full lips and between her brows. Time, toil, and Papa.

"Liesl."

I shook my head.

She sighed, and a world of meaning lay within that sound. Anger, frustration, hopelessness, resignation. Mother still had the gift of conveying every shade of emotion through voice and voice alone.

"Well," she said. "Let us pray Master Antonius won't take offense to his absence."

"I'm sure Papa will be back in time." I picked up a knife to hide the lie. Trim, twist, tie. Trim, twist, tie. "We must have faith."

"Faith." My mother laughed, but it was a bitter sound. "You can't live on faith, Liesl. You can't feed your family with it."

Twist, trim, tie. Twist, trim, tie. "You know how charming Papa can be," I said. "He could coax the trees to bear fruit in winter, he can be forgiven any slight."

"Yes, I certainly know how charming your father can be," Mother said drily.

I flushed; I had been born only five months after my parents said their vows.

"Charm is all well and good," she said, straining the sausages and setting them on a towel to dry. "But charm doesn't put bread on the table. Charm goes out with his friends at night when he could be showing his son to all the great masters himself."

I did not reply. It had been a dream of the family's once, to take Josef to the capital cities of the world and play his talent for better, richer ears. But we never did tour Josef. And now, at fourteen, my brother was too old to be touted as a child prodigy the way the Mozarts or Linley had, too young to be appointed to any sort of permanent post as a professional musician. Despite his skill, my brother still had years left to learn and perfect his craft, and if Master Antonius did not take him on as an apprentice, then it would be the end of Josef's career.

So there was a great deal of hope riding on Josef's audition, not just for Josef, but for all of us. It was my brother's opportunity to rise beyond his humble beginnings and show the world what a talent he was, but it was also our father's last chance to play for all the great audiences of Europe through his son. For Mother, it was a way for her youngest child to escape the life of drudgery and hardship that came with an innkeeper's lot, and for Käthe, it was the possibility of visiting her famous brother in all the capital cities: Mannheim, Munich, Vienna, and possibly even London, Paris, or Rome.

For me . . . it was a way for my music to reach ears beyond just Josef's and mine. Käthe might have seen my secret scribblings hidden in the box beneath our bed, but only Josef had ever heard its contents.

"Hans!" Mother said. "I didn't expect to see you here so early."

The knife in my hand slipped. I cursed under my breath, sucking at the cut to draw out the blood.

"I wouldn't miss Josef's big day, Frau Vogler," Hans said. "I came to help."

"Bless you, Hans," Mother said affectionately. "You're a godsend."

I ripped a strip from my apron to wrap around my bleeding finger and continued working, trying my best to remain unnoticed. *He is your sister's betrothed*, I reminded myself. Yet I couldn't help but steal glances at him from beneath my lashes.

Our eyes met, and all warmth left the room. Hans cleared his throat. "Good morning, *Fräulein*," he said.

His careful distance stung worse than the cut on my finger. We had been familiar, once. Once upon a time, we had been *Hansl* and *Liesl*. Once upon a time we had been friends, or perhaps something more. But that was before we all grew up.

"Oh, Hans." I gave an awkward laugh. "We're almost family. You can still call me Liesl, you know."

He nodded stiffly. "It's good to see you, Elisabeth."

*Elisabeth.* It was as intimate as we'd ever be now. I forced a smile. "How are you?"

"I am well, I thank you." His brown eyes were guarded. "And you?"

"Fine," I said. "A little nervous. About the audition, I mean."

Hans's expression softened. He came closer and took a knife from the cutting board, joining me in twisting, trimming, and tying the sausages. "You needn't worry," he said. "Josef plays like an angel."

He smiled, and the frost between us began to thaw. We settled into the rhythm of our work—trim, twist, tie, trim, twist, tie—and for a moment, I could pretend it was as it had been when we were children. Papa had given us keyboard and violin lessons together, and we had sat upon the same bench, learned the same scales, shared the same lessons. Though Hans never progressed much beyond simple exercises, we spent hours together at the klavier, our shoulders brushing, our hands never touching.

"Where is Josef, anyway?" asked Hans. "Out playing in the Goblin Grove?"

Hans, like the rest of us, had sat at Constanze's feet, listening to her stories of kobolds and *Hödekin*, of goblins and Lorelei, of *Der Erlkönig,* the Lord of Mischief. Warm feelings began to flicker between us like embers.

"Perhaps," I said softly. "It is the last night of the year."

Hans scoffed. "Isn't he too old to be playing fairies and goblins?"

His contempt was a dash of cold water, quenching the remnants of our shared youth.

"Liesl, can you come watch the vat?" Mother asked, wiping the sweat from her brow. "The brewers are to arrive at any moment."

"I'll do it, ma'am," Hans offered.

"Thank you, my dear," she said. She relinquished the stirring rod to Hans and walked out of the kitchen, wiping her hands on her apron, leaving us alone.

We did not speak.

"Elisabeth," Hans began tentatively.

Twist, trim, tie. Twist, trim, tie.

"Liesl."

My hands paused for the briefest moment, and then I resumed my work. "Yes, Hans?"

"I—" He cleared his throat. "I had hoped to catch you alone."

That caught my attention. Our eyes met, and I found myself staring at him, bold-faced and direct. He was less handsome than I was wont to remember him, his chin less strong, his eyes closer set, his lips pinched and thin. But no one could deny that Hans was a good-looking man, least of all me.

"Me?" My voice was hoarse, but steady. "Why?"

His dark eyes studied my face, a wrinkle of uncertainty appearing between his brows. "I . . . I want to make things right between us, Lies—Elisabeth."

"Are they not?"

"No." Hans stared at the swirling vat in front of him before setting his stirring rod aside, stepping closer to me. "No, they're not. I . . . I've missed you."

Suddenly it was hard to breathe. Hans seemed too big, too close, too much.

"We were good friends once, weren't we?" he asked.

"We were."

I could not concentrate through the nearness of him. His lips formed words, but I did not hear them, only felt the brush of his breath against my own lips. I held myself rigid, wanting to push into him, knowing I should pull away.

Hans grabbed my wrist. "Liesl."

Startled, I stared at where his fingers were wrapped around my arm. For so long, I had wanted to touch him, to take his hands and feel those fingers entwined with my own. Yet the moment Hans touched me of his own accord seemed unreal to me. It was as though I were looking at someone else's hand and someone else's wrist.

He was not mine. He could not be mine.

Could he?

"Katharina is gone."

Constanze had wandered into the kitchen. Hans and I leaped apart, but my grandmother did not notice the flush in my cheeks. "Katharina is gone," she said again.

"Gone?" I struggled to gather my fallen composure and cover my exposed longing. "What do you mean? Gone where?"

"Just gone." She sucked at a loose tooth.

"I sent Josef to fetch her."

She shrugged. "She's not anywhere in the inn, and your red cloak is missing."

"I'll go look for her," Hans offered.

"No, I will," I said hurriedly. I needed to put my mind and body back into their proper spaces. I needed to get away from him and find myself in the woods.

My grandmother's dark eyes bored into me. "How did you choose, girlie?" she asked softly. She was hunched over her gnarled cane like a bird of prey, her black shawl draped over her shoulders like crow's wings.

The memory of the goblin fruit's bloody flesh running down my sister's face and fingers returned to me. *Josef is not the only who needs looking after.* I felt sick.

"Hurry," Constanze urged. "I fear she is for the Goblin King now."

I ran out of the kitchen and into the great hall, wiping my hands on my apron. I took a shawl from the rack, wrapped it about my shoulders, and went in search of my sister.

I did not venture far into the woods, thinking Käthe would keep close to home. Unlike Josef or me, she had never felt any particular kinship with the trees and stones and babbling brooks in the forest. She did not like mud, or dirt, or damp, and preferred to stay inside, where it was warm, where she might primp and be pampered.

Yet my sister was in none of her usual haunts. Ordinarily, the farthest she ventured was to the stables (we owned no horses, but the guests occasionally traveled on horseback), and sometimes to the woodshed, where the tame grasses surrounding our inn ended and the wild edges of the forest began.

There was the faint, impossible scent of summer peaches ripening on the breeze.

Constanze's warning echoed in my mind. *She is for the Goblin King now.* I wrapped my shawl tighter about me and hurried off the footpath into the woods.

Past the woodshed, past the creek that ran behind our inn, deep in the wild heart of the forest, was a circle of alder trees we called the Goblin Grove. The trees grew in such a way as to suggest twisted arms and monstrous limbs frozen in an eternal dance, and Constanze liked to tell us that the trees had once been humans—naughty young women— who displeased *Der Erlkönig*. As children we had played here, Josef and me, played and sang and danced, offering our music to the Lord of Mischief. The Goblin King was the silhouette around which my music was composed, and the Goblin Grove was the place my shadows came to life.

I spied a scarlet shape in the woods ahead of me. Käthe in my cloak, walking to my sacred space. An irrational, petty slash of irritation cut through my dread and unease. The Goblin Grove was *my* haunt, *my* refuge, *my* sanctuary. Why must she take everything that was mine? My sister had a gift for turning the extraordinary into the ordinary. Unlike my brother and me—who lived in the ether of magic and music—Käthe lived in the world of the real, the tangible, the mundane. Unlike us, she never had faith.

Mist curled in about the edges of my vision, blurring the distance between spaces, making near seem far and far seem near. The Goblin Grove was but a few minutes' walk from our inn, but time seemed to be playing tricks on me, and it felt as though I had been walking both forever and not at all.

Then I remembered time—like memory—was just another one of the Goblin King's playthings, a toy he could bend and stretch at will.

"Käthe!" I called. But my sister did not hear me.

As a child, I'd pretended to see him, *Der Erlkönig,* this mysterious ruler underground. No one knew what he looked like, and no one knew what his true nature was, but *I* did. He looked like a boy, a youth, a man, whatever I needed him to be. He was playful, serious, interesting, confusing, but he was my friend, always my friend. It was make-believe, true, but even make-believe was a sort of belief.

But those were the imaginings of a little girl, Constanze told me. The Goblin King was none of the things I knew him to be. He was the Lord of Mischief—mercurial, melancholy, seductive, beautiful—but he was, above all, dangerous.

*Dangerous?* little Liesl had asked. *Dangerous how?*

*Dangerous as a winter wind, which freezes the marrow from within, and not like a blade, which slashes the throat from without.*

But I was not to worry, for only beautiful women were vulnerable to the Goblin King's charms. They were his weakness, and he was theirs; they wanted him—sinuous and fey and untamable—the way they wanted to hold on to candle flame or mist. Because I was not beautiful, I never felt the weight of Constanze's warnings about the Goblin King. Because Käthe was not imaginative, she never had either.

And now I feared for us both.

"Käthe!" I called again.

I picked up my skirts and my pace, running after my sister. But no matter how quickly I ran, the distance between us never closed. Käthe continued walking in her slow, steady way, yet I never managed to overtake her. She was as far from me as when I had first set out after her.

My sister stepped into the Goblin Grove and paused.

She glanced over her shoulder, straight at me, but she never saw me. Her eyes scanned the woods, searching for something—or someone—specific.

Suddenly she wasn't alone. There in the Goblin Grove, standing by my sister's side as though he had always been there, was the tall, elegant stranger from the marketplace. He wore his cloak and hood, which hid his face from me, but Käthe gazed up at him with a look of adoration.

I stopped in my tracks. Käthe had a strange little smile on her face, a smile I had never seen before, the thin, weak smile of an invalid facing a new day. Her lips looked bitten, and her skin was wan and pale. I felt bizarrely betrayed, by Käthe or the tall, elegant stranger, I wasn't sure. I did not know him, but he had seemed to know *me*. He was just another thing Käthe had taken from me, another thing she had stolen. Wasn't he?

I was about to march straight into the Goblin Grove and drag my sister back home to safety when the stranger drew back his hood.

I gasped.

I could say the stranger was beautiful, but to describe him thus was to call Mozart "just a musician." His beauty was that of an ice storm, lovely and deadly. He was not handsome, not the way Hans was handsome; the stranger's features were too long, too pointed, too alien. There was a prettiness about him that was almost girly, and an ugliness about him that was just as compelling. I understood then what Constanze had meant when those doomed young ladies longed to hold on to him the way they yearned to grasp candle flame or mist. His beauty *hurt*, but it was the pain that made it beautiful. Yet it was not his strange and cruel beauty that moved me, it was the fact that I *knew* that face, that hair, that look. He was as familiar to me as the sound of my own music.

This was the Goblin King.

I came upon that realization with no more surprise than if I had come across the local baker. The Goblin King had always been my neighbor, a fixture in my life, as sure as the church steeple and the cloth merchant and the poverty that dogged my family's heels. I had grown up with him outside my window, just as I had grown up with Hans and the milk-maid and the purse-lipped ladies of the village square. Of course I recognized him. Had I not seen his face every night in my dreams, in my childish fancies? Yet . . . hadn't it all been just that—pretend?

This was the Goblin King. That was my sister in his arms. This was my sister tilting her head back to greet his lips. That was the Goblin King bending down to receive her kisses like sacred offerings made at the altar of his worship. This was the Goblin King running long, slender fingers down the line of my sister's neck, her shoulder, her back. That was my sister laughing, her bright, musical bell of a laugh, and this was the Goblin King smiling in return, but looking at me, always looking. I was entranced; my sister was enchanted.

*Enchanted.* The word was a dash of cold water, and my senses returned with a jolt. *This was the Goblin King.* The abductor of maidens, the punisher of misdeeds, the Lord of Mischief and the Underground. But was he also not the friend of my childhood, the confidante of my youth? I hesitated, torn by conflicting desires.

I shook my head. I had to rescue my sister. I had to break the spell.

"Käthe!" I screamed. The woods resounded, and a raucous

cacophony of startled crows took up my cry. *Ka-kaw! Ka-kaw! Ka-Käthe!*

This time the Goblin King took note. He raised his head and we locked gazes over my sister's stupefied form. His pale hair surrounded his thin face like a halo, like a thistle cloud, like a wolf's shaggy mane, silver and gold and colorless all at once. I could not tell what color his eyes were from where I stood, but they were likewise pale, and icy. The Goblin King tilted his head in a duelist's nod and gave me a small smile, the tips of his teeth sharp and pointed. I clenched my fists. I knew that smile. I recognized it, and understood it as a challenge.

*Come rescue her, my dear,* the smile said. *Come and rescue her . . . if you can.*

# VIRTUOSO

**K**äthe!"

I rushed forward as my sister collapsed. Panic galvanized me, turning my blood to steel, and I ran to catch her before she fell. My sister leaned against me, her body limp, her pallid face tight and drawn.

"Käthe, are you all right?"

She blinked slowly, her blue eyes glassy and unfocused. "Liesl?"

"Yes." I frowned. "What are you doing here?"

We knelt in the Goblin Grove, which was not my sister's usual haunt. She had led me on a merry chase, searching over hill and dale for her when so much needed to be done before Master Antonius awoke. I was vexed with her—should have been vexed with her—but my thoughts were curiously sluggish, as though thawing after a long winter.

"Here?" Käthe struggled to sit up. "Where are we?"

"The Goblin Grove," I said impatiently. "Where the alder trees grow."

"Ah." A dreamy smile touched her lips. "I came because I heard it."

"Heard what?"

Her words shook something loose in my mind, my thoughts scattering to the floor like falling leaves. But they were only scant impressions—feathers, ice, pale eyes—that disappeared as soon as I tried to hold them, like snowflakes in my hand.

"The music."

"What music?" That half-woken memory tickled again, an itch I could not scratch.

"Tut," she said, turning her smile on me. "You, of all people, should have recognized it. Can you not hear the sound of your own soul singing?"

A grotesque grin crossed my sister's face, bloodless lips stretched thin over a gaping, wine-dark maw. I recoiled.

"Is something the matter?"

I blinked and her smile was gone. There was a little pucker to Käthe's lips, petulant and pouting, and she was wide-eyed, apple-cheeked, and beautiful once more. But there were dark smudges beneath her eyes, her complexion pale and wan.

"Yes," I said irritably. "The fact that we're here and not there, back at the inn." I helped my sister to her feet. "What were you doing out here?"

Käthe laughed, but it did not sound like her own. There were hints of dark winter woods and cracking ice beneath those bright, pealing tones, and my skin prickled, my mind itched.

"Having words with an old friend."

"What old friend?" I focused on getting Käthe to her feet, and draped her arm about my shoulders. Her skin was cold and clammy beneath my touch, and she felt more like a corpse than a living girl.

"Tut," she said again. "How you've forgotten the old days, Elisabeth."

I froze. Käthe made no move to continue on without me. She watched me, her head tilted to one side, a half smile on her lips, both mocking and sweet.

My sister never, ever called me Elisabeth.

"You always spoke of him as a friend, you know," she said in a soft voice. "A friend, a playmate, a lover." Her expression changed, sharper, sly. Her chin seemed pointed, her cheekbones like a knife. "You said you would marry him someday."

*Hans.* No, not Hans. He was back at the inn. An old friend in the wood, a girl in a grove, a king in his kingdom . . .

That itch in my mind grew unbearable. Desperately, I clawed at it, scrabbling and digging for a memory I could not find. Something was missing. Something was gone. What had we been doing before this? How had we gotten here? Foreboding rose within me, foreboding and fear, rising like dark waters in a flood.

"Käthe," I said, voice cracking. "What—"

A mane of silver and gold, a pair of eyes as cold as ice, a challenge in a smile. I almost had it, almost uncovered it—

Then my sister laughed. It was her own proper laugh, bright and musical. "Oh, Liesl," she said, "you're too easy to tease."

Darkness and shadow were gone, the feeling a spell had been broken. "I hate you," I groaned.

Käthe smiled. I thought I saw that flash of bloodless lips

and a wine-dark maw, but it was her own sweet smile. "Come," she said, taking my arm in hers. "We've wasted enough time. Master Antonius will awake at any moment and I'm sure Mother has worked herself into a frenzy."

I shook my head and gathered myself, letting my sister lean upon me as a crutch. Together we limped back home, back toward reality, back toward the mundane.


Käthe was right; Mother was in a frenzy. Master Antonius had awoken from his nap when we returned and the entire inn was in an uproar. Constanze and Mother were the midst of a screaming match, while Hans hovered awkwardly in the corner, broom in hand, too polite to intervene, too cowardly to leave.

"Absolutely not!" A loose curl slipped from Mother's cap and she pushed it aside with a floury hand. "I will not permit it! Not tonight of all nights."

Constanze held a large burlap bag in her hands. A queer jolt ran through me as I saw she had been pouring salt along the windowsill, every threshold, every entrance.

"It is the last night of the year!" She pointed an accusatory finger at Mother. "I will not let this night pass without protection, whether you will or no."

"Enough!" Mother struggled to wrest the salt from Constanze's grip, but the old woman's hands, as gnarled as oak roots, were surprisingly strong. "I have no patience with this today, not with Master Antonius and Georg disappearing on us again." She caught sight of us. "Käthe! Come help me."

My sister took the broom from Hans and began to sweep.

"You!" Constanze shot me a dirty look. "You must help me. You mustn't let *Der Erlkönig* in."

I flinched, and looked from my mother to my grandmother.

"Liesl," Mother said with exasperation. "We've no time to indulge these childish fancies. Think of your brother. What would Master Antonius say?"

"And what of that one?" Constanze nodded her head at Käthe. "Think ye she needs no protecting? Mind how you choose, girlie."

I glanced from the spilled salt to my sister. Protection against the Goblin King. Then I thought of Josef, and chose not to risk his already precarious position with the maestro. I took the broom from my sister's hands and began sweeping the salt away. Constanze shook her head, her shoulders slumped with resignation.

"Now," Mother said with satisfaction. "Käthe, go make sure your brother is ready for his audition, and I will put my husband's *elderly mother*"—she glared at Constanze—"to bed."

"I'm not tired," Constanze snapped. "I'm not infirm or feeble in my wits, despite what my son's *harried wife*"—she matched Mother glare for glare—"might say."

"Listen, old woman," Mother began. "I have given up my career, my family, and my children's futures for you, and a little gratitude would be appreciated—"

Just then Papa returned. He returned with a song on his lips and violin case in hand, jingling and rattling with every step.

"Got to go, got to go, got to leave this town, leave this town!"

"You!" Mother's nostrils flared. "Georg, where have you been?"

"Käthe," I whispered. "Why don't you and Hans take

Constanze upstairs to her room? I'll make sure Josef is ready once I'm finished here."

My sister gave me one long, unreadable look, then nodded. Hans gently took Constanze's hands as he and Käthe led our grandmother away.

"And you, my dear, stay here; when I'm back, when I'm back, when I'm back again, back again, on your doorstep I'll appear!" Papa leaned forward to plant a kiss on Mother's lips, but she pushed him away.

"Master Antonius has been here these several hours past, and the man of the house nowhere to be seen! I could just—"

The rest of her tirade was lost in the sounds of a muffled kiss. Papa dropped his case to the floor, holding his wife close as he whispered beery blandishments in her ear.

"'Tho I can't be with you all the time, my thoughts are with you, my dear," he sang in a soft voice. "When I'm back, when I'm back, when I'm back again, back again, on your doorstep I'll appear!"

I could see Mother's body bending, growing pliant in Papa's embrace, her protests more and more halfhearted as Papa plied her with a kiss, and another, and then another, before she broke at last with a laugh.

Papa grinned with triumph, but it was only a temporary victory. He had won a laugh from Mother, but by the look in her eyes, he would lose the war.

"Go clean yourself up," Mother told him. "Master Antonius waits in the main hall."

"You could join me," Papa said, waggling his brows outrageously.

"Shoo," she said, giving him a shove. Her cheeks were pink. "Go."

Mother started when she caught sight of me in the shadows. "Liesl!" she said, smoothing her hands over her hair. "I didn't think you were still here."

I swept the last of the salt into the dustpan and tossed it into the fire. Even in the midst of my own family I was easily forgotten.

"Here, I'll take that." Mother took the broom and dustpan from my hands. "Heaven knows where else that old witch got to before we stopped her." She shook her head. "Salt, pah."

I shrugged, picked up a damp rag, and wiped down the countertops. "Constanze has her beliefs." I was overcome by a sudden stab of misgiving. Salt was an old superstition, and I was not usually one to gainsay superstition, but I had just broken faith with my grandmother.

*Mind how you choose.*

"Well, she's welcome to them on days when a famous violin master is *not* here," Mother said. She nodded to the countertops. "Once you're finished in here, go find your brother and make sure he's ready for tonight."

She left the kitchen, grumbling as she went. "Salt. Honestly."

As I finished cleaning the kitchen, I tripped over something on the floor. Papa's violin case. It lay open on the flagstones, empty of its instrument, but littered with a handful of silver *Groschen* in its place.

It seemed as though I was not the only one to pay a visit to Herr Kassl today.

I shut the case, took the money, and put both away in a safe place.

For a moment, I considered chasing after Käthe instead of Josef. Ignoring Constanze's warnings had unsettled me more than I cared to admit, and the guilt scratched at me from within. I frowned. There was something I could not remember, but the more I grasped at it, the more it slipped away. Then I shook my head. No, it was not a time for childish fancies. I set my concerns about my sister aside and went in search of my brother instead.

He was in none of the usual places: his bedroom, the footpaths in the woods, the Goblin Grove. Dusk was falling and Josef was nowhere to be found. I returned from the forest, tearing at my hair in frustration.

A hand reached out to grab my wrist as I made my way up the stairs. "Liesl."

I jumped. It was Josef, hiding beneath the stairwell. All that was visible was the reflected shine of his eyes, a wolf's in the dark.

"Sepperl!" I said. "What are you doing?"

I came down around the stairs and crouched before him. The shadows carved Josef's face into hard planes and angles, sharp cheekbones and pointed chin.

"Liesl," he said in anguished tones. "I can't do this."

Word of the old violin master's arrival had spread like wildfire throughout the village. Josef would have an enormous audience for his audition tonight. I minded my brother's fear of strangers.

"Oh, Sepp," I said. Slowly, gently, as though I were coaxing a baby bird from its nest, I took my brother by the hand and led him down the hall to his room.

His quarters were in complete disarray. Josef's clothes were strewn about, and someone—perhaps Papa—had brought down a trunk from the attic. His violin case lay open on the bed beside him, the instrument still nestled in its velvet lining. By the looks of it, he hadn't played it all day.

"I can't audition for Master Antonius, Liesl. I just can't."

I said nothing, only opened my arms to hug him close. My brother felt slight and frail in my arms. We were both small and bird-boned, but I was hale and full of life where my brother was delicate. As a babe he had been taken with scarlatina worse than either Käthe or me, and he had been prone to fevers and agues ever since.

"I'm scared, Liesl," he whispered.

"Shh," I soothed, stroking his hair. "You'll be marvelous."

"It should be you, Liesl," he said. "It should you before Master Antonius. Not me."

"Shush," I said. "*You* are the virtuoso. Not me." It was true. While Papa had taught us all to play the violin, it was Josef whose playing sparkled with brilliance. I was a composer, not a performer.

"Yes, but you are the *genius*," he said. "You are the creator; I'm just an interpreter."

Tears started in my eyes. My brother told me my music was worth something every day of his life, but it still hurt to hear him say it.

"Don't hide away," he pleaded. "You deserve to be heard. The world needs to hear your music. You can't be so selfish as to keep it to yourself."

Oh but I could, but it was not out of selfishness; it was shame. I was untrained, untaught, untalented. It was easier— safer—to hide behind Josef. My brother could prune my wild imaginings into a beautiful garden, smooth their rough edges, and present a work of art to the world.

"But I wouldn't keep it to myself," I said softly. "You would play my music for me."

That was how it had always been. Josef was my amanuensis; through him I could play the music I heard in my soul.

I was the violin, he was the bow. We were the left and right hands of a single fortepianist, meant to be played together and not apart. I wrote the music; Josef played it for the world. This was how it would always be.

He shook his head. "No. No."

Anger flared through me, anger and frustration and jealousy. Josef could have it all, all we had ever wanted, if he would only take the chance. And he *had* the chance, something I would never have. Could never have.

Sensing my shift in mood, my brother turned to hug me harder. "Oh, Liesl, I'm sorry, I'm sorry," he said into my shoulder. "I'm a terrible person. I know I'm being selfish."

My anger faded, leaving me drained and exhausted. No, it was not my brother who was a terrible person; it was I. I, who begrudged him the opportunity of a lifetime because it would never be mine.

"You're not selfish, Sepperl," I said. "You're the least selfish person I know."

Josef glanced at the window of his bedroom, toward the forest surrounding our inn. The sun was setting, lending a bloody cast to everything. My brother absentmindedly ran his fingers over the bridge of his violin. It was a del Gesù, one of the few valuable violins we had left after Papa sold the others to Herr Kassl to settle his debts. The Amatis, Stainers, and Stradivarii were long gone.

"What if," he said at last, "I made a wish, and had it answered?"

The reddish light threw all the hollows and shadows of his face into ghastly relief. The bruises beneath his eyes and jaw where he rested it against the chin rest were the color of old blood.

"What wish, Sepperl?" I asked gently.

"To be the greatest violinist in the world." Josef traced the f-holes, lightly sliding his fingers up the neck to rest on the scroll. The scroll was one of the violin's more unusual parts, carved into the shape of a woman. It was not the woman that was unusual; it was the fact that her face was carved into an expression of agony. Or ecstasy. I was never quite sure. "To play with such beauty as to make angels weep."

"Then your wish was granted." I smiled, but the smile twisted in my mouth. *If only our wishes had power.* I thought of being young and sitting by Käthe's side in church, our bony thighs pressed into the hard wooden pews. I remembered looking at my sister's golden hair haloed by the sun, and wishing—no, *praying*—that I would grow up to be beautiful too.

"That's what I'm afraid of," he whispered.

"Afraid? Of your God-given gift?"

"God has nothing to do with it," he said grimly.

"Josef!" I was shocked. We might have been indifferent churchgoers, but God was as ritual and routine as washing up in the morning. To deny Him utterly was blasphemy.

"You, of all people, should know this, Liesl," Josef said. "Think you that our music comes from *God*? No, it comes from below. From *him*. The Ruler Underground."

I knew my brother did not speak of the Devil. I had always known that Josef had faith—kept faith—with Constanze and the Goblin King. More than Papa. More than me. But I had not understood just how deeply his belief in the uncanny was stitched into his bones.

"How else can you explain the wildness, the abandon we feel when we play together?"

Was Josef afraid he was *damned*? God, the Devil, and the

Goblin King were larger figures in my brother's life than I had realized. More than either Käthe or me, Josef had been sensitive to the moods and emotions around him. It was what made him a superb and sublime interpreter of music. Perhaps this was why he played with such exquisite clarity, agony, frenzy, ecstasy, and longing. It was fear. Fear and inspiration and divine providence all in one.

"Listen to me," I said firmly. "The abandon we feel—that is not sin. That is *grace*. Grace is not a gift bestowed upon you that can suddenly be taken away. It is within you, Sepperl, a part of you. You carry that grace inside. And you will carry it with you all your life, no matter where you go."

"But what if it's not grace?" Josef whispered. "What if it's a favor to be repaid?"

I said nothing. I did not know what to say.

"I know you don't believe me," he said miserably. "And I wouldn't, either. But I remember a dream, and it returns to me piece by piece, night by night. I dream of a tall, elegant stranger who comes to me."

Josef turned his head, and although it was dark, I could imagine the blush staining his cheeks. My brother had never confided in me outright about his romantic inclinations, but I knew him better than anyone else. I knew, and I understood.

"The stranger places his hand upon my brow, and says I will carry the music of the Underground with me, so long as I never leave this place." Josef turned his eyes to me, but he didn't seem to see me. "I was born here. I was meant to die here."

"Don't say that," I said sharply. "Don't you dare say that."

"Don't you believe so? My blood belongs to the land, Liesl. Yours too. We draw our inspiration from it, from the ground beneath our feet, as surely as the trees in the wood. Without it, how can we continue? How can I still play my music when my soul rests here, in the Goblin Grove?"

"Your soul rests within you, Sepperl." I lightly touched my hand to his breast. "Here. That's where your music comes from. Not from the land. Not from the woods outside."

"I don't know." Josef buried his face in his hands. "But I am afraid. I am afraid of the bargain I struck with the stranger in my dreams. But now you understand why I'm too terrified to leave."

I understood, but not in the way my brother intended. I saw his fear, and saw the demons he conjured to justify his fear. Unlike me or Käthe, Josef had never seen anything of the world beyond our little corner of Bavaria. He did not know what delights the world could offer, what sights, what sounds, and what *people* he could encounter. I did not want my brother to stay home, to stay confined to the Goblin Grove and Constanze's apron strings. Or mine. I wanted him to go out and live his life, even as it pained me to let him go.

"Come." I walked to the klavier. "Let us play. Forget our woes. Just you and me, *mein Brüderchen*." I felt, rather than saw, my brother smile. I sat down on the bench and played a simple repeating phrase.

"Don't you want the light?" Josef asked.

"No, leave it." I knew where the keys were anyway. "Let's just sit in the dark and play. No sheet music. Nothing we know by heart. I will give you the *basso continuo*, and you will improvise."

I heard the faint *plink* of strings against the soundboard as Josef pulled the violin from its case, the soft *shush* as he ran his bow over the rosin cake. He settled the instrument beneath his chin, touched the bow to the strings, and began to play.

Time passed in waves, and my brother and I lost ourselves in music. We improvised on established structures, embellished on some of the sonatas we knew from memory, and then gradually segued into what Josef was to play for Master Antonius. Papa had decided on a Haydn sonata, though I had suggested Vivaldi. Vivaldi was Josef's favorite composer, but Papa claimed he was too obscure. Haydn—a composer with critical and popular acclaim—was the safer choice.

The music wound down. "Feeling better?" I asked.

"Just one more?" Josef begged. "The largo from Vivaldi's *L'inverno*. Please."

By now the enchantment the music had woven over us was fading. Käthe had accused me of loving Josef more, but it was not Josef I loved more; it was music. I loved my sister as much as I loved my brother, but I loved music most of all.

I glanced over my shoulder. "We should go," I said. "Your audience awaits." I closed the lid of the klavier and rose from the seat.

"Liesl." Something in my brother's voice gave me pause.

"Yes, Sepp?"

"Don't leave me alone," he whispered. "Don't let me go into that long night alone."

"You won't go alone." I gathered him close. "You will never be alone. I am always with you, in spirit if not in flesh. Distance won't make a difference to us. We will write each other letters. We will share our music with each other, in paper, ink, and blood."

It was a long time before he spoke. "Give me a little something, then," he said. "Just a little melody, to hold your promise."

I pulled at a scrap of melancholy and hummed a few notes. I paused, waiting for him to tell me my opening chords.

"Major seventh," was all Josef said. His smile was wry. "Of course that's what you start with."

## THE AUDITION

the sounds of the gathered guests in the main hall flooded the corridor outside Josef's room. My brother shrank back, but I pulled him along, bringing him out from the darkness and into the light.

Our little inn had never seen this many patrons before. Many of the assembly were burghers from town, including Herr Baumgartner, Hans's father. Mother bustled back and forth between the tables, serving the customers alone. Käthe emerged from the kitchen with platters of food a few moments later, Hans on her heels with steins of beer.

"There's our little Mozart!" One of the guests rose to his feet, pointing excitedly in my direction. My heart leaped with both excitement and fear, but then I saw he was pointing to Josef hiding behind me. "Come, *Mozartl,* play us a jig!"

Of course the guest wasn't referring to me. I was no one, the forgotten Vogler child with neither looks nor talent to recommend her. But the truth did nothing to lessen the sting of disappointment.

Josef gripped my skirts. "Liesl—"

"I'm right here, Sepp." I gently nudged him in Master Antonius's direction. "Go on."

Our father and the violin master were sitting by the fortepiano near the hearth. It was the nicer of our two klaviers; Papa had used it when he was still teaching. Our father stood over the celebrated musician, animatedly reminiscing about the time they'd played with the "greats" during their erstwhile Salzburg careers. They spoke in Italian—Master Antonius's mother tongue, and one Papa did not know particularly well. I noticed the scattered steins by Papa's side and winced; when our father had a few drinks in him, it was impossible to get him to stop.

"Is this the boy?" Master Antonius asked when Josef stepped forward. He spoke German passably well.

"Yes, maestro." Papa proudly clapped my brother on the shoulder. "This is Franz Josef, my only son."

Josef gave me a frightened glance, but I nodded encouragingly.

"Come closer, boy." Master Antonius beckoned Josef to his side. To my surprise, the old master's fingers were gnarled and bent with rheumatism; it was amazing he was still able to play the violin. "How old are you?"

Josef quailed. "Fourteen, sir," he managed after a few swallows.

"And how long have you been studying?"

"Since he was a babe," Papa said. "Since before he could speak!"

"I'll have the boy speak for himself, Georg," Master

Antonius said. He turned back to Josef. "Well?" he har-rumphed. "How do you answer?"

My brother first looked to me, then to Papa. "I have been studying since I was three years old, sir."

Master Antonius snorted. "Let me guess: keyboard, the-ory, history, and composition, eh?"

"Yes, sir."

"And your father also schooled you in French and Ital-ian, I presume?"

Josef looked stricken. Aside from Bavarian and German, we spoke the barest bit of French, and what little Italian we knew was musical Italian.

"Never mind, I can see that he didn't." Master Antonius waved his hand dismissively. "So," he said, nodding at the violin in Josef's hand. "Let's see what you can do."

There was no disguising the skepticism and contempt in the old maestro's voice. He must have been wondering why Georg Vogler had never taken his son to any of the capital cities for further instruction, if Josef's skill was indeed of any worth.

*Because,* I thought with despair, *Papa can't see farther than the bottom of his next drink.*

"Well?" Master Antonius prompted when Josef hesitated. "What are you going to play, boy?"

"A Haydn sonata," my brother said, stuttering a little. My stomach clenched in sympathetic misery.

"Haydn, eh? Never did compose anything of worth for the violin. Which one?"

"The—the one in D major. N-number two."

"I suppose you'll be needing accompaniment. *Fran-çois!*"

Both Josef and I jumped when a slender youth materialized by Master Antonius's side, astonished by the valet's sudden appearance. But I didn't know what astonished us more—the young man's beauty, or his dark skin.

"This is my assistant, François," Master Antonius said, ignoring the gasps and gapes from the assembled masses. "He is regrettably not a violinist, but he fingers the keyboard masterfully."

My brows lifted at the sneer in the old man's words. The youth, impeccably and garishly dressed in a gold and ivory frock coat, buckskin breeches, and powdered wig, seemed more like a pretty pet than a musician's assistant. My stomach began to sink with fear; just what sort of man was Master Antonius?

Josef cleared his throat and gave me a panicked look. We had practiced together, and had therefore expected to be performing together. I stepped forward.

"If you please," I said. "I would like to accompany my brother."

Master Antonius noticed me for the first time. "Who is this?"

"My daughter Elisabeth is also educated in music," Papa said. "You must forgive her, maestro; I indulged her fancies as a child."

I winced. Yes, Papa had taught me music—not on my own merits, but as a means to an end. I was an afterthought, an accompanist, not a musician in my own right.

"A veritable family of musicians," Master Antonius remarked in a dry voice. "A regular Nannerl to yon boy's Wolfgang, is it?"

Papa shook his head. "We will, of course, defer to young master François here, if that is your wish, Antonius."

Master Antonius nodded. *"François, assieds-toi et aide le*

*petit poseur avec sa musique, sonate de Haydn, s'il te plait. Numéro deux, majeur D.*"

François gave a sharp bow and walked to the fortepiano, flipping out his coattails as he sat down at the bench, giving us all a flash of sky-blue silk lining. His poise in the midst of the audience's all-too-curious and none-too-friendly stares was incredible. The youth readied his hands over the keyboard and nodded at my brother, awaiting his cue.

Josef was agog. The youth was beautiful: his skin smooth and completely flawless, his lips full, his eyes dark, his lashes long. We had never seen a black person before, but I didn't think it was the color of François's skin that captivated my brother.

I cleared my throat, and Josef flinched. He immediately busied himself with his violin, his cheeks flaming, unable to meet François's gaze. The youth had a slight, bashful smile about his face.

My brother managed to regain his composure, and nodded at François, setting the tempo with his bow. The two began to play, and a hush fell over the room.

To the untrained ear, it might have been hard to distinguish Josef's—or even François's—playing from any other professional musician. They hit all their notes with precision and clarity, their phrasing impeccable. But if you knew my brother as I did, or even if you loved music at all, you could *feel* the intelligence, the *intent*, behind his performance. He interpreted what was written into something almost like speech, as if he could wring words and sentences from the notes and phrases.

But the majority of the assembled guests were not trained in music, and shortly after the two started playing, the low buzz of conversation arose once more. Most returned to their food and drink, keeping their voices down to a respectful murmur. A polite few kept their attention focused on Josef and François: Master Antonius, my family, and Hans. But I spied another in a darkened corner of the room, and my heart stopped.

It was the Goblin King.

He sat among us, brazen and bare-faced, inconspicuously dressed in leather trousers and a roughspun woolen coat. Yet it was difficult to miss his unusual height, his slender physique, his strange coloring, so starkly different from the rest of us stocky, dark-haired peasants. The Goblin King caught my eye. His gaze reached right through me, touching some private core deep within me no one else could see. His lips twisted to one side, a sardonic smile.

His presence scratched that itch in my mind, that niggling sense of something lost. And then it all returned to me in a rush of fear: spindly fingers and bloody fruit, my sister in a red cloak in a winter wood, a forgotten conversation among the alders. Suddenly, it was just the two of us, suspended in a moment. Time, like memory, was just another one of his toys.

I was torn. I wanted to confront him. I wanted to ignore him. But I was afraid to approach the Goblin King, afraid to acknowledge his existence. To confront him was to make him real, and I wanted to keep him my beautiful, indulgent secret.

"Yes, yes," Master Antonius murmured, nodding approvingly.

The moment burst, and the sounds of Josef's and François's playing returned to me, beautiful and pure.

"Very impressive. Very impressive indeed."

My hopes lifted. Master Antonius wore a smug, self-congratulatory expression on his face.

"François is quite a specimen, no?"

Disgust roiled through me. *Specimen.* This was the man into whose hands we were entrusting Josef's career.

"Astonishing," Master Antonius continued in a conspiratorial whisper, sotto voce, to my father. "I picked him up as a babe from a traveler from Saint-Domingue. His mother was a slave back in Hispaniola, and his father some no-account sailor. Not a shred of musical ability between the two of them, and look at him now! Proof that if you get them young, you can train these Negroids like any other person."

I was going to be sick. Of all people, the old virtuoso should know that music was God's gift to man. Music, and a soul. Skills could be taught, but talent could not. François's fingers flew over the keyboard with ease, and the proof of his soul lay in his playing, more human than Master Antonius.

I could not bear to watch any longer. Unbidden, my eyes went to the darkened corner where I had last seen the Goblin King, but there was no one there. Perhaps I had imagined him after all.

Two more movements in the sonata to go, but I could see that Master Antonius had already made up his mind. No one could deny Josef's skill, but there was something missing from the notes, something special, something *more.*

*Papa made a mistake,* I thought. Haydn was too cerebral for my brother; Josef would have been better served by Vivaldi, as I had suggested. Vivaldi *was* a violinist; he had known of the instrument's capabilities and wrote for them. Josef knew this. I knew this. Papa had known this too, once.

The main hall was overly warm now, stuffed with bodies comfortably digesting their *Kraut, Wurst, und Bier*. Josef and François played on, oblivious to everything but the joy of each other's performance. I noted how they responded to each other's cues: the sway of my brother's body, the tilt of François's shoulders, they played like lovers who knew every nuance of the other's sighs. Tears started in my eyes.

Polite applause rose from the assembly as the movement wound to a close. Josef and François smiled at each other, a glow of joy bathing both their faces. Papa clapped like a fiend, but Master Antonius hid a bored yawn behind his hand.

"Very good, very good," the old virtuoso said to Josef. "You are quite talented, young man. You will go far with the right teacher."

My brother's face fell. Josef was naïve, not blind, and he knew exactly what Master Antonius hadn't offered along with his congratulations: an apprenticeship.

"Yes, sir." His blue eyes shimmered in the firelight. "My thanks for the opportunity to play for you."

The sight of my brother's unshed tears was the last straw. "And just who is the right teacher, maestro?" My voice cut through the chatter and applause like a scythe. "Who could possibly take Josef on as a pupil if not you?"

A hush fell over the room. I felt the astonished stares like daggers at my back, but I ignored them. Master Antonius's eyes sharpened as they focused on me.

"Ignore her, Antonius," Papa said. "She overreaches herself."

The old virtuoso waved him off. "I have my reasons for taking the pupils I do, *Fräulein*," he said. "And while your brother is a very talented musician, he lacks a certain, how do you say, *je ne sais quoi*?"

His pretension was as odious as his condescension; his French was scarcely better than mine, and with a decidedly Italian accent. "And what is that, maestro?" I asked.

"Genius." Master Antonius looked smug. "True genius."

I crossed my arms. "Pray, be more specific, maestro," I said. "I'm afraid we rustic peasants have not your worldly experience." Grumbles from the audience, and their pointed daggers of curiosity were aimed at Master Antonius now.

"Liesl," Papa warned. "You overreach yourself."

"No, no, Georg," the old violinist said. "The young lady has a point." He smirked. "True genius is not just technical skill, yes? Any fool could learn to play all the right notes. It takes a certain . . . *passion* and brilliance to bring the notes together to say something true. Something real."

I nodded in agreement. "Then if true genius is performance and ability and passion," I said, not daring to look at Papa, "perhaps my brother was ill-served by the choice of music."

This piqued the old master's interest. He lifted his bushy brows, his dark eyes beady in his fleshy face. "So the little *Fräulein* fancies herself a better tutor than her father! Well, I am tickled. You amuse me, girl. Very well, then, I shall humor you. What will you have your brother play?"

Josef turned panicked eyes on me. I gave him a small smile, the one he called my *pixie smile,* playful and mischievous.

I walked to the fortepiano. François graciously gave way. Josef looked nervous, but he trusted me, trusted me completely. I placed my hands against the keys and began to play a set of repeating sixteenth notes, trying my best to imitate the pizzicato sound of a violin.

My brother's eyes brightened when he recognized the ostinato.

*Yes, Sepp,* I thought. *Now we shall play the* L'inverno.

He tucked his violin under his chin, his bow poised over the strings. After another measure, Josef closed his eyes and began to play the second movement, the largo, from Vivaldi's *L'inverno.*

The melody was gentle and a little melancholy; when we were babies, Papa used to play the largo as a lullaby. The piece was simple enough that three-year-old Sepperl had learned it by ear on his quarter-size violin, but it was a piece to grow on. My brother had experimented with flourishes and improvisations, refining the music until it became something solely his own. No one could wring shades of nostalgia and wistful longing from this movement like Josef. As he grew older and more skilled, he'd continued to practice it over and over until he and his violin were one. Of all the sonatas and concertos Josef knew, this was the one that sounded the closest to his own voice, the one in which his violin sounded the most human.

The violin sang, serenading all those who listened, weaving a spell that made the silence around it sound reverent. Holy.

The largo movement of the winter suite wasn't long, and all too soon, Josef and I approached the end of the piece. His body was slowing down, taking the last trill ritardando. I strove to match him, slowing down my accompaniment as the last note faded away with a tremulous shimmer.

The quivering memory of that final note held us rapt. Then thunderous applause broke the spell, started by Master Antonius himself. François leaped to his feet with shouts of *"Bravo! Bravissimo!"*

Josef colored, but his eyes shone as he grinned at François. Without warning, he launched into the third movement of Vivaldi's *L'estate,* the presto. Intense and fast, it called for all his abilities as a virtuoso player, and I could not keep up with him. I had adapted the accompaniment to the *largo* myself, but I hadn't done the other seasons. François nodded at me and I relinquished my seat to him.

Within a heartbeat, he found Josef in the music and launched into the performance. He pounded the chords where my brother emphasized the shivering trills, he relented when my brother dropped a phrase sotto voce. He knew when to pause to allow Josef's incredible playing to take flight, where to supplement the holes in the accompaniment to sound seamless. My throat was tight; this slender, dark-skinned youth knew my brother's unspoken cues even better than I. He could fall into Josef's rhythms without thought, and he could adapt and modify music he knew and music he didn't.

Somehow, incredibly, they finished exactly in unison. The hall erupted with praise. Papa clapped Josef on the back, shouting loudly for all to hear that he had *taught the boy everything he knows,* while Master Antonius could be heard congratulating François's astonishing impromptu performance.

"I didn't even know you knew Vivaldi, François, you sly dog!" The violin master turned to Josef. "You!" he said. "Now *you* are a young man of taste and vision. Vivaldi! *Il Prete Rosso,* or the Red Priest, as we called him back home. He did much for the violin, you know, even as *some people*"—Master Antonius shot a look at Papa—"no longer recognize his genius."

Never mind that it had been I who suggested Vivaldi, not

Josef; it was lost in the rush and aftermath of my brother's playing.

"Thank you, maestro." Josef's face was flushed, his eyes aglow. I sought out his gaze to congratulate him, but he had eyes for François and François alone. The youth looked back.

I turned away. Papa shouted and toasted and drank to celebrate his son, and Mother—stern, stoic, unsentimental Mother—wept unashamedly into her apron. Constanze nodded her approval from her nest by the hearth, while Käthe . . .

My heart stopped.

Where was Käthe?

*Gone,* a soft voice murmured in my ear.

Startled, I looked over my shoulder. No one was there, but my ear tingled from the brush of someone's lips. The jubilation continued on around me, but I was excluded, standing outside everyone else's excitement.

"Käthe," I whispered.

*Gone,* the voice said again.

This time I saw him.

He was standing in a far corner of the main hall, leaning against the wall with his arms crossed. The tall, elegant stranger.

The Goblin King.

He was the still point around which everything revolved. He was reality where everything else was a reflection. He stood out in sharp relief when everything else was muted, as though we were the only two alive and present in a world of illusion and shadow. He smiled at me, and every fiber of my being reached for him. His very grin could command my flesh to dance.

He nodded, indicating the door that led outside. He moved through the crowd like a wraith, a *geist* passing through the revelers like mist. They never noticed the touch of his hand as he gently moved them out of the way, only pausing in their conversations as if they felt an unexpected chill. But not a soul saw the Goblin King as he walked among them—it was me, and me alone.

He paused at the threshold of the door, glancing over his shoulder. He lifted a pale brow.

*Come.*

It was more than a summons; it was a command. I felt the call in my bones, the tug upon my flesh, but still I resisted.

Those icy eyes glittered, and I was afraid. I trembled, but not with cold. I ached, but not with pain. My feet began to move of their own accord, and I followed the Goblin King out of the light and into the darkness.

# THE TALL,
# ELEGANT STRANGER

h e plays well, your brother."

I blinked. The world around me was dark, and it was a long time before I began to make shapes out in the gloom. Trees, and a full moon. The Goblin Grove. I had no memory of how I had gotten here.

A velvet voice stroked down my spine. "I'm quite pleased, quite pleased indeed."

I turned around. The Goblin King was lounging against one of the alder trees in the grove, one arm draped against the trunk, the other resting casually against his hip. His hair was in wild disarray, ruffled and feathery, like thistledown, like spiderwebs, illuminated by the full moon into a halo about his head. His face held all the beauty of angels, but the grin upon his face was positively devilish.

"Hello, Elisabeth," he said softly.

I stood dumb and silent. How did one respond to *Der Erlkönig*, Lord of Mischief, Ruler of the Underground? How did one address a legend? My mind spun, trying to reel in my emotions. The Goblin King stood before me, in flesh and not in memory.

"*Mein Herr*," I said.

"So polite." His voice was as dry as autumn leaves. "Ah, Elisabeth, we need not stand on formalities here. Have we not known each other your entire life?"

"Liesl," I said. "Then call me Liesl."

The Goblin King grinned. The tips of his pointed teeth gleamed. "I much prefer Elisabeth, thank you. Liesl is a girl's name. Elisabeth is the name of a woman."

"And what do I call you?" I strove to keep my voice from shaking.

Again that predator's smile. "Whatever you like," he murmured. "Whatever you like."

I ignored the purr in his voice. "Why did you bring me here?"

"Tsk, tsk." The Goblin King waved one long, slender finger at me. "I had thought you a worthy opponent. We were playing a game, *Fräulein,* but you don't seem much inclined to engage me."

"A game?" I asked. "What game?"

"Why, the best game in the world." He leaped from his languid pose by the alder tree, suddenly alert, suddenly sharp. "One where I take something you love and hide it. If you don't come find it, it's mine to keep."

"What are the rules?"

"The rules are simple," he said. "I find it, I keep it. I'll note that you haven't made much of an effort to play. A pity," he pouted. "We used to play so often when you were a child. Don't you remember, Elisabeth?"

I closed my eyes. Yes, I had played with *Der Erlkönig*

when I was young, after Käthe had gone to bed, before Sepperl was old enough to talk. Back when I was still myself, whole and entire, before time and responsibility had whittled me to a sliver of myself. I would run to the Goblin Grove to greet the Lord Underground. I would be dressed in a gown of the finest silk and satin, he trimmed in lace and brocade. The musicians would play and we would dance, dancing to the music I heard in my head. It was when I first began to write down my musical scribblings, when I first began to compose.

"I remember," I said in a low voice.

But did I remember something I had imagined, or something real? There was pretend, and then there was memory. I could see little Liesl dancing with the Goblin King, a Goblin King who was always just a little older, just a little out of reach. A Goblin King who fulfilled all her childish fantasies, who told her she was pretty, who told her she was cherished, who told her she was worthy of being loved. Was that a memory? Or a dream?

"But not everything." He leaned in close. He was not my size now; he was tall and reed-thin. Had he been an ordinary man, he might have been called lanky. But he was not an ordinary man; he was *Der Erlkönig*, possessed of a preternatural grace. Every movement of his body was smooth, fluid, purposeful. He stood by me, hovering over my shoulder, breathing into my neck. "Do you remember, Elisabeth, the little games of chance we used to play?"

*Wagers.* Constanze said goblin men loved to gamble. If you could trick them into playing with you, they bet everything until they lost.

I recalled the games the Goblin King and I had played, simple enough guessing games with simple enough stakes.

Wishes and favors and hopes laid out on the betting table like cards.

*Guess which hand holds the golden ring.*

I remembered laughing and picking a hand at random.

*What will you bet, little Liesl? What will you give up if you lose? What will you gain if you win?*

What answer had I given? I was suddenly, terribly, horribly afraid of what young Liesl had been willing to give. What I had unwittingly sacrificed.

"You lost the game." The Goblin King circled me, a wolf stalking a hart. "You lost every game."

I never chose right. The prize was never in the hand I thought. Perhaps the game had been stacked against me from the start.

"You promised me something I desperately needed," he continued, drawing out his syllables into a drawl. "Something only you could give." His eyes glowed in the dark. "I am a generous soul, Elisabeth, but no man waits forever."

"And what did I promise?" I whispered.

The Goblin King chuckled, and the sound rippled through my body.

"A wife, Elisabeth. You promised me a bride."

The word fell between us, a drop of water in a bowl, sending ripples of fear through me. *Now the days of winter begin, and the Goblin King rides abroad, searching for his bride.*

"Oh, God," I whispered. "Käthe."

"Yes," the Goblin King hissed. "I am patient, Elisabeth. I have waited a long time. A long time during which you never came. A long time during which you grew distant. A long time during which you forgot me."

"I never forgot you." It was true. If I no longer played pretend, then the memory of *Der Erlkönig* remained lodged in my soul. I could no more remove him from my life than I could remove my heart and live.

"No?" He lifted a hand to brush an errant curl from my face, but hesitated. He curled his hand into a fist and dropped it back to his side. "Then you denied me, and that is an even greater betrayal than forgetting."

I turned my head away, unable to look at him.

"First your father, then you, and now your brother," he said. "Only Constanze keeps faith with me now. The days of the Wild Hunt draw to a close, and no one heeds its call anymore."

"I heed it," I said. "What do you want from me?"

"Nothing." His voice was almost sad. "It's too late now, Elisabeth. The game was played, and you are forfeit."

*Käthe.*

"Where is my sister?" I quavered.

The Goblin King did not respond, but I sensed, rather than saw, the knife-edged smile on his lips.

There was only one place Käthe could be. Far beneath the earth, in the realm of *Der Erlkönig* and his goblins.

The Underground.

"The game isn't over," I said. "You've but made the opening gambit."

This time, I made myself look him directly in the eyes. In the bright moonlight, they were two different colors: one as gray as a winter sky, the other a hazel-green, the color of moss peeking through dead loam. Wolf's eyes. The Devil's eyes. He could see into the darkness. He could see into me.

"I chose the wrong hand the first time." The salt. The audition. Guilt gripped me in a vise; I had chosen Josef over Käthe. Again.

His smile grew wider. "Very good."

"Fine," I said. "I'll play." I tilted my head back. "I'll play your game. If I find Käthe, you will let my sister go."

"Is that all?" he said petulantly. "Not much of a game if there's nothing interesting you're willing to sacrifice."

"The rules were simple, so you said. Finders, keepers. You take, I lose. You hide, I find. Whoever fails is the loser. Let's say . . . best of three."

"Very well then." He huffed his shoulders. "But remember, Elisabeth, our childish games are behind us now." Those wolf's eyes glittered. "When I play, I play for keeps. Should you fail to bring your sister back to the world above by the next full moon, she will be lost to you forever."

I nodded.

"You lost the first round," the Goblin King said. "You must win the next two in order to win."

I gave another nod. From Constanze's stories, I knew how it would go. I had failed to protect my sister from the goblin men. I must not fail to find my way to her in the Underground.

"No tricks," I said. "No cheating. No taking away my memories. No playing with time."

The Goblin King tutted. "I make no such promises. You knew the stakes when you chose to engage with me."

I shuddered.

"However," he said. "I *am* generous, after all. I shall promise you one thing, and one thing only. Your eyes will remain open. But you cannot deny me the power to cloud the minds of others as it suits my purposes. "

I nodded again.

"Oh, Elisabeth," he said. "You foolish, foolish girl. How easily you give me your trust."

"I play the hand I am dealt."

"Yes, and by my rules." The tips of his teeth glinted. "Beware, Elisabeth. You may prefer the pretty lie to the ugly truth."

"I am not afraid of ugliness."

He watched me and I steeled myself against his scrutiny. "No," he said softly. "You're not." He straightened his shoulders. "Until the next full moon." He pointed to the moon in the sky, and for a moment, I thought I saw the hands of a clock pass over its face. "Or your sister is lost forever."

"The next full moon," I repeated.

The Goblin King moved closer. His hand cupped my chin, and I raised my eyes to his multicolored gaze. "I shall enjoy playing with you," he said in a low voice. He bent down, and the touch of his breath against my lips was cold.

*Viel Glück, Elisabeth.*

Then he was gone.


"Liesl!"

The voice was muffled, as though heard through ice or water.

"Liesl! *Liesl!*"

I tried to open my eyes, but they were frozen shut. After a few moments, I managed to crack one open, and through the ice and tangled lashes, I could see a blurred shape running toward me.

"Hans?" I croaked.

"You're alive!" He pressed his hand to my cheek, but I felt nothing: no warmth, no sensation of touch, nothing but light pressure. "By God, Liesl, what happened to you?"

I could not answer. Even if I could, I did not want to

answer. Hans scooped me up in his arms and carried me back to the inn.

I felt nothing but cold, nothing of life, of warmth, or of Hans's arms around my legs, beneath my back, his hands curled around my chest. It was as though I were dead. I might as well be dead. I had sacrificed my sister for my brother. Again. I deserved to die.

*Käthe,* I said. But Hans did not hear me.

"We must get you inside and warm immediately," he said. "God, Liesl, what were you thinking? Your mother and Josef have been frantic with worry; Josef even threatened he would not join with Master Antonius until you were found."

*Käthe,* I tried again.

"Your father was beside himself; I thought he had gone mad! I never want to see him that drunk again."

How long had I been gone? It couldn't have been more than an hour—two at most—that I had spent in the grove with the Goblin King.

"How—how long—" My throat was hoarse, my voice creaky with disuse.

"Three days." The calmness of Hans's tone did not disguise the very real fear and panic in his voice. "You were gone for three days. Josef's audition with Master Antonius was three days ago."

Three days? How could that be possible? Hans must be exaggerating.

*No tricks. No cheating. No taking away my memories. No playing with time.* The Goblin King had broken his promises already.

But he had not made me any. *I shall promise you one thing, and one thing only. Your eyes will remain open.* My eyes were open. I remembered it all.

"Käthe," I said again, but Hans shushed me with a finger against my lips.

"No talking now, Liesl. I'm here. I shall take care of you," he said. "I shall take care of all of you, never you fear."

Back at the inn, everyone was in a tizzy. Mother embraced me and wept, an untoward display of emotion. The age-old tracks of beery tears stained the grooves in Papa's cheeks, and Josef, dear Sepperl, said nothing and clenched my hand with white-knuckled ferocity. Only Constanze stood apart, her dark eyes boring into mine.

My sister was gone.

I was responsible.

Mother coddled and fussed over me as though I were a babe, wrapping me in woolen blankets, demanding that Papa place me in his favorite chair by the hearth, bringing me soup and even tea with just a dash of rum.

"Oh, Liesl!" she said tearfully. "Oh, Liesl!"

Her intense outpouring of affection discomfited me. Mother and I had never been particularly close; we were each too preoccupied with holding our lives together— Mother the business, me the family. I found it hard to express my love for my mother; we shared an understanding, but we did not share hugs.

Seeing my discomfort, Mother wiped at her eyes and nodded. "It's good to see you safe, Liesl." She was once again practical, no-nonsense Frau Vogler, innkeeper's wife. All hints and signs of her previous breakdown had vanished, save for her reddened eyes.

"Mother was worried you had run away from home," Josef whispered.

I was incredulous. "Why would I run away from home?"

Josef gave a sidelong glance to Papa, who was hunched in the corner. He looked years older, suddenly haggard and worn and sad. He had always been blithe and gay, a shambling semblance of the bright, vivacious, promising young man he had been. His cheeks, reddened by years of drink, lent him a childish air, and his convivial nature disguised his graver shortcomings to all but those who knew him best.

"Because . . . because you had nothing left to live for," Josef said.

"What?" I struggled to sit up, but the myriad of blankets draped around me trapped me in a cocoon of knitted wool. "Don't be ridiculous, Sepperl."

Hans's hand stayed me in my seat. "Liesl." His voice was kind. "We know how hard you worked to keep this family together. We know what you did for Josef, how you worked your entire life to further his career. We know you neglected your own hopes and dreams for his future. We know your own parents often passed you over in favor of him."

A prickling sensation overcame me. Hans was echoing all my selfish and unkind thoughts, validating my every frustration. Yet I felt no relief, no triumph, only a vague sense of dread.

"That still doesn't explain why you all thought I would run away," I said crossly.

Hans and Josef exchanged looks. I distrusted this new sympathy between them.

"You haven't been well lately, Liesl," Hans said. "You've taken to spending long periods of time alone and in the woods."

"That's not so unusual," I said.

"Of course not," Josef said. "Only . . . you keep telling us you're searching for someone, someone who needs your help desperately."

I stiffened. "Käthe."

The boys exchanged another look. "Yes, Liesl," Hans said carefully.

The thought of my sister sharpened all my senses and mental faculties. "Käthe!" I said again, and this time I managed to disentangle myself from my nest of cloaks and blankets. "I must find her."

"Hush," Hans soothed. "There is no danger. Everything is all right."

I shook my head. "If I've been gone for three days, then Käthe must be in even greater trouble. Have you sent any search parties after her? Have you had any luck in finding her?"

Josef worried his lower lip. His blue eyes shone with tears as he took my hand. "Oh, Liesl."

The cold hand of fear gripped my heart. I misliked what I saw in my brother's face. "What is it?" I asked. "What have you to tell me?"

Over my brother's shoulder, Constanze hovered over us like a bird of prey. Her face was dark, her expression both smug and grave.

"Oh, Liesl," Josef said again. "I'm so very glad you're safe. But I must ask you: who have you been searching for? None of us understand what you've been talking about. Who, my dear, is Käthe?"

# Intermezzo

## THE IDEAL
## IMAGINARY

*n*o *promises,* the Goblin King had said. *Your eyes will remain open, but you cannot deny me the power to cloud the minds of others as it suits my purposes.*

As Josef prepared for his departure with Master Antonius and François, Mother insisted I keep to my rooms and "recuperate."

"You deserve a rest, my dear," she said. "You've worked so long to take care of us; let us now look after you."

*I'm not ill!* I tried to say, but it was no use. The harder I searched for everyone's missing memories of my sister, the more convinced they were that reason had abandoned me.

It was not my mind that had broken.

Or was it?

Käthe was gone, but she was more than gone; she had never existed. All traces of her were wiped completely from our lives and nothing remained, not even a strand of her golden hair. No dried wildflowers from the meadow. No ribbons. No lace. Nothing. She had simply never been.

*Your eyes will remain open.*

My eyes were open, but they could no longer trust what they saw, for it was not what they remembered.

One morning I awoke to find the klavier from Josef's rooms had been moved to mine.

"Who put that there?" I asked Hans. "How did you move it without my hearing?"

Hans frowned. "The klavier has always stood in your room, Liesl."

"No," I said. "No, it has not. How could it? Josef and I practiced in his rooms upon it."

"You and Josef always practiced on the fortepiano downstairs," Hans said. His tone was patient, but his eyes were worried. "This is your own personal klavier, Liesl. See?" He pointed to a stack of music laid across the lid, with notes scrawled in my hand.

"But I never—" I picked up the notes. It looked to be the start of a composition, one I could not recall ever having written. I lightly tapped out the melody on the keyboard. *Major seventh,* my notes said.

The memory of a stolen moment before my brother's audition returned to me. *A little something to hold your promise,* he'd said. *Major seventh, of course that's what you start with.*

But was it a true memory, or a false one? Had I already begun writing this before our conversation? Or was this yet another dream I had wished into existence?

Hans placed his hands on my shoulders and guided me to the bench. His touch was intimate, but my mind recoiled. He was not mine. He had never been mine.

"Here, Liesl," he said gently. "Play. Compose. I know how much your music brings you solace."

*Liesl.* Had I always been thus? I thought I could remember the words *Fräulein* and *Elisabeth* upon his lips, a distance so vast it could only be bridged by awkwardness.

"Hans—Hansl." The endearment tasted strange upon my tongue.

"Yes?" His gaze was tender, and wrong. Hans had never looked at me this way, never regarded me as anything but a sister.

"Nothing," I said at last. "Nothing."


I had awoken into a new world, a new life. Reality had snapped in half: truth on one side, lies on the other. But which was which? I struggled to match its jagged edges, but the pieces did not fit.

My "convalescence" kept me confined to my room, where I could do little else but compose. My attempts to leave my confinement, to find Josef, to find Constanze, to run to the Goblin Grove, were all met with kind but firm rebuttals. The Goblin King had said he would not make it easy. I had expected inhuman tasks, supernatural quests, epic battles to bar my path, but what I had not expected was plain, ordinary human compassion. *Rest, dear,* was their repeated refrain. *Rest.*

And I . . . I could not help but be seduced.

It was easy, so damnably easy, to sit at the klavier and let the world outside continue with its twisted regularity. So easy to tinker upon the ivory keys and let my mind take flight, to turn my confusion and longing and unsettled desires into *music.* So easy to compose . . . and forget.

This was the way life should have been.

This was the way life had always been.

The scrap of melancholy, the promise I had begun for Josef, grew into a mournful little bagatelle. I had decided on the key designation and tempo—A minor and common time—but try as I might, the rest of the piece would not fall comfortably into place.

The melody and themes were the easiest to write, and were therefore laid to paper first. Then came the work of figuring out chord progressions and subordinate harmonies, for which I relied heavily on the klavier. I was not Josef; I could not pull them from my head, but I could notate which sounded—no, *felt*—right to me.

After a while, I abandoned writing down my thoughts one phrase at a time and let myself play without pause. I improvised, I experimented, I wandered. Papa said real composers worked within the strictures set upon them, but I wanted to be free. I would shape the world to fit the music in my soul.

I had never composed something solely on my own before; Sepperl usually sat on the bench with me, correcting my mistakes in structure and theory. The music of Bach, Handel, and Haydn had been composed from the mind; I composed from the heart. I was not Mozart, infused with divine inspiration; I was Maria Elisabeth Ingeborg Vogler, mortal and fallible.

A shadow cut the light seeping in from beneath my door.

I immediately stopped playing.

"Who's there?"

There was no response, but the light, shuffling footsteps gave her away.

Constanze.

"What is it?" I repeated.

The footsteps faltered, then stopped. A cold knot of dread formed in my stomach, and I was a child again, caught with my hand in the sugar. Music was an indulgence, and too much sweet would spoil me. I had other tasks, other chores, other duties to attend to.

Käthe.

For a moment, there was utter clarity. I rose from the bench and ran to the door. Constanze kept faith with *Der Erlkönig*. Constanze would remember.

But . . .

I thought of my grandmother pouring salt along the windowsills. I thought of her leaving a tin of milk and a slice of cake out each harvesttide. I thought of her strange and eccentric oddities, more ritual than religion, and thought of Mother's exasperated grumblings, Hans's pitying looks, the villagers' scornful gazes. Constanze kept faith with the Goblin King, and what had her faith availed her?

Nothing.

I glanced about my room, at the klavier in the center, at the dinner tray Mother had set on a low table beside it, at the sachet of dried, sweet herbs from Hans.

Time to compose. Favors from the handsomest man in the village. No shame, no judgment upon who I was, and what I loved. It was only the very beginnings of all the things I had ever wished for, and the possibility of happiness—*real* happiness—stretched out before me, a fork in the road.

What had my lack of faith availed me?

Everything.

Suddenly the clarity was gone.

We stood on either side of the threshold, my grandmother and I, each waiting for the other to cross.

# A PRETTY
# LIE

**a** s the days passed, it was harder and harder to keep hold of my resolve, my convictions, my sanity. Too often I would turn a corner expecting to see a flash of gold or hear the echo of a tinkling laugh. The memory of Käthe in these halls was fading fast, leaving nothing but dust motes in the fading light. Perhaps I had never had a sister. Perhaps I was mad. Perhaps my reason had, in fact, abandoned me.

*Sepperl, Sepperl, what should I do?*

But if reason had abandoned me, then so had my beloved baby brother. More often than not, Josef was to be found with François, the two of them conversing in a mix of French, German, Italian, and music. Master Antonius was anxious to leave, but an unseasonably early ice storm had stopped all travel for a few more days. But the old virtuoso had more to worry about than a few impassable roads; French soldiers crawled our countryside like an infestation of roaches, and the troubling rumors of impending war hung over our heads.

I shouldn't have been jealous. I had promised I wouldn't be jealous. But envy ate me up inside anyway. I saw how Josef's eyes sparkled whenever he beheld François, how the dark-skinned youth smiled in return. My brother was leaving me behind in more ways than one. Like Käthe and Hans, like Mother and Papa, Josef was stepping into a world that seemed forever barred to me.

The future sparkled ahead of Josef, a shining city at the end of a long road. His life stretched out ahead of him, exciting and unknown, whereas mine began and ended here, at the inn. With Josef gone, who would listen to my music? Who would listen to me?

I thought of Hans and his sweet, chaste gestures toward me. I imagined stifled giggles, shared and private jests, *basso continuo* and treble improvisation. I dreamed of fleeting touches, sloppy kisses, whispered breaths and pants in the dark of the night when we thought no one could hear. I wished for love, the ethereal and the physical, the sacred and the profane, and wondered when I, like my brother, like my sister, would cross that threshold into knowledge from innocence.

I retreated into the comforting embrace of my klavier more and more as the date of my brother's departure approached. Without Josef's guiding hand, the bagatelle grew wild and unchecked. Its musical phrases did not resolve themselves according to a logical, rational progression; they went where my flights of fancy took them. I let them go where they will. The results were slightly dissonant, eerie, and unsettling, but I did not mind. After all, I was not a child of beauty; I was a child of the queer, the strange, and the wild.

I had the shape of the piece now, its rise, fall, and resolution. It was simple enough, especially for a virtuoso like Josef. I had written it with the violin in mind, to be accompanied by the fortepiano. I wanted to hear my brother play it, wanted to hear how it would transform in his hands.

A few days later, I got my wish.

François was attending to Master Antonius, who had taken a "mild chill," although it seemed more a fit of jealous pique—he wasn't the only one to have been abandoned by someone he loved, I realized. I found Josef in a rare moment alone downstairs in the main hall, lovingly tending to his violin. Twilight was falling, and the shadows carved the planes of his face into sharp relief. My brother looked like an angel, a sprite, a creature not quite of this world.

"Think you the kobolds will be out tonight?" I asked softly.

He startled. "Liesl!" He set down his oiling rag and wiped his hands on his trousers. "I didn't see you there." He rose from his seat by the hearth, arms out to embrace me.

I walked straight into them. With a pang, I realized he was of a height with me. When had that happened?

"What is it?" he asked, sensing my heartache.

"Nothing." I smiled at him. "It's just . . . you're growing up, Sepp."

He chuckled. It rumbled deep in his chest, a man's chuckle, a bass. Though Josef still retained a boy's sweet soprano, his voice walked the edge of breaking. "It's never nothing with you."

"No," I admitted. I wrapped my hands around his. "I have something for you. A gift."

His brows lifted with surprise. "A gift?"

"Yes," I said. "Come with me. And bring your violin."

Bemused, Josef followed me upstairs to my room. I led him to the klavier, to where the bagatelle rested against the music stand. I had stayed up late the previous night, wasting precious candlelight to make a fair copy.

"What is this?" He squinted and leaned closer.

I didn't say anything, but waited.

"Oh." Josef paused. "An entire new piece?"

"Don't judge too harshly, Sepperl." I tried to laugh off my sudden embarrassment. "It's full of mistakes and errors, I'm sure."

Josef tilted his head. "Do you want me and François to play it for you?"

I flinched. "I had thought," I said, unexpectedly stung, "that we would play it together."

He had the grace to blush. "Of course. Forgive me, Liesl." He took his violin and rested it beneath his chin. He scanned the first few lines and then nodded at me. I was suddenly nervous. I shouldn't be; this was Josef, after all.

I nodded back and Josef lightly bounced his bow up and down, setting the tempo. We gave it a measure, and then began.

The first notes were tentative, unsure. I was nervous and Josef was . . . Josef was unreadable. I faltered, my fingers slipping on the keyboard.

Josef continued to play, reading the notes I'd written with mechanical precision. You could have set a watch by his playing, exact and ruthless. Numbness began to spread from my fingers, traveling through my hands, up my arms, my shoulders, my neck, my eyes, my ears. I had written this piece for the Josef I had known and loved, for the little boy who never skipped out on an opportunity to run away to find the *Hödekin* dancing in the wood. For the child who had shared half my soul, strange and queer and wild, for the brother who kept faith with *Der Erlkönig*.

He wasn't there.

It was as though my brother had been replaced by a changeling. The music did not transform, did not transcend in his hands. The notes were muddy, mundane, terrestrial. Suddenly it was as though I could see the cobwebs of delusion I had woven about myself, through which I could see another world and another life.

Josef finished the piece, holding the last note's fermata with exacting length.

"A good effort, Liesl." He gave me a smile, but it did not quite reach his eyes. "A definite start."

I nodded. "You'll be leaving for Munich tomorrow," I said.

"Yes." Josef sounded relieved. "At first light."

"Get some rest, then." I patted him on the cheek.

"And you?" he asked, inclining his head toward the piece on the klavier, the piece he had just finished playing. "You will write, won't you? Send me more music?"

"Yes," I said.

But we both knew it for a lie.


Energy was high when the coaches arrived to bear Josef, Master Antonius, and François to Munich. Guests and patrons and friends from the village turned out to bid them farewell. Papa wept as he embraced his son, while Mother—stoic-faced and dry-eyed—laid her hands over Josef's head in a quiet benediction. I avoided Constanze's gaze. Her eyes were dark and clouded, her mouth set in a mutinous line.

"*Glück*, Josef." Hans pounded my brother good-naturedly

on the shoulder. "Don't worry about your family; I'll take care of them." He caught my eye and gave me a bashful smile. My heart fluttered, but with nervousness or guilt, I wasn't sure.

"*Danke,*" Josef said absently. His eyes were already distant, already gone.

"*Auf wiedersehen,* Sepp," I said.

My brother looked startled to see me standing beside him. I was easily lost in the shadows—plain, drab, unremarkable—but Josef had always managed to find me. Tears started in my eyes.

"*Auf wiedersehen,* Liesl." He took my hands in his, and for a moment, it was as though the world had never changed, and he was still my beloved Sepperl, the other half of my soul. His blue eyes shone bright as he wrapped me in his arms. It was a boy's hug, unself-conscious and sincere, the last my little brother would ever give me. When—if—we next saw each other, he would be a man.

François came to escort Josef to the coach, to Munich, to greatness, to acclaim. Our eyes met over my brother's head. We did not share the same tongue, but we spoke the same language nonetheless.

*Take care of him,* I said.

*I will,* he replied.

I made myself stand and watch as the coach drew away, as it disappeared down the road, swallowed up by mist, distance, and time. One by one, my family returned to their lives: Papa to his chair by the hearth, Mother to her place in the kitchen. Hans lingered longest, his hand on my shoulder. At last I turned to join what remained of my family inside, but Hans stopped me.

"Hans," I said. "What is it?"

He shushed me. "Come. I have something—something I want to show you."

Frowning, I let him lead me past the creek toward the woodshed. Once there, he pushed me against the wall.

"Hans." I struggled against him. "What—"

He shushed me. "It's all right," he said. This was the most of Hans's body I had ever felt against my own: his hand on my wrist, his chest against mine, his thighs against my hips, the heat of his skin warming mine. "It's all right," he repeated, and gripped me closer. There was an urgency to his touch, a need that stirred my blood.

"What are you doing?" I asked.

But I knew. I had both dreaded and desired it.

His hand pressed against my lower back, pushing our lower limbs together. His right hand released my wrist to slowly come up to caress my cheek. "What I've wanted to do ever since I met you," he breathed.

And then he kissed me.

I closed my eyes and waited, waited for the fires within me to ignite. I had imagined, dreamed of, and yearned for this moment for a long time: the moment Hans would take me in his arms and press his lips to mine. Yet in the precise moment it came to pass, I felt cold. I could feel his lips, his breath, and the tentative brush of his tongue against mine, but he aroused no emotion save vague surprise and detached curiosity.

"Liesl?"

Hans had pulled away, trying to read my expression. I thought of Käthe, but it was not the shape of my sister's body that lay between us.

*You might prefer the pretty lie to the ugly truth,* the Goblin King had said.

I had. This entire life was a pretty lie, and I had thought myself strong enough to resist it. What a fool I'd been, to fall for the Lord of Mischief's tricks.

"Liesl?" Hans repeated, hesitant and unsure. This was all a lie, but what a beautiful, beautiful lie it was.

So I kissed him back.

In the dark of the night, with my back turned to my sister so she would not notice, I had pretended to feel Hans's hands on me, his fingers questing for all the secret hollows and crevices of my body. I imagined his lips and tongue and teeth, I imagined desire so forceful he nearly burst with it, matching the roughness in my restless limbs with his own violence.

The intensity of my kisses startled him, his surprise resonating through him from head to toe. He released me.

"Liesl!"

"Was this not what you wanted?" I asked.

"Yes, it is, but—"

"But what?"

"I didn't expect you to be so forward."

Somewhere, deep in the forest, I thought I could hear an echo of the Goblin King's laugh.

"Is this not what you wanted?" I repeated, angrily wiping at my mouth.

"Of course," Hans replied, but I heard the uncertainty in his voice. The fear, the disgust. "Of course it is, Liesl."

I shoved him away. Fury unfurled from me, a rising wave of frustration.

"Liesl, please." Hans grabbed my sleeve.

"Let me go." My voice was as dead as I felt inside.

"I'm sorry. I just—I just thought you were pure. Chaste. Not like all those other girls, easily spent, easily satiated."

I went rigid. *Käthe.*

"Oh?" I asked tightly. "What other girls, Hans?"

His brows furrowed. "You know," he said vaguely. "The others. But they don't matter to me, Liesl. They're not the sort of girls you marry."

I slapped him. I had never raised my hand against anyone in my life, but I hit him with all the strength I had. My palm stung where it struck his cheek.

"And what sort of girl am I?" I asked in a low voice. "What sort of girl do you marry, Hans?"

He sputtered, but did not form a response.

"When you said pure, you meant plain. When you said chaste, you meant ugly."

My words hit him in all their hideous truth, exposing him for what he truly was. I half expected, half wanted Hans to react, to grab my arm and tell me I was overreaching my bounds. But instead he stumbled back, his hands going limp, submissive.

My lip curled. "I wanted you once," I said. "I thought you were a worthy man, Hans. And deep down, I think you are. But you are not worthy of *me*. All you are is a pretty lie."

Hans reached for me, but I kept my hands to myself.

"Liesl—"

I looked him straight in the eye. "What was it your father used to say?"

Hans said nothing. He turned his head away.

"What's the use of running, if we are on the wrong road?"

## THE UGLY
## TRUTH

I ran straight to Constanze's room.

I should have gone to my grandmother before. Gone the moment I returned from the woods, gone the moment I knew Käthe was stolen. Instead, I had let my grandmother hover on the edges of my awareness like a ghost, unable or unwilling to face the ugly truth. Guilt crawled up my throat, leaking from my eyes.

The door to her quarters was shut. I raised a hand to knock when a querulous voice called, "Well, come in, girl. You've dawdled long enough."

It was true.

I pushed open the door. Constanze sat in her chair by the window, looking out into the forest beyond.

"How did you know I—"

"Those of us touched by the hand of *Der Erlkönig* recognize his own." She turned to face me, her eyes dark and sharp. "I've been expecting you for weeks."

Weeks. Had it truly been that long? I tried to count the days I had lived in this false reality, but they blurred together, connecting seamlessly without end.

"Then why not come seek me?" I asked.

Constanze shrugged. "It is not for me to meddle in his affairs."

Angry words beat against my lips. I swallowed them down, but a few emerged as a choked, incredulous laugh.

"And you would have him change the world as you know it?" I asked. "You would let *Der Erlkönig* win?"

"Win?" She thumped the floor with her cane. "There is no winning with *Der Erlkönig*. Or losing. There is only sacrifice."

"Käthe is not a sacrifice!"

My sister's name boomed like a thunderclap between us. I felt the seams of this false reality come apart at her name, tearing holes in the fabric of my confusion. *Käthe.* I remembered her sunshine hair and bell-like laugh, her jealousy of Josef and her admiration of me, the way only a little sister could admire me. *Grace,* she had said. *Cleverness and talent. That's much more enduring than beauty.* I thought of her thousand thoughtless hurts and kindnesses and the ache of missing my sister, muffled by misdirection and lies, flared into sharp relief.

I buried my face in my hands.

I heard Constanze stir in her seat, turning to face me. If she were a different sort of grandmother, she might have beckoned me close so that she might place her gnarled hands upon my head, stroking my brow while murmuring comforting words.

But Constanze was not that sort of grandmother.

"Well, girlie, what is it you want from me?" she snapped. "Tell me quickly so you'll leave me in peace."

Constanze hardly ever called either Käthe or me by our names, given or otherwise; we were always "girl" or "you," as though we were extraneous, superfluous, or otherwise unimportant.

"I want . . ." My voice was hoarse, barely a whisper. "I want you to tell me how to gain entrance to the Underground."

She said nothing.

"Please." I lifted my head. "Please, Constanze."

"There is nothing you can do," she said, and the finality of her words was worse than her contempt. "Haven't you been listening? Your sister is for the Goblin King now. *It is too late.*"

*Until the next full moon, or your sister is lost forever.*

How much time had passed in this fever dream? Had the full moon risen? I tried to count the weeks, but the passage of time had gone unmarked in my halcyon daze.

"It is not too late." I prayed it was true. "I have until the next full moon."

This time Constanze's silence was less scornful than surprised. "Did he . . . did he speak to you?"

"Yes." I wrung my hands. "In the Goblin King's own words, I have until the next full moon to find my way into his realm."

But she did not seem to hear a word I said. "He spoke . . . to *you*?" she repeated. "Why you?"

I frowned. Acid no longer etched her tones with biting distaste, but a lingering vulnerability traced her words. In them, I heard, *Why you . . . and not me?*

"Have you—have you met *Der Erlkönig*?" I asked.

It was a long moment before she replied. "Yes," she said. "You are not the only maiden to have had foolish, girlish dreams of *Der Erlkönig,* you know. You are not the only one to have danced with him in the wood. Like you, I once dreamed he would take me away, to be his bride in the Underground." She looked away. "But he never did. Perhaps," she said sardonically, "I was not pretty enough for him either."

Sympathy beat in my chest for Constanze. Unlike Käthe, unlike Mother, Constanze understood what it was to be plain, overlooked, ignored. Käthe's and Mother's beauty ensured they would never be forgotten; their stories would live on in someone else's narrative, as beautiful women always did. People would remember their names. Women like Constanze and me were relegated to the footnotes, to the background, nameless and unimportant.

"What happened?" I asked softly.

She shrugged. "I grew up."

"All children do," I said. "And yet, you still believe."

Constanze returned my gaze with a long, hard stare. Then she gestured to the footstool beside her with a nod. I came and knelt at her feet, just as I had when I was young.

"I believe because I must," she said. "Lest the consequences prove disastrous."

"What consequences?"

It was a long while before Constanze spoke.

"You don't know," she croaked. "You could never know what the world was like when *Der Erlkönig* and his subjects walked among us. It was a dark age, an age before reason, enlightenment, and God."

I resisted the urge to ask how she knew. Constanze was old, but not *that* old. Instead, I let myself be young again in her presence, to settle into the rhythms and cadences of her story, lulled by the rise and fall of her speech.

"It was an age of blood, violence, and war," she continued, "a time when man and goblin fought—over land, over water, over flesh. Beautiful flesh, sweet and tempting, the flesh of maidens, full of light and life. The goblins saw them as sustenance, men saw them as otherwise."

Pointed teeth over razor-thin lips. I shuddered, remembering how juice from the enchanted peach had flowed over Käthe's mouth and throat like blood.

"Blood spilled as easily as rain, soaking the land, salting the earth, turning it red beneath our feet with the remains of the dead, burying the harvest beneath rage, grief, and sorrow. *Der Erlkönig* heard the cries of the land, stifled by death and war, and stretched out his hands. In his right, he gathered Man; in his left, the goblins, dividing one from the other. And so, *Der Erlkönig* has ever stood between us and them, between the world of the living and the dead, the ordinary and the uncanny."

"How lonely," I murmured. I thought of the tall, elegant stranger in the marketplace, the first guise in which the Goblin King had shown himself to me, more man than myth. Even then, he had stood alone and apart, and his loneliness called to my own. My cheeks flushed with the memory.

Constanze gave me a sharp glance. "Lonely, yes. But does the king serve the crown, or the crown serve the king?"

We sat in silence.

"How then, Constanze," I said at last, "do I gain entrance to the Underground?"

For a long moment, I was afraid my grandmother would not give me a straight answer. Then she sighed.

"*Der Erlkönig* is bound by an ancient sacrifice," she said, "so we honor him with our own."

"A sacrifice?"

Her eyes softened. "An offering," she amended. "When I was a girl, we used to leave bread and milk as a tithe, a portion of our hard-earned work. But these are not the lean times they were when I was young. You must bring the Goblin King an offering that costs you something; after all, is that not the meaning of sacrifice?"

"I don't have anything," I said. "Only people. And I've already sacrificed one I love to *Der Erlkönig*, Constanze; I'll not risk any more."

"Do you truly have nothing?" There was something in the tone of my grandmother's voice that chilled my blood.

"Nothing," I repeated, but my voice was less sure than before.

"Oh, but I think you do." Her words were soft, sinister. "Something you love more than your sister, more than Josef, more than life itself."

My mind did not comprehend her meaning, but my body knew. My body was cleverer than I. It went cold, and then numb with stillness.

My music.

I would have to sacrifice my music.

## SACRIFICE

i should have known it would come to this.

As dusk began to fall outside, I knelt before the bed— the bed my sister and I had shared our entire lives— and reached for the lockbox I knew would be hidden there. My fingers scraped and searched, but stopped when they brushed over something smooth and polished.

The elegant stranger's gift.

I had all but forgotten about it since we returned from the market that fateful day Käthe had taken that bite of goblin fruit.

*I do not offer this gift to you out of the goodness of my heart, but out of a selfish need to see what you might do with it.*

And what had I done with the Goblin King's gift? I had taken it and hidden it away, like it was something secret, something shameful. Perhaps my lack of faith had cost me everything after all.

I drew out my box of compositions from beneath my bed

and opened it. It looked like nothing: bits of foolscap, pages torn from my father's unused accounting books, the backs of old hymnals—the sad, pathetic treasure hoard of an unlovely, untalented child.

Closing the lockbox, I got to my feet and walked to the klavier. Its presence in the room was both bane and balm, a reminder of all I had dreamed of and all I would never gain. I ran my hands over its surface, feeling the hours that had chipped away at the ivory keys and twisted and warped the strings within.

My latest composition still lay open on the music stand. Across the top, in my best handwriting: *Für meine Lieben, ein Lied im stil die Bagatelle, auch Der Erlkönig.*

For my loved ones, a song in the style of a bagatelle, or The Goblin King.

Below that, in a hasty scrawl:

*For Sepperl, may he never forget.*

*For Käthe, all my love and my forgiveness.*

I shuffled the leaves together, stacking them neatly, before tying them with a length of twine from my sewing kit.

The pages looked plain and forlorn, sitting unadorned on my keyboard. If I were Käthe, I would have dressed them with a bit of ribbon or lace, or some dried wildflowers from the summer meadow. I had nothing but a few catkins dropped from the alder trees in the Goblin Grove.

But perhaps that was the most fitting decoration after all.

With my shears, I snipped a lock of hair and tied it with the catkins to the sheet music. My latest composition, and my last. My gift to my loved ones, my farewell. If I could not give them one last embrace, one last kiss, then I could give them this: my truest expression of self, to safeguard in their keeping. I left the composition on the bed.

Then, gathering both the flute and the lockbox, I turned from the klavier, from the room, from home, toward the Goblin Grove and beyond.

Constanze stood at the bottom of the stairs.

"Are you ready, Elisabeth?"

It was the first time my grandmother had ever called me by name. Shivers ran through me, not of dread, but of anticipation.

"Liesl," I said. "Call me Liesl."

Constanze shook her head. "Elisabeth. I like the name Elisabeth. It's a name for a grown woman, not a girl."

In her words I heard the echo of the Goblin King. But I chose to draw strength from them. For all our differences, Constanze believed in me. She handed me a cloak and a lantern. To my surprise, she also handed me a slice of *Gugelhopf,* which she had not made for me since I was a child.

"An offering for *Der Erlkönig.*" She wrapped the cake in a piece of linen. "From me. He will not have forgotten the taste of my *Gugelhopf* so soon, I should think."

I smiled. "Nor will I, Constanze."

We faced each other one last time. No tears, no farewells. My grandmother did not countenance sentimentality. She merely patted me on the shoulder.

"*Viel Glück,* Elisabeth." She did not say we would meet again.

I followed Constanze through the back door of the inn. She did not direct me on my way, but it did not matter. I knew exactly where I was going.

"*Servus,* Constanze," I said softly. "Go with God. And thank you."

Constanze nodded. She had no words of encouragement, no blessing for my journey. But the cake in its linen wrapping was as good as a benediction from my grandmother. I took it, and left.

The night was clear, and the air had the breath of winter upon it, death and ice and slumber. I held the lantern aloft, illuminating the path ahead.

The Goblin Grove lay in the distance, the only bit of the forest wreathed in mist. The mist formed spectral shapes before my eyes, suggesting the hump of a goblin's back or the curve of a nymph's cheek, but nothing—no one—materialized. I would have no audience tonight.

*Very well, then,* I thought, walking into the Goblin Grove itself. It was a circle of twelve alder trees, almost perfectly round, as though planted by some tender gardener ages ago. It had the whiff of some place holy or sacred, fed by the stories we told each other. Of Frau Perchta. Of the Wild Hunt. Of the White Ladies. Of *Der Erlkönig.*

I set down my lantern and began combing the grove for deadfall. I found plenty of wood within reach, but the wood had gone to damp and the coming winter. It would not light without tinder. I managed the best I could, arranging the sticks into a small pyramid over a small pile of kindling. But try as I might, I could not get a fire lit, and as match after match sputtered out in my trembling fingers, so too did my hopes.

I could not play for him like this. I could not give him my music with hands half frozen and lips blue with cold. I had promised the Goblin King a sacrifice, but he was not going to make it easy for me. *Turn back,* whispered the spectral breezes. *Give up.* I reached into my satchel for the flute.

The instrument felt alive in my grip. It was carved from some sort of wood, possibly alder wood, which was sacred to the Goblin King. The flute unsettled me; it was like holding someone's hand, a touch that felt back. The instrument was old, built on a simpler design, without the keys and metal joins of the newer flutes I had seen the musicians play in church. Yet it had the right holes that allowed chromatic fingering, not like the fifes and old transverse flutes in our inn that had belonged to our grandfather. Papa had taught me the rudiments of the flute; I knew how to play all the notes, but whether or not I could get them to sound as I wished remained to be heard.

I wet my lips, brought the instrument to my mouth. Nothing but a hollow whistling noise emerged, the sound of the wind in the trees. I gently blew into the instrument itself, attempting to warm the air within, the wood of which it was made. It helped but little; my hands trembled too much to hold the flute straight, my numb fingertips scarcely feeling the holes beneath them.

In the silence of the forest beyond, I thought I heard the mocking echo of a laugh.

*You have not defeated me yet.*

Fire. I needed fire. I could not keep going like this. The mist grew thicker, droplets of moisture forming on my hair. They would be droplets of ice before long.

I looked at the lantern Constanze had given me. It had a small well of oil at its base, along with a wick of flame. Perhaps I could spill a little bit onto the woodpile I had made, just enough to prompt a fire. But I worried that the damp would defeat that too, and what little light I had would be gone with it.

No, I needed something else to burn: something dry, something seasoned, something like . . . paper.

I remembered my box of compositions.

I wanted to laugh. I thought I had known the meaning of sacrifice. I thought I had known the meaning of suffering. But no, I had been a fool. What did it mean to sacrifice my music to the Goblin King? I had thought a few tunes would be enough. But I was wrong. So very wrong. He wanted more. He wanted my very soul.

Hands shaking with more than cold, I reached into my satchel and pulled out my box of compositions. It was nothing but an old lockbox I had found in the garret—long emptied of its coins but filled with treasure nonetheless. The lock was rusted through, but the clasp still worked, and the box stayed shut until I opened it. I opened it now.

My compositions were scattered in its depths, dead leaves on autumn loam. Music scribbled hastily on foolscap, on parchment stolen from my father's account books, on fancy stationary our guests sometimes left behind. All paper. All flammable.

"Is this what you want, *mein Herr*?" I asked. "Is this the sacrifice you asked for?"

No response from the wood but a waiting silence, as if the air held its breath.

With a cry I scattered my music over the woodpile. Then before I could lose my nerve, I splashed the burning oil from my lantern over it.

The pages caught fire immediately. Flames flared into life,

then died down. No, I would not burn my life's work for nothing. I kicked their burning ashes further into the kindling, and the rest began to catch light. Twig after twig, branch after branch, a small, smoky, but steady fire began to grow.

*For you, mein Herr,* I thought. *Is this enough?*

Nothing again but that waiting silence. First the pages, then my soul. This last scrap of self, he demanded it all. This was the meaning of sacrifice.

I pulled out the slice of cake Constanze had given me. Unwrapping it, I broke off a piece and cast it into the fire. The sweet smell of its ashes rose into the night air. I took one bite. Subtle sweetness melted across my tongue, subtle sweetness and strength.

"Let us share a meal, you and I," I said to the waiting stillness. "But first, some music."

I lifted the flute and began to play.


I played everything I knew, every étude and écossaise, every chaconne and concerto, every sonata and song. I embroidered, I embellished, I improvised, I improved. I played and played and played until the flames died down, until my fingers turned white with frost, until my throat grew hoarse with ice. I played until the darkness creeping in on the edges of my vision became the entirety of it, until I could no longer see the approaching dawn.


Someone takes me in his arms.

"Hans?" I ask weakly.

There is no reply.

Only the sensation of long fingers running along the length of my neck, soft and gentle as spring rain. They rest against my collarbones. The caress is light, and somehow reminds me of the flute in my hand.

Then I know no more.

# Part I

## THE GOBLIN BALL

A linnet in a gilded cage, -
A linnet on a bough, -
In frosty winter one might doubt
Which bird is luckier now.
But let the trees burst out in leaf,
And nests be on the bough,
Which linnet is the luckier bird,
Oh who could doubt it now?

—CHRISTINA ROSSETTI,
*A Linnet in a Gilded Cage*

## FAIRY LIGHTS

The sound of giggles woke me.

"Käthe?" I murmured. "It is early yet." It was too dark to be dawn, too dark for my sleepy sister to be awake. I reached under the covers for her warmth, but there was nothing.

My eyes opened with a snap. The room was dimly lit, but I wasn't home, wasn't in my bed. I was comfortable, for one thing. The mattress Käthe and I shared was old, full of lumps and sags, and no matter how many hot bricks wrapped in wool we cuddled, no matter how many blankets we piled over our heads, it was never warm enough.

I sat up. The room brightened. Small twinkling lights hovered beside me, and I gasped with delight. I reached to touch one, but was met with an angry *zzzzzzzt!* and a sharp, sizzling pain that lasted half a moment. The light pulsed irritably before resuming its steady glow.

"Fairy lights," I breathed.

Fairy lights.

The fey. Goblins. *Der Erlkönig.*

"Käthe!" I cried, throwing off my covers and scattering the fairy lights into a frenzy.

But there was no reply.

I was Underground.

I had done it. I had won this round.

Now fully awake, I saw I was in some sort of barrow, the ceilings, floors, and walls made of packed dirt. But there were no doors, no windows, no way to escape. The room was as sealed as a tomb. The bed was carved from the roots of a very great tree, the roots curved and bent into sinuous shapes, almost as if it had been grown.

I got to my feet. A crackling fire gave off cheery pops and hisses in a beautiful travertine fireplace. I ran my hand over the mantel. The creamy white stone was shot through with gold, the joins seamless, as though it had been laid from one continuous slab of stone. Such fine craftsmanship seemed incongruous in this tomb of roots and dirt.

I wandered every inch of my barrow, searching for a window, a threshold, some means of escape. The barrow was well-appointed with little luxuries and creature comforts, outfitted like a graceful lady's private quarters. An upholstered chair and table in the Louis Quinze style graced the hearth, and a beautiful rug woven with glittering threads covered the packed-earth floor. Above the mantel hung a large painting of a winter landscape, and scattered about here and there on side tables and dressers were delicate, decorative objets d'art.

At first glance, it was all harmonious elegance and feminine delicacy. Yet upon closer inspection, little grotesqueries revealed themselves. Instead of smiling cherubs, little hobgoblins leered from the carved furniture finials. The carpet beneath my feet depicted stylized spiderwebs and flowers dying on the vine. The pretty little objects decorating my room were not charming little china shepherdesses; they were demon-faced nymphs with a flock of hunchbacked goblins. Their shepherds' crooks had been replaced with reapers' scythes, their dresses torn and ravaged, revealing breasts and hips and thighs. Instead of pretty pouts, their lips were twisted into satyrs' smiles. I shuddered.

The winter landscape above my mantel was the only bit of art in my barrow that did not reveal itself to be full of hidden ugliness. It showed a forest shrouded in fog, disconcertingly familiar. The mist seemed to move and writhe at the corners of my vision. I peered closer. With a jolt I realized it was a painting of the Goblin Grove. The painting was so skillfully rendered that its brushstrokes were practically invisible, more like a window than a work of art. My fingers reached to touch it.

Giggles erupted behind me.

I whirled around. Sitting on my bed were a pair of goblin girls. They stared at me, tittering behind their hands. With a twist of the stomach, I noticed they had too many joints in their long, twig-like fingers. Their skin had the greenish-brown tint of a spring wood just waking from its winter slumber, and their eyes had no whites about the pupils.

"No, no, mustn't touch." One of them waggled an unsettlingly long finger at me. "His Majesty wouldn't be pleased."

I dropped my hand to my side. "His Majesty? The Goblin King?"

"Goblin King," the other goblin girl scoffed. She was the

size of a child, but proportioned like an adult, a little stocky, with shining white hair like a thistle-cloud about her head. "King of the goblins, feh. He's no king of *mine*."

"Shush, Thistle," the first goblin girl admonished. She was longer and thinner than her counterpart, built like a slender birch tree. Her hair was branches wound with cobwebs. "You mustn't say things like that."

"I'll say what I want, Twig." Thistle crossed her arms with a mutinous expression on her face.

Thistle and Twig carried on as though I were nothing more than another fixture in the barrow. Even among the goblins, I faded into the shadows. I cleared my throat.

"What are you doing here?" My voice cracked through their conversation like a whip. "Who are you?"

"We are your attendants," said the one called Thistle. She grinned, her smile row upon row of jagged teeth. "Sent to prepare you for the fête tonight."

"Fête?" I did not like the way she said *prepare*, as though I were a kill for the feast, a roast to be trussed. "What fête?"

"The Goblin Ball, of course," said the one called Twig. "We host revels each night during the days of winter, and tonight promises to be special. Tonight *Der Erlkönig* introduces his bride to the Underground."

*Käthe.*

"I must speak with *Der Erlkönig*," I said. "Immediately."

Twig and Thistle laughed, branches rubbing against each other in a sudden storm. "And so you shall, maiden. So you shall. All in good time. You are his guest of honor at the ball tonight, and you shall meet with him then."

"No." I tried to impose my will upon them; I was bigger, after all, although not by much. "I must speak with him *now*."

"All you mortals are so impatient," Thistle said. "I suppose that's what comes with feeling the hand of Death upon your neck at all times."

"Take me to him," I demanded. "Right now."

But both Twig and Thistle were implacable, ignoring my words and circling me with curious eyes. I wanted to shy away from their scrutiny, from their judging eyes, from the sense that they were measuring me against some invisible mark.

"Not much to work with," Thistle remarked.

"Hmmm," Twig agreed. "Don't know what we could do to improve her appearance."

I bristled. Plain as I was, at least I wasn't grotesque, not like these goblin girls.

"I shall address him as I am, thank you," I said sharply. "My appearance needs no improving."

They gave me a look of pity mingled with contempt. "It's not your choice, mortal," Thistle said. "It pleases our *esteemed* sovereign to have you properly dressed tonight."

"Can't this wait?"

Twig and Thistle exchanged looks, then laughed, another burst of branches in a storm.

"There are rituals, and there are traditions," Twig said. "The Goblin Ball is a tradition. There is a time and place for boons and audiences, and the Goblin Ball is not the appropriate time or place for either. You are *Der Erlkönig's* guest of honor; this night is for you. Enjoy yourself. All other nights belong to him. And to us."

A shiver of foreboding ran up my spine. "Fine," I said. "What do you need me to do?"

Despite my reluctance, a part of me tingled with anticipation. A ball, a beautiful gown. I had dreamed of such things once. I had dreamed of dancing with *Der Erlkönig*, a queen to his king.

Twig and Thistle gave me identical grins. Their teeth were pointed and jagged. "Oh, you shall see, maiden. You shall see."

The goblin musicians struck up a minuet when I entered.

Thistle and Twig had pushed, prodded, pulled, and cajoled me into an elaborate construction of a gown. It was a little out of date from the current fashions of the world above, something a fine lady might have worn fifty or sixty years ago. The gown was a russet and bronze damask, lined with a stomacher of watered silk striped with cream and violet. It was trimmed with rosettes cunningly shaped like alder catkins. Little as I was, the waist of the gown was even littler, the stays pinching my lower ribs so painfully I could not draw a deep breath. Even more impressive was the décolletage the bodice was able to give me. Despite the yards of fabric, I still felt naked.

My face was also naked; I had declined the powder and rouge Twig and Thistle had offered. I did not think pinching my cheeks for color was necessary—with the heat, the constricting nature of my dress, and the excitement quickening my breath, I was flushed.

The main hall was cavernous—it *was* a cavern. A large one, formed from stone, unlike the dirt-packed barrow that was my room. Icicles of stone dripped from the ceiling, embedded with glowing, glittering chips. The same grew from the ground, atop which tables and boards laden with food were laid. Centerpieces were created from the antler horns of stags and cobwebs and gems, and bubbling springs rose up like fountains at intervals, giving off a faint, sulfuric, mineral smell.

A myriad of fairy lights twinkled against the inky darkness of the cavern ceiling, so high out of reach I could almost believe I was looking up at the night sky. Bare branches and dried leaves still vibrant with the brilliance of autumn were hung like chandeliers halfway above our heads. Bolts of silk and brocade cascaded down the walls, as well as tapestries depicting scenes of rapacious goblin men and virginal maidens. Gold, silver, and jewels were scattered like confetti, catching the light of dancing candle flame, of fairy lights, and of flickering torches, glittering like new-fallen snow. Bits of silvered glass and mirrors were embedded into the stone floors and walls of the cavern, reflecting fractured images: a sliver of a face, broken limbs, a million blinking eyes.

Everything was opulent, sumptuous, and excessive. I moved unnoticed among the partygoers, each fitted with a mask shaped like a human face. There was something sad and melancholy about this ghoulish gathering of goblins, playacting like they were humans in the world above. Each mask was modeled after the same face—the men incredibly handsome, the women incredibly beautiful. All the men looked like Hans; all the women looked like Käthe, their faces frozen into bland, personable smiles.

The goblin musicians started another minuet, their twisted hands gripping the oboe, the fife, the violoncello, and the violin awkwardly. The minuet, while adequately performed, sounded stiff and rote. None of the attendees danced, the music too dull to be much inspiration.

It was all wrong. Music of the rational, human mind with its rules and structure was all wrong in the hands of the goblins. It was lifeless, joyless, constrained. It did not breathe, take flight, or live. If only I could have taken their stacks of sheet music, I would have changed the tempo, the key, or else do away with the notes and paper altogether and let the music flow.

My skin prickled, my fingers twitched. I itched to join the musicians, but could not scrub away the hesitation of painful inadequacy that clung to me. I was unheard, uneducated, unpublished. Papa would say I was overreaching myself.

And yet . . . Papa was not here. Master Antonius was not here. Not even Josef was here. No one would judge me if I walked to the first chair, took his violin, and began to play.

As though sensing my intent, the violinist lifted his head and glanced at me. The goblin musicians were not masked; their queer, puckish faces were made uglier by concentration.

"What, maiden?" the violinist leered. "Think you could do better than me?"

"Yes." The certainty of my reply surprised me.

My reply certainly surprised the musicians, who immediately stopped playing. I plucked the bow and violin from the first chair's hands and tucked the instrument beneath my chin. The others gaped at me, but I ignored them. Instead, I touched my bow to the strings and began a simple country air.

A *Ländler*, instantly recognizable to all assembled in the goblin ballroom. The musicians picked up the beat and the dancers picked up their feet. Once we were comfortable in the music, I began to embroider and expand the piece, adding a harmonic line to the melody. This was a game Josef and I had played when we were children: taking songs we knew and adding harmonies. The harmonies were usually simple thirds, but sometimes they were perfect fifths. This was how my little brother began to teach me the rudiments of theory.

The musicians looked to me once we finished the *Ländler*. As though they expected me to lead. As though I were the *Konzertmeister*. I swallowed hard. I had hidden for so long in my brother's shadow that the light of their regard was almost too much to bear. Then I brought my bow to the strings and picked another song from my childhood, this time a simple canon. I began, then nodded to the flautist, the oboist, and the violoncellist as we played the melody as a round. The goblin musicians were enchanted by the web of sound, their unmasked, puckish faces made uglier with glee.

As we grew accustomed to each other, the musicians and I began to improvise, taking the sounds and turning them inside out, upside down. A game. Music was just a game. Somehow, I had forgotten.

A seed began to unfurl deep within me. Long ago, I had planted my music in the dark places of my soul, away from the light. There was Josef, the gardener of my heart, but not even his gentle encouragement had been enough to coax that little seed into life. I could not let it grow. Not in the world I lived in. Not in the world above. That world needed Liesl, dutiful daughter and protective sister. To let that seed bloom would encourage a weed to grow, choking out the other lives that needed my care.

But now I was free. The music inside grew into a weed, a wildflower, a meadow, a forest. I spread my roots out, feeling the rush in my limbs. My breathing was erratic, my bowing languid.

A bright laugh shattered my concentration. My bow

stuttered and stumbled over the string. At once everyone paused, heads turning one by one toward the ballroom entrance. There, atop the great staircase that seemed both carved and grown at once, stood the Goblin King.

With my sister Käthe on his arm.

# EYES OPEN

iesl!"

My sister found me straightaway. If we had been in the world above, I would have marveled at how quickly she discovered me in this sea of faces. But in the Underground, I understood. I was mortal, and so was she, and here among the goblins, our lives pulsed with intensity. I had sensed Käthe before I saw her.

But even without the telltale beat of our hearts that marked us human, I would have sensed my sister's presence. Her beauty was polished like a gem, every facet of her sparkling appearance enhanced by the dress she wore, and the aura of glamour about her. Unlike the rest of the ballgoers, dressed in earthen shades and jewel tones, my sister was in summery pastels. She wore a sky-blue gown that shimmered with gold where the light hit it, and her own sunshine curls were piled high atop her head, dressed with pale pink roses and other spring flowers. Her face was powdered and rouged, and she looked like a painting, a portrait, a porcelain china doll.

Käthe had come in on the Goblin King's arm, but she dropped it at the sight of me. She ran down the steps, parting a path between the sea of identical Käthe faces, holding out her arms to embrace me. In her hand she carried a mask fashioned into the shape of a goblin's face.

"Liesl, my darling!" My sister wrapped her arms about my waist.

"Käthe!" I hugged her tightly, feeling the thud of her heart against mine.

"I was so afraid you wouldn't come," she said.

"I know, I'm sorry." Tears clotted my throat. "I'm sorry I took so long. But I'm here now, my dear, never fear."

"Wonderful!" Käthe exclaimed, clapping her hands together in delight. "Now we must dance."

"What?" I drew back to give her a proper look. "No, no. We must leave. We must go home."

She screwed up her face in a childish pout. "Don't be such a spoilsport, Liesl."

Beneath the maquillage, Käthe's complexion was wan and pale. No amount of powder could disguise the bruised hollows beneath her eyes, no amount of rouge distract from the bloodlessness of her lips. Only her eyes were bright and brilliant: the shine of fever. Or enchantment.

I believed I had abandoned my sister to the goblins' untender mercies. I had imagined her in torment or agony, crying out for the world above. I had thought I would find her, and we would run back home, back to the inn, back to safety.

My gaze met the Goblin King's over my sister's head. He

leaned against the entrance, his arms crossed, his smile mocking. Even from where I stood, I saw the tips of his pointed teeth gleaming in the fairy lights.

*Did you think I would make it so easy?* his smile seemed to say.

I had won the second round. I had made my way to the Underground. This was the third and final round of our game: getting Käthe back to the world above.

*Well,* I thought. I would drag my sister back to life, even if I had to drag her out by her hair. The Goblin King had his tricks, but I had my stubbornness. We would see who prevailed in the end.

"All right, then," I said to Käthe. "Let's dance."

On cue, the goblin musicians struck up a tune. The violinist took back his instrument with a sour expression. The musicians played another old air from my childhood, a fast-paced *Zweifacher.* Even Käthe stirred when she heard it, and I smiled at her.

"Just like when we were little," I said. "Come!"

Käthe fitted her goblin mask over her face, and we clasped our arms together. *One-two-three, one-two-three, one-two, one-two,* our bodies followed the turns and pivots in the music. The other ballgoers took up the *Zweifacher,* and soon the entire cavern was filled with twirling, whirling dancers.

My sister and I laughed as we stumbled over each other's feet and collided into other dancing pairs, out of breath and giddy. As we turned about the dance floor, I tried my best to maneuver Käthe toward the exit. My eyes kept darting to where the Goblin King was standing. He alone did not join the throng, apart and untouchable.

"Do you remember," I said, breathing hard, "when you,

me, Sepperl, and Hans used to dance the *Zweifacher* while Papa played his fiddle?"

"Hmmm?" Käthe seemed distracted, her eyes wandering over to the tables laden with food. "What did you say?"

"I said, do you remember when you, me, Hans, and Sepperl danced to this when we were young?"

"Who's Hans?"

A laugh stuck in my throat. "Handsome Hans, you used to call him," I said. "Your betrothed."

"Me, betrothed?" Käthe giggled. "Whyever would I do a thing like that?" She cut a glance at a tall, slender goblin man and gave him a coquettish wink.

Cold pins of guilt pricked me. Whyever would she do a thing like that, indeed? "Yes, betrothed," I said.

She raised her brow. "And who is Sepperl?" Another goblin man caught her hand and dropped a quick kiss as we spun past.

"Käthe." Despair slowed my limbs, weighing them down. "Sepperl is your brother. Our younger brother."

"Oh," Käthe said indifferently. She blew a kiss to yet another goblin man.

"Käthe!" I stopped dancing, and my sister stumbled. Another swain was there to catch her before she fell.

"What?" she asked irritably. A goblin server offered us a platter of hors d'oeuvres. Käthe smiled at him and grabbed a few grapes. To my horror, the "grapes" on the platter were staring eyeballs, the chocolate bonbons beetles, and the luscious bloody peaches that had been my sister's downfall were putrid and rotten, their split flesh looking like spilled guts in the goblin's hands.

"Käthe." I grabbed her wrist, and she dropped the food in her hand. Her blue eyes behind the goblin mask were startled, and behind the fever-spell, I caught a glimpse of my sister, my *real* sister. "Wake up. Wake up from this dream and come back to me."

Her gaze wavered, and for a moment, flesh and life returned to her face. But her eyes turned glassy once more, and her color faded.

"Oh, come off of it, Liesl," she said gaily. "Let's enjoy ourselves. There are men to dance with and men to flirt with!"

With that, one of the goblin swains hovering over her shoulder whisked her away.

"Käthe!" I cried, but a press of bodies suddenly swarmed in front of me. I reached out for my sister, but there was always another person, another goblin in my way. I pushed through the dancing crowd, following the flash of sky blue through the revelers. But each time I thought I drew near, it was another woman, another lady wearing Käthe's face, those humanlike masks ghoulishly realistic in the flickering fairy lights of the ball.

In the tumult of heated bodies, a sea of identical faces stared back at me. But they no longer looked like Hans or Käthe; they looked like the Goblin King. And me. My face, reflected back at me, a million little mirrors. His face, many of his faces, laughing and mocking me. His face, more human than the others, sharp, languid, and cruel. A beauty that cut like a blade. A dozen knife wounds slashed me to the heart.

"Why are you not partaking of my generosity, Elisabeth?"

A cool breath upon my neck. It smelled faintly of the wind before a snowstorm.

"There is a feast laid before you, yet you touch nothing." The Goblin King came into view. In the shifting, mercurial fairy light, he was even more beautiful than he was in the world above, and even more frightening. "Why?"

"I am not hungry," I lied. I was starving. I was starving for food, for music, for gluttony.

"Does the food not tempt you?"

I thought of the "bonbons" on the table. "No, *mein Herr*."

"A pity." His smile was a snarl. "Well, I did promise that your eyes would remain open, but my gifts do have consequences, my dear."

"What consequences?"

The Goblin King shrugged. "Goblin glamour has no effect on you. You see things as they are."

"How is that a consequence?"

"Depends on whom you ask." He ran his tongue lightly over his pointed teeth. "Your sister," he said, nodding toward Käthe in the crowd, "would prefer pretty enchantments to the stark ugliness of reality, I think."

My sister danced with not one, but several of the tall goblin men. They spun her from man to man, pressing their lips to the inside of her wrists, up her arms, along her collarbone, up her throat. She laughed and tried to kiss one of them on the mouth, but he turned his face away.

"Don't we all?" I thought of the uncounted days spent at my klavier, before I had come to my senses, before I had come Underground. "Sometimes it is easier to pretend."

"It is," the Goblin King said in a low voice. His words vibrated all the way down my spine. "But aren't we too old for our games of make-believe, Elisabeth?"

There was a wistful note in his words that belied his cool command of composure. Startled, I turned to face the Goblin King. His mismatched eyes looked vulnerable. Fallible. Almost . . . human. Those remarkable eyes searched mine, and in the space of a breath, I recognized the boy for whom I had played my music in the Goblin Grove.

A bright, musical laugh. I turned to see Käthe trip and fall into a dancer's arms. She threw her head back, exposing her neck and bosom to his kisses. I wanted to rush to my sister's defense, but froze at the touch of a hand upon my shoulder.

"Wait." Fingertips brushed the skin of my neck. "Stay."

"But Käthe—"

"Your sister will come to no harm, I promise."

I held myself still, unwilling to face his eyes again. "How can I trust you to keep your word?" My voice did not sound like mine, husky and dark. "Are you not the Lord of Mischief?"

"You wound me, Elisabeth," he said. "I thought we were friends."

"You became my enemy the moment you stole my sister."

It was a long time before the Goblin King replied.

"Tonight is for indulgence without consequence. Tonight you are my guest, Elisabeth, and your sister shall come to no harm. Tomorrow," he said, arch and sly once more, "we can return to being enemies."

The sound of my sister's laughter returned to me, echoing about the cavernous ballroom. "Your word, *mein Herr.*"

"I said your sister will come to no harm," he said. "Do not press me further than that. Now," he said, turning me to face him. "Let us dance, Elisabeth."

The musicians struck up another song, one I didn't recognize. The tempo was slow and in a minor key, seductive and sinister. The Goblin King pulled me into his embrace.

He pressed his hand to my lower back, pushing our hips

close together. Our hands met palm to palm, fingers inter-twined. He was not masked and neither was I. Our eyes met. Despite the closeness of our bodies, it was the touch of our eyes that made me blush.

"*Mein Herr,*" I demurred. "I don't think—"

"You think too much, Elisabeth," he said. "Too much about propriety, too much about duty, too much about everything but music. For once, don't think." The Goblin King smiled. It was a wicked grin, one that made me feel unsafe and excited at the same time. "Don't think. *Feel.*"

We swept around the ballroom floor, our feet keeping rhythm with each other, even as my heart kept a frenetic pace. I flinched whenever our legs entangled themselves within the folds of my gown, whenever a step caused his chest to brush against mine, whenever more of him touched me than necessary.

"Breathe, Elisabeth," he said softly.

But I could not. It wasn't the stays trapping my lungs in an iron grip; it was the Goblin King. His proximity, his un-bearable nearness. I had wanted Hans to know me inti-mately, but I was familiar with him. I could imagine his body beneath my hands—solid, comforting, dependable, predictable, just like the rest of him. But I did not know the Goblin King, not as a man, not as someone with flesh and hands and hips. My soul thrilled with recognition at the sight of his face, but the reality of him frightened me. He was an old friend in myth and legend; he was a stranger in breath and body.

The Goblin King sensed my discomfort. After the dance was over, he stepped back and gave me a courteous bow, kissing the back of my hand.

"I thank you for this dance, my dear," he said formally.

I nodded, unsure of my voice. I tried to pull my hand out of his grip, but he held on all the tighter.

"But we are not finished yet." He leaned in, lips moving against the curve of my ear. "The game resumes tomorrow."

With that, he released me and melted into the crowd. I stood, dazed, wanting to follow him, wanting to crawl back to my barrow room and hide. Every face in the room belonged to him; I found an echo of his cheekbones, his chin, his arched brows in the masks of the attendees.

"Wine, *Fräulein*?" A goblin servant materialized by my side, holding a tray with several goblets. I hesitated. Years of watching Papa struggle with drink had made me wary of intoxication. And yet, the burden of being Liesl, responsible older sister and dutiful eldest daughter, wore on me. I wondered what oblivion was like.

A responsible older sister. I scanned the room for Käthe. I found her straightaway; she was like a flame in darkness with her golden hair, her bright, pastel-colored gown. She sat upon an enormous carved throne at the head of the ballroom, surrounded by a bevy of fawning suitors. They fed her "grapes" and "bonbons" as she took sips of wine from a crystal-studded goblet. Her gorgeous gown was in disarray, her hair falling loose from its elaborate pompadour. She kicked out at one of them, giggling and showing quite a bit of leg. One of her swains caught her foot, and then ran a hand along her delicate ankle, slowly moving up her stockinged leg to her calf, then along her bare thigh . . .

"Mistress?" The goblin servant had not moved. I stole another glance at Käthe, then looked at the goblets on the tray. I had wished for wantonness, hadn't I? I fingered the edge of a wineglass. I wanted to be like Käthe, to turn off my rational mind just for one minute, one hour, one day.

*You think too much.*

I lifted a goblet of wine off the tray.

*Your sister will come to no harm.*

"Ooh—*ooh!*" Käthe said in a scandalized voice.

I brought the goblet to my lips. The wine was a dark red, darker than rubies, darker than blood, the deep black-red of blackberries. And sin.

*Don't think. Feel.*

I drank.


The taste is heady on my tongue. The world is bright, the sounds are clear, and everything is beautiful. Touches, touches everywhere. A hand on my waist. Fingers in my hair. Wine-red lips that taste of temptation. They leave stains on my neck, where my skin meets my clothes, the rising swell of my breasts and the valley between them. Ticklish brushes against my ankles, a rising breeze. My skirt above my knees, games of bluff. Yes, no. Yes. No. Yes. Fingers walk up the inside of my thigh. No.

His face. I wrap my arms around him, but it is not the Goblin King, only another wearing a mask. I let him taste my skin, but I am looking. I am still searching.

I twirl around the room, passed from arm to arm, partner to partner. With each switch I look, I search, I yearn. My stays are loosened, my shoes are lost. I am not thinking now. The freedom is headier than the wine.

*Elisabeth.*

A breath on the back of my neck. I am dizzy, I sway, but I stand. A breath, then a kiss. I cannot see, but I know it is him. The Goblin King.

I lean into him, but he holds me upright. He murmurs

my name down my neck, down my spine, his long, elegant fingers traveling along the curves of my hips, my waist.

*Elisabeth.*

I do not know what to call him, but I cry out his name. My fingers reach, but he is gone.

# THE GAMES
# WE'VE PLAYED

I opened my eyes.

And immediately regretted it.

The room tilted and spun, the bed rocking back and forth like a boat on the sea. I shut my eyes and moaned. I was dying. Or worse.

Presently, my wits began to return. I was not dying; I was merely suffering the ill effects of my lapse in judgment. I tried to recall the events of the previous night—day?—but nothing returned. Hazy memories, the remembered sensation of bare skin against skin.

Bare skin. I sat up, clutching my head as pain shot through my temples. To my horror, I was naked beneath my sheets. Where was I?

The bed was my bed, the barrow my barrow. The portrait of the Goblin Grove hung over the fireplace, the same Louis Quinze table and chair set, the same grotesqueries. I took stock of myself, running a trembling hand over my body.

Aside from the headache, I was unharmed. Intact. Untumbled. I did not know whether to be relieved or disappointed.

My beautiful ball gown lay rumpled on the floor, discarded in haste with little regard for preservation. There were wrinkles and tears in the fabric, and the stays had been shredded. It was beyond salvaging.

I cast my eye about for my old dress and chemise, but there were no other clothes in my room. Despite the nausea roiling through me, I was desperately thirsty and hungry. I pushed back my bedclothes and got up.

"Mortals look so different naked, don't they?"

I threw up my hands, trying to cover my nakedness as best I could. I had not seen Twig and Thistle enter my room; had they always been there?

"Yes. Pink," Twig said, agreeing with Thistle.

"How did you get here?" My throat was hoarse and dry, and squeaked like a badly played oboe.

Thistle and Twig shrugged in unison. Twig held an earthenware jug and a cup, while Thistle had a loaf of bread. "We thought you might need this."

They set their offerings on the Louis Quinze set. Twig poured me a cup of water. I eyed the cup; after the goblin wine, I was wary of any drink the goblins might offer me.

"It's not poisoned," Thistle said irritably, seeing my hesitation. "His Majesty told us not to, ah, tamper with your food."

I needed no more urging. I gulped down the water: ice-cold, delicious, and tasting of alpine springs. I poured myself a few more cups. Once my stomach was settled, I tore into the bread.

After I had eaten and drunk, I felt more human. More alive. It was only then I noticed that I was still stark naked.

"Look, she's growing pinker!" Twig pointed out my flush of embarrassment. I hurried back to my bed and pulled off one of the sheets to wrap around me.

"Stop staring at me," I snapped.

Twig and Thistle cocked their heads. They were clothed in scarce more than rags and leaves stitched together. Their clothing seemed less about modesty and more about status—indeed, the goblins I had seen at the ball were more humanlike in appearance than these two, and dressed in clothing much like ours.

"What have you done with my clothes?"

Thistle shrugged again. "Burned them."

"Burned them!"

"His Majesty's orders."

I was furious. He had no right to dispose of my things like that. My clothes had been my last link to the world above. The longer I stayed Underground, the more I felt as though I were being skinned and peeled alive, little bits of human Liesl stripping away.

"Take me to him," I said. "I want an audience with the Goblin King. Now."

The goblin girls exchanged looks.

"Is that what you wish?" Twig asked.

"Yes," I said firmly. "I wish for you to take me before the Goblin King."

"All right." Identical pointed grins spread over their faces. "As you wish, mortal," they said. "As you wish."


I blinked.

I was in an entirely different room, naked but for the bed-sheet draped about me. This room was much larger than my barrow, its packed-dirt ceilings supported by the great roots of a spreading tree, like the buttresses of a cathedral. *An audience chamber,* I thought.

Despite the spaciousness, the chamber was cozy: the furnishings simple, the decorations spare. No tapestries, no statuaries; the only thing that dominated the room was the enormous bed at its center, wrought of roots and rock.

Then I realized I wasn't in the Goblin King's audience chamber. I was in his *bedroom.*

Thistle and Twig had granted me my wish. They had taken me before the Goblin King the exact moment I demanded it. I had wished and now I was here.

Constanze always told me to never play games with the goblin folk. *Never say* I wish, *never give them an opening.*

Panicking, I scrambled for a way out. I had to leave before he awoke, before he saw me.

A moan from the bed stopped me, a disconcertingly familiar sound. It was the sound of Papa trying to make it through the day. The sound of Mother's disappointment in her husband's failures. The sound of Josef after a long day of practice. The sound of Käthe during her monthly courses. The sound of pain.

I should have left. I should have run. This was *Der Erlkönig.* This was the Lord of Mischief, the Ruler Underground. This was the creature who had abducted my sister, who made me sacrifice my music to his capricious whims. This was the stranger who lured me Underground for the sake of his wagers and games.

But I thought of the soft-eyed young man with whom I had danced at the ball, the man who had called himself my friend. I hesitated.

*Well,* I thought. *Today we go back to being enemies.*

I approached the bed. All that was visible was a shock of messy, pale hair, a pile of rumpled sheets, and the curve of a bare shoulder. I tucked the edges of my bedsheet more securely about me. Gathering my courage, I grabbed the silken linens wrapped around the Goblin King, and pulled.

The force of my pulling hurled him out of bed. He awoke with a volley of curses, his voice roughened by wine and lack of sleep. The Goblin King swore at Heaven, at Hell, at God, and the Devil. I was amused.

A disheveled head peered over the edge of the bed, eyes bleary, cheeks creased with sleep. He looked surprisingly young. I had always thought of *Der Erlkönig* as ageless, neither young nor old, but seeing him like this—he seemed near to me in age.

The Goblin King shot me a glare before realizing just who it was in his chambers, alone and undressed.

"Elisabeth!" Unbelievably, his voice cracked, like a schoolboy's.

I crossed my arms. "Good morning, *mein Herr*."

He scrambled for the covers. He wrapped the sheets about his slim hips, leaving his chest bare. The Goblin King was tall and slim, but well-muscled. I had seen other men bare-chested before—tan, broad-shouldered, well-worked— but their half-naked bodies did not stir me like the Goblin King's. There was a grace to every line of his body; elegance was not only in his air, but in the way he moved. Even when he was awkward. Even when he was unsure.

"I—I—" He was flustered. I relished this bit of power over him, this ability to unsettle him as much as he unsettled me.

"Is that all you have to say to me?" I asked, struggling to keep a straight face. "After all we shared?"

"What did we share?" There was definite panic to his voice now. Suddenly the game was not so fun anymore; if we had indeed taken a tumble in his bed, would he truly be so horrified? I was not Käthe, with her inviting walk and her smile that promised indulgence. Despite my plainness, I thought that the Goblin King and I had shared a spark, but perhaps it was only I who was ready to blaze into flames.

"Nothing, nothing." I was done playing.

"Elisabeth." His wolf's eyes demanded answers. *"What did I do to you?"*

"Nothing," I said. "You did nothing. I woke alone in my own chamber."

"Where are your clothes?"

"In a pile of ashes, I've been told. On your orders, I might add, *mein Herr.*"

He ran a sheepish hand through his tangled locks. "Ah. Yes. I will send the tailors to you to take your measurements. Is that why you are here?"

I shook my head. "I asked to be brought before you, and the servants you sent to attend to me are rather literal-minded." Relief crept over his face, slowly hiding the vulnerable young man from view. "They whisked me here before I could even blink."

During the course of our conversation, the Goblin King had slowly donned his affected armor, piece by piece. First the smirk. The raised brow. The twinkle in his eyes. Then the nonchalant pose, as though it were nothing to him to be found naked in his bedroom by an equally naked young woman in a bedsheet. As though he had not shown me more nakedness of the soul than the brief glimpse of his thighs as he tumbled out of bed.

"Well, then." Even his voice had resumed its usual dry

tone. "I do apologize you caught me with my pants down, my dear. Rather literally too. I had not thought to resume our game so quickly."

"Will you not offer me a seat?" I was determined to conduct myself with all the dignity I could muster, despite my sleep-mussed hair and disheveled appearance.

The Goblin King tilted his head in a courteous bow and waved his hand. The earth parted beneath my feet, and the roots of a young tree burst forth, growing and twisting themselves into the shape of a chair. Louis Quinze style. So that was where the furniture in my room had come from.

I sat down, primly rearranging the sheet about me.

"To what do I owe this honor, Elisabeth?" The soft-eyed young man was gone; he wore the mantle of *Der Erlkönig*, distant and dangerous. I missed that soft-eyed young man. I wanted him back. He seemed real, not like *Der Erlkönig*, all illusion and shadow.

"Where is my sister?"

He shrugged. "Asleep, I presume."

"You presume?"

"It was a rather raucous night." His lips curled. "I imagine Käthe is back in her own bed. Or perhaps someone else's. I can't be too sure."

Panic gripped me. "You swore she would come to no harm!"

He gave me a curious look. Before, he had merely glanced at me, unable to meet my gaze, but now that he was back in his trickster skin, he truly *looked*. He took in my flushed cheeks and tumbled hair, his eyes tracing the curve of my neck where it met my shoulder. Heat crept up the back of my neck.

"And so I did, my dear. So I did. Your sister is perfectly safe. She is whole, intact"—he placed a slight emphasis on the word *intact*—"and hale. My subjects were under orders not to touch her."

It had not seemed that way the night before. I remembered a bevy of fawning swains, illicit kisses, and inappropriate touches.

"Very well, then." I would not show him any sign of relief, any weakening of my dignity. "I shall collect her and go."

"Oh ho ho." The Goblin King conjured himself a chair and table and sat to face me. "We are not finished. We've but just played the second round."

"Which I won," I reminded him. "I am here in your domain now."

"Yes, you are," he said softly. "You are here at last." There was an inviting edge to his words, an edge that caressed.

"Here at last," I agreed. "Soon to be gone." I spread my hands flat on the table between us. "And so the final round begins. What are the rules?"

The Goblin King laid his hands on the table as well. His fingers were long, slender, beautifully articulated, and—I saw with relief—with the proper number of joints. Our hands were where we could both see them, an old gesture to prove we were laying down honest wagers. Our fingertips brushed. The whisper of a memory touched me.

"The rules are simple," he said. "You found your way in. Now find your way out."

"Is that all?"

He smirked, smug and self-satisfied. "Yes. If you can."

"I found my way Underground; I shall find my way back to the world above," I said. " 'For we walk by faith, not by sight.' "

The Goblin King raised an eyebrow. "Are you confident," he asked, finishing the verse, "and willing to be absent from the body?"

I was startled. I had not expected a king of goblins to recognize words from the Scripture.

"I am willing," I said in a low voice, "to do anything that is required of me."

A slow smile spread over his face. "What will you play, Elisabeth?"

I had no answer. I had given him my music; I had given him my all. I did not know what else I had left.

"You first," I said instead. "What will you lay down on the table?"

He watched me closely. "Shall we call each other's reckoning then?"

I swallowed. "If you wish it."

"Then what would you ask of me?"

He was laying a vast amount of power at my feet. He was *Der Erlkönig,* magic and myth and mystery. I could ask him for anything I wished. I could ask for riches. I could ask for fame. I could ask for beauty.

"My music," I said at last. "I am not greedy, *mein Herr.* I will ask only for what was mine to start."

He studied me for a long time, so long that I thought he would refuse me. "That is fair," he said with a nod.

"And you?" My scalp tingled, and an ache began at the base of my spine, fear or eagerness, I did not know. "What would you ask of me?"

His eyes held mine. "I would ask the impossible."

I struggled to let the Goblin King hold my gaze as heat stained my cheeks. "Bear in mind that I am no saint," I said, "and cannot work miracles."

His lips twitched. "Then I would ask for your friendship."

Startled, I removed my hands from the table.

"Oh, Elisabeth," he said. "I would ask that you remember me. Not as we are now, but as we were then."

I frowned. I thought back to our Goblin Grove dances, to the simple wagers we had made when I was a little girl. I struggled to find the truth hidden within my past, but I was unsure which was memory and which was make-believe.

"You do remember." He shifted closer in his seat. There was something like hope in his voice, and I could not bear it.

The Goblin King lifted his hand. The table beneath us vanished, swallowed up by the earth once more.

He placed a finger against my temple. "Somewhere within that remarkable mind of yours, you kept those memories safe. Too safe. Hidden away."

Was the Goblin King the friend I had imagined—remembered—as a child? Or was he truly the Lord of Mischief, blurring the lines between fantasy and reality? I was restless and itchy within my own mind.

He left his seat and kneeled before me. His hands rested on the armrests of my chair, but he was careful not to touch me.

"All I ask, Elisabeth," the Goblin King said, "is that you remember." His words were a bass, their notes resonating in my bones. "Please, remember."

I shrank from the longing in his voice. "I cannot give you that which cannot be given," I said. "I could more easily cut off my hand to give you than my memories."

We stared at each other. Then the Goblin King blinked and the tension that quivered tight between us snapped.

"Well," he said, drawing out the vowel. "Then I suppose we shall have to make do."

I nodded. "What would you claim of me?"

His eyes glittered. "Your hand in marriage."

The blunt proposal hit me harder than a blow. "What?"

The Goblin King crossed his arms and leaned back, his pose insouciant, a smile quirked to one side. Yet somehow his eyes seemed sad.

"You asked, I answered," he said. "The answer is you. What I want is you—entire."

I swallowed hard. The air Underground was suddenly hot, close, suffocating.

"What of Käthe?" I whispered.

For a moment, the Goblin King seemed confused, but then he laughed. "Ah well," he said. "A bride is a bride. You or your sister, it matters not to the old laws." He leaned closer. "But if either of us had the choice, would we not rather it be you instead, Elisabeth?"

I would. But I threw myself upon that thought before it was fully formed, stuffing it back into my heart's compartments, shutting it firmly closed. "A poor choice you have given me," I said. "My life, or my sister's."

He shrugged. "All you mortals die in the end."

His callousness was a chilling reminder that the Goblin King was not my friend. That despite the soft-eyed man I yearned for, he was still *Der Erlkönig*, ruthless, indifferent, immortal.

I'd had enough. "All right," I said. "The stakes are laid. Is there anything else you need from me, *mein Herr*?"

The Goblin King shook his head. "No," he said softly. "Just know this: you have but the days of winter to escape. The barrier between worlds is thin, but only until the year begins anew."

"What will happen if I don't?"

His face was grim. "Then you are trapped here forever. My power is great, Elisabeth, but I cannot change the old laws. Not even for you."

I took his warning for truth. I nodded and rose to my feet.

The Goblin King inclined his head at me. *"Pfiat' di Gott.* Godspeed, Elisabeth."

"I had not thought goblins believed in God."

A small wrinkle appeared between his brows. "They don't," he said. "But I do."

## THE BRIDE

**W**ell?"

I blinked. I was back in my barrow, whisked there before I could finish my next thought. Twig and Thistle waited for me, perched on my bed.

"Well, what?" I asked.

An unholy glee painted both their faces. "Was he angry with you?"

My mind was still in the Goblin King's chambers, even as my body stood in my own barrow. Humans were not meant to be whisked to and fro like this; my grasp of time and space was simple, linear, uncomplicated.

I shook my head, more to regain myself than to respond. "No."

My goblin attendants' ears pricked up with interest, their knobby fingers reaching for my skin. I shrank from their inquisitive touch.

"No," I said in a firmer voice. Twig and Thistle pushed

closer, their sharp-pointed teeth twinkling beneath the fairy lights. "He was not angry with me."

Their ears drooped with disappointment. "He wasn't?"

I minded that these goblin girls were not my friends; they, like the Goblin King, were my enemies in this wearisome game.

"He was not," I repeated. "And I do not appreciate your little tricks, putting me in that position."

"So calm," Twig remarked, running a shiny black claw over the back of my hand. I snatched my hand away, wrapping the bedsheet tighter about my body. "So calm despite the passion shimmering beneath this fragile, mortal skin."

"Mmm," Thistle agreed, her long nose disconcertingly close to the crook of my neck, where my pulse fluttered erratically. "I like this one better than the other one. This one could sustain us for a very long time."

*The other one.* Did they mean Käthe? I needed to find her, and soon.

"Enough." I pushed Twig and Thistle away. They both retreated with a snarl, disappointed by my composure. There was something unsettling about their . . . eagerness for me. It looked like desire, but felt like hunger. I shuddered, still feeling their ghostly fingers crawling over my skin. "Find me something to eat, something to wear, and take me to my sister."

My attendants exchanged glances, their inky eyes blank.

"*I wish* you would find me something to wear and *I wish* you would find me something to eat."

A sour expression crossed both their faces; I had said the magic words. I allowed myself a triumphant smile as the goblin girls faded away, leaving nothing but scattered leaves behind.

After they left, I studied every inch of my barrow, but my room stubbornly remained windowless and doorless. How did goblins travel? Did they simply wish themselves to and fro? I laughed.

If only our wishes had power indeed.

Within a few moments my attendants returned, Thistle carrying a dress, Twig carrying a cake and some wine. The dress was a gaudy confection, more suited to a public salon than workaday practicality. The cake looked appetizing, but I remembered the "treats" from the Goblin Ball and did not trust it.

"No," I said. "Go back and find me something more suitable."

Thistle looked mutinous. "And what do you consider suitable, mortal?"

I rubbed the fabric of the gown between my fingers. Silk. It was beautiful, but the hoops and panniers and corsets Thistle had brought along seemed more trouble than they were worth, especially if I were to go traipsing Underground with my sister.

"Something simple," I said. "None of this silk and satin frippery. Nothing that would take a bevy of servants to sew me into. Something practical."

"So boring," Thistle pouted.

"Yes." I didn't deny her. "And if you can't find me a dress, bring me a skirt and blouse and I shall make do."

Thistle crossed her arms. "I don't understand. The other mortals loved all the pretty dresses we could find for them."

"I am not my sister." I paused. "The other mortals?"

"The other brides, of course."

I knew that the Goblin King had taken other brides. Constanze was a veritable fount of cautionary tales about women who were too bold, too intelligent, too beautiful, too different. Yet jealousy pricked me with its needle-sharp sting; I was none of those things, and the Goblin King had made me believe he had wanted me—me entire, me alone.

"What, jealous?" Thistle grinned.

"No." But my flush betrayed the lie.

"Look how pink she is now!" Twig said with delight.

"What happened to the other women?" I was determined not to let my attendants get the better of me. "What happened to the other brides?"

"They failed," Thistle said simply. She went about the business of dressing me.

"Failed?" I was too surprised to swat her away. "What do you mean, *failed*?"

"Stand *still*," Thistle growled, trying to lace me into the stays and panniers. The matter was clearly of no great import to her, but the game had changed somehow. I felt I had turned a familiar corner to find a completely different path than the one I expected. Constanze's stories had never mentioned *this*.

"What do you mean, *failed*?" I repeated the question to Twig.

The taller goblin girl lifted her bushy brows. "They failed to escape," she said. "What else would we mean?"

"Escape the Underground, you mean."

Twig shrugged. "*Der Erlkönig*, the Underground, Death. They are one and the same."

"Stop wriggling!" Thistle pinched me with her sharp little claws, and I yelped. "If you let me dress you, then you can go see to your sister. I can tell you *she's* already dressed in whatever her retinue have put out for her, *and* eaten of whatever they have brought."

Was she trying to *guilt* me? I bit back a laugh. If I started laughing, I would cry.

"Fine," I said. "I'll get dressed. But not in this. Find me another dress." My stomach rumbled. "And bring me a loaf of bread and some water. Some sausage if you can find it. None of these fairy-made sweets. I will not have my senses clouded by your magic."

Twig and Thistle opened their mouths to protest. I glared at them. "I wish . . ."

They disappeared without a word, leaving behind nothing but the echoes of a disgruntled sigh.


Once I was properly dressed and suitably fed, I felt much better equipped to face whatever was to come. After questioning both Twig and Thistle, I discovered that the world underground had corridors and thresholds, but no windows or doors. Goblins had no concept of privacy, and there had never been a need to shut an entrance. My barrow room had been sealed for my comfort. Orders of the Goblin King.

"Can you also conjure things from the earth?" I asked my goblin girls.

They nodded.

"Then conjure me a door. With a lock on it."

It was a while before they understood exactly what I needed. Thistle and Twig took my descriptions and fitted me with a circular door, odd but satisfactory. The lock was a strange device of their own invention, but serviceable. We three were the only ones with a key.

My barrow opened into a corridor. Like my room, it was

a mixture of natural and unnatural elements: dirt-packed floors and wrought-iron decorations. Goblin art was both frightening and beautiful; it emulated human art with an extraordinary degree of skillful imitation, but the subjects were not lofty. They were entirely terrestrial. The sconces along the wall were carved not into the shapes of flowers and angels; they were grown from tree roots into the shape of an arm clutching its torch. The paintings on the wall did not depict the traditional scenes of grandeur and glory; they were mostly landscapes. Woods and mountains, streams and brooks, rendered with such precision they seemed like windows to the world above. It alleviated the sense of being trapped underground.

Thistle and Twig led me along the corridor to a grand hall. Like the ballroom, this space was a cavern of stone with tall, arched ceilings and dripping icicles of glittering rock. Above, the fairy lights danced like stars in the night sky. But I saw not a single goblin, not of Twig and Thistle's ilk, closer to the earth than humankind.

"Where is everyone?" I asked.

"Working," Twig said, as though it were the most obvious answer in the world.

"Working?" I had not thought that goblins worked; at least, not in the way humans did in the world above. It made me wonder: where did goblin food come from? Where did their clothes? Their furniture? Did they have goblin farmers? Goblin craftsmen? Constanze's stories never told me much about the Underground itself, only what happened when its denizens trespassed into the world above. Always fighting, always tricking, always stealing, the goblins always sought to take away what did not belong to them.

"What," Thistle said sourly. "Did you think all this was

created by *magic*?" She waved her long, many-jointed fingers about the great hall.

"Well, yes," I admitted. "Couldn't you just . . . wish this all into existence?"

The goblin girls laughed, their cackling giggles echoing up the walls like skittering roach feet.

"Mortal, you know nothing about the power of wishes," Thistle said. "What the old laws giveth, they taketh in return."

I thought of the careless wishes I had thrown around, and a whisper of foreboding touched me.

"All must be in balance," Twig explained. "Ever since we were sundered from the world above and driven Underground, we were granted the power to travel as we wished. But nothing comes for free, mistress, and we built this kingdom with our own hands. Now, you must excuse us, mistress," she said. "We have other duties to which we must attend." She pointed above our heads. "The fairy lights will guide you to your sister."

I looked up at the ceiling. A shower of bright motes began to fall about me like snow, resting lightly on my shoulders and hair. I laughed; magic or no, it was enchanting. It tickled. The fairy lights spun about me before resolving into a golden stream of light. I followed the path down the hall and into another corridor.

Käthe's barrow room was on the other side of the great hall. The corridor leading to her room looked very much like mine, but the human touch on this side of the Underground was stronger. The paintings hung on the walls were similar to what we might see in the gallery of a great estate: portraits and pastoral scenes, all showing the Goblin King.

At first I was inclined to dismiss them as yet another self-aggrandizing display of *Der Erlkönig*, but as I walked farther down the timeline of portraits, I noticed something curious. The fashions and artistic hand changed and shifted through the centuries—as to be expected—but so too did the sitter.

I did not notice the changing faces at first, for each successive portrait showed kinship with its predecessor. Yet there were subtle differences between them all that one could not simply attribute to differing artists. They all shared similar features—the long, elfin face, high cheekbones, preternatural and relentless symmetry—but the slope of the jaw, the set of the eyes, as well as the colors of the irises, were each as distinct as a snowflake in a storm. They were all different men, and yet, at the same time, they were all *Der Erlkönig*.

Brown eyes, blue eyes, green eyes, gray eyes, but none were the mismatched wolf's eyes of my Goblin King. I walked up and down the gallery, studying each face, looking for the pair I knew.

At last I came across a portrait at the very end of the corridor, unlit, secluded, and shadowed, as though hiding in shame. It was the most recent in the long line, painted in the style of the old Dutch masters: light and dark in exaggerated contrasts, the details sharp and painstakingly realistic. Its sitter was a young man, dressed in velvet academic robes and a round cap with a tassel. Despite the richness of the material, there was something austere about him, especially as he had one hand clasped around a wooden cross hanging from a cord on his neck. In the other hand, he held a violin upright in his lap, his long, beautiful fingers resting along the neck. I squinted. The scroll of the instrument looked familiar, but its edges faded into shadow, and I could make nothing of it but the vague impression of a woman's face contorted in agony. Or ecstasy.

I shivered.

I could not bring myself to meet the sitter's gaze until the very end. I thought I knew what I would find—two differently colored eyes, one green, one gray—but what I saw arrested me.

It was a younger Goblin King in the portrait, his cheeks fuller and not so sharp, his features less defined. A young man my age. A youth. The difference in color in those eyes was in stark relief in the portrait: the left, the bright green of spring grass, and the right, the blue-gray of a twilight sky. Yet I recalled them being the muted hazel-green of dying moss and the icy gray of a winter's pond. Faded. Old.

Presently the fairy lights tugged at my hair and at my clothing until I moved on. The image of the Goblin King's younger self stayed with me as I walked away. The expression in his eyes made my breath come short. Unguarded. Vulnerable. *Human.* I recognized those eyes from my childhood, in the soft-eyed young man I'd stumbled across in the Goblin King's bedchamber. I saw that expression when my Goblin King looked at me now.

I was all shaken up, my emotions upturned and in disarray. I continued walking down the corridor, suddenly eager to put as much distance between the portrait and me as I could.

It wasn't until the portrait gallery was far behind me when a disconcerting thought came to me:

When had he become *my* Goblin King?


"Liesl!" Käthe enthusiastically greeted me when I appeared in her room. Like mine, her barrow chamber had no door, but one had appeared when I wished it.

Her changed appearance was shocking. My sister had always been full-figured and plump, her cheeks cherubic, her arms full and healthy. Now she was thin, gaunt, and sickly. She wore a dressing gown over her chemise, but it hung off her shoulders, as though the body within it was nothing. Käthe was disappearing before my eyes.

"Come sit by the fire and take tea with me," my sister urged. She seemed at home in the Underground, playing hostess in her suite of packed-dirt rooms.

"Käthe," I said. "Are you all right?"

"Of course I'm fine." A tea set had already been laid out on the table by the hearth, and she gestured to the chair and bade me sit. Then she poured me a cup of tea and offered me a slice of cake. "How are you, my dear?"

I accepted the slice of cake. "I don't know," I admitted. "I don't know at all."

Käthe gave me an indulgent smile, and added another spoonful of sugar to her tea. "Eat," she said, nodding at the untouched slice of cake on my plate.

I studied my sister. She seemed clear-eyed and conscious; present, in a way she hadn't been at the Goblin Ball.

"Käthe," I said carefully. "Do you know where we are?"

She laughed and sliced herself another piece of cake. "Of course I do, you ninny. We're in my quarters, enjoying a spot of tea and some time together. Now tell me," she said, gesturing to the bare, earthen walls, "what do you think of the wallpaper?"

"The wallpaper?"

"Watered silk imported from Italy, of course," she said loftily. "Just like we always imagined, Liesl."

My heart fluttered in my chest. The color was high in my sister's cheeks, her movements heightened and exaggerated, as though she were playacting the role of a gracious lady. As though she were playing pretend. *What if?*

"Yes," I said slowly. "Your quarters are beautiful." I picked up my teacup and took a sip to hide my frown. "My compliments, my dear."

Käthe's eyes were alight. "Why, thank you, darling. My husband is a very generous man, as you know."

My cup rattled in its saucer. "Your husband?"

She pouted. "Don't you remember? We had the most beautiful wedding in the Munich Frauenkirche, with the archbishop presiding. Josef played your wedding mass to thunderous applause."

I set down my tea. "My . . . wedding mass?"

Käthe gave me a pitying look. "Oh, Liesl, you must have had a rough night if you can't remember. The wedding mass you wrote for us. Mother sang the Benedictus so beautifully it moved everyone to tears."

"My . . . music."

She nodded. "You're a success all over the Holy Roman Empire now, thanks to my husband's connections. He had the good sense to hire Josef at court too, and even funds our brother's tours across Europe. He even has Papa on retainer as a *Konzertmeister,* although it's more a courtesy than an active position."

"At . . . his court?" My voice was strangled, thin.

"Of course his court," she said, as if it were the most obvious thing in the world. "He couldn't very well hire for someone else's, could he?"

"Käthe," I said. "Just *who* is your husband?"

She blew out a huff and rolled her eyes. "Manók Hercege. The Hungarian count? Honestly, Liesl, perhaps you ought to let yourself have a bit of fun more often if a little indulgence will set you back like this." Käthe traced her fingers absentmindedly along her collarbone, and I found myself mirroring the gesture, half-remembering the revels of the Goblin Ball.

A count. A rich, Hungarian count. Käthe's fantasy husband was a wealthy, foreign nobleman. This was not the sort of man I thought my sister would imagine herself in love with.

"Is Man—Manók Hercege good to you?" I asked.

"Of course," Käthe beamed.

"What is he like?"

"Kind. Gentle." Her voice was misty, distant. "Generous. Not just to me, but to all of us. Eat up," she said again, pushing the cake at me. "Chocolate torte. It's your favorite."

Then it became clear just what Käthe's greatest dream had been: to marry rich. Not for fancy gowns or expensive jewels, but to provide for her family. My throat tightened and I gathered my sister in my arms, holding her close.

"Liesl," Käthe said with surprise. "Is everything all right?"

"No," I choked. "Everything is not all right. It's not right at all."

She swatted me away. "Have some cake," she insisted again. "After all the trouble I went through to get it for you, you should at least have a bite."

I nodded and picked up the plate and a fork. I recoiled. What had seemed, at first glance, like a moist chocolate torte was layer upon layer of crumbling dirt, with stripes of slime for buttercream. I pretended to tuck in for Käthe's sake, but the moment my sister looked away, I cast the cake into the fire. The impossible scent of summer peaches rose with the smoke.

"Did you like it?" she asked, eagerly searching my face for an answer. Her blue eyes were steady, but seemed overlarge in her pale face. Despite the high color in her cheeks, she looked sicker than ever. "My husband went all the way to Bohemia for the recipe."

"Delicious." I managed to swallow my bile. "My compliments to your husband."

Käthe beamed, then deflated. "He travels so often, my husband," she said. "I wish I could go with him sometimes. To see the world beyond this beautiful palace. It *is* beautiful," she continued, a trifle defensively, "but it can be stifling. Almost like a prison, rather than a palace."

I straightened in my seat. That was the real Käthe speaking, my true little sister beneath the wish-spell that surrounded her. The young woman who wanted to experience the world beyond the edges of the rustic life she had always known.

"Where are Manók Hercege's holdings?" I asked.

"Hungary, of course."

"But *where* in Hungary?" I pressed.

A vague expression crossed her face. "I—I'm not sure."

"Where did you go on your wedding tour? Vienna? Rome? Paris? London? Did your husband take you to all the greatest cities in Europe, as you had always dreamed?"

"I—" A little wrinkle appeared between her brows, a wrinkle of pain and concentration. "I can't remember."

"Think." I grabbed Käthe's hands. "Where we are. Where we aren't. Where we must be."

My sister closed her eyes.

"The market, the fruit, the ball, the Goblin King . . ."

"Liesl." Käthe's voice was strained, as though coming from an incredible distance. My pulse thrummed in my ears. "Yes. I—I think I remember. The taste of peaches in winter. The sound of music. I think—I think—"

"Go on," I urged. I was getting to the heart of the enchantment. If only I could get closer and cut it away entirely.

"It hurts," she whispered. She opened her eyes and looked at me. "Sometimes I think I know where I am and I am afraid. But it's easier not to be. Is this what it is like to be dead?"

A trickle of blood over her lip; a nosebleed. Frightened, I wiped it away with the hem of my skirt.

"No, dearest," I said, gripping her hands tighter. "You're alive."

The blood wouldn't stop. Panic threaded its way about my heart, my hands, my throat.

"You're alive, Käthe," I repeated. "Just hold on for a little while longer."

A suite of bells began to play, their bright, tinkling sound akin to my sister's laugh. At once my sister's demeanor changed; she grew animated and agitated, her bloodless lips stretched thin in a grotesque smile.

"That must be him!" she said happily. "My Manók." She rose from her chair, and stood in the middle of her barrow, waiting with her arms outstretched. I wondered who would appear—which of her tall, elegant swains from the Goblin Ball would play the Hungarian count. "Come in, my love!"

I turned, half expecting a door to appear and let in this mysterious Hungarian husband. But no door materialized. Instead, with a breeze that sent the fairy lights swirling, the Goblin King swept into view.

"Hello, my darling," he said, taking Käthe's hand in his. Those wolf's eyes glinted at me as he met my gaze over my sister's head. "How did you enjoy your cake?"

# THE OLD
# LAWS

the Goblin King and I locked eyes with each other as my sister made our introductions.

"Darling," she said. "You remember my sister, Elisabeth, of course?"

"Charmed, *Fräulein*." He brought my hand to his lips. I resisted the urge to snatch it away and deliver it back with a slap.

"Liesl." Käthe turned to me. "My husband, Manók Hercege."

"A pleasure," I said through gritted teeth.

"I do believe your sister does not approve of me, my dear," the Goblin King said to Käthe. "She stares daggers into my soul. They stab." He pressed his hand to his heart.

"Liesl!" Käthe reprimanded.

"Now, now," the Goblin King soothed. "I'm sure Elisabeth is only doing her duty, as an elder sister must. Since she is doomed to a life of spinsterhood, she might as well pass judgment on all your swains, yes?"

"Manók!" Käthe slapped him hard on the wrist. "Be kind. The both of you."

"*Mein Herr*," I said tightly. "A word?"

The Goblin King inclined his head. "Of course. Madam?" He turned to Käthe, asking to be excused from her presence. My sister nodded her consent and waved us off.

"Manók Hercege?" was the first thing out of my mouth when we were alone.

The Goblin King gave an elegant shrug. "I know a little Hungarian."

"What does it mean?"

He grinned. "What you think it means. I am not so creative as all that, Elisabeth."

I frowned. "Is that your name? *Have* you a name?"

The Goblin King stiffened. "That is not the topic at hand."

I raised my brows. But his face was shuttered tight as a house in a storm.

"No," I agreed. "The topic is why and how you've made my sister believe she's married to you."

"Jealous?" He looked pleased.

"Did you force her? Coerce her somehow? Or is this all an elaborate fantasy you've orchestrated to trap her here with you forever?"

"Coerced is such a strong word," he said. "I like to think I am persuasive on my own merits."

"She thinks you are a Hungarian count."

He waved his hand. "We all have our flaws."

"You can play your games with me," I said. "But leave Käthe alone. She is not equipped to deal with you."

"Oh, and you are?" The Goblin King leaned forward. I willed myself to stillness. "Do tell; I am intrigued."

"The game is between you and me," I repeated. "Leave my sister out of this. She's innocent."

His eyes darkened. "Is your sister truly innocent?"

"Yes."

"A girl well acquainted with temptation, a girl with an inviting laugh, a fickle heart, and an adventurous soul," he said in a low voice. "A girl given to self-indulgence, who reaches for the low-hanging, forbidden fruit and eats of it against the wisdom of her older sister—can such a girl truly be called innocent?"

I went rigid with rage. "It is not for you to judge."

"But it is for you?" he returned. "Are you responsible for your sister's virtue?"

"No," I said. "But I will safeguard her good name."

"Oh, Elisabeth." The Goblin King shook his head. "When will you be selfish? When will you ever do anything for yourself?"

I was silent.

"You cannot leash yourself to your sister's quim and whims." All pretense of charm or chicanery were gone from the Goblin King. "Someday she must make her own choices. Without you. What will you do when there is no one left to take care of, no one left to look after? Is that when you will finally look after you?"

He had a way of attacking me with compassion. His unexpected kindness, more than his charm or beauty, was seductive. I disliked the truth in his words. And his pity. I did not want his pity.

The Goblin King sighed. "Käthe is part of the game. The pieces have been set in motion, and she is one of them."

"You gave me the days of winter to escape the Underground." I crossed my arms. "And you've gone and married my sister behind my back."

That smug grin returned to his face. "You *are* jealous. Well, well, well; that bodes well for me."

When I did not rise to his bait, he shook his head.

"No, Elisabeth, I have not married Käthe. The old laws are binding, and when I take a bride, it is forever. She may never set foot in the world above again. This pretty vision is a spell of her own making, a beautiful fantasy to bring her comfort. I have very little power, you know."

I scoffed. "You are *Der Erlkönig*. You have all the power."

The Goblin King lifted a brow. "If you think that, then you know less than I gave you credit for," he said. "I am but a prisoner to my own crown."

*Does the crown serve the king or the king serve the crown?*

"Why a bride?" I asked after a moment. "Why—why Käthe?"

Why not me? Why hadn't he come for *me*?

It was a while before he answered. He ran his fingers over one of the figurines on one of the side tables in the corridor. It was a wood nymph, wide-hipped, buxom, earthy. He traced the curve of her waist, down the hillocks of her thighs, and back up the shape of her leg before resting on the nymph's collarbones, where the line of her neck met her bosom.

"Shall I tell you a story?" he said at last. He released the nymph figurine and stared into one of the landscapes that hung in the corridor. "A story such as Constanze might have told you and your siblings when you were children."

I held my breath.

"Once upon a time, there was a great king who lived underground."

My grandmother's fairy tales often began this way. I had always thought her stories were her own invention, but hearing the rhythm of the Goblin King's words, I wondered where Constanze first had learned them.

"This king was the ruler of the dead and the living," he continued. "He brought the world above to life every spring, and brought it back to death every autumn."

The Goblin King stared at the landscape as the trees and living things blossomed and bloomed, growing green and bright before withering away.

"The seasons turned, one after another, and with time, the king grew old. Weary. Spring came later and later and autumn earlier and earlier, until one day, there was no spring at all. The world above had gone quiet, dead, and still, and the people suffered."

The enchanted portrait returned to winter and snow. The seasons had stopped changing.

"One day, a brave maiden ventured into the Underground." His eyes turned from the portrait back to me. "To beg the king to return the world above to life."

"Brave?" I laughed, a thin, defiant bark of a laugh. "Not beautiful?"

His lips twisted to one side. "Brave or beautiful, it matters not. Let Constanze tell it one way; I shall tell it in mine."

The Goblin King moved closer. I held my ground, pushing back against his insistent presence.

"She offered the king her life in exchange for the land. *My life for my people,* she said. She begged him to accept her bargain. She knew the old laws: life for life, blood for harvest. Without it, the Underground would wither and fade away, taking with it every last trace of green from the world above."

He hovered over me, his fingers outstretched, reaching

for the pulse in my throat. My breathing grew shallow. I waited—wanted—for him to touch me, to seize my lifebeat in his hands and take it.

But he did not. His fingers curled in on themselves and he retreated.

"Her life would sustain the king's, the king's life would sustain the denizens of the Underground, and their lives would sustain the earth and make things grow. The king accepted her bargain, and when the new year turned, spring came again."

In its own way, it was a beautiful story, more like the parables and fables of good Christian martyrs Mother told us than Constanze's tales of hobgoblins and mischief. Virtuous people, persistent people, people who sacrificed themselves for the greater good of all, these were the heroes of Mother's stories. Like the brave maiden of the Goblin King's tale.

But Käthe was not the brave heroine of Mother's stories; she was the foolish, beautiful girl of Constanze's. Who was the brave maiden of the Goblin King's tale?

"But the story doesn't end there, does it?" I asked.

"The story has no end," he said roughly. "It goes on and on and on and on unto eternity."

The Goblin King's eyes were sad, or regretful. His eyes were not like those of the other goblins—those dark, ink-black orbs that hid all intent. It was difficult to read the faces of the goblins around me; their eyes flat and inscrutable, their features twisted and alien to the natural eye. But there was sympathy between myself and the Goblin King, a language of our bodies that I understood.

"So you want my sister to die," I whispered, "so the world can live."

He said nothing.

"If," I began, and then cleared my throat. "If you lose the game, what happens? Will—will spring never come? Will the world above live under eternal winter?"

His face was grave. "Are you willing to take that risk?"

An impossible choice. The life of my sister . . . or the fate of the world. I had thought my stakes were high, but I saw now that the Goblin King's was even higher.

"What will happen to you if I win?" I whispered.

A smile crossed his lips, but the corners were down-turned, more sad than satisfied. "You know," he said. "You're the only one who's ever asked."

Then he vanished in a swirl of wind and dead leaves.

I was running out of time.

With no sunrise or sunset to mark the passing of days, I counted the hours by the fading of Käthe's hair, the wither-ing of her flesh, the growing pallor of her complexion. The curves about her breast and hips disappeared, and the skin beneath her eyes thinned to a bruise-black.

My sister was dying.

The Goblin King paid frequent tribute to her in his role as the Hungarian count. I watched my sister and the Goblin King fawn and simper at each other at these outings, at dinner, at the goblin revels he insisted on holding every night. Another night of goblin wine, another night lost to indulgence.

Every moment lost was another victory gained for the Goblin King.

His eyes seemed to tell me so, whenever our gazes met over my sister's head. Which was often. I felt the touch of his eyes on my skin at all times, an insistent caress that compelled me to look at him. Although I did not admit it aloud, the sight of Käthe on his arm drove me mad with envy. She was a pawn in our game, and I knew it; she was the bait to my temper, and I knew it, yet I could not brush off the nettle-stings of jealousy. I missed my klavier, where I could let those staccato notes of frustration and futility burst forth in a torrent of song.

In my moments alone, I wandered the labyrinthine passages of the Underground. Goblins scuttled back and forth underfoot, their black eyes shining at me from the corners like beetle carapaces. At my request, Twig and Thistle brought me stacks of paper and a lead pen. I tried to mark the various pathways in the Underground, but the tunnels shifted and twisted and changed every time I thought I traversed down a familiar way. More often than not, I scribbled little throwaway melodies and musical thoughts in the margins of my maps.

Käthe too was determined to distract me. She had seen my maps, but her eyes lingered on the notes, not the paths. She insisted I sit at her desk and compose, and supplied me with pretty paper and fancy nibs, her fantasy of how a composer truly worked: in beauty, in isolation, and in silence. My sister, so kindhearted, so blind.

"Come!" she said one day—night?—clapping her hands. "I have a gift for you!" She gestured to her goblin attendants, who brought in gown after gown after gown.

"What's all this?" I asked as Käthe shooed her attendants away again.

"For your debut, you ninny," she said.

"What debut?"

She gave me an exasperated eyeroll. "Honestly, Liesl, it's

a wonder you're even able to function sometimes. The debut of your latest symphony, of course. Manók has arranged for a concert to be held in the receiving hall."

The strength of my sister's fantasy world overwhelmed me sometimes, so much I could no longer tell where the edges of her dream ended and mine began.

I let Käthe dress me in whatever gown she thought best suited me and let her fuss with my hair. For a moment, it was like we were children again, the touch of her gentle fingers on my scalp as familiar as the lullabies Josef and I used to play for each other.

"There," she said once she had finished. "Beautiful."

"Beautiful?" I laughed. "No need to flatter me with lies, Käthe."

"Stop it." She slapped my shoulder. "Just because you grew up in a backwater town doesn't mean you have to dress like a peasant all the time, you know."

"If it were only feathers that could transform a sparrow into a peacock."

"A sparrow is beautiful in its own way," Käthe said severely. "Don't force yourself to be a peacock, Liesl. Embrace your sparrow self. Look." She gestured to the bronze mirror before me.

It was not my reflection that caught my eye, but hers. The full scope of my sister's transformation hadn't been clear until I saw her face in the bronze mirror. How many times had I watched Käthe primp and prepare before the mirror in our bedroom, her apple-plump cheeks and sparkling eyes glowing with health? The bones of her cheeks and jaw jutted painfully now, angular and almost masculine. Her chin was as sharp as a dagger, her nose long, her lips thin. Her eyes were overlarge in that wasted face, and with a start, I realized I was looking at me. No, my sister. Faded away to a wisp of her former self, Käthe and I looked the same, save for our different coloring.

"See?" She smiled, a rictus grin. "Ready to face the whole, wide world."

Käthe hadn't done much in the way of face paint or powders; she'd merely touched my lips with rouge and brushed out my brows. In the flickering fairy lights of the Underground, my sallow complexion evened into a creamy pallor, the angles of my face imposing rather than thin. This was the face I had seen every day of my life growing up—plain, angular, horsey—yet in this new environment, I glowed with an otherworldly light. A sparrow in its nest.

"I wish . . ." Käthe began, then frowned.

"What is it?" I asked.

She shook her head. "Nothing. It's just . . ." She bit her lip. "I wish, just once, we might venture beyond these palace walls. To hear your music played before a wide audience. To see works of art by the great masters. To feel . . . real sunshine, taste strawberries sun-sweet from the meadow, to—oh!"

Drops of blood fell to stain the rug beneath our feet. Another nosebleed. I jumped up, rushing to grab a cloth or a bandage, but there was nothing in the room save for yards and yards of expensive fabric. I grabbed a discarded stocking—clean, I hoped—and helped clean her up.

"I need to lie down," she murmured weakly.

"All right." I helped her to her bed. She felt even thinner and frailer in my arms than before.

"Liesl." Käthe's voice was a thready whisper. "Liesl, I don't . . . feel so well. I—"

"Shush," I said. "I'll call for your attendants."

Käthe shook her head. "I want Mother," she whimpered. "I want—"

I did not know what to do. Mother was far away; life was far away, and slipping ever further from my sister's grasp. Despair and rage choked me, but I swallowed them down. Käthe looked at me with large, frightened eyes, and I smiled for her. Mother's smile. Calm in the face of adversity.

Smoothing her hair as she rested against her pillows, I hummed a bit of a lullaby Mother used to sing for us. My voice held none of our mother's sweetness, but Käthe seemed soothed nonetheless. To my surprise, she joined in, her unmusical, tone-deaf ear struggling to find the right pitch along with me. As a little girl, she had refused to sing or play other musical games with the family, painfully conscious of her inadequacies.

"Liesl."

Behind the strained voice, I heard her. My *real* sister, behind the enchantment. I faltered.

My sister seized my hand. "No, don't," she said. "Keep singing. Keep going."

I stopped playing with Käthe's hair. I took up the lullaby once more, substituting the lyrics with a wordless *ooh* as I tried to figure out what to do next.

*Are you here, Käthe, my love, my dear?*

The question fit awkwardly into the lullaby's rhythm and beat, but it seemed to be the best way to speak with her without breaking the music.

"Yes, I'm here," she said, struggling. "Your music . . . it helps keep the fog away."

*We must flee, we must fly, your bridegroom awaits to take his prize.*

"My bridegroom?" Her blue eyes clouded and I silently

cursed myself for slipping in my own spell that I tried to weave about her.

*No matter, no worries, come with me; let's hurry!*

"Hurry," she repeated. Her eyes roamed the barrow chamber, as though seeing it for what it was for the first time. "Yes, we must hurry."

*Are you well, are you hale? You are so weak, you are so pale.*

"Yes." She nodded stiffly. Then, almost as if by strength of will, color returned to her face, and her blue eyes were hard with determination. "I am."

*Then follow me, my sweet, follow me.*

Käthe nodded again.

"I'm coming, Liesl," she said faintly. "I will follow."

# STRANGE,
# SWEET

I wasted no time. Once I got Käthe out of bed, I dressed us both in the most practical gowns I could find. I had nothing with me, not even my rudimentary and contradictory map of the Underground. But the time for planning was past. Whether or not we got lost mattered little now; time had run out. So, like the Pied Piper of Hamelin, I strove to lead my sister away.

My voice was already growing hoarse. I could not sing forever; I needed some other way to keep my sister under *my* spell.

When the idea came to me, I almost dropped my song within a laugh. My flute. The gift of the tall, elegant stranger. I had played it into his lair; I would play it out.

*I wish, I wish, for anyone near*
*To bring me my flute, quick!*
*Bring it to me here.*

Within the twinkling of an eye, Twig and Thistle appeared before me. Thistle seemed irritated by the summons, but Twig seemed amused. The tall, spindly goblin offered me the instrument with an almost reverent look on her face.

*Thank you, my friend*
*My thanks to you.*
*Please help me find my way*
*Out of this tomb?*

I could not figure how to work *I wish* into my improvised song, which grew more tuneless and shapeless by the measure.

"There is no way out, mortal," Thistle said. "It is futile to try."

I shook my head, still humming a wordless tune. I turned to Käthe, whose drawn face was pale and sheened with cold sweat.

"I'm here," she said in that strained, distant voice of hers. "I'm still here."

Twig gazed at me with those flat, inhuman, unreadable eyes. I wanted to read kindness into them. "Know this, mortal," she said. "All paths lead to the beginning and to the end in the Underground. It is for you to find which is which. Stay true; be swift. Remember, what the old laws giveth, they also taketh. It will not be easy for you to escape."

"She will fail," Thistle sneered. "No mortal on earth has the power to upset the ancient balance." She bared her teeth in a ghoulish grin. "Good luck. You will need it."

I ignored Thistle, and nodded my thanks to Twig. Both goblin girls faded away.

*Talk to me, darling,* I sang to Käthe, *Stay with me. Sing!*
Then I placed the flute to my lips.


The Underground was a labyrinth. I followed corridors that led upward, corridors that doubled back on themselves, corridors that disappeared into a wall. I could not hold Käthe's hand as I played the flute, but she tied herself to my apron strings. Every time she faltered, I played something from our childhood. A canon. A skipping song. A silly little nonsense ditty.

"You'll never win, you know."

Ahead of me, wreathed by shadow and torchlight, stood the Goblin King. He wore the hood and cloak he had when I first met him in the marketplace, when he was just a tall, elegant, and mysterious stranger.

I stopped in my tracks. Käthe tripped into me.

"What is it?" she wobbled. "Are you all right?"

I stared at the Goblin King, but Käthe's eyes darted about, blind to his slender form blocking our path. He raised one side of his mouth in a smirk and brought a gloved finger to his lips. *Shhh.*

A breeze picked up in the Underground, bitter and cold, bringing with it the tantalizing scent of the world above: leaves, loam, ice, and freedom. My sister pressed against me and I could feel her trembling against my back. The wind darted about us like a little sprite, tugging at our hair, our skirts, our blouses, playful and mischievous.

"Liesl," Käthe said. "Are we getting close?"

I dared not lower my flute to comfort my sister. The Goblin King's eyes glittered beneath his hood. I raised my chin and met his gaze squarely.

There was nothing of my soft-eyed young man in him now; this Goblin King was all shadow and illusion, *Der Erlkönig* in his most elemental form. Trickster. Seducer. King. I searched his face for any hint of the austere youth from the portrait in the gallery, *my* Goblin King. But he was not there.

I squared my shoulders and turned to Käthe, playing a jaunty little *Ländler*. It was one of the most cheerful melodies I knew, and I playe it with all the lightheartedness I could muster. The little wrinkle of concern never left my sister's brow, but her face relaxed into a tentative smile. Käthe wasn't one to dissect the moods and tones of a piece of music, but even my non-musical sister could respond to what I was saying without words.

*All is well. Do not worry.*

Käthe followed in my footsteps as we approached *Der Erlkönig*. The wind grew stronger, no longer a playful sprite, but a malicious spirit. It pushed, it pulled, it argued, it threatened. It bit at my fingertips and lips, turning them stiff, numb, insensitive. The sound of its wuthering rose higher than the thin voice of my flute, drowning out my melodies. Käthe huddled close as I struggled to play over the wind, but it was a battle we were losing. My sister slipped farther and farther away from me, my apron strings leaving her grasp. So close, we were so close . . .

"Give up, Elisabeth," *Der Erlkönig* crooned. "Let go, my dear. Lay down your flute and rest. Stay with me."

I closed my eyes. I could no longer feel the instrument between my numb fingers. I was tired, out of breath, and out of ideas.

"Yes," he hissed. "Gently, slowly—"

My lips left the flute, my hands slowly lowered to my

side. But to yield was not always to lose. I was not defeated yet.

Mother had taught us all to sing, just as Papa had taught us all to play. While none of us had her gift of song, she taught us all how to control our breathing, how to project our voices, how to shape the air within us to produce an enormous sound. I took a deep breath, filling my lungs down to my stomach with air. I found a pitch I could comfortably sustain: high enough to be shrill, low enough not to shred my vocal cords.

I opened my mouth and screamed.

I let the sound fill my head, resonate in the hollow spaces of my face, and pushed outward. *Der Erlkönig* faltered, stunned by the intensity of my scream. He stumbled back, throwing his hands up against the sound.

I took one step forward; *Der Erlkönig* took one step back. I kept moving forward, but the distance between us never closed. I wanted to meet him, confront him, push him out of the way with my bare hands, make him admit defeat at my feet. I reached for him, but my fingers passed through the fabric of his cloak. He was as insubstantial as a will-o'-the-wisp. He vanished in an instant.

Käthe and I were alone in the passageway. The air grew still and warm, the silence about us stifling. I began humming, a tuneless hum that was more resignation than reassurance. Käthe slid her hand into mine and squeezed it comfortingly, her palm surprisingly warm.

I glanced down at the flute by my side. It was smoking slightly, but not from heat. Frost rimmed its joins, the frozen wood of its body almost too painful to hold. I brought it back up to my mouth, my lips sticking to the ice-rimmed metal embouchure. A sigh misted across the surface as I began to play once more, my breath forming clouds before me.

It was my first encounter with *Der Erlkönig* on that long, endless night, but it would not be the last. Over and over again, he appeared before me, taunting me, misleading me, tricking me. I stood stalwart and unwavering, walking past his apparitions and through his illusions. It was easier, somehow, when I thought of him as the terrifying and enigmatic figure of myth from Constanze's stories, rather than the Goblin King with whom I had danced as both a child and a young woman. There was nothing of *my* Goblin King within *Der Erlkönig*.

Each triumph against *Der Erlkönig* strengthened my resolve and determination, but I grew overconfident. I had bested his supernatural tricks; I had not reckoned on his psychological ones.

I was playing the flute again—I alternated between singing and playing in an effort to preserve both my voice and my breath—when I heard the violin.

I who had grown up with Papa, I who had nurtured Josef's developing virtuoso talent, had never, *ever* heard such playing as this. The violinist played a piece I did not know. I did not recognize the composer, though I thought I could hear Bach's contrapuntal intricacy, Vivaldi's elegant expressiveness, and Handel's grandiose charm within the piece. There was devotion in every strain—devotion, reverence, ecstasy—and I nearly wept from the beauty of it. I stopped humming.

The scent of summer peaches filled the corridor.

Even Käthe seemed moved, though she couldn't tell the difference between a concerto and a chaconne. My sister swayed on her feet, closing her eyes as though trying to listen with greater attention.

The music came from somewhere just beyond reach. Hand in hand, Käthe and I followed the sound to where it seemed loudest, the most clear, the most affecting. But there was no musician standing before us, no one to congratulate on the exquisiteness of his or her playing. In fact, the music seemed to come from behind the earthen wall of the passageway, in another room, another hall, another world. I pressed my ears to the dirt, struggling to get closer to the source of that sound.

I clawed at the earth, digging, digging, searching, reaching. The music grew louder as I pressed myself into the dirt, burying myself deeper and deeper into the Underground. The moving earth shifted and stirred about me, the dirt falling back on my shoulders as I dug and tunneled closer to the music.

I did not know to where I was digging, or to whom. I did not know if it was to freedom, to the world above, to the unknown musician, to Josef, or to the angel of music himself. I only knew that I could not die without having beheld the face behind the magic.

"Sepperl!" I cried. Or perhaps it was the name of God. Dirt filled my mouth and my nostrils, but I did not care.

"Liesl!"

Through earth-packed ears, I thought I heard a cry. My name, perhaps. A voice I once knew.

"Liesl, please."

Hands on my shoulders, pulling and tugging and dragging me away.

"No!" My throat was clogged with dirt, and I choked on it. The music was fading and I wept at its loss.

"You can't do this. You can't leave me here to do this alone."

Something wet fell on my face. Rain? How it could possibly rain underground?

A few more drops. Then another. They were warm, so warm. Almost living. Like no rain I had ever felt. A drop slid to the corner of my mouth and I tasted it. Salt.

Tears. They were tears.

Käthe was crying.

"Liesl, Liesl," she keened, clutching me to her chest, rocking us back and forth.

"Käthe," I croaked, then coughed, spitting out bits of dirt, mud, and even leaves. My lungs were raw, each breath drawn over gravel and charcoal. As my wits returned, I saw I was buried up to my neck in the loose dirt and rocks of the corridor floor, digging my grave with my bare hands.

"Oh, thank God!" My sister worked furiously at my bodice and stays, trying to loosen the strings to help me breathe. I coughed and retched and coughed and retched until the bile ran clear.

In the distance I could still hear the ghostly strains of that angelic violin, but my sister held me tightly in her grip, my face in her palms.

"Stay with me." Her blue eyes searched mine. "Right here. Don't listen. It's not real. It's not Josef. It's not Papa. It is the Goblin King. It is a trick."

*It's not Josef. It's not Papa. It is the Goblin King. It is a trick.*

I repeated those words like a refrain, drowning out the sweet music that enveloped me and threatened to steal my senses. The scent of summer peaches was stronger than ever, only now it held the whiff of putrefaction.

*Goblin glamour,* I realized.

Käthe brushed the mud and blood from my face and helped me to my feet, leading me down the long, labyrinthine corridor.

Dear, sweet, unmusical Käthe. Each time the spell of the violin tightened its stranglehold about my wits, my sister gripped my hand all the harder. It hurt, but I relished the pain; it reminded me of who I was and what I was doing. I was Liesl. I was Käthe's older sister. I was rescuing her from the Goblin King. I was saving her life. Only now it was my little sister saving mine.

Presently, the peach perfume faded from the air, my senses cleared, and I heard the music with a mind entire. The magic was gone. There was no angel of music, no divine presence, only the fallible sounds of mortal performance. Beautiful, but human.

Curiosity had returned along with my wits. Something— some*one* was playing the violin, and the music was closer than ever.

Light shone through a large crack in the wall of the maze ahead of us. A slim, slender silhouette cast a shadow against the passage floors. *Der Erlkönig.* I did not marvel then that I knew the shape of his body as well as my own reflection.

I watched the Goblin King's shadow play his violin, his right arm moving in a smooth, practiced bowing motion. Käthe tried to pull me away, but I did not go with her. I moved closer to the light, and pressed my face to the crack. I had to look, had to see. I had to watch him play.

The Goblin King's back was turned to me. He wore no fancy coat, no embroidered dressing gown. He was simply dressed in trousers and a fine cambric shirt, so fine I could see the play of muscles in his back.

He played with precision and with considerable skill. The Goblin King was not Josef; he did not have my brother's clarity of emotion or my brother's transcendence. But the Goblin King had his own voice, full of passion, longing, and reverence, and it was unexpectedly . . . vibrant. Alive.

I could hear the slight fumblings, the stutters and starts in tempo, the accidental jarring note that marked his playing as human, oh so human. This was a man—a young man?— playing a song he liked on the violin. Playing it until it sounded perfect to his imperfect ears. I had stumbled upon something private, something intimate. My cheeks reddened.

"Liesl."

My sister's voice sliced through the sound of the Goblin King's playing like a guillotine, stopping the music mid-phrase. He glanced over his shoulder, and our eyes met.

His mismatched gaze was unguarded, and I felt both ashamed and emboldened. I had seen him unclothed in his bedchamber, but he was even more naked now. Propriety told me I should look away, but I could not, arrested by the sight of his soul bared to me.

We stared at each other through the crack in the wall, unable to move. The air between us changed, like a world before a storm: hushed, quiet, waiting, expectant.

A moan broke the tension. Käthe. The hooded expression fell over the Goblin King's eyes, and he was distant and untouchable, *Der Erlkönig* once more.

"Liesl," Käthe whispered. "Let's go. Please."

I had forgotten my sister's existence. I had forgotten why I was there. I had forgotten everything but the sight of the Goblin King's eyes, gray and green and blue and brown together. Käthe pulled at my sleeve, and I followed, running down the corridor hand in hand with my sister. Running before *Der Erlkönig* could catch us, running before he could trap us again with sweet words and sweet enchantments, and running before I could quite understand the strange, syncopated beat of my sympathetic heart.

## PYRRHIC
## VICTORY

the sky was dark when we emerged from the Underground at last, spangled with endless stars. The moon
had not yet risen and I did not know how much time
had passed. Were we too late?

I glanced about me. The surrounding forest was unfamiliar, lit with the otherworldly glow of starlight. The trees
grew into twisted shapes, sculpted by centuries of wind—
or a goblin-led hand. They grew as though striving to dance
and roam free, only to be rooted fast and trapped by the
earth beneath them. I thought of the stories Constanze had
told us of maidens turning into trees and shivered, although
the night was curiously mild.

No, we were not too late. I stared at the great open
expanse above me. The sky above me was proof, proof I had
won. My eyes burned against the light; after what seemed like
days buried beneath dirt and roots and rock, the sight of
stars was enough to move me to tears.

"Oh," I murmured. "Oh, come and see!"

I had crawled out from the roots of an enormous oak tree, through a rabbit hole scarcely large enough for the rabbit. Käthe and I had wandered the endless corridors for what had seemed like days on end. The tunnels had grown narrower and narrower, the finishes rougher and rougher, the niceties of civilization gradually disappearing until we crawled on our hands and knees. I was proud of my sister; she never once complained of the dirt on her dress, the rocks beneath her palms, or the roots tearing at her hair. I had taken heart from her courage, and never faltered, even when despair clung to my ankles as the passageways began shrinking around us.

"Käthe," I called. "Come and see!"

I turned to help my sister out, but all I could see were her beautiful blue eyes in the shadows of the oak.

"Käthe," I repeated. "Come."

She did not move. Her eyes darted to a point behind me.

"What is the matter with you?" I knelt before the tree and reached for my sister. "We're done. We're finished. We've escaped the Goblin King."

"Have you?"

I turned around. The Goblin King stood before me in a clearing, dressed in leather trousers and a roughspun jacket. Were it not for the pallor of his skin, or the sharp tips of his teeth poking through his smirk, I might have taken him for one of the local shepherd lads. But he was not a shepherd lad. He was both too beautiful and too terrible.

"Have I not?" I gestured to the night sky. "I have beaten you and your godforsaken labyrinth."

"Ah, but are we not, in some ways, all trapped in a labyrinth of our own making?" the Goblin King asked lightly.

"A philosopher as well as a king," I muttered. "How charming."

"Do you find me charming, Elisabeth?" His voice was a velvet purr.

I searched his face for the soft-eyed young man, a hint, an anchor I could cling to. But I could find none. "No."

The Goblin King pouted. "You wound me." He moved close, bringing with him the scent of ice and sweet loam. He took my chin in his long, elegant fingers and raised my gaze to his. "And you lie."

"Release me." I trembled, but my voice was steady.

He shrugged. "As you wish." He pulled away, and the absence of his touch was a sudden chill. "I don't see your sister with you."

I sighed. Käthe, so brave until now, had suddenly turned mulish in his presence. She remained hidden in the roots of the great oak, unwilling to come out into the open.

"Then help me free her from the tree," I said.

He raised his brow. "With nary a *please*? Tsk, tsk, where are your manners, Elisabeth?"

"*I wish* you would free Käthe from the tree."

The Goblin King bowed. "Your wish is my command."

The oak tree split open from root to tip, revealing a terrified Käthe at its heart. She was tightly curled into a ball, hiding her face between her knees, her shoulders shaking with fright.

"Käthe, Käthe." I took her into my arms. "It's all right. It's all over. We can go home now."

"Not so fast." The Goblin King stepped forward. "We are not yet finished."

My sister cringed and buried her face into my shoulder.

"Yes, we are," I said. "We had a wager."

"Did we? Remind me."

Sometimes it was all too easy to forget that *Der Erlkönig* was ageless, ancient, older than these hills. "That I would find my way out of the Underground and bring my sister," I said through gritted teeth. "And lo, here we stand, in the world above."

"Is that what you think?"

Dread began to grow inside me, rising waters of panic, drip by drip. "What do you mean?"

"A valiant effort, Elisabeth," the Goblin King said. "But you have lost."

At his words, the forest about me changed. What I had taken for trees smoothly changed into columns of stone, leaves into bits of ragged cloth, and the night sky froze and cracked, like a pond icing over in winter. Käthe gave a quiet sob against my shoulder, and what I had taken for the chattering of her teeth was in fact a repeated refrain: *too late, too late, too late.*

"No," I whispered. "Oh no."

We were still Underground.

"Yes," he said, the word a soft, sibilant caress. "I win."

I gripped my sister tighter to me.

"Well," the Goblin King amended. "I will win, once the full moon rises on the new year."

I stiffened. "It hasn't risen?"

"Not yet," he admitted. "You are close. Too close for comfort, in fact." He waved his hand. The icy sky rippled, and the stars returned, weak and watery, as though seen through a reflection upon the surface of a lake.

"We stand upon the threshold, you see," he said. "The world above lies beyond that veil."

Käthe sucked in a sharp breath as she turned to face the

stars. They bathed her face and hair in silver and she closed her eyes, as though to shut out the sight of freedom, so close yet so far.

"How long before the moonrise?" I asked.

"Not long," the Goblin King said. A grin spread across his face. "Not long enough for you to escape, at any rate."

"You have to give me a chance."

He crossed his arms. "No."

"A gentleman would honor the rules."

"Ah, but I am not a gentleman, Elisabeth." The Goblin King was all affectation and languid sarcasm. "I am a king."

Realization swept over me in a wave. "You were never going to let me win."

"No." He bared his teeth. "After all, am I not the Lord of Mischief?"

The Lord of Mischief. Of course.

"Then why play this game?" I asked. "Why bother with all this when you could have simply taken what you wanted?"

An unfathomable expression flashed across his eyes. Suddenly he seemed terribly old—old and weary. I was reminded that *Der Erlkönig* had existed in these mountains and woods longer than I, longer than time itself.

"I do not want this." The words were soft, so soft I might have imagined them. "I never wanted this."

Surprise slashed through me, leaving me cold and breathless. *"Mein Herr,"* I said. "Then what . . ."

The Goblin King laughed. His face, previously old and haggard, took on a puckish expression. His features sharpened: his gaze hard and glittering, his cheekbones a slash of shadow.

"What did you think the answer would be, Elisabeth? I

toy with you because I can. Because it gives me great pleasure. Because I was bored."

An inarticulate scream of rage strangled me. I wanted to destroy something, to spend my anger against the unfairness of everything. I wanted nothing more than to grapple with the Goblin King, to tear him from limb to limb, a Maenad against Orpheus. I tightened my hands into fists.

"Yes," he murmured. "Go ahead. Hit me. Strike me." The invitation was not just in his words, but his voice. He advanced. "Use your rage against me."

We stared at each other, scarcely half a breath between us. This close, I could see that his gray eye was flecked with silver and blue, his green one ringed with amber and gold. Those eyes mocked me, inviting and inciting me into a passion. If I were a smoldering ember, he was the poker, stirring me into flames.

I retreated. I was afraid. Afraid to touch him for fear of starting a fire within me.

"What," I asked tightly, "do you want from me, *mein Herr*?"

"I already told you what I want," he said. "You, entire."

We did not relinquish each other's gaze. *Let go,* his eyes seemed to say. But I couldn't; if I surrendered to my fury, I wasn't certain what else I would give up.

"Why?" My voice was hoarse.

"Why what, Elisabeth?"

"Why me?" My words were barely audible, but the Goblin King heard them. He had always heard me.

"Why you?" Those sharp, pointed teeth glistened. "Who else but you?" Even his words were sharp, each slicing through me like a knife. "You, who have always been my playmate?"

Childish laughter rang in my ears, but it was more memory than sound, the memory of a little girl and a little boy, dancing together in the wood. He, the king of the goblins, and she, an innkeeper's daughter. No, a musician's daughter. No, a musician herself.

*A wife,* said the little boy. *I need a wife. Will you marry me someday?*

The little musician laughed.

*Just give me a chance, Elisabeth.*

"A chance," I whispered. "Give me a chance to win. The moon has not yet risen."

The Goblin King said nothing for a long moment. "The game is unwinnable," he said at last. "For either you or me."

I shook my head. "I must try."

"Oh, Elisabeth." The way he said my name reached out and stroked some inner part of me. "One could almost admire your tenacity, if it weren't so foolish."

I opened my mouth to speak, to plead my case, but he placed his long fingers against my lips and silenced me.

"Very well," he said. "One last chance. One last game. Find your sister, and I shall let the both of you go."

"Is that all?"

His only response was a smile, more scary than soothing.

"Fine," I said, my voice shaking. "Come, Käthe, let us be gone from here."

But she did not come.

"Käthe?"

I whirled around, but I was alone, my sister vanished. Again.

*Find your sister.*

I did scream then. The cavern shook with my screams,

of rage, of self-loathing, of hatred, of despair. The world around me shifted again, and I was once more in that strange and eerie forest, out in the cold with the stars above. The sky was clear, and the stars watched from a dispassionate distance.

I was in the world above.

"Oh no," I said. "No, no, no, no."

In the woods, only the echoes of *Der Erlkönig*'s mocking laugh lingered.

"You bastard!" I raged. "Come out and fight fair!"

And there he was, standing in a distant grove with Käthe in his arms, her limp body draped across his arms like an altar cloth, her head falling back, her arms splayed. They formed a twisted sort of pietà: the Goblin King the smirking mourner, my sister the dead martyr.

I ran forward, but the instant my fingers touched her skirt, both she and the Goblin King vanished. Where my sister had lain, there was nothing more than a scrap of silk fluttering in the breeze, caught in the branches of a birch tree.

"Liesl!"

Käthe's voice was muffled. I whirled around, desperately following the sound of her cries. There she was, caught in a cage of branches; but no, it was nothing but a tree growing from a net of brambles. Then I saw her at the mercy of several goblin swains, her arms pinioned behind her back. They no longer looked human despite their comely forms, their lascivious grins no longer inviting, but threatening.

I chased after them, but it wasn't Käthe in their clutches; it was me. I was surrounded by tall, elegant goblin men, made in the mold of their king—languid, beautiful, cruel. I felt the touch of their lips against my skin, little love bites against my throat, as though they meant to devour me. But no, they weren't goblin men at all, but dead winter branches: their twigs shredding my clothes and hair to ribbons.

"Liesl!"

Käthe's cries were faint, but somehow closer. As though she were beneath me, buried somewhere deep in the earth. I fell to my knees and clawed at the dirt, digging frantically.

"Give up, Elisabeth," the Goblin King urged. "Give up and surrender to me."

His voice was everywhere and nowhere at once. He was the wind, he was the earth, he was the trees, the leaves, the sky and the stars. I fought against him and the forest fought back, confusing my sense of time, distance, and even self.

"Liesl!"

A muffled thumping. I cleared away the leaves and twigs and rocks and dirt before my hands hit something as hard and smooth as glass.

"Liesl!"

Beneath my hands was Käthe, trapped behind a sheet of ice. A frozen pond? I ineffectually beat at the surface, calling her name. Was she drowning? I screamed with frustration, clawing and scratching and pounding until my palms cracked and bled, leaving bloody smears over the ice.

Suddenly, the frost cleared beneath me, revealing a frantic Käthe. But for the panic on her face, she seemed hale. Yet when I peered closer, everything was all wrong. My head spun; beneath me was not the depthless black of a frozen pond, but the starry infinity of a winter sky. Käthe was not staring up at me, but down, as though kneeling beside the pond instead of floating within. Her hands struck the ice in rhythm with mine, but I could no longer tell which way was up. Was I trapped underground? Or was she?

"Give up, Elisabeth." The Goblin King's face was reflected in the smooth surface of the ice, but when I turned, there was no one behind me. "Let go."

But I would not. I searched for something—anything—I could use to smash the ice between my sister and me. But there was nothing. No stone, no branch, no twig.

Then I remembered the goblin-made flute. I had thrust the instrument through the waist of my skirt once we passed from corridors to tunnels in the Underground, when I was no longer able to play it for crawling about on my hands and knees. My hands fumbled for the flute, untying the strings that held my apron, skirt, and modesty together. I did not care. I tore at my clothes and freed the instrument.

A flicker of uncertainty crossed the Goblin King's eyes, still reflected in the ice beneath me. "Don't, Elisabeth—"

But I never heard what he was about to say. I raised the flute above my head with both hands. The wind caught in its myriad keys and stops, playing a sweet whistling melody, drowning out all other sounds.

Then I brought the flute down like an ax with all my strength.

# RESURRECTION

i opened my eyes to a bright light. I flinched and lifted a hand to shade them, but could make out nothing. It was bitterly cold, but the air was crisp and fresh and carried with it the scent of openness.

"I'm impressed."

I squinted into the shadows. I could just make out the lanky, willowy form of the Goblin King in the darkness, but it was his eyes that caught the light and gleamed like a wolf's.

"Against all odds, you've managed to break me, Elisabeth."

My laugh was as rough as the gravel beneath my hands. As my eyes adjusted, I saw that the Goblin King and I were slumped against the ground, like two soldiers fallen in battle. We lay in an earthen chamber, illuminated by a bright light overhead.

The full moon.

I sat up, wincing as my body—cold-stiffened and battered—gave a mighty protest. "Käthe," I croaked.

The Goblin King rose and nodded his head. "Yonder."

A small, rumpled form lay on the ground a few feet away from me. I tried to stand, but the world spun beneath me, and I collapsed. I brought myself to my hands and knees and crawled to my sister's side.

Käthe was unconscious, but her breath misted lightly into the chilly air around us, the pulse of her heart faint but steady. I glanced at the Goblin King.

"She's alive," he said. "And well. Well, maybe a little worse for wear. But she is unharmed, and will come to no harm, once she wakes up in the world above."

I stroked Käthe's brow. Her skin was cool, but beneath my touch, her flesh felt like living, breathing skin.

"Is this it, then?" I asked. "Have I won?"

He was quiet, quiet so long I feared he would never speak again. "Yes," he said. There was more than fatigue in his voice; there was defeat. "You win, Elisabeth."

Somehow the declaration did not bring the sense of victory or triumph I expected. My body was bruised and bloodied, and I was tired, so tired. "Oh," was all I said.

"Oh?" Though I couldn't see his face clearly in the shadows, I knew his eyebrow was raised. "You who faced me in all my power, you who rent the fabric of my world asunder, you who broke the old laws—all you can say is *oh*?"

Of all things, this brought a smile to my face. "May I go, then?"

"You don't need my permission, Elisabeth." His voice was soft. "You've never needed my permission for anything."

I turned my head away. "How could I possibly trust that, after everything you've done to me?"

There was a long silence, before a small, jagged voice returned to me. "I've done terrible things, yes," he said. "And you've borne the brunt of it. Yes, you were right not to trust me." The space between us, empty of words, was nevertheless filled with past regrets and painful memories. "I was your friend, once," he said. "I had your trust, once. But I've squandered that horribly, haven't I?"

"Yes." I saw no reason to lie. But even as I told him the truth, a part of my heart protested the pain, both his and mine. I slumped over, my head against my sister's shoulder. Our bodies rose and fell together.

"There." The Goblin King pointed. "That is your avenue of escape."

Moonlight streamed in from an opening above our heads, moonlight and starlight and the cold winter air.

"You are so very near to the end, you need only take the merest step to find your freedom."

The merest step. Twenty feet above our heads, a way out into the world above. No great distance after what I had been through. But I was spent, wrung of every last drop of determination and resolve.

"Well," said the Goblin King, a hint of impatience in his voice. "What are you waiting for? Leave me here, and go. Go back to your family, your mother and father and inimitable grandmother. Go back with your sister, go back to your brother, go back to that insufferable, stolid lover of yours and be happy."

Mother. Papa. Constanze. Hans. Somehow, sitting here with the Goblin King was preferable to facing the world above. After all, what world would I be returning to? I thought of that false reality that had so nearly seduced me, a world where I was not Liesl the innkeeper's drudge, Liesl the discarded sister, Liesl the lesser. That was not the world waiting for me.

"Elisabeth," the Goblin King said. "You must leave now. The way is open as long as the moon is risen. You don't have much time."

"If you are so anxious for me to be gone, *mein Herr*," I said, "then conjure me a ladder of vines, or a stairwell of tree roots. I am not so tall as to reach the end myself."

"You broke me, my dear. I can scarcely conjure my name, let alone a ladder."

"Well, you did tell me the game was unwinnable. I should have taken you at your word."

Even his laugh was tired. "Ah, the winner's curse," he said. "It cost you more to win than to lose." Then he sobered. "It cost us both."

"What will it cost you?" I did not have the strength—or the heart—to mock him now, not when we were both broken. "What will it cost you but a bride?"

"Oh, Elisabeth. It will cost us both everything."

I waited. I laid my head against Käthe's soft flesh, listening to the slow thump of her beating heart.

"As the old year dies, so too does the world. Without sacrifice, nothing good can grow. Without death, there can be no rebirth. A life for life, that is the cost."

"You have heard that it hath been said: An eye for an eye, and a tooth for a tooth," I murmured.

"Aye," he said. "The old laws and God's laws are not so different."

"You could," I began, but the words stuck in my throat. "You could find another bride, couldn't you?"

"Yes," the Goblin King said. He sounded almost hurt. "I suppose I could."

"You suppose?"

It was a long time before he answered. "Would you like another story, my dear? It isn't as pretty as my last, I'm afraid."

"Before moonset?" I glanced through the threshold to the world above.

He laughed. "We have time enough for this."

I nodded.

"Once upon a time, a savage, violent time, humans, goblins, kobolds, *Hödekin*, and Lorelei lived side by side in the world above, feeding, fighting, preying, slaying. It was, as I had said, a dark time, and Man turned to dark practices to keep the blood tides at bay. Sacrifices, you see. Man turned against brother, fathers against daughters, sons against mothers, all to appease the goblins. To stop the needless deaths, one man—one stupid, foolish man—made a bargain with the old laws of the land, offering himself as a sacrifice."

"The last time, it was a beautiful maiden," I said from my spot by Käthe's side.

"A brave maiden," the Goblin King corrected.

I smiled.

"His soul was the price," he continued. "The price he paid to sunder the goblins and the fey from the world above. His soul—and his name. No longer a mortal man, he became *Der Erlkönig*. For his bargain, the foolish man was granted immortality, and the power to manipulate the elements as it suited his needs. He restored order, seasons progressed in their normal manner. But the further away from mortality he grew, the more capricious and cruel he became, forgetting what it was like to live and love."

He was right; it wasn't a pretty story. What did immortality do to one who was once mortal? It stretched him thin.

I watched what little I could see of the Goblin King from my vantage point. In this half-light, in this half-space between the Underground and the world above, I thought I could see the mortal man he might have been. The austere young man in the portrait gallery. That soft-eyed young man who had been my friend.

"It isn't just the life of a maiden I needed, you know," the Goblin King said quietly. I glanced sharply at him; his tone had changed. "It was what a maiden can give me."

"And what is that?"

His smile was crooked. "Passion."

Heat flared in my cheeks.

"Not that sort of passion," he said quickly. Did I imagine things, or were his cheeks tinged a faint pink? "Well, yes, that too. Passion of all sorts," he said. "Intensity."

"Goblins do not feel the way mortals do," he went on. "You humans live and love so fiercely. We crave that. We need that. That fire sustains us. It sustains me."

"Is that why you stole Käthe away?" I looked at my sister, thinking of her voluptuous body and inviting laugh. "Because of the passion she inspired?"

The Goblin King shook his head. "The sort of passion she inspires in me is all flash and no heat. I need an ember, Elisabeth, not a firecracker. Something that burns longer, to keep me warm for this night and all other nights to come."

"So Käthe . . ."

I could not finish my question.

"Käthe," he said in a low voice, "was a means to an end."

The way he spoke of my sister vexed me. *A means,* as though she were cheap. Disposable. Worthless.

"To what end?" I asked.

"You know the answer, Elisabeth," he said softly.

And I did. The goblin merchants, the flute, all the way back to when he had granted my wish to save Josef's life—everything he had done, he had done for me.

"A means to an end," I whispered. "Me."

He did not deny it.

"Why?"

The Goblin King was silent for a long while. "Who else but you?" he asked lightly. "Whose life would you rather it be?"

He was avoiding answering my question. We did not look at each other. The darkness was too complete, and the light from the world above too harsh. But I could feel an answer between us, pulsing like a heartbeat. It made my breath come faster.

"Me," I said, a little more loudly. "Why me?"

"Why not you?" he returned. "Why not the girl who played her music for me in the Goblin Grove when she was a child?"

He had said so much, yet nothing I wanted to hear. That he desired *me*. That he had chosen *me*. That he . . . I wanted to hear the truth in his eyes said aloud. I could feel his gaze upon every part of my body: on my neck, where my shoulder disappeared into the torn sleeves of my blouse, the line of my collarbone as it led to my décolletage, the swell and ebb of my breasts as I breathed. I had waited for this my entire life, I realized. Not to be found beautiful—but *desirable*. Wanted. I wanted the Goblin King to claim me as his own.

"Why me?" I repeated. "Why Maria Elisabeth Ingeborg Vogler?"

I held his eyes with mine. He had his pride, but so had I. If I were to make good on the promise I made that little dancing boy in the wood all those years ago, I needed to hear validation from his own lips.

"Because," he said. "Because I loved the music within you."

I closed my eyes. His words were the spark to the tinder lining my blood; they touched my heart and warmth blazed from within, spreading through me like wildfire.

"A life for a life," I said. "Does that mean . . . does that mean the sacrifice must die?"

"What does it mean to die?" the Goblin King asked. "What does it mean to live?"

"I told you I don't find the philosopher charming."

A laugh, a real, startled, human laugh. "There is," he said, "no one like you, Elisabeth."

"Answer my question."

The Goblin King paused. "Yes. The sacrifice must die. She must leave the world of the living and enter the realm of *Der Erlkönig*, enter the Underground." He lifted his eyes to mine, those mismatched eyes, so startling, so beautiful. "She will be dead to the world above."

Dead to the world above. I thought of Papa, Mother, Constanze, Hans, and, with a painful twinge, Josef. In many ways, I was already dead.

"We have both lost," I said.

He gave me a sharp glance. "What do you mean?"

"You win, I lose my sister. I win, I condemn the world above to eternal winter. Is that not the true outcome of our game, *Mein Herr*?"

He could not deny it.

"Then I propose we call a draw. Then we both get what we want. I, my sister's freedom and you"—I swallowed—"will have me. Entire."

He was silent for a long while. "Oh, Elisabeth," he said. "Why?"

I looked at where Käthe lay, still senseless on the floor. "For my sister." I pulled her into the circle of light. "For my brother." I looked from Käthe to the hollow above us. "For my family. And the world above."

The Goblin King moved closer, slowly and haltingly, as though in pain. "That is not enough, Elisabeth."

"Is it not?" I asked with a dark laugh. "Is the world not enough? Could I condemn everyone to an eternal winter, spring and life never returning?"

He hovered on the edge of the circle of light. I could see the figure of his body outlined in silver and black, and the slim shape of his hand just beyond the circle's edge.

"Always thinking of others," the Goblin King murmured. "But that's still not enough. Don't you ever make any wishes for yourself, Elisabeth?"

What would be enough? He had an answer he wanted to hear, but I withheld it. Games and more games. We would always be dancing with each other, the Goblin King and I.

"All right, then," I said. "For love."

It was a while before he spoke. "For love?" His voice was rough.

"Yes," I said. "After all, we all make sacrifices for love." I leaned over and kissed my sister on the forehead. "We make them every day." I lifted my eyes to where his shadow stood beyond the edge of light. The two-toned eyes gleamed at me and while I could not see the rest of his face, the hope-fulness in them moved me. "You called me selfless," I said. "So I claim selfishness. Because for once, I want to love myself best, instead of last."

He said nothing. He was silent so long I feared I had made a mistake, but then he opened his mouth to speak.

"Think well on this, Elisabeth." There was a fervor in his voice I could not quite discern. "Your choice, once made, cannot be unmade. I am not so generous as to offer you your freedom again."

I hesitated. I could fight him. I could force his hand, make him bring Käthe and me back to the world above. I'd defeated him before and I could do it again.

But I was too tired to fight. Moreover, I did not *want* to fight. I wanted to surrender, because surrender was the greater part of courage.

"I offer myself to you." I swallowed hard. "Free and of my own will."

"For yourself?"

"Yes," I said. "For myself."

The longest pause of all. "All right." His words were scarcely audible in the large cavern. "I accept your sacrifice." By my feet, Käthe began to murmur and moan. "I shall bring your sister to the world above and then"—his breath caught—"will you consent to be my queen?"

I turned my face away.

"Elisabeth." The way the Goblin King said my name made my heart flutter. "Will you marry me?"

This time, it was a long time before I replied.

"Yes," I said. "Yes, I will."

# Part II

## THE GOBLIN QUEEN

My life is like a broken bowl,
A broken bowl that cannot hold
One drop of water for my soul
Or cordial in the searching cold;
Cast in the fire the perish'd thing;
Melt and remould it, till it be
A royal cup for Him, my King.

—CHRISTINA ROSSETTI,
*A Better Resurrection*

## CONSECRATION

the Goblin King took Käthe away without another word. She was in my arms one moment and gone the next, gone before I could say goodbye, before I could tell her I loved her.

I do not know how long I sat there in the oubliette. My mind was blank, devoid of any sorrow or thoughts or music. I should have felt grief. I should have felt fear. But instead I felt nothing but immense weariness, an exhaustion so profound it was like death. Hours, or days, or minutes passed before I felt the light touch of a hand on my head.

"Elisabeth."

A young man looked down at me, his mismatched eyes soft, the tilt of his mouth tender. It was the tenderness that undid me, undid the strings I'd bound about my heart. Longing, fear, grief, resentment, and desire came tumbling out. I began to cry.

The young man reached out to wipe my tears away, and

in his touch there was nothing but kindness. I wanted to take his compassion and wrap it about me for comfort.

An apology hung in the space between us, though he did not speak.

*I'm sorry, Elisabeth.*

But why would he sorrow for me? My grief belonged to me and me alone, and I could not, did not want to share it with anyone. I did not mourn my life, for it had not been a life worth living. But I mourned the lives I would not have: my sister's, my brother's, my family's. I would never see Josef find acclaim as a musician. I would never travel with Käthe to see the great cities of the world. I would never again hear my name upon their lips.

The Goblin King gathered me in his arms, and I let him carry me back to my barrow room. His way through the Underground was short and straight, but he could bend time and distance to his will, after all. He set me down before my door, still locked with that absurd contraption. Then, with a courteous bow, the Goblin King disappeared.

It was a pleasure to open that door and turn the lock, hearing the solid *thunk* and *clang* as the mechanism slid into place. I had done this so many times to my own heart; it was a pleasure to do it to the world.

I was empty. A vessel filled with nothing. Whatever spirit filled me had fled years ago, leaving me with ghost and body alone.

I lit a candle.

I had heard acolytes at the nunnery held a candlelight vigil the night before they consecrated themselves to Christ, much as young brides did the night before their wedding, before they consecrated themselves to their husbands. But how far was I from His grace, deep beneath the earth? While

I had dutifully attended Mass with the rest of my family on Sundays, I had never felt the presence of God or His angels. It was only when I heard Josef play that I believed in Heaven.

I would endure this vigil alone, with no prayers in my heart. For what could I possibly pray? A fruitful marriage with lots of children? Could I even bear any, a monstrous thing half-human, half-goblin? Or could I pray for something altogether more selfish, like the life I had never had, a life lived to the fullest?

So I prayed for nothing. I knelt with my hands clasped before the candle, and watched as the flame burned low into the night.

I say goodbye to the world above.

> *Farewell, Mother, careworn and abiding,*
> *Farewell, Papa, faded brightness hiding.*
> *Farewell, Constanze, I took your tales to heart,*
> *Farewell, Hans, and your fumbles in the dark.*
> *Farewell, Käthe, I'm sorry I did you wrong.*
> *Farewell, Josef, may you play ever-long.*
> *Farewell, all, to you I give my love.*

# THE WEDDING

there was a bright light in my bedroom when I awoke. I did not remember falling asleep, but at some point during my vigil, I had stirred from my place before the candle and sat by the hearth in my room. I watched the flames flicker and dance before my eyes and composed a hymn—my first—humming and working at the melody until I had gotten it right. I had had no paper on which to write down my thoughts, but it did not matter. That hymn was sacred to that night and that night alone—no one would ever sing it, for God or for me.

The light shone down from the fireplace, slanting in like the morning sun. I squinted. The painting of the Goblin Grove above the mantle—which to my last recollection had depicted a dark landscape—now showed the woods in all their daylight glory. It appeared as though snow had fallen, and the sun shone crisp and bright on its blank whiteness.

I frowned. The light was shining *through* the painting into my barrow, like a window to the outside world. I got to my feet, bones aching, fingers poised to touch this miraculous thing.

"Tut, tut, what did we say about touching?"

Twig and Thistle were in my room.

"What did I say about knocking?" I returned.

"You didn't," Thistle said cheerfully. "You wished for a door and a lock. You didn't wish us to *use* it."

"A problem that shall be rectified immediately."

"Your wish is our command, Your Highness." Twig bent her impossibly long and slender body into a bow. The tops of her tree-branch hair scraped the barrow floor.

"My wish is your command regardless," I said mildly.

Thistle made a face. "Hmph," she said. "She's not Her Highness *yet*." Her black, beady eyes took me in, from the top of my disheveled head, down my tearstained cheeks, to the tips of my unshod feet. It was hard to discern any recognizable emotion in such a strange and alien face, but I thought I detected a hint of contempt.

"She will be soon enough," Twig replied. Her words sent a bolt of—of some strong emotion through me. It was not quite fear, but it was not exactly pleasure either.

"Are we—are we to be married soon? The Goblin King and I?"

"Yes. You are to meet His Majesty in"—Twig and Thistle exchanged glances—"the chapel."

"The chapel?"

"That's what he calls it," Thistle said indifferently. "He holds on to his quaint human rituals, but it's not as though it really matters. What matters," she continued slyly, "is the consummation."

I blushed. Of course; in the world above, consummation also sealed a marriage. Then I frowned. *Quaint human rituals.*

I thought of the austere young man in the portrait gallery with the cross and violin in his hands.

"How . . . how did he—His Majesty come to be *Der Erlkönig*?" I asked. But it was not the question I held in my heart.

How had that austere young man become *my* Goblin King?

But neither Thistle nor Twig answered my questions, voiced and unvoiced. Instead, Thistle produced a fine silk dress out of thin air and ordered me to put it on.

"What for?"

"All the other queens came prepared in their finest gowns," she sneered. "Unless you want to go to your funeral dressed in filthy rags."

"My funeral? I thought it was my wedding."

Thistle shrugged. "There is no difference here."

I took the dress from Thistle's hands. It was made of a white silk so fine it was nearly sheer, the cut simple, made to drape rather than fit. A shroud. Thistle also brought out a long veil, even more transparent than the dress and spangled with tiny diamonds, and affixed it to my hair.

Meanwhile, Twig produced a wreath fashioned of branches and alder catkins. I thought of the wedding wreaths I had seen for sale in the village markets, and remembered with a pang the dried wreath and ribbons I had thought to buy for Käthe that fateful day she stumbled upon the goblin merchants. There would be no flowers or ribbons for me, only a coronet made of dead twigs. There would be no sister or mother to act as my attendants, only a pair of goblin girls, one of whom hated me and the other who pitied me. And there would be no blessing made holy by God, only a promise made in the dark.

Once I was suitably attired, Twig and Thistle led me out into the corridor. Thistle marched on ahead, Twig picked up my veil and train, and the three of us wound our way through the labyrinthine passages, deeper and deeper into the heart of the Underground, where my immortal bridegroom awaited me to bring him to life.

Deep below the labyrinth was a lake.

After descending what seemed like an endless spiral of stairs, we came upon its desolate shores. Its black expanse appeared suddenly from nowhere, its dark waters lit by candelabras fashioned like arms holding torches. Dripping stone teeth glittered as they bit into the lake, and beautiful pools of blue-green light rippled from where rock met water. Fairy lights danced in the grotto, and a barge floated at the bottom of the stairs as though waiting for me to enter.

"Where does this lead?" I asked. My voice echoed in this watery underground cavern, scattered like light in a prism.

"The lake itself feeds into small rivers and streams down here," Twig explained. "And then on to springs and wells in the world above."

"But that is not your destination." Thistle pointed to the barge. "This will lead you straight to where the Goblin King awaits you on the other side."

"Am I to cross alone?" My words trembled.

"For now, yes," Thistle said.

"Who will guide me?"

"There is only one place to go," Twig said gently. "Straight across. The Lorelei will take you there."

"The Lorelei?"

"Listen not to their songs," she warned. "They lure mortals

to a watery grave with the sweetness of their music. Not even we are completely immune."

"Are they not of your kind, then?"

Twig shook her head, the cobwebs of her hair quivering. "The Lorelei have been here long before goblins found the hills and mountains of this land. Once they were as populous as the leaves in the trees, but more and more of them were driven underground by the spread of you humans."

"It's been a very long time since they've had a mortal in their midst," Thistle said with a toothy grin. "I don't much like your chances."

"Shush," Twig admonished. "The Goblin King needs her. *We* need her."

"Hmph," was all Thistle said. She looked expectantly at the barge at my feet.

I hesitated.

"Scared?" she sneered.

I shook my head. It wasn't the nixies under the black water of the lake that frightened me; it was the dark figure who waited for me on the other side. This long journey, the last of my maidenhood, I was to take alone with no one beside me. The loneliness of it all pierced my heart.

Twig and Thistle helped me into the barge and gently pushed me from the mooring. A bright trail of blue-green light stirred in my wake, the ripples of movement waking the glowing luminescence into life. The multicolored light played against the sheer white of my gown and veil, and the glittering beauty of this underground grotto stole my breath away.

As soon as the barge embarked from its mooring, a high, thin, sweet singing sound rose into the air around me. The sound of fingers running over the rim of a crystal glass, but clearer, more bell-like. There were no words to this enchant-ing music, no structure, but the web of sound ensnared me in its haunting spell.

Despite the warnings, I leaned over the edge of my boat for a closer look. Dark shapes stirred beneath the trail of light, and against my better judgment, I reached out to touch it. Where my fingers dipped into the water, more glittering ripples grew, the glowing droplets clinging to my skin when I lifted my hand from the surface. Something soft caressed my palm as I let my hand drift farther and farther into the water, gentle fingers wrapping themselves around my wrist.

The shapes beneath the surface grew clearer, and I saw a young woman peering back at me. Her eyes were an inky black, her hair a pale spring green. Her skin was a marvel: pale and shimmering with a myriad rainbow shades like the scales of a fish. But it was her face that arrested me: wide cheekbones, a flat nose bridge, and pouting lips. She was the loveliest creature I had ever seen.

She emerged from the water, a creature of light and shad-ows. Her hand lifted to caress my cheek and the singing intensified with her touch. Her glistening lips moved in the changing lights of the grotto, and I leaned even closer to drink in the whispering sounds of her mouth. I wanted to feel that impossible singing in my body. I closed my eyes, and breathed her in.

A discordant screech cut through the music.

Startled, I tumbled back into my barge, sending the boat rocking. The Lorelei hissed in annoyance and dove back underwater. I lifted my fingers to my mouth, still feeling the cool touch of her lips against mine. The nixies thrashed beneath the boat, threatening to capsize me. The discor-dant screech sounded again and the waters stilled.

The barge had stopped moving now that the Lorelei had abandoned me, and I was alone in the middle of a black lake. The grotto still rang with the echoes of that harsh screech, shattering the crystalline singing that had filled it moments earlier. I sat in my barge, trembling with fear and something more—a shivery sort of anticipation brought on by the near-kiss and near-drowning by the beautiful young woman.

As the disturbances in the flat, glassy surface faded away, so too did the glowing light. Darkness fell over me, broken only by the twinkling of fairy lights and the strange, carved-arm torches at the edges. I did not know how to move forward; I was too wary now to risk putting my hands back in the water, and my barge had no pole or oar with which to propel myself. I wondered what inhuman creature had cried out to drive my seducers away, whether it would come swooping to claim me, now that its rivals had gone.

And then, in the distance and impossibly far away, was the warm, grainy voice of a violin. Suddenly I recognized that discordant screech; it was the sound of a violinist running his bow indiscriminately over his strings, wielding their harsh squeal like a scythe. My treacherous heart lifted—Sepperl, come to rescue me!—but my mind knew better. It was not my little brother. It was the Goblin King.

As the violin continued to play, the barge began to move of its own accord, as though it too were drawn to the music. I held my breath as the Goblin King played a processional, a stately entrance for his mortal bride as the boat bore her smoothly over the dark, glassy water.

It was a long journey to the far shore, and as I drew closer, the music changed. It transitioned from stately processional to something simpler: a repeating melodic motif, a jaunty little tune, something like the warm-up exercises Papa had me and Josef play when we were younger. I frowned. I recognized this little piece. The little notes galloped and skipped about me like children around a maypole, tugging at my memory.

It was mine. The piece was mine.

I had composed a number of little écossaises when I was a young girl, after some traveling French musicians had played at the inn. It was a dance in the Scottish style, they told me, and I had been charmed by its liveliness. The compositions were simple enough and I had written them for the klavier, but hearing them played on the violin brought me images of Josef practicing in the back bedroom. He could not have been much older than six, and me ten.

I had all but forgotten the existence of this little piece, which was probably my best effort in the series. It was gone now, gone with the rest of my compositions in a blaze. And yet, it still lived in the Goblin King's hands.

The écossaise faded into a *Lieder*, one I had written in a romantic fit when I was a girl of fourteen. The heat of shame and embarrassment singed me, and I cringed to remember the moody, melancholy maiden I had been, mooning over Hans like the lovestruck child I was.

The Goblin King continued playing my repertoire as the boat reached the far shore. He played from my childhood, through my foolish girlhood, and on to my burgeoning womanhood. Listening to him play was hearing my mind made tangible. He knew exactly when and how to push and give, to give shape to my musical musings as I had imagined them. He played my music like a sculptor, fashioning and molding and building it until it produced a perfect image of myself. Josef played like an angel, but whatever

I had composed for my brother was written around him: his strengths and flaws. The Goblin King interpreted me, and showed me a vision of Liesl I had heretofore not known. He played *me*.

It hurt. Hearing my music like this, played in the hands of someone who understood me so completely—in a way not even my brother had known—hurt. My music was elegant, transcendent, ethereal, and I could not bear to behold its beauty. I longed to pull it back beneath my skin, to hide it away in the shadows where it properly belonged, safe where no one could judge it for its flaws.

The last notes of my music faded over the lake as the barge soundlessly glided to a halt on the opposite mooring. Ahead stood the Goblin King, haloed by the flickering torches behind him. From this distance he seemed forbidding, his tall height accentuated by the long black cloak draped over him and the crown of antlers at his brow. I could not see his face, but the violin and bow hung loose at his sides.

For a moment, we stood and stared at each other in silence. The beat of my excitable heart thumped louder at the sight of him. The awkward and self-conscious way he held his instrument made my blood pulse harder. Was this my soft-eyed young man? But the Goblin King put his violin and bow away, and he was as mysterious and implacable as a statue once more.

He walked down to the quay to meet me, his footfalls silent. He moved like a shadow, a shadow that bent down to take my hand and help me from the barge. He led me from the lakeside, up through a series of passageways, and into a large, well-lit chamber. We did not exchange a word.

As my eyes adjusted to the brightness, I took in the

chamber. It was the chapel. The ceilings were tall and arched—formed by nature, not by man—and beautiful stained glass windows were placed at regular intervals around the chamber. The windows did not open to the outside world, but were instead lit from within. There was an altar at the head of the chamber, and a modest crucifix hung in the sanctuary.

Tears stung my eyes. Goblin-made and Underground as this chapel might have been, it was still a church. A church like many I had seen in the world above. Here there were no strange goblin-made statuaries. Here there were no fantastic creatures, no leering satyrs, no ecstatic nymphs. Here there was nothing but Christ, the Goblin King, and me.

"It's all right to grieve, Elisabeth." His voice was gentle as I wiped away my tears. "I did, when I first came to the Underground."

I nodded, but his sympathy only made my tears flow harder.

There was no priest to bless us, no one to conduct the service. But we were in the presence of God nonetheless. Here, before the altar, the Goblin King and I were to exchange our vows.

"I do—" I began, then stopped. What could I say to *Der Erlkönig*, the Lord of Mischief, the Ruler Underground? What vows could I offer that mattered? I had already made him the greatest promise, the greatest sacrifice: my life.

He saw my hesitation, and took my hands in his. "I do solemnly swear," he said, "that I accept your sacrifice, the gift of your life, selflessly and selfishly given."

I looked at our entwined fingers. The Goblin King had a violinist's hands: long, dexterous fingers, the tips of his left one callused and rough where they pressed against the strings. They were hands that could be both gentle and cruel, and they were familiar.

"Do you swear, Elisabeth?" I glanced up at his face. Those mismatched eyes were uncertain, and I saw not *Der Erlkönig*, but the austere young man. "Do you swear that you make this bargain of . . . of your own free will?"

We kept each other's gaze, unblinking and unbroken. Then I made my vows.

"I do solemnly swear," I said softly, "that I give of myself unto you of my own free will. Body . . . and soul."

Those mismatched eyes sharpened. "You, entire?"

I nodded. "Myself, entire."

The Goblin King took a ring from his finger. It was wrought of silver, and fashioned into the shape of a wolf. Its paws swept around the band, and its eyes were gems of two different colors: one an icy blue and the other a silvery green.

"With this ring," he said, taking my hands in his, "I make you my queen. To hold sovereignty over all that I rule, and the power to bend the will of the goblins to your every wish."

He slid the ring onto my finger. It was too big, but I tightened my hand into a fist so I would not lose it. He wrapped his own hands over mine.

"Sovereignty over my kingdom, over the goblins, and over me," he said. Then he knelt. "I beg your compassion, my queen. Your compassion, and your grace."

I freed a hand from his grasp, the hand that bore his ring. I laid it over his brow, and I could feel him tremble beneath my touch.

Presently, he rose and retrieved a chalice from the altar.

"Let us drink." He offered the goblet to me. "To seal our troth."

The wine was as dark as blackberries, or sin. I remembered the heady rush of goblin wine, the sweet, full-bodied taste on my tongue. I remembered the loose-limbed, wanton self I had become at the Goblin Ball, and a slow, languorous heat began to warm me from within. I brought the chalice to my lips in a hasty swallow, a few drops falling onto the white silk of my wedding gown. They looked like drops of blood in the snow.

The Goblin King took the goblet back and drank a little himself, his eyes never leaving mine. There were promises of nights to come, and I swore to myself then that I would hold him to every single one.

He set the cup back on the altar, and slowly wiped the wine away from his mouth with the back of his hand. I swallowed hard. Then the Goblin King offered me his arm and we walked out of the chapel, into the Underground, as husband and wife.

## WEDDING NIGHT

We emerged directly into the goblin revels.

At the center of the large cavern that had served as the ballroom was an enormous bonfire, around which the twisted shapes of goblins danced. A gigantic boar was speared and spitted over the fire, and the smell of roasted meat was overpowering. There were no lights in this cavern: no torches, no fairy lights, no candles burning away in their unsettling candelabras shaped like human arms. Only the flames of the bonfire, its bloody, inconstant fire growing shadows instead of throwing light.

I shrank away from the scene, but the Goblin King held my hand firmly.

"Don't be afraid," he murmured into my ear. "Remember my troth."

But I was afraid. I had danced and feasted at the Goblin Ball, but this was something entirely different: wild, untamed, and feral. The Goblin Ball, hosted by the Goblin King, had had a veneer of civilized behavior overlaying its orgiastic abandonment, but there were no such niceties now. This was not hedonistic indulgence; this was savagery. I could smell blood—freshly spilled. It smelled of copper and iron and flesh. Twining, writhing shapes copulated in the corners of my vision, and I thought of the little objet d'art in my barrow room that depicted the nymph and the satyr. Music wailed on pipes and horns and catgut lutes— rude, rustic, without refinement. The goblin wine took the edges off my fear, but the chill of it still ran through my veins.

"Come," the Goblin King said. "Let your subjects pay tribute to their new queen."

He led me down the steps into the throng. Bodies and fantastical faces crowded me on all sides, leering and cheer- ing at me, their spindly fingers like brambles in a hedge, catching on the edges of my dress, my veil, my hair. A little hunchback of a hobgoblin skipped up beside us and offered me a flagon of wine.

"Ah, the music maiden," it said. "She smolders still. Tell me, mistress"—it winked at me—"does His Majesty fear to set you alight?"

I blinked, trying to place where I had seen its face be- fore. The hobgoblin hummed a familiar little tune, and I caught the scent of summer peaches.

The goblin market.

It cackled when it saw recognition bloom across my face, and cackled even harder at the blush on the Goblin King's cheeks. "Only a breath, Your Majesty. A breath, and she bursts into flame."

The Goblin King grabbed the flagon from the hobgoblin's spindly hands. He threw back his head and downed the wine, heedless of whatever spilled from his lips and coursed down his throat like blood. Then he offered me the flagon, and grinned.

I was taken aback by that grin. It was all sharp edges and pointed teeth. His hooded eyes twinkled maliciously, and he was the Lord of Mischief once more. Which was the mask and which was the man? *Der Erlkönig* or the austere young man to whom I had said my vows? I stared at him as I took the flagon from his grasp. Neither his expression nor his manner changed or softened, but something flashed across his eyes when our fingers brushed.

The goblins hooted and called as I threw back my head and gulped down the wine. It burned down my mouth and throat, staining my dress. The room wheeled and spun, and for a moment I thought I might be sick.

Eyes watched me as I struggled with the effects of the wine, judging my reaction. I took a deep breath, threw back my shoulders, and smiled. If it could be called a smile. It was more like a challenge met, a grimace, the way a dog bares its teeth in its last extremity. I might have even snarled.

The goblins whooped their approval, hissing appreciatively. They rubbed their long, spindly fingers together to make a *shushing* sound, the sound of the wind in the trees. They did not clap the way humans did, and I suppressed a shudder of revulsion. The Goblin King's hooded gaze rested on my wine-stained and dripping lips, and I stared back, bold for the first time in my life. He inclined his head.

"Let us join the revels, my queen." He extended me a pale, elegant hand. His palm was cool and dry, but the living touch of his skin against mine sent my heart racing.

Without warning, the Goblin King swept me onto the cavern floor. The goblin musicians had not ceased playing their savage melodies, and we danced. No prescribed steps to follow, no restrained and civilized conversations to be held, we let the music overtake us. I danced with wild abandon, my veins running with wine, falling into the throng of goblins as they embraced me, kissed me, and worshipped me. I was passed from hand to hand, goblin to goblin, each wanting to steal a bit of me, my life, my fire. I was their queen, their sacrificial lamb placed atop the altar, and they paid homage to me with their bodies, their gifts, their offerings. They offered me food, fruit, and drink: flesh fresh-charred from the spit, overripe peaches and plums bursting to the touch, and wine so rich it spilled from tongue to tongue.

Somewhere in the fray I lost track of the Goblin King. I wanted him, reached for him, but could not find him.

Panic overtook me. Like wolves scenting blood on the wind, the goblins closed in around me, nipping, grabbing, biting like I was a hart in the hunt. My fear drove them into a frenzy. I cried out as they tore at my dress, my veil, my hair, but it wasn't my modesty I was concerned about. I could feel life draining from my limbs, I was turning languid, liquid, dissolving into nothing as the goblins fed on my emotions, growing bigger, more powerful, *more*.

"No," I said feebly, but my protests went unheard. "No."

My subjects did not listen, lost in the bloodlust and life-lust of my mortal existence in their midst.

"Stop!" I cried. "I wish you would stop!"

My voice rang out, echoing in the cavernous chamber. At once, all movement stilled. The goblins held their positions, frozen by my command. Their faces still contorted into expressions of desire, their limbs still twisted into grasping gestures. Their flat, black eyes moved and quivered, their inhuman chests rising and falling with each breath, the only movement in a still room.

I walked through the goblins, but not a single one stirred, bound by my wish. Only their eyes traced my path as I wound my way through the cavern. One poured an endless stream of wine into a goblet that overflowed onto the floor, another had sunk its teeth into the carcass of a raw and bloodied deer, yet another bent its back in the midst of a wild and savage dance.

Curious, I pushed at one of them. The flesh gave way beneath my fingers and offered me no resistance. I pinched the skin of its arm, rather cruelly, to see if I could make it react. No sound, no cry, no grimace, only a slight tightening of its mouth. Then, without warning, I shoved the goblin over with all my might.

The creature went careening into his fellow goblins, scattering them like tenpins. I laughed. I did not recognize the sound of my own laugh—high, wild, and cruel. I sounded like a mad woman. I sounded like one of *them*.

My laughter broke the spell that held them. The goblins began bowling into each other, sending each other flying, the crash of shattering dinnerware and the clatter of falling cutlery punctuated by the sharp, high laughter of the goblins. And me.

I surveyed my kingdom. Chaos. Cruelty. Abandon. I had always been holding back. Always been restrained. I wanted to be bigger, brighter, better; I wanted to be capricious, malicious, sly. Until now, I had not known the intoxicating sweetness of *attention*. In the world above, it had always been Käthe or Josef who captivated people's eyes and hearts—Käthe with her beauty, Josef with his talent. I was forgotten, overlooked, ignored—the plain, drab, practical, talentless sister. But here in the Underground, I was the sun around which their world spun, the axis around which their maelstrom twirled. Liesl the girl had been dull, drab, and obedient; Elisabeth the woman was a queen.

Across the room, I spied my king. He was not part of the throng, off to the side, half-forgotten in the shadows. This night—my wedding night—was about me. I was the center of the goblins' world, their savior, their queen. Yet a part of me longed for my adoring subjects to disappear. Longed to be alone with my husband. To be the subject of *his* adoration, the center of *his* world. Freed of my inhibitions by attention, power, and the goblin wine, I could finally admit how much I desired *Der Erlkönig*.

I had always desired him, even when he had been a shadowy figure from Constanze's stories, and even more when he had been my friend from the Goblin Grove. How had I forgotten? I *knew* that face, those eyes, that build. I *knew* how his lips thinned into an approving smile, how those eyes crinkled into a twinkle of pleasure. I had watched those fingers run themselves along an imaginary fingerboard, seen those arms hold an invisible bow as I shared my music with him. I had watched him study me, and knew now how he had become the most sublime interpreter of my art. He was as familiar to me as the sound of my own voice.

Around us a chorus of goblins screeched and shrieked their ribald comments and bawdy suggestions. While my cheeks were flushed, I drew my head up high and met *Der Erlkönig's* gaze. Although my laughter had broken the spell of *I wish* over the goblins, the Goblin King stood paralyzed, powerless against me. My mouth stretched in a grin, and I imagined my teeth growing sharper and pointed, the smile of a predator.

Fairy lights followed the path I cut through my gay, cavorting goblins, illuminating my husband's face as I drew near. His face was blank and expressionless, his hooded eyes giving nothing away. No tremor nor tremble betrayed him, his hands loose and careful by his sides. Yet I noted the tension in his arms and shoulders, and wondered if my bridegroom was afraid.

Was he frightened of *me*? Somehow the thought excited me to greater heights. I was the Goblin Queen. I could force or coerce any goblin to do my bidding, including my king. The power was more intoxicating than the wine. I drew myself up tall, moved closer to claim my husband as mine.

I stopped just a handsbreath away from the Goblin King. My bare toes brushed the tips of his polished black boots. He did not shrink or withdraw, but he made no move to meet me either. I lifted my chin and studied his face. His eyes were . . . wary? excited? pleading? I could not read him, I could not parse his features into an expression I understood.

I lifted my fingers to touch his cheek. He was trembling, so slightly I could not see it, but felt it beneath my hand.

"Elisabeth," he murmured, and his voice quivered too. Those quivers traveled all the way down my arm, down my chest, down to a secret, deep part of me. "Elisabeth, I—"

I shushed him with a finger across his mouth. He was shaking even harder now. I ran my hand down his lips to his jaw, and then farther down his neck to rest on his chest. I could feel the flutter of his heart beneath my palm; it felt like a baby bird in my hand.

*I beg your compassion, my queen, your compassion and your grace.*

Suddenly, I understood. He had put his trust—his faith—

in me, and he was afraid of my mercy. My tender, sympathetic heart twinged, beating in time with his.

So I grasped his cloak and pulled him close, crushing our lips together in a kiss.

The kiss is sweeter than sin and fiercer than temptation. I am not gentle, I am not kind; I am rough and wild and savage. I bite, I nip, I lick, I devour. I want and I want and I want and I want. I hold nothing back.

*Elisabeth*, he exhales into me, and I feel my lungs, my body, my loins fill with his breath. He fills me and I want to be filled by him. I open my mouth to let him in, but his hands come up and wrap themselves around my arms.

*No, no, no*, I think. *Don't push me away. Light my fire. Make me burn.*

But the Goblin King doesn't push me away. He grips me closer, and I am met. Our lips part and greet like partners in a dance, meeting, twining, clinging. When he pulls away, I moan, but his mouth never travels far, kissing the corners of my lips and my chin, his nose brushing the skin of my cheek.

I am sloppy, artless. I run my tongue along the upper edge of my teeth, the lower edge of his lip. He tastes like a winter wind, but the heat of our mouths warms him up, and then everything is languid, humid, hot, like a still summer night. His hands, wrapped tightly about my arms, loosen and slide down. His fingertips trace a line down my back, resting where the curve of it meets my backside.

Oh, God. I have no words and I am far from Heaven, but I do not care. I want to lie with the Devil and would do so again and again, just to feel like this. I am gripping his cloak so tight, I imagine the impression of the embroidery will be left on my palms for days.

*Elisabeth*, he breathes again. *Elisabeth, I*—

But I don't let him finish.

*I wish . . .*

He pauses, tensing.

*I wish you would take me. Ravish me. Right now.*

Right now.

## PRICK

## AND BLEED

the power of a wish. In the world above, wishes were will-o'-the-wisps: beautiful, but insubstantial and always just out of reach. Here in the Underground, will-o'-the-wisps were very much real. Tricksy little creatures: sly, deceitful, but tangible. Touchable. My wishes had weight.

Sounds faded, lights dimmed. It was a moment before I realized we were no longer in the great cavern. Swept up in the powerful current of our kiss, I had not noticed when the Goblin King and I were no longer surrounded by jeering, leering hobgoblins. I had not noticed that we were alone. I only noticed that his lips were no longer on mine, and I suffered their loss like a child deprived of its sweets: *no—more, please, more.*

I whimpered when the Goblin King withdrew, clutching and clinging to him. He stopped my amorous advances with a gentle hand on my mouth. I nuzzled into his fingers, craving whatever bit of him I could touch.

"Elisabeth, Elisabeth," he shushed. "Elisabeth, wait."

Wait? I had waited my entire life for this moment. Not for consummation, but for validation; I desired so hard I wanted to be found desirable in return. The Goblin King saw me—all of me—and now I wanted him to *know* me. I pushed away his restraining hand and leaped forward; I was a cat, a wolf, a huntress. I was out for blood and flesh.

"Stop." His voice was firmer now. I ignored him, pulling at his cloak, his shirt, his breeches. "Stop, Elisabeth. Please."

It was his *please*, not his protestations, that broke through my determination.

"Stop?" My voice was thick. "Why?"

"Because," he said, his words slow and sluggish, "because you know not what you do."

My mind was slow to parse his words. *I know not what I do.* Then my cheeks burned. "Oh."

Clarity burned away the haze of lust that fogged my senses; my embarrassment stung worse than any slap to the face. I turned my back to him.

"If I know not what I do," I said, my voice quavering. "It is only because I am unschooled and untutored. Untouched." I swallowed. "I could be taught, *mein Herr*. I am a quick study."

"I don't doubt that."

I sensed his presence behind me, near enough to touch, but not nearly near enough. I cringed at how desperate I sounded. I did not want to be desperate. But I was. *Oh, God, please touch me,* I thought. *Please.*

He stepped closer to me. I could not see him, but I could imagine him. I could imagine those mismatched wolf's eyes staring down at me, at my neck, down the low line of my wedding gown to where my shoulder blades were exposed.

I could imagine his fingers, long and slender, reaching out to trace them, stopping just short of actual contact. I could imagine this all so clearly, but what I could not imagine was the expression on his face.

"Elisabeth." His tone was steady. "There's so much you don't know. Would you still want this if you knew?"

A laugh burst from me. I could no more disguise my wanting than I could my eagerness. Neither could he. I had felt the shape of him through his trousers, pressed against me.

"Yes," I breathed. "Yes, I would. Yes, I do. I want this."

The Goblin King gripped my shoulders tight and pulled me against him. One arm snaked across my neck, the other wrapped around my waist. I felt every last bit of him through the thin cloth of my wedding gown. He trembled as he held me. I was breathing hard, my breathing made harder by his arm pressing against my throat.

I arched my back and closed my eyes. I covered his hand about my waist with my own, and brought my other hand up to touch his face. Beneath my fingers, the feathery pieces of his hair, the curve of a cheekbone, the strength of his jaw. His head bent, bringing his mouth to graze against where my neck met my shoulder. A soft kiss, a light bite. A nip. I moaned. The echoes of that moan ran up and down his body.

Slow, too slow. I wanted him to devour me, break me with the urgency of his lust. If he could not give that to me, then I would take it from him. I took the hand at my waist and moved it lower, closer to where I wanted him. His fingers clenched at the skin of my hipbone, rucking up the sheer material of my dress, exposing my bare leg to the air inch by inch. I struggled against him—not to run away, but to hurry him along. With agonizing slowness, his fingers explored my body below my waist, dipping, stroking, caressing. *Not enough,* I thought. *Not enough.*

My hand threaded through his hair tightened with impatience. He let out a slight hiss of pain. Moans of pain, moans of pleasure—to my ears, they were all sung in the same key. His fingers buried in my secret crevices tightened in response and I gasped—or tried to—my inarticulate cry lost in his stranglehold about my neck.

My other hand—the one guiding his course across my thighs, my hips, between my legs—reached behind me to touch him. I slid my hand down the length of his hardness, the proof of his desire unmistakable through his leather breeches. His hips bucked and a long shudder ran through him. I gripped him harder, staking my claim on him. *Mine,* I thought. *Mine.*

But he was shying away from my touch, pulling out of my grasp and away from me. I growled in frustration, but suddenly he wasn't there. I opened my eyes and turned around.

The world tilted, and for a moment, I could not find my equilibrium. The Goblin King stood only a few yards from me, but the distance was infinite. His feathery hair was a bird's nest of ratted tangles, his lips swollen, his cheeks flushed. His wolf's eyes glowed.

"Enough, Elisabeth." He was short of breath. "Enough."

I massaged my sore throat and gaped at him. "Enough?" I rasped.

"Yes." He nodded. "No more. Not tonight. I will have your attendants escort you back to your chambers."

"What?" The question burst from me before I could help myself. "Why?"

"Because," he said again. "I don't want this. Not now. Not like this."

The humiliation of his words burned. The flimsy silk of my wedding gown would go up in flames from its contact with my skin. Humiliation, shame, lust, desire, all burning. I was burning. How could he send me away? The room smelled of our mutual passion, musty and warm, and I had held the proof of his wanting me in my hand.

An old wound opened up inside me, and all my feelings of worthlessness came pouring out. I was bleeding shame. I should have known better than to place my heart before him; I had exposed my innermost self to someone I trusted once before, only to have it ridiculed for being untutored, unschooled, unremarkable.

I hid my face from the Goblin King so he would not see me cry.

His hand touched my shoulder, and in his touch I felt nothing but gentle consolation. That hurt most of all.

I threw him off. "Don't touch me," I hissed. "You don't get to touch me. Not like—not like that."

"Like what?" His voice was kind.

"Like—like you don't care." My skin was raw. Everything was tender to the touch, my entire body yearning and reaching for sensation and meeting nothing but rejection. I smoothed down my wedding gown over my hips. My wedding veil—that diamond-spangled gauze—had fallen off during our embrace, and it lay pooled at my feet.

"Elisabeth," he said. "I abstain because I *do* care—"

"Then why won't you touch me?" A sob hitched in my throat and I hated myself for my weakness. "Why won't you take what is yours?"

"It's not mine to take," he said, much more fiercely than I expected. "It's yours to give."

"And I'm giving it to you now!" I gathered the fallen wedding veil to me, as though I could hide my humiliation in its spangled gauze.

"And I do not want you," he said quietly. "Not like this."

It was so unfair. Despite the evidence of his lust straining against his leather breeches, he hid it all behind a cloak, behind a mantle of sarcasm and a disaffected air. I could have screamed.

I turned around. "You said you wanted me—entire." I hurled his words back at him with all the bitterness I could muster.

The Goblin King closed his eyes, as if he could shut out my words along with the sight of me. My heart thudded in my chest—was I truly so distasteful to men that not even a king of hobgoblins wanted me?

"This is not you entire," he said. "This is you, desperate."

His words were salt in my wounds.

"What do you want from me, then?" I *was* desperate, but I was beyond the point of caring now. "Why did you marry me, if not for this?"

This time it was the Goblin King who stumbled back, as though I had slapped him. "If you thought that I wanted—"

But I did not want to hear what he had to say.

"Perhaps you are now afflicted with buyer's remorse," I said. "Perhaps you should have taken the beautiful sister instead."

"Elisabeth," the Goblin King said warningly. "Stop."

I should have stopped, but I did not want to stop. My tongue, once loosened by goblin wine, could not be tightened back into submission.

"Well, *mein Herr,*" I said. "You married the ugly one. And," I continued with a high, shrill titter, "you've made your bed. Now you'd better sleep in it. So come, my lord," I said coyly, running my hands down the curves of my body— what few I had. "Come sleep with your new bride. If you can stomach it."

The Goblin King made a disgusted sound, a sound that shattered what little confidence I had left. A lump rose in my throat and I swallowed it back with a hiccough.

"Go to bed, Elisabeth," he said. "You're drunk."

Was I? I had drunk wine and beer before, had even stolen a little bit of the schnapps Constanze kept in her secret cupboard when I was a child, but I had never drunk myself into indulgence. Not like Papa. Never like Papa.

The ground was unsteady beneath my feet. The room spun, and I was falling. The Goblin King rushed forward to hold me up.

"Twig, Thistle!" My goblin attendants appeared in an instant. "Take my bride back to her chambers and make sure she is well rested."

"No." I threw up a hand. I drew myself up to my fullest height and tried to muster a little dignity. "I can see myself out, *mein Herr.*"

I stumbled away from him, but long fingers twined themselves in my hair, forcing my head back and into the Goblin King's embrace.

"I *do* want you," he whispered in my ear. "But I want the part of you that you will not give me. This"—and he ran his hand down the column of my exposed throat, my chest, my waist—"this is only part of you. When I said I wanted you entire, I meant it."

"What part of me have I not given you?"

He smiled into my hair.

"You know what it is, Elisabeth." He hummed a bit of a melody.

My music.

I wrenched myself from his grasp and shoved him away. I wished for a door to appear. Then I wrenched the handle open and slammed it shut, its loud, satisfying *clang* the last word in our conversation.

My bravado lasted only as long as the walk to my own chambers. The paths in the Underground rearranged themselves so I found myself in the corridor outside my room. I unlocked the door and threw myself inside, eager to outpace the howls of rage and disappointment that dogged my heels.

I could not breathe. The burn of tears scalded my lower lashes, but none came. I wanted to scream, I wanted to tear my room to shreds. I wanted to destroy something. I wanted to destroy *him*.

I grasped the Louis Quinze set by my hearth and hurled it against the earthen walls with all my might. The table and chairs, delicate as they seemed, were sturdier than they looked and merely bounced off. I did scream then, and picked up one of the chairs by its legs before smashing it against the gleaming travertine of the fireplace. It was a few blows before the chair splintered, sending chips and shards of the white stone with it. I threw what was left of the ruined chair into the fire. The table and the other chair soon followed.

Then the other objects in my room. The candelabras, the console tables, the beautiful and ugly objets d'art. I picked up the statuette of the leering satyr and orgiastic nymph and threw it as hard as I could against the solid wood of my door. Made of porcelain, it shattered immediately.

I screamed and raged and kicked and shrieked and cried and destroyed until my anger and frustration were spent. I lay on the floor and debris of my bedroom, my breath coming in short gasps.

My wedding dress choked me. I made a feeble attempt to rip the fine silk off me, but could not muster enough hatred for strength. I was empty. After a whirlwind evening of hopes and disappointment, the emptiness was blessedly comforting. I listened to the crackle of the fire, searching for patterns in the sound. For music. For structure. For sense.

A handful of notes came to me, a short rise, a rushed fall. The motion of a hand reaching out, only to fall uselessly by my side. It repeated over and over, faster and faster, until the storm of sixteenth notes rushing out of me crashed into a jangling chord. I had never written something like this before. It wasn't pretty; it was messy, discordant, ugly, and it perfectly suited my mood.

Paper. I ought to write it down. But I had destroyed everything in my room. A laugh escaped me. Tripping myself up at every turn. How like me.

I glanced at the mostly white expanse of my wedding gown, unsullied and untorn, save for a splash of wine and dirt here and there. I reached for a large splinter near me and charred the end in the fire before cooling it quickly with breath and fingers.

Then I used the ash to write.


An incomplete musical phrase wormed its way into my sleep, begging me to finish it. But I could not grasp its shape.

I did not know how to resolve the questions it posed. The phrase seemed familiar, like a half-whistled tune from my childhood, but I could not place where I had heard it before.

I startled myself awake. The fire in the hearth had died down to embers, and I was cold and naked on my debris-strewn floor. My wedding gown hung from my bedpost, the white silk covered with ashen scribbles—remnants of my moody masterpiece. I ran my grubby hands down its silken length. So fragile. So temporary. One smudge of my dirty fingertips could erase hours of work. I teased my fingers along the edges of my notes, the temptation to destroy even this rising strong within me. I swallowed it down.

The silk gown rustled gently. There was a draft in my barrow room. Shivering, I rose to my feet in search of that spectral breeze when I stumbled across a threshold.

I blinked. My barrow room had been sealed, shut, and locked with a key. The door was still there, but next to the hearth was an arch that had not been there before. The breeze came from the space beyond the threshold.

I glanced over my shoulder. Evidence of my fury and frustration was still scattered over the floor. This was my room. That was my bed. That was my wedding gown, still hanging from its post. Not wanting to put the dress back on, I wished for a dressing gown. I found one on my bed, rumpled and wrinkled as though it had been tossed rather than magicked there. I put it on, and stepped into the darkness.

Fairy lights winked into existence the moment I crossed into this new room, fluttering slowly, as though they struggled to wake. Their soft glow illuminated another set of rooms, larger and grander than my barrow bedchamber, yet somehow still small and intimate in scale. Standing in the center was a klavier.

My breath caught. The instrument was beautiful, made of a rich, warm, dark wood that gleamed under the fairy lights. I ran my hands reverently over the keys, polished to a dull shine. It was a full octave larger than the klaviers in our inn, and when I pressed a key, a clear, full sound filled the room. None of the tinny, brassy resonance that plagued the instruments at home.

I lightly tapped out a melody, allowing myself to fall into a reverie. I had been lost, but now a piece of myself had been returned to me. Then I noticed the stack of paper and ink on a small table beside the klavier.

Staff paper. Parchment already lined with a musical staff, waiting only for a clef, a key, and a signature. I stiffened.

*Another trick,* I thought. *Another taunt of the Goblin King.*

The room held the silent echoes of a mocking laugh. I was tempted to dash the inkwell against the keyboard and tear the staff paper to shreds. But the memory of a tall, elegant stranger in a marketplace stayed my hand. A tall, elegant stranger who approached a plain, homely girl because he had heard the music within her and wanted to set it free.

My fingers twitched, longing to work my hands into the keys, longing to set my feelings to paper. The wedding gown hung in my bedchamber, so close, yet so far away. I wanted to take its ash and turn it to ink.

But I didn't.

I turned and walked back to my barrow room, the fairy lights winking out one by one, snuffed out like candles. I did not know what time it was. The painting of the Goblin Grove above my hearth showed the thin gray scene of snow falling. The hour could be predawn. It could be late dusk.

It was hard to tell, the light flattened by the gentle snow falling down on its black branches.

I squinted. I could swear the snow *was* falling. Moving. The snowflakes were coming down, settling across the wintry landscape. Whether it was the lack of sleep, or the crusty remnants of tears blurring my vision, I could not tell. I moved closer.

My eyes were not playing tricks on me. The snow was falling on the Goblin Grove in the world above. It was like a window, a view I might have seen from my bedroom back at the inn. I was pierced with a sudden yearning for home. For Josef. For Käthe. Mother and Papa. Even Constanze. I even missed the girl I had been: Liesl the dutiful daughter, the loving older sister, the secret composer. If my life had been stunted, at least I had known my place. What place had I here? Who was I in the Underground? A neglected queen, an unloved, unravished wife. A maiden still. I found rejection wherever I went, even among the goblins.

My humiliation was still raw and tender within me, so I focused on the enchanted painting instead. The Goblin Grove beckoned, and I reached for the portrait, against the warnings of Twig and Thistle.

I was startled when my fingers met glass. I leaned forward to examine it, and my breath covered its surface in mist, completely obscuring the Goblin Grove in fog.

When the mist cleared, the scene had changed. I stumbled backward, tripping over the broken furniture and shattered knickknacks in my chamber. I cut my palm on something sharp, but I scarcely noticed the pain. Instead of the Goblin Grove, a young man sat at a writing desk, scribbling furiously.

"Sepperl!"

He did not hear me. Of course he did not hear me. My little brother was taller than when I saw him last—taller, thinner, leaner. He dressed like a gentleman now, his frock coat of pastel blue brocade, his breeches of fine satin, fine lace crowding his throat. He looked prosperous and, I thought with a pang, like a person I would not recognize in passing.

The door behind him opened, admitting François. Josef's face brightened, and my breath hitched in my throat. My brother had once looked at me that way, as though I held his soul in my hands. But his soul was no longer in my care; I had been replaced.

Josef asked something, and François shook his head. Josef's shoulders slumped, his fingers crumpling the parchment in his hand. A composition? No, no notes. Words. A letter—

Fog covered the glass once more. "Sepperl!" I cried, but when the mist disappeared again, my anguished call died in my throat.

A young woman knelt beside a bed. For a moment, I thought I beheld my own reflection, until I noticed the gleam of gold peeking out from beneath her headscarf.

Käthe.

Wearily, she put aside her stained apron and made ready for bed. She was about to pull back the covers and crawl beneath them when she paused. Reaching beneath the pillow, Käthe pulled out a sheaf of paper.

With a jolt I realized it was the little *Lieder*, the composition I had left behind. *Für meine Lieben*, I had written. For my loved ones.

My sister fingered the lock of hair tied with twine to the piece. Her blue eyes swam with tears and she hugged the piece to her chest. I was not dead to the world above. The mist closed in again.

The sacrifice I had made, my marriage to the Goblin King, seemed foolish now. My life, my future, my loved ones—I had thrown it all away for selfishness. Because for once, just once, I had wanted to be wanted. Desired. The Goblin King had said he wanted me, and I had taken that desire and staked my entire life on it.

Was my sacrifice worth it? I felt hollow and bereft, yet the grief in my heart had palpable weight, bearing me down to the ground. I could not breathe. I carried the burden of my love for my family, and it threatened to suffocate me.

# THOSE WHO HAVE
# COME BEFORE

s she all right?"

"Don't know. It's hard to tell with mortals. They wither and fade so quickly."

"She's filthy."

"Must have been a fine night then." A snicker. "Well, that bodes well for us."

"Should we wake her?"

I stirred at the sound of voices in my room. Twig. Thistle.

"Sure. Lazy layabout." Thistle. I recognized the contempt in her voice through my haze of exhaustion and grief. Her dislike was comfortingly reliable, like Constanze's.

Constanze. The stab of homesickness roused me, and I groaned and sat up. Thistle leaped back with surprise, her hand poised for a slap.

"What is it?" I rasped. The painting above my fireplace once again showed the Goblin Grove. Several hours must have passed; the snow was much thicker now.

"Can't spend the entire day lying in bed," Thistle said. "Or on the ground, as the case may be. Funny." She grinned, showing all her sharp teeth. "I thought you mortals preferred the comforts of a bed, but here you are, sleeping in the dirt like a proper goblin."

I rolled my eyes as Twig helped me to my feet. My half-tied dressing gown fell off my shoulders as my joints creaked and protested against the abuse. Human bones were most certainly not meant to sleep on dirt floors.

"She *has* gone native," Thistle said to Twig. "Not even a second thought for those quaint mortal notions of modesty!"

I tied the dressing gown properly about myself. "If you've come to wake me, at least have the decency to bring me a proper breakfast," I groused. Twig made a motion to go, but I shook my head. "Not you, Twig." I pointed to Thistle. "You. You go."

Thistle made a face, but disappeared in a twinkling. Twig gave a deep bow, her cobweb-and-branch-laden hair scraping the floor.

"Twig," I began. "What is that painting above my fireplace?"

An inscrutable expression crossed her face. Between my two attendants, Twig had seemed the more sympathetic one, but I was reminded that despite her kindnesses to me, she wasn't my friend. But she was the closest thing I had to a confidante in the Underground, and I sorely missed the companionship. I sorely missed Käthe.

"You touched it, didn't you?" Twig asked.

I nodded.

She sighed. "It's a mirror, Your Highness."

"A mirror?" I glanced at it again, but all I saw was the Goblin Grove, blanketed in white. "Then why . . . ?"

"That one," Twig said, inclining her head toward the gilt-edged piece above the mantel, "was brought from the world above. Like most of the mirrors there, it's silver-backed. Silver follows her own laws here in the Underground. She won't show you your reflection; she'll show you what she wants you to see."

Josef. Käthe. My heart twisted with pain.

"That's why we warned you not to touch it," she said. "Your thoughts, your feelings, your questions—that's what gets reflected back at you, not your face."

"Is what the mirror shows me not a true vision, then?" I desperately needed this magic mirror to be real. So I could watch Josef grow up to be the man he was meant to be. So I could see Käthe blossom into the woman I knew she could become. So I would not forget what it was to live, even as life itself forgot me.

Twig's lips twisted. "I wouldn't necessarily trust what you see in it, Highness. Silver won't lie, but it can conceal truths as much as it can reveal them."

The ghosts of my family sat around us in my chamber, crowding in on the edges of our conversation. I had to talk around them.

"If silver won't show me my reflection," I said, "then what will?"

"Still water is best, of course, but in the absence of that, polished jet, bronze, or copper will do." Twig picked up a round copper basin from the floor. She turned its convex side toward me.

I looked worse than I thought. Tearstains cut grooves through the ash and dirt encrusting my cheeks, but could not disguise the gray shadows beneath my eyes. My face looked sunken, haggard, old, and the copper basin distorted my image back at me—long, pointed nose; stubby, weak chin. Or perhaps I truly was this ugly.

I swallowed. "I look a right mess."

"That you do," Twig said cheerfully. "I've been told mortals like to bathe, so I've been instructed to bring you down to the hot springs. Come," she said, gesturing to me. "You won't even have to say *I wish*."

I laughed. It felt good to laugh, even for a feeble joke; it relieved a bit of the pressure of grief and homesickness on my heart. It felt good to laugh with someone again, even if she wasn't my sister. Even if she wasn't a friend.

Humans were not meant for isolation. We were not meant for loneliness. I glanced back at the ghosts of my family sitting with me in my bedchamber, invisible to the eye, but visible to my heart. I was dead to the world above, but I could not help but reach for comfort and companionship, the way a flower yearns for sunshine in the dark.


After my bath, Twig and Thistle took me deep into the heart of the Underground, to the center of the goblin city for some proper gowns and dresses. I was curious about goblin ateliers—Thistle and Twig did not wear human clothes; they preferred to wear little skirts woven of leaves and branches and twigs. The fact that goblins had tailors and seamstresses at all intrigued me.

The corridors changed as we wound through the various passageways. Where my room was situated had curved hallways, tunnels rather than broad passages, paintings and portraits and other objets d'art, and dirt floors lined with rugs. The paths by the underground lake were smaller, tighter, and damper—less earthen and more rocky.

As we neared the center of the goblin city, the hallways broadened and expanded into passable avenues. The floor became paved with enormous gemstones, each the size of my head. They glittered beneath our feet as we passed, their surfaces polished by thousands—millions—of feet smoothing them over centuries. On each side of these broad avenues were elaborately carved thresholds, with "windows" cut into the second- and third-story walls to overlook the streets below.

It was wrong. The city was strange, forced, and artificial. It did not teem with life; it was empty. This city had not been grown—it had been made. There was a symmetry to these buildings that seemed antithetical to the goblin aesthetic, a rigid sameness and grace that was as ordered as a Baroque symphony.

"Does anyone live here?" I asked.

"Goblins don't live in cities," Thistle said. "We're not like you humans, wanting to live on top of each other. Most of us are solitary, and we live in barrows connected by family and clan. This," she said, gesturing to the storefronts around us, "is where we trade."

"Trade?" I was surprised. "Goblins conduct business with each other?"

The sour look was back on Thistle's face. "Yes. Obviously."

There were signs above each open threshold, goblin sigils. Family crests, perhaps. Perhaps this one indicated gold work, that one gem-cutting. I had seen some astonishing works of art in the Underground, works that were far more deftly made than those made by human hands. Goblin-made objects of legend had always been treasure beyond measure in Constanze's stories; wars had been waged for their possession, empires had fallen to acquire them.

"A lot of effort to build a city that will never be lived in," I murmured. My eyes swept over the elaborately carved arches, the graceful façades and storefronts—all for nothing.

"It wasn't always this way," Twig put in. "Goblins never gathered in cities; we always conducted our business in the open air, in groves and other sacred places in the world above."

"What changed?"

Twig shrugged. "*Der Erlkönig*. When he took the throne, he brought many strange customs with him."

I frowned. "My Goblin King?" I corrected myself. "*This* Goblin King?"

Thistle wore a dark look. "*Der Erlkönig* is *Der Erlkönig*. It is only you mortals who care where one ends and the other begins."

"Look here, we've arrived at the clothier," Twig said jovially. She bustled me past a dark threshold into a large room. I was about to admonish Twig for her transparent attempt to distract me, when I became distracted indeed.

The clothier was laid out like a large shop, with dresses in the "window displays," and gowns hanging on dress forms. A large mirror made of polished copper stood in the corner, and fairy lights illuminated the space: glowing, floating dust motes that gave everything a soft, diffuse look. Käthe would have loved this.

The thought of my sister was sharper than needles and pins, my heart a pincushion of sorrow. I thought of her running her hands over the sumptuous bolts of fabric at the clothier's in our village, her summer-blue, beauty-loving eyes drinking in the rich velvets, the elaborate brocades, the vibrant colors, the shimmering silks and satins. How I both loathed and loved visiting the shops with my sister. Loathed because I would never be as lovely as she, loved because her delight was infectious. I brushed away the moisture from my lower lashes.

"Ah, fresh meat."

I jumped when another goblin materialized at my feet. He wore a knotted measuring ribbon about his neck, with a few pins in his mouth. The tailor. Upon closer inspection, I realized the pins in his mouth were in fact whiskers. Steel-tipped whiskers.

"Yes, this is *Der Erlkönig*'s latest." Thistle pushed me forward.

The tailor sniffed. "Not much to look at." He peered into my face. "Looks familiar, though."

I shrank beneath his scrutiny.

"Well!" the tailor said, sweeping his hand over the shop. "Welcome to my humble atelier. We've been dressing brides of *Der Erlkönig* since time immemorial, so you've come to the right place if you are in need of attire befitting a queen. What can I do you for?"

My eyes wandered over the beautiful gowns on display. They were all several years out of date—some even older than that. I ran my hands over the gowns. Although the fabrics were sumptuous, rich, and beautiful, the gowns themselves had been skillfully repaired. Nothing, not even goblin hands, could stop the wear and tear of time on these gorgeous pieces. The more I looked, the more I realized that everything around me was crumbling, decaying, dying.

It was only then that I understood these dresses had

belonged to my predecessors. My rivals. I immediately quashed the thought.

The tailor sidled forward, his long, multi-jointed fingers caressing the dress form closest to me.

"Ah, yes," he said. "Beautiful, isn't it? The color of storms and oceans, or so we've been told. This dress," he continued, "belonged to Magdalena. She was beautiful—the way you mortals reckon, anyhow—beautiful, but stupid. Oh ho, we had fun with this one, we did, but we used her up too soon. Her fire died, leaving us cold and dark."

The dress form beneath the gown was tall and well-formed, the bosom and hips generous, the waist tiny. The dress, a *robe à la française*, was made from a deep, jewel-toned blue silk, and I could imagine the dramatic coloring of the woman who had worn it: pale skin, dark hair, and blue eyes to match her gown. A breathless beauty, a glittering jewel, and I imagined the Goblin King partaking of her loveliness over and over again, biting the sweet peaches of her cheeks until she was gone.

"And this one," Thistle chimed in, pointing to another dress form, "belonged to Maria Emmanuel. Prissy, she was. Refused to do her duty by her lord. She was consecrated to someone else—a carpenter? Something like that. Don't know what the king saw in her, but they were both possessed of a strange devotion to a figure nailed to a wooden cross. She lasted the longest, this prudish nun, not having given herself to king and land, and during her rule, our kingdom suffered. Yet she lasted the longest for that, although she too died in the end, pining for the world above she could see but not touch."

This dress form was slim, the gown that hung on it made of an austere gray wool. I could imagine the woman who wore this dress—a pious creature, veiled like a bride of Christ. No beauty, but her eyes would be a clear, luminous gray, shining with the fervor of her passion and faith. Not like Magdalena, whose loveliness would have been carnal and earthly; Maria Emmanuel would have glowed with an inner light, the beauty of a saint or a martyr. The Goblin King was a man of varied tastes, it seemed.

On and on, Thistle and the tailor went through the litany of brides, but their names and histories blurred quickly from my mind, their lives faded from memory. This was not a clothier's shop; this was a mausoleum, the dress forms all that remained of each previous bride. Reduced to the fabric she wore. I wondered what gown my dress form would wear, once the Goblin King had used me up.

"What of the first Goblin Queen?" I asked. "Where is her dress form?"

Three pairs of black eyes blinked at me. Then Thistle and the tailor exchanged looks.

"She doesn't have one," Twig said.

"She doesn't?" I glanced around the shop, mannequins of all shapes and sizes standing in an array. "Why not?"

Thistle gave Twig a vicious pinch, but the taller goblin girl waved her off.

"Because," Twig said, "she lived."

The room spun around me, the mannequins and goblins tilting and twirling in a swirl of color and shadow.

"She lived," I echoed. "How do you mean?"

The goblins were unwontedly quiet. The brave maiden must have found a way to escape the Underground with her life, without having condemned the world above to an eternal winter. How was that possible?

"What was her name?" I whispered.

"Her name is lost to us," Twig said.

"Forgotten, not lost," Thistle interrupted. "Stricken from our memory. We do not honor her."

"Understand this, mortal," the tailor said. "What the old laws giveth, they taketh away. Do not think she walked away from us unscathed, unbroken, or whole. You are dead, maiden. Your life is ours."

"I thought my life belonged to the Goblin King."

The goblins burst into their strange laughter. "And to whom," Thistle said, "do you think his life belongs?"

Their smiles were row upon row of jagged teeth. I shuddered.

"Now, why don't we find you a nice gown for your dinner with *Der Erlkönig*?" the tailor asked. "We have some lovely new fabrics taken from the world above. Still warm from their owners' now-cooling bodies, if I don't miss my guess."

I recoiled. "What did—how did—" I could not finish for the horror that strangled my throat.

"Ah, the days of winter," the tailor said, licking his steel-tipped whiskers. Did I imagine things, or were there bloodstains upon his clothes? "The earth belongs to us as the old year dies, mortal. Walk away from the Underground, and the earth belongs to us forever."

Magdalena, Maria Emmanuel, Bettina, Franziska, Ilke, Hildegard, Walburga; my predecessors and rivals and sisters. Every single one of them had married *Der Erlkönig*. Every single one of them had given up her life. Had they known the true cost of their sacrifice? Had I? They had long since faded away to dust, but something of their spirits lingered, the seams of their threadbare gowns holding in the last remnants of their souls. Their ghosts surrounded me now, and

I could hear the whispers of their voices across time, beckoning, pleading, calling. *Join us. Join us.* But one voice was absent. The nameless, brave maiden.

*She lived,* I thought. *She walked out of the Underground, and lived.*

## COME OUT
## TO PLAY

the dining hall was another cavern, much like the ball-room. Its tall ceilings rose high above me like the arches of a cathedral, while icicles of stone dripped down low, strung with fairy lights. It was like standing in a monster's giant maw, its teeth threatening to close down on me at any moment, as I waited for my lord and husband to escort me to my seat.

I strove to calm myself. It was difficult with the stays about my ribs, holding my lungs in their iron grip. The breaths I took were restricted, doing nothing to slow my fluttering heart. Did it flutter with nervousness or excitement? I wasn't sure.

Thistle, Twig, and the tailor had brought back an array of gowns for me to choose from. Most were terribly ill-suited to me—the colors too bright, too pale, the shapes all wrong, the fit made for someone taller, someone more slender, someone simply *more*. The thought of wearing another woman's—another dead woman's—castoffs made my skin crawl, and I refused them all, driving my attendants mad. The tailor finally tossed me a drab old robe and threatened to dress me in it.

To his surprise, I accepted. The tailor took the robe and fashioned it into a simple dinner gown. His long, spindly fingers clacked as he worked, ripping the seams until he had enough material to stitch into something wearable. The speed and dexterity of his fingers astonished me; within a few moments he had put together a dress with a full skirt and modest bodice. The gown was dull and ashy brown in color, the color of dirt, the color of mud. It was also, I thought, the color of sparrow feathers.

"Good evening, Elisabeth."

The whisper of a cool breath against my neck. I shivered, icy fingers traveling down my spine. I faced the Goblin King and dropped a curtsy.

"Good evening, *mein Herr.*"

He brought my hand to his lips, all courtesy and charm. He was as resplendent as a peacock in a beautiful moss-green frock coat made of silk brocade, gold and copper thread woven into a pattern of autumn leaves. His satin breeches were cream, his stockings snow white, the toes of his pointed black shoes turned up like goblin feet in illustrations I had seen as a child. He was stunning, both as a king of goblins and as a man. My breath caught in my throat.

"How are you, my dear?" The Goblin King held both my hands in his own. His were gloved; mine were bare. "Was the klavier to your liking?"

I stiffened. I thought of the gleaming instrument in the room next to mine, waiting for me to sit down and compose.

The beauty of its shape and sound had pushed at me, pressing down on my defenses.

"Are you mocking me?" I asked.

The Goblin King was surprised. "Why would I mock you? Did you not enjoy my gift?"

I pulled my hands out of his grasp and turned away. I could not accept this gift from him; its very existence reminded me of the hollowed-out space inside me that longed to be filled.

"Don't, please," I said. "It wasn't a gift; it was an assault."

Those mismatched eyes immediately shuttered, turning his face cold and pitiless. I did not realize until he disappeared that I had been speaking with the soft-eyed young man. *Der Erlkönig* appeared in his place.

"Shall we, my queen?" His distance was colder and bitterer than a winter wind. He offered his arm and I took it as he guided me to the great table in the middle of the hall. Once I had been seated on one end, the Goblin King disappeared and reappeared at the other end within a blink.

The large table was situated next to an enormous hearth, larger than I was tall, in which a monster of a boar was spitted and roasting over a roaring fire. Out of the shadows came a multitude of servers, each bearing a dish or a platter I had never seen or heard of before. Two servers lifted the boar from the fireplace and set it, still steaming and smoking, on a lake-sized plate surrounded by an assortment of goblin fruits.

"Let us say grace," the Goblin King said, once the servers had retreated.

My fingers were already wrapped around the fork and knife in front of me, and I shamefacedly returned them to my lap. My husband was more devout than I. I was curious about his faith, but kept silent as I bowed my head. The Goblin King asked for the Lord's blessing upon our meal—in Latin.

Where had he learned Latin? My own Latin was rudimentary at best, half-remembered from Sunday school lessons I had given up in favor of hobnobbing with Josef and the goblins in the wood. *Heathens,* our mother had called us, *with no care or concept for God.* But Josef and I hadn't minded; we were *Der Erlkönig's* own, and he did not believe in God. And yet this Goblin King sat before me, learned in Latin and schooled in music. Just who *was* he?

"Amen," he said once he had finished the benediction.

"Amen," I intoned. We commenced eating. I was amused by the shape of my utensils: the fork, fashioned into a thin, slender goblin hand with its many-jointed fingers and pointed claws serving as the prongs; the knife, suggesting a long fang slipping from a smiling mouth. The servers returned, carving up the boar and transferring the meat—steaming, red, undercooked, still dripping a little with blood—onto a large platter.

We ate without speaking, as I picked at the roast and other winter root vegetables. I spied assorted dishes, custards and flans and other delicacies, but they all turned my stomach. Cooked with a goblin flair, they looked strange, unnatural, rotten: the chocolates muddy, the pastries frosted with slime.

"What, does the food not please you either, my queen?"

I looked up from my repast. The Goblin King wore a sour expression, his lips pulled tight. He picked at his own plate, a meager portion barely touched.

"No, *mein Herr.*" I rephrased my words. "Your offerings do not tempt me."

"No?" He drove his fork into his roast with increasing force. "And what would it take to please you, my dear?"

He was in a sullen mood, his lower lip pushed into a pout that rivaled Käthe's. He was like a child denied his favorite toy, a spoiled child accustomed to getting his way.

So I said nothing, giving the Goblin King a nonchalant shrug as I took a large sip of wine.

"So particular, my queen," he remarked. "You will be here for the rest of your life; you might as well enjoy yourself."

I had no response to that, so I took another sip of wine.

The meal progressed in silence, a silence that stuck in both our throats. Neither of us ate much, but the goblin servers continued to bring out course after course after course. I tried my best to honor each dish, but the Goblin King had given up all pretense of eating. He drank cup after cup after cup of wine, growing more and more irritable when his servers did not refill his goblet quickly enough. It was the most I had ever seen him drink, but he seemed completely sober. Papa would have been laughing—or crying—by now.

I watched the Goblin King fidget from beneath my lashes. I knew he longed to break the stillness that was not still between us. His mood grew fouler with each passing moment. He slid the platters and bowls on the table back and forth, watching the food slop on the surface and onto the floor, forcing the goblins to clean up after him. I could see the words forming on his tongue, but he clamped his lips shut and swallowed them down, determined not to be the one who broke first.

But he did anyway.

"Well, my dear," he said at last.

He wanted to fill the empty spaces with sound, with meaningless conversation. He was a little like Josef in that way; Josef, who always played because he could not bear the silence. I was content to shape the quiet into the structures I wanted.

So I waited.

"What scintillating topics shall we discuss over supper?" the Goblin King continued. "We have the rest of your life to reacquaint ourselves, after all." He took another sip of his wine. "How about the wine? A very good vintage, if I do say so myself."

Again I said nothing. I methodically took bite after small bite of my food, chewing slowly and carefully.

"What about the weather?" he continued. "Ever-unchanging here in the Underground, but winter in the world above, or so I've been told. Spring, they say, is slow to come this year."

I paused with my fork halfway to my mouth. I thought of what the tailor had said, of the earth belonging to the goblins during the days of winter. The food turned to ash on my tongue, crumbling all the way down my throat. I took another sip of wine.

The Goblin King had had enough. "Will you not speak?" he demanded.

I cut myself another piece of roast. "You were doing a fine job by yourself," I said mildly.

"I had not thought you would be such a dull conversationalist, Elisabeth." He sulked. "You were always willing to speak to me before. Back in the Goblin Grove. Back when we were young."

Had *Der Erlkönig* ever been young? He was ageless and ancient, yet I seemed to remember his face, round and fleshed out with youth. I remembered a little girl in the wood, and a little boy.

"A little girl's idle chatter is not the same as scintillating conversation, *mein Herr*." I set down my utensils. "But what did I tell you?"

The Goblin King smiled, but I could not tell whether it teased or soothed. "Many things. You wanted to be a famous composer. You wanted to have your music heard in all the great concert halls of the world."

Pain flared out from my breast, lightning quick, but the burn of it lingered after its initial strike. It was true I had dreamed those things once. Before Josef stole our father's attention with his gifts. Before Papa had made it abundantly clear to me that the world had no interest in hearing my music. Because it was strange. Because it was queer. Because I was a woman.

"Then you know the very heart of me," I said. "And there is no more to be said."

The Goblin King's face darkened. "What is wrong with you, Elisabeth?"

I lifted my eyes to his. "There is nothing wrong with me."

"There is." He shifted in his seat, and although there was an endless array of food and feast between us, he was too close. A storm was brewing behind those mismatched eyes, and the air between us crackled with electricity. "You're not the Elisabeth I remember. I thought that if you—that if you became my—" He cut himself off abruptly. "This," he said, gesturing to the space between us, "is not what I was hoping for."

"People grow up, *mein Herr*," I said shortly. "They change."

He gave me a hard look. "Evidently." He stared at me for a beat longer before leaning back in his chair and crossing his arms, resting his feet on the table. "Ah, well, my mistake. Time passes differently Underground than in the world above. Mere moments for me, several years and a lifetime ago for you, apparently." The storm in his eyes grew darker.

A hapless goblin attendant tried to move one of the Goblin King's feet to clean beneath it. "What are you doing?" he snapped.

The goblin gave him a beetling look and tried to scurry out of the way, but not before the Goblin King grabbed the poor thing by the scruff of its neck and gave it a malicious kick, sending it ear over toe across the room.

I was horrified. "How could you?"

His eyes glittered dangerously. "It would do the same to me if it could," he said mulishly.

"You're *Der Erlkönig*," I said. "You are their king, and hold untold power over them. You are the reason they cannot leave the Underground. Have a little pity, why don't you?"

He snorted. "They are as much my jailers as I am theirs," he retorted. "If I could lay down my burden as warden of the Underground, I would. If I could wander the world above as a free man, I would. Instead, I am a prisoner to my crown."

That brought me up short. He had always seemed to come and go at my beck and call in the Goblin Grove, but in his own way, he was trapped. Like me.

"What would you do, if you were a free man?" I asked.

The question struck him in the chest, spreading through his throat and face like the blush of dawn. With life and color to his features, he looked once more like the austere young man in the portrait gallery: young, idealistic, and vulnerable.

"I would take my violin and play." The words were spoken almost before his lips could catch up to what he was saying. "I would walk the world and play, until someone called me by name and called me home."

His name and his home. What had my Goblin King left behind in the mortal world? Was it a greater torment to watch everything you had known and loved transform and disappear before your eyes while you remained alive and unchanging? Or was it worse to die before you could witness that change for yourself?

The Goblin King's eyes met my own, and for the briefest moment, I saw him—truly *him*—behind the mask of *Der Erlkönig*, down to the boy he had been. But he blinked, and the mantle was upon him once more.

"And what of you, Elisabeth?" he drawled. "What would *you* do, if you were free?"

I turned my head, eyes stinging. He had returned my question with a particularly vicious volley, and we both knew it.

"We can play this game all you like," he said. "Question for question, answer for answer."

"You can keep your answers to yourself," I replied. "I have no further questions."

"Oh, Elisabeth." His voice was sad. "What happened between us? What happened to you? You were once so passionate and open with me, and now I can barely see the friend I once knew. Why won't you come out and play, Elisabeth? Why?"

He had all the questions, but I had no further answers. We finished our meal without another word between us.

After the goblins had cleared the last of our dishes away, the Goblin King invited me to join him in his retiring room.

A slight tingle of excitement began at the base of my spine at the prospect of being in his private chambers again, and I agreed. I wished I could sort out my feelings for him, my lord and jailer, friend and foe. Part of me yearned to draw him close, while another wanted to keep him at arm's length. The Goblin King offered me his arm and we left the dining hall on a breeze.

When I caught my breath, we were in a beautifully appointed space with two fireplaces, the near wall lined with bookshelves, the far wall lined with enormous silver mirrors that showed snow falling on a winter wood. A klavier stood at the center. A white gown smudged with dirt hung from a rack beside the instrument. I frowned.

"This," I began, but my voice squeaked. I cleared my throat. "This is your retiring room?"

The Goblin King nodded. "Of course, my dear. What do you think of it?"

"But it's—it's the one connected—" I could not finish the sentence.

"The one connected to your bedchamber?" he asked dryly. "But of course; we *are* married, after all."

A flush heated my cheeks. "And then your bedchamber—"

"Is on the other side of this wall." He gestured to the wall on the opposite side from my bedroom. I noted no threshold connecting his quarters to the retiring room. The Goblin King saw me searching and lowered his voice.

"There is no direct path from your bed to mine," he said softly. "And I could remove them even farther from each other, if that is your wish."

My cheeks flared even hotter, but I shook my head. "No, no," I said. "It's fine." I straightened my shoulders and lifted my eyebrow, matching his dry tone as best I could. "After all, we *are* married."

A twitch at the corners of his lips. He conjured two chairs and a reclining couch before one of the fireplaces. "Relax, my dear."

I sat on the reclining couch. Two comely youths crawled from the shadows, one bearing a decanter of brandy, the other a tray with two cut-crystal glasses. I was startled by their appearance, not just because I hadn't seen them in the dark, but because of their humanlike appearance. Most of the goblins I had seen were of Twig and Thistle's ilk: more creature than kin.

One of the attendants presented me with a glass of brandy. I gasped; for the space of a breath, I thought it was Josef beside me.

Then I blinked. The face waiting so very patiently by my side did not belong to my younger brother; the skin was too pale, the cheekbones too angular, the features altogether too pretty. Yet there was something of Josef in this youth's face, in the sensitive tilt of his mouth, the cant of his brows. But the eyes were pure goblin: a flat black that left no room for the whites about the pupils.

The Goblin King gave me a sharp glance. "What is it, my dear?" He saw me staring at his attendants. "Oh, Elisabeth," he said, "surely you've not forgotten my changelings?"

He rested his hand on the youth nearest him, affectionately caressing the boy's face. The attendant's expression betrayed nothing, but when the Goblin King tilted back his head for a kiss, the youth complied with a razor-toothed smile. It was a lascivious, knowing sort of smile. Then I realized he was one of the goblin swains I had met at the goblin ball, one with whom I had played games of bluff.

I took a sip of the brandy to disguise my discomfort. It tasted of summer peaches, of sunshine, of life, and it burned all the way down. I coughed.

The Goblin King studied my face, burning bright and red, and nodded at the changelings. They vanished without a word.

"So," I said, trying to smooth the awkwardness between us, "what shall we do to pass the time?" I couldn't tell if it was the room or the brandy, but I was suddenly warm—too warm.

The Goblin King shrugged. His eyes flitted to the klavier, where it gleamed in the glow of the fire and fairy lights. "It is up to you," he said. "I am at my lady's command."

It felt all so surreal and strange to be sitting with him, in this beautifully appointed room with a glass of brandy in her hand. When Käthe and I pretended to be rich noblewomen, we had played at their airs and graces, their refined and elegant tastes. But when confronted with the reality of it, I was at a loss. At the inn, there was never any time for leisure. After dinner had been served, there were dishes to wash, tables to clean, and floors to sweep and mop. It had always been Mother and me, working our hands to leather while Papa went out with his friends, while Constanze rested in her room upstairs, while Käthe primped and preened, while Josef played.

"What would you do?" I asked.

The Goblin King poured himself a glass of brandy, his silver-white-gold hair falling to cover his expression. "I would play some music."

I held my glass in both hands, as though it could protect me from what I knew he would ask next. He would ask me to play. He would ask to listen to my music.

"All right," I said. He lifted his eyes to meet mine, a knife-slash of a gaze that cut deep. But it was the hope and delight in his face that cut deeper. "Why don't you play a little something on the klavier for me, *mein Herr*?"

The light in his eyes dimmed. "As you wish, my queen."

The Goblin King set down his brandy and walked to the klavier, flipping out the tails of his coat as he sat down on the bench. He ran his fingers lightly over the keys and began to play.

At first I didn't recognize his choice of music. Gradually it revealed itself as a simple children's skipping song, one Käthe and I had sung as we played in the wood. The Goblin King elaborated on the theme in a few variations, and I listened politely, my toe tapping the floor beneath me.

The variations were not particularly inspired, nor his execution on the klavier especially clean. For a man of myth and legend, the Goblin King's playing was astoundingly ordinary. But his touch on the keys was light and nimble, and he had a wonderful sense of rhythm, moving in and out with the rise and fall of the melody.

My fingers twitched, and a hitching sensation clawed its way out of my breast. I wanted to go to him, to suggest a different variation, to sit next to him on the bench and share in the act of creation. I wanted my hands on his, I wanted to guide those long, slim fingers, and I wanted to change the tenor of the music, to push here and draw out there. The Goblin King sensed me watching him, and the faintest blush of pink tinted his cheeks. His fingers slipped on the keyboard.

"Well," he said once he had finished. "I hope that was to your satisfaction, my dear. I have not your gift for improvisation, and my hands are much more accustomed to the feel of strings and a bow beneath them."

"Who taught you to play?" I was trembling, but I was not cold; I was hot. I could feel the heat rising from my cheeks, my throat, my chest.

His only answer was an enigmatic smile. "And now it is your turn, Elisabeth."

From too hot to too cold. A wash of fear drenched me from head to toe in a nervous sweat. "Oh no." I shook my head. "No."

Annoyance began to harden his face. "Come, Elisabeth. Please. I am asking nicely."

"No," I said again, a little more firmly.

The Goblin King sighed, and rose from his seat. "I don't understand," he said. "Why are you so afraid? You were always so fearless, so brazen in your own way when it came to this. You never held anything back when we played together in the Goblin Grove."

The small tremors in my body had grown into bone-shattering shakes. The Goblin King studied me, watching my complexion change from pale to flushed to pale again, and walked over to me. His hands took mine and I let him lead me from the couch to the klavier.

"Come." He sat me down on the bench and set my hands on the keyboard. I snatched them away as though I'd been burned, hiding them in my lap.

"Elisabeth," the Goblin King said. "It's just us."

That was the problem. It wasn't just me. It was me and the Goblin King. I could not play for him. He was not Josef, who was the other half of my soul. He was another person, whole and entire.

I shook my head.

He made a frustrated sound and moved away. "Here," he said, pushing a bundle of white silk at me. "Why don't you play what you were working on before? This—"

The words died in his throat as he spread the fabric before his inquisitive eyes. Too late, I saw it for what it was: my wedding gown with my smudged-ash composition. I leaped to my feet, but he was too quick, or I was too slow, for he read every last bit of me on that dress.

"Hmmm," he said, scanning the marks on the gown, the music I had notated there. "You were angry when you wrote this, weren't you? I can see the rage, the impotence, in your notes." Then he looked up. "Oh, Elisabeth," he breathed. "You wrote this on your—on our wedding night, didn't you?"

I slapped him, hard, across the face. My aim was sure, and he staggered back, hand on cheek.

"How dare you," I said. "How *dare* you?"

"Elisabeth, I—"

"You make me give up my music, force me to sacrifice my last bit of self and sovereignty to you, and you throw it back in my face?" I asked. "You have no right! No right to look at my music like that." I reached to snatch the wedding gown out of his hands, to rip the fabric to shreds, and to throw the pieces into one of the hearths, but he held me back.

"I didn't mean—I mean, I just thought—"

"You thought *what*?" I returned. "That I would be grateful? That you can bring an instrument like this—so beautiful and so perfect—out of nowhere and expect me to be all right with it? I can't—I cannot—" But I did not know what it was I could not do.

"Isn't this what you wanted?" Color slashed his cheekbones. "Isn't this what you wished of me? Your music? Time to compose? Freedom from your responsibilities?" He dropped the gown and stepped closer to me. The Goblin King was slim, but tall, and he towered over me. "I've given you everything you've ever wanted. I'm tired of living up to your expectations."

"And I'm tired," I said. "Of living up to *yours.*" We were so close we could feel the brush of each other's breaths on our lips.

"What have I ever asked of you?" he asked.

Sobs choked my throat. "*Everything,*" I hiccoughed. "My sister. My music. My *life.* All because you wanted a girl who ceased to exist a long time ago. But I'm not that girl, *mein Herr.* I haven't been in a very long time. So what do you want from me?"

Stillness overcame him, the calm in a storm, but I was the rage and wind and the fury. "I told you what I wanted," he said quietly. "You, entire."

I laughed, a high and hectic sound. "Then take me," I said. "Take all of me. It is your right, *mein Herr.*"

The Goblin King sucked in a sharp breath. The fury inside me changed key, minor to major. The sound of his breathing transformed me, and I stepped closer.

"Take me," I insisted. I was not angry anymore. "Take me."

I yearned and I burned. There were scant inches between our flesh, separated only by the thinnest layers of silk brocade and linen. Every bit of my skin leaped and hoped for his touch; I could feel the radiance of his warmth against my skin, the space between just as alive as we were. My trembling hands seemed to lift of their own accord, fingers sliding along the buttons of his waistcoat, burying themselves in the lace cravat at his throat.

"Elisabeth." His voice quivered. "Not yet."

I wanted to tug at the lace at his throat, to pull him to me and crush our lips and our bodies together. But I didn't.

"Not yet?" I asked. "Why?"

I could feel how much he wanted me, wanted this, but still he held back. "Because," he whispered. "I want to savor this." One hand twined itself in my hair. "Before you are gone too soon."

I laughed bitterly. "I'm not going anywhere."

The corner of his lips twisted. "The longer you stay, the sooner you leave."

That damned philosopher again. "What does that mean?" I asked.

"Life," he said softly, "is more than flesh. Your body is a candle, your soul the flame. The longer I burn the candle . . ."

He did not finish.

"A candle unused is nothing but wax and wick," I said. "I would rather light the flame, knowing it will go out, than sit forever in darkness."

We both stood in silence. I waited for him to close the distance between us.

But he didn't. Instead, the Goblin King gently pushed me away.

"I said I wanted you, entire." He pressed a finger against my breast, where my heart beat erratically beneath his touch. "And I will have you, when you truly give your all to me."

Again, that hollow place within me echoed with pain.

"When you finally free that part of you that you so desperately deny," he said, cupping his free hand around the back of my neck, "the part of you I have wanted ever since I first met you, then I *will* have you, Elisabeth." He leaned his head close to mine. "You, entire."

I could feel the feathery strands of his hair against my lips. I turned up my face to meet his, mouth half-open to receive his kiss.

But he did not kiss me. Instead he withdrew, leaving me bereft and empty.

"Only then," he said. "I won't settle for second best. I won't settle for half your heart when I want your whole soul. Only then will I taste your fruit, and savor every last drop until it is gone."

I shuddered with the effort of holding back my tears. His smile was crooked.

"Your soul is beautiful," he said softly. His eyes swept over the wedding gown on the klavier. "And the proof is there. In your music. If you weren't so afraid to share it with me, if you weren't so scared of that part of you, you would have had me long ago."

And then the Goblin King was gone, gone in a swirl of silk, and the faint scent of ice on the breeze.


I sit at the klavier, minutes or hours later, fingering the smudges on the fabric of my wedding gown. The words of the Goblin King echo in my mind's ear—*you, entire; you, entire*—a refrain I cannot shake. It is not my body he demands; it is my music. I am more than the flesh and bones that house my spirit. I want to give him that innermost part of me now, more intimate than any carnal knowledge we could learn together. But I do not know how. It is easier to give him my body than to give him my soul.

I pull a sheet of staff paper toward me and pick up the quill. I dip it into the inkwell, but do not write. I see the marks I made on the night of our wedding, but the notes blur together. This is all so secret, so sacred, and I do not know if I can bear to share it with anyone else. I am my wedding gown—fragile, flimsy, ephemeral—the ash smudges that are my music will fade and disappear with time. And still I cannot bring myself to write.

Tears, along with drops of ink, stain the paper before me, dotting the staff like a measure of eighth notes. Somewhere in the distance, on the other side of the far wall perhaps, a violin begins to play. The Goblin King. I bring my hands to the klavier and follow. Without our bodies to get in the way, our true selves take flight and dance. His is intricate complexity and mystery; mine is unconventional and emotional. Yet somehow we fit, harmonious and complementary, contrapuntal without dissonance. I think I'm beginning to understand.

I dip my quill into the inkwell once again, and join up my teardrops into a song.

# CHANGELING

*iesl!*

Someone called my name, and I struggled against the weight of darkness pressing me into sleep.

*Liesl!*

The voice was familiar—dear—to me, but I could not remember where I had heard it before. When I had heard it. With one great effort, I wrenched my eyes open.

I was in the Goblin Grove. A bright red shape walked toward me and I knew her before I even saw her face. Who else would steal my red cloak?

*Käthe!* I called, but I was voiceless.

My sister scanned the forest, as though she had heard some echo of her name. But her eyes did not settle on me, did not find me standing in front of her.

*Käthe!* I tried again, but I was invisible.

"Liesl." Käthe paced the Goblin Grove. "Liesl, Liesl, Liesl."

My sister chanted my name over and over, a summons or an incantation. With shaking hands, she reached into her satchel and withdrew a sheaf of papers. My heart leaped in my chest. It was the piece of me I had left behind, the composition I called *Der Erlkönig*.

Then Käthe reached into her satchel again, drew out a piece of foolscap and a lead pen. To my surprise, the paper was covered with little figures—hands, eyes, lips, dresses. I had not known my little sister could draw, and draw well.

Resting the foolscap against her knee, Käthe began scribbling furiously. I leaned closer to see what she was sketching—a tree?—but Käthe wasn't drawing; she was writing.

*Dear Josef.*

A letter. She was writing a frantic, hurried, panic-filled letter.

*Liesl is gone. Liesl is gone. Liesl is gone.*

Käthe ignored both her spelling and her penmanship in a rush to get down her words. *Liesl is gon and no one rememburs her name. I am not going mad. I am not. I hav held the pruf of our sister in my hands, and I am riting nao to entrust it into yurs. Pubblish it, Josef. Play it. Play her music. Then rite me bac, rite Mother bac. Tell everyone that Liesl exists. That Liesl lives.*

She did not even bother to sign her name. Then, holding the letter before her like a precious artifact, Käthe took one trembling, hesitant step beyond the Goblin Grove.

A strangled, inarticulate cry ripped through the forest. I jumped back as Käthe tore the foolscap in her hands, violently, angrily. She threw the pieces away and they scattered about her like falling petals. Bits of paper floated toward me, and I reached out to touch one, afraid I would pass through it like mist.

The paper was solid in my hand. I gathered them all, and tried to piece them together; a bit of a hand, the tip of a finger, the corner of a smile, the shine of an eye. I searched for me, for evidence of my existence, but there was nothing. Only blank, empty space where my name used to be.

The world grew dark around me. I covered my face, and wept.


The sound of a violin. My heart thrilled, recognizing its sweet strains, its exquisite emotional clarity.

Josef.

I removed my hands from my face. My brother and François stood before me, playing for an audience. As they finished together—in sync, in unison—the audience leaped to their feet. I could feel the applause but not hear it; I could see the cries of *Encore! Encore!* etched on their lips, but the room was as silent as a tomb.

After a cursory bow, Josef removed himself from the salon with an abruptness that bordered on rudeness. François said something placating to the confused listeners and then hurried after Josef. I followed them into an adjoining chamber, small, private, and intimate. François furiously gestured to the audience outside. The boys argued, François agitated and incensed, my brother curiously laconic and morose. Josef shook his head and said something that stopped the black boy short.

*Liesl.*

I did not hear my name, but I felt it, resonating in the chambers of my heart. Josef repeated my name, and François softened. He went to Josef and gathered my brother up in his arms. He let my brother cry, smoothing away his tears as I might once have done. Then François began to kiss him, but not as I would have done; with passion, with tenderness, with artfulness. I averted my eyes to give them privacy and drifted back outside, where my brother had left his violin, his bow, and his music score open on the stand.

*Für meine Lieben, ein Lied im stil die Bagatelle, auch Der Erlkönig.*

My heart gave a queer jolt, as though someone had reached into my breast and shaken it in their fist. My music. My brother was playing my music, not just for himself, but for the world to hear.

I smiled. I sat down at the klavier and ran my fingers over its shining ivory keys. I began to play a Mozart sonata, one Josef and I had practiced for ages when we were both little. Little by little, with each note I played, sound began to return.

Behind me, I could sense someone pick up the violin and join me in the music. I turned to face him and smiled, my pixie smile.

Sepperl.

He was as beautiful as ever, my baby brother, his golden curls shining in the light of some distant sun, his blue eyes large and bright. His face had lost much of its baby fat already, the angles of his cheekbones and jaw chiseled and sharp. We played together, just as we always had, but there was something different about his playing.

Sepperl's music had always been crystal-clear, a bell-drop of a sound, exact and transcendent. His playing was of another world, a clarity that was almost ruthless in its precision. So, so beautiful. So ethereal. So otherworldly. But as he drew closer, the tenor of his playing changed. It grew warmer, more languid, more mysterious, more . . . human. My fingers faltered on the keyboard.

The music pushed me, prodded me, lifted me up. This was not Josef's voice; it was mine. It was the voice I heard in my head when I composed, the voice I listened to when I was angry or joyful or sad. I squinted into the haze; was it not Sepperl after all? The figure playing the violin resembled my brother, but as he moved closer, I wondered how I could have made that mistake. Golden curls gave way to a silver mane, blue eyes to contrasting gray and green.

The Goblin King.

But was it the Goblin King? Or Josef? They resembled each other, though they looked nothing alike, the way the men in the portrait gallery Underground were individuals, yet were all *Der Erlkönig* at the same time. My hands slipped from the klavier. The violinist drew closer and smiled, pointed teeth and sly lips. His eyes faded from blue to gray and then disappeared altogether into the opaque, solid black of goblin eyes.


I awoke with a gasp. The remnants of a song broke apart, vanishing along with my dream. I was playing with someone—Sepperl? No, someone else. Someone tall and slender, someone who shaped the sounds inside me in a way that was utterly foreign and achingly familiar all at once. An unsettling realization stirred within me, but I did not want to think of it, to bring the revelation into the light and examine it. I chased it away, along with the remnants of sleep.

Despite the blazing fire that roared merrily away in my hearth, I was cold and sheened with sweat. I sat up in my bed, my body aching and trembling, as though I were recovering from a bout of influenza. I was thirsty and hungry, but moreover, I was painfully, desperately homesick. I wanted to call for my mother, have her bring me a mug of warm milk with herbs, wrap myself up in the soothing touch of her work-worn hands. *Mutti, Mutti,* I wanted to sob. *Mutti, I am unwell.*

Back in the world above, Mother and Constanze would have chastised me for lying abed so long. *The sun doesn't rest, and neither do we,* Mother always said. Even on my worst days, the days when my monthly courses pressed down upon my womb with an iron-hot weight, the days when the futility of my existence threatened to suffocate me, I always found the strength to face the next hour, the next task, the next chore. It was easier not to think of the long road ahead, lest I drown in the mire and muck of my mundane life.

Now without purpose, without responsibility, I did not know how to order my unlife. How to arrange my hours into something meaningful, something worthwhile. The thought of the klavier in the next room taunted me; the notes stained onto my wedding gown cried out to be recorded, remembered. *Write it down,* a voice inside me urged. It sounded like the Goblin King. *Write your music down.*

I wanted to. I absolutely wanted to. But a part of me was too raw to even think about looking at the notes I had scrawled on the silk, the rejection, humiliation, and frustration I had laid there. The music I made with Sepperl was safe; my brother had been there to guide me through my errors and correct my mistakes. The bagatelle I had written for him, the piece I had named after the man who inspired the both of us, was also in Josef's more educated, capable hands. But this—the beginnings of this wedding night sonata—was too shameful.

*It is great because it is shameful,* the voice inside me said again. *It is great because it is true.*

I rose from the bed and walked to the retiring room. My weakness did not pass; it grew worse the longer I was awake. I thought about calling for Twig or Thistle, to have them bring me something to eat or drink, but I wanted to be alone. I wanted to cry. I had spent tears of rage, frustration, and sorrow since becoming the Goblin King's bride, but I hadn't allowed myself the indulgence of a good sob. The undignified, broken-hearted, mournful wail of ugly tears. The weight of that unreleased cry pressed down upon my lungs and my heart.

I sat down at the klavier. The cry was there, crawling up the edges of my throat, the corners of my nose and eyes, but it would not free itself. I thought of Mother, of Papa, of Constanze. I thought of Josef, and of Käthe.

Missing Josef was a stab to my heart, sharp, piercing, a grave and mortal wound. Missing Josef was learning to live without a part of myself, like losing a limb or a hand. How did one live without a limb or a hand? You learned to live around it, to absorb its emptiness as a part of yourself.

Missing Käthe was yearning for a summer's day on a winter night. My love for my sister was a constant thing, just as she had been a constant presence in my life, my bedmate since childhood. If Josef was a part of who I was, then Käthe defined me, shaped my borders, filled my negative spaces. She was the sunshine to my darkness, the sweetness to my salty disposition. I knew who I was because I knew who I was not: my sister. Without my sister to define me, I was unsteady, unstable. I had lost the crutch that propped me up.

I could not let them out. I could not let them go. The ghosts of my family were trapped, and I needed someone to turn me inside out, break me apart, rip me open. *Let them out. Let them out. Let them out.* I could not do it alone. I needed to unburden myself, push that pain into someone else, relieve myself of the unbearable weight of grief. I needed someone to pull my grief from me, draw the poison from the wound. I needed someone to carry my pain for me. I needed a friend.

I buried my head in my arms, tears dotting the black and white keys of the klavier, a slow, steady leak that did nothing to relieve the pressure building inside me.

My time in the Underground took on a sort of clockwork of its own: sleep, eat, sleep, wander, sleep, eat, sleep, sit at the klavier, sleep, wander, sleep. I spent much of my time in the abode of the goblins asleep. It seemed a luxury at first, after years of rising before dawn. But in time, not even sleep could pass the time quickly enough. I had my first taste of boredom, and I hated it.

Twig and Thistle suggested a picnic down by the shores of the Underground lake. We watched the Lorelei emerge and disappear beneath the surface as a group of changelings played on the far side. Unbidden, the memory of Josef's face with goblin eyes returned to me. I frowned.

"What are the changelings?" I asked.

Thistle gave me a sharp look. "Why do you ask, mortal?"

I could have punished her for not addressing me properly— I was Her Highness—but Thistle, like Constanze, called me whatever she wanted.

"I'm just curious," I said. "Are they—are they children? Of the Goblin King?"

Twig and Thistle laughed, their high-pitched cackles

splintering and echoing on the shores of the Underground lake.

"Children?" Thistle sneered. "No. No union of mortal and *Der Erlkönig* has ever been fruitful."

"Actually—" Twig began, but the other goblin girl cut her off.

"The changelings are nothing, poor fools," Thistle said. "Neither fish nor fowl, human nor goblin."

"How can that be?" I watched the changelings on the far side skipping rocks, sending luminescent ripples across the surface. In the shifting, mercurial light of the grotto, they seemed more like a ragtag bunch of children than the elegant creatures with whom I had danced at the Goblin Ball. There was an innocence as well as an agelessness about them. They could have been fifteen. They could have been five hundred. "If they aren't the children of humans and goblins, then what are they?"

"They are," Twig said quietly, "the product of a wish."

Silence louder than a bell gong rang throughout the grotto. Thistle gave Twig a dark look.

"A wish?" An image returned to me, half-remembered and mostly forgotten: the sound of my baby brother's crying in the room down the hall, a plea to save his life.

One of the changelings, a comely young female, sidled toward me.

"What did we tell you before, Your Highness?" Twig said. "Whatever the old laws giveth, they also taketh."

I nodded.

"Say you are a young girl," Twig began. "And the black death is sweeping through the world above, taking with it every man, woman, and child it comes across. You watch your father sicken and die, you watch your mother swell up and bloat, you watch your little brother grow thin and fade away into a wisp. You bury them all, one by one, into the frozen ground and wonder where they have gone. To Heaven? Or someplace worse? So you make a wish—a wish, not a prayer—that you will never suffer their fate. That you can hide where not even the hand of Death can find you."

The changeling near me reached out her hand and I took it. She was a sickly little thing, with pointed ears and teeth.

"Careful," Thistle said. "They bite."

At my touch, the changeling's entire countenance brightened; the paleness of her cheek no longer pallid, the painful thinness of her body a languid slenderness. The pinched expression on her face smoothed into one of hunger. The changeling breathed deep, and the world around me grew just a little bit darker. I snatched back my hand. Thistle snickered.

"Say also," Twig continued, "you are a young man. You are the younger of a beautiful pair of siblings renowned throughout the village for your beauty. Your mother was a beauty in the generation ahead of you, but time has not been as kind to her. She dresses in fashions much younger than are appropriate, cakes her face in powder and rouge. Your older sister is happily married to a wonderful man, until one day, she is stricken with smallpox, leaving her face scarred and her beauty marred forever. So you stare into the mirror and make a wish: to remain young and beautiful for all time."

"How sad," I murmured. Trapped and tormented by your own wishes. I knew intimately how that felt; I was often strangled by the tyranny of my desires.

"Oh, you of the tender heart," Thistle sneered. "Don't waste your pity on them; they brought it on themselves, as all you mortals do."

"Can they walk the world above?"

"No," said Twig.

"Then how . . ." The rest of the question died in my throat, choking on my brother's name.

Thistle sniggered, but Twig stared at me with her blank, black eyes. I could read nothing in them, but she heard the unspoken question on my tongue. "The wishes they made were selfish," she said simply. "Yours was selfless."

I did not want to dwell on this uncomfortable thought further. A restlessness overcame me and I rose to my feet. "Let's go."

"Go where, Your Highness?" Twig asked.

"Somewhere," I muttered. "Anywhere."

I wanted to crawl out of my skin. Boredom and futility pressed on me, and I wanted to rip, shred, tear, scream. But the scream was bottled within me, and I could not let it out. I could not let it out. I could not let it out.

"Mmmm." I recoiled when I noticed Thistle's face hovering over my shoulder. She had climbed up the stone wall of the grotto and was poised over me, breathing deeply as though inhaling the scent of some delicious perfume. "Such strong emotions," she purred. "Such fire. It's so warm."

"Get away from me." I shoved her away, and she tumbled down the rock wall to Twig's crackling laughter.

Twig's laugh caught the attention of the changelings, who left off their rock-skipping games and slid toward me, silent and smooth. They had the form and feature of young men and women, but they moved with a sinuous grace that was not of the world above.

As they drew closer, the changelings brightened. Their faces shone with vivid expressions; their movements became more animated and less preternatural. I reached for them.

Their features—both familiar and foreign—reminded me of my own human ones. I longed for them. I longed to be among them like they were kin.

One of the changelings, a young man—a youth—took my hand in his. He nuzzled his face into my palm. My heart softened and I wanted to hold this changeling. I yearned to draw comfort from his presence, the way I would have turned to Käthe or Josef. The changeling even looked a little like Josef: the same high cheekbones and sharp chin, the same heart-shaped face.

He snapped at my fingers.

"Ouch!" I cried. The changeling had managed to draw blood.

"Didn't I say they bite?" Thistle giggled cruelly.

The changelings took up her laughter. It sounded like one laugh, broken into a myriad pieces, echoing against each other into a cacophony of mocking jeers. The changeling licked my blood off his hands.

Long, spindly fingers wrapped themselves around my ankles like brambles in a hedge. Twig. A sickening expression crossed her face, half of hunger and half of pity. *No, I* thought. *No. Not Twig. Not her too.*

Goblin and changeling lurched closer, the scent of my blood drawing them to me like moths to the flame. The intensity of my emotions, my mortal life, sustained them. Fed them. Fueled them. I kicked out, trying to shake them off, but they clung tighter than burrs.

"Stop," I said. "Please, stop!"

But they were gone, their black eyes blank in a haze of hunger. I wrenched Thistle's fingers off the skirt of my dress, pried myself from Twig's grip, but they were relentless. Skittering from the shadows came other goblins, the flickering waves of my fear drawing them out of the darkness.

*This is it*, I thought. *This is how I die. Unremembered, unsung, torn apart by ravenous hands.*

A blast of anger returned strength to my limbs. Beyond the edges of panic and fear, there was clarity. There was sharpness. This would not be how I died. If I were to die, it would not be in this ignominious way. If I were to die, *I* would choose how. Was I not the Goblin Queen? My subjects were bound by *my* desire, by *my* wishes.

"Enough."

My word was my command. They froze, bound by my will and the wish I hadn't needed to speak aloud. Not anymore. I pushed them all away, and they toppled over where they stood. I stepped on their fingers out of spite, hearing the bones snap like twigs underfoot. They flinched with pain, and I relished the agony on their faces. I wanted them to fear me, to be afraid to trespass upon my person.

It wasn't just the goblins. It was everyone. The Goblin King. Master Antonius. Papa's condescension. Hans's bored expression whenever I left him to practice on the klavier. The incredulous looks on the villagers' faces when they remembered that I, too, had talent. I even wanted to rise above Josef's shadow on my music. I wanted to bend the entire world—both above and below—to what *I* needed. For once. Just once.

Just once.

*Light my flame*, mein Herr, I thought. *Light my fire, and watch me burn.*

## MERCY

"You are not attending, my dear," the Goblin King said from the klavier.

I looked up from my glass of wine, the stem of which I had been listlessly twirling between my fingers for the past several minutes. An open book sat on my lap, but I had not read a single word in the past hour.

"Hmmm?" I quickly turned the pages. "I am."

The Goblin King raised a brow. "I've stump-fingered my way through three pieces and you've not said anything about the notes."

I coughed to hide the blush creeping up my neck.

Since that first, disastrous evening after dinner, our time together had taken on a comfortable, almost comforting routine. Sometimes we would pass the time by reading aloud to each other. I preferred poetry, but the Goblin King—unsurprisingly—preferred his philosophers. He read Latin, Greek, Italian, French, and German, and spoke a dozen other languages as well. He was astonishingly well learned; he might have been a scholar in the world above.

On other occasions, the Goblin King would play some short pieces on the klavier while I read by the fire. Those were my favorite evenings, when music, not words, filled the silence between us. Tonight my husband played a few Scarlatti *sonatinen* while I took up a volume of Italian poetry. I did not read Italian, and only understood as much as I needed to know how quickly, how slowly, or how elegantly I ought to play a piece of music. The book was for show; it allowed me to watch the Goblin King from beneath lowered lashes under the pretense of reading.

After that first evening, he never invited me to play my music for him again.

In the beginning, it had been a relief. But as the evenings wore on, the relief turned into guilt, then annoyance, then anger. He was so maddeningly, infuriatingly complacent. He was so assured I would come to him of my own volition, that I would break and lay my music at his feet like a gift, that he could afford to watch me from the klavier with that distant, compassionate look on his face.

But he was wrong. I was already broken, and the music was still trapped inside. It prickled, tickled, and itched in my gut, threatening to claw out of my throat in a scream.

"Is everything all right, Elisabeth?"

No, everything was not all right. It had not been all right since I became *Der Erlkönig*'s bride, since he stole my sister away, since he gave me that flute in the marketplace, since before I could remember. It had not been all right since I locked my music away, both in my box and in my heart.

But I could not tell him so. "I'm fine," I said instead.

His gaze sharpened, the pupils of his eyes dilating to drown the gray and green in black. The Goblin King knew how to interpret my breaths before pauses, the lengths of my measures of rest, my caesuras of speech. He followed my cues as attentively as a musician in an orchestra, waiting for the maestro to take the lead. And he knew whenever I broke tempo.

His eyes swept me from head to toe, lingering on my exposed shoulders and arms, the expanse of my collarbones and décolletage. "What's the matter?"

I suppose I had not been particularly subtle. For the first time, I had taken care with my appearance; after the encounter by the Underground lake, I had forced Twig and Thistle to take me to the tailor to stitch me a new gown. To stitch me some armor. I had had the tailor modify a gown made of a beautiful cream and gold silk taffeta. It was fashioned like a chemise, the skirt gathered beneath what little bosom I had before flowing out behind me in a train. The entire construction was held together by diaphanous straps at my shoulders, leaving my arms bare. Diamonds were craftily sewn into the bodice—hundreds, thousands, a myriad—twinkling like stars in a night sky. Twig and Thistle arranged my hair into a coronet of braids about my head, fitted with more little diamonds that sparkled brightly against my dark locks. For the first time, I found myself hoping the Goblin King would find me pretty.

It seemed ridiculous; I was plain and he was gorgeous, but the desire that throbbed between us was real and had nothing to do with beauty or the lack thereof. And it was there, always there, smothering me, strangling me, until I could not breathe for wanting.

So I answered the Goblin King's question the only way I could. "Do you not like my new dress?" I blurted out.

That certainly surprised him. "I—uh—*what*?"

"My dress," I said. "Is it not to your liking?"

His eyes were both bewildered and wary. "It is lovely, Elisabeth."

"And me? Am I lovely?"

The Goblin King frowned. "You *are* in a mood tonight, my dear."

He had not answered me. Suddenly I could not bear to remain seated. I rose to my feet and paced back and forth before the fire. I *was* in a mood—for a fight.

"Answer me," I said. "Do you think me lovely?"

"Not with the way you're acting at the moment."

I laughed, a nigh hysterical sound. "You sound like my father. It's a simple question, *mein Herr*."

"Is it?" The Goblin King gave me a sharp look. "Then tell me, my dear, what would you like to hear? The simple answer, or the honest one?"

I trembled, although whether it was from hurt or fear, I did not know. "The truth," I said. "You're the one who showed me that the ugly truth is preferable to a pretty lie."

It was a while before he spoke. "I think you know the answer, Elisabeth," he said in a low voice.

I closed my eyes to stop the tears. Despite everything, I had hoped it would be different. That his desire could somehow make me lovely, could transform me from a sparrow into a peacock.

"Then *why*?" My voice tripped over the jagged edges of my sorrow. "*Why* do you want me?"

"I've answered this before, Elisabeth, I—"

"Yes, yes, I've heard it all before. You loved the music in me. My soul is a beautiful thing. Once I give you myself, entire, you'll—" I hiccoughed. "You'll give yourself, entire."

The Goblin King said nothing, only watched me with his mismatched gaze.

"But that means nothing to me, *mein Herr*. Your words mean nothing to a queer, unlovely little girl."

There was a scrape across the floor as the Goblin King pushed back the bench to get to his feet. His treads were light and nearly soundless, a wolf's in the snow. Yet I could sense him cross the space between us. He placed a hand upon my brow.

"Loveliness of the spirit is worth more than loveliness of the flesh," he said gently. "You know that."

I opened my eyes and slapped his hand away. I felt the shock of that slap reverberate through both our bodies, from his startled expression to the stinging of my palm.

"Now that," I said, "was a pretty lie."

For a moment, I thought the Goblin King would try to console me, soothe me the way a parent would placate a cranky child. Then a spark lit his eyes, a glint of malice. His mouth twisted, and the sharp tips of his teeth gleamed in the firelight.

"You want the ugly truth, Elisabeth?" he said. "Very well then, you shall have it." He paced the floor before me, a wild creature pacing its cage. A wolf prowled in his heart, and it wanted very badly to be free. "I wanted you because you are queer and strange and unlovely. Because a man could spend an age—and believe me, I have—with an endless line of beautiful brides, their names and faces blurring before him. Because you—queer, unlovely you—I would remember."

The Goblin King smiled at me by way of a snarl. My pulse quickened in response, and deep within me, the knots I had tightened about my heart began to loosen. My blood rose to meet his and I stood from my chair, breathing hard.

But he turned away before I could touch him, before his wildness could mingle with mine. I let my hand drop.

"What is eternal life but a prolonged death?" the Goblin King asked. "I live in tedium unending, dying just a little more each day, unable to truly *feel*." He walked back to the klavier and ran his hand lightly over the keyboard.

I had no response. We were as far from each other as we could be in that moment; he on one end of forever, me on the other.

"Your intensity, your ferocity," he said quietly. "I crave it, Elisabeth. I do."

He sat down on the bench and pressed a key, then another, and another. Each note resounded in my breast, echoing in that hollow, hallowed place where my music lived.

"I would give anything to feel again." His voice was low, so low I could scarcely hear it. "And for a long time, I thought I never would. Then I heard you play your music for me back in the Goblin Grove. For the first time in an eternity, I hoped—I thought—"

Another silence fell over us, thick with secrets and things unsaid. I could taste the questions at the back of my tongue, but swallowed them down.

"Your music," he said at last. "Your music was the only thing that kept me sane, that kept me *human* instead of a monster."

A breeze raised goose pimples along my arms and down my back. The Goblin King did not look at me as he continued to play, stringing notes together like beads on a necklace.

"And that," he said, "is the ugly truth, my dear. I could have your hand in marriage, your mind, your body, but what I truly want, I cannot have." He turned his head away. "Not unless I break you."

Not unless he broke me.

It wasn't until this moment that I understood.

"I am not afraid of you," I said quietly.

"Oh?" The Goblin King lifted his head. "I am the Lord of Mischief, the Ruler Underground," he said, mismatched eyes glinting. "I am wildness and madness made flesh. You're just a girl"—he smiled, and the tips of his teeth were sharp—"and I am the wolf in the woods."

*Just a girl.* Just a maiden. But I wasn't just a girl; I was the Goblin Queen. I was *his* Goblin Queen, and I wasn't afraid of the wolf, that untamable wildness that could tear me limb from limb and bathe itself in my blood.

I walked toward the klavier and sat down on the bench beside him. The Goblin King's eyes flashed with surprise, pleasure, and not a little wariness.

"I may be just a maiden, *mein Herr*," I whispered. "But I am a brave maiden."

I raised my shaking fingers to the keyboard and formed a chord. C major. I felt the Goblin King's body bend in a long sigh.

"Yes, Elisabeth," he breathed, lifting his hand to cup my cheek. "Yes."

But I did not play. Instead I brought my right hand up to cover his, then pushed it down to rest against the column of my neck.

"Elisabeth, what—"

He tried to pull away, but I had him in my grip. I leaned into him, daring him, tempting him, to push against where

my life fluttered beneath his thumb. I could sense the wolf shaking in him, chafing at his bonds. I wanted the wolf; I wanted his hunger, a ravenous desire that could obliterate me. I wanted to be obliterated. I wanted to be made anew.

"You are," I said, "the monster I claim."

He was trembling now. "You do not know what you ask." Panic touched his words, even as savagery played across his features.

"Oh, but I do."

A memory rose to the surface: little Liesl waiting patiently on the landing at the top of the stairs. Waiting for her Papa to return from an audition with a famous impresario. Sepperl was only three years old then, already showing incredible promise on the violin, and Liesl was eager to show her father just what she could do. She had diligently practiced a Tomasino chaconne on the quarter-sized violin until it was perfect. But when Papa came home, he came home stinking of ale, his Stainer violin missing from its case. Liesl played for him as he entered the inn, a triumphant piece of welcome, but he snatched away the violin and snapped it in half over his leg. *You will never amount to anything,* he said. *You are half the talent your brother is.*

"I could hurt you," the Goblin King said, and I felt that promise in his hands. My lifeblood in his grip, my throat bared to him in submission.

"I know."

Another memory, bubbling up from beneath the pain of the previous one. Josef playing a piece I had written, Papa coming into the back room to praise his son for his efforts. *So wild, so untamed!* Papa had said. *We must get this published, my boy; you have the potential to change music as we know it!* Josef demurring, telling our father that the true

author of the piece was me. Papa's face hardening. *A decent effort. But you must be less lofty in your ideals, Liesl. You must grow up and stop indulging in these romantic flights of fancy.*

"Then why, Elisabeth?" the Goblin King murmured. "Why?"

Ten years ago. Ten years ago, when I was nine, and composing alone, and in secret. I had stolen two candles we could ill afford and was up until the wee hours of the morning, profligate with my music, my papers, my flames. And Papa, Papa asleep in bed with Mother, a rare occurrence that was sure to leave Mother smiling and Papa generous. The world was asleep, and I was alone.

Until Josef found me. *Liesl?* he'd asked in his sleepy baby's voice. *Liesl, why are you awake?*

Anger, anger and jealousy, flaring as quick as lightning. My hand twitching, knocking a candle over, sending burning wax everywhere.

It hit Josef in the face.

His cries waking the house, Papa shouting, Mother crying, Käthe trembling, Constanze hiding, and all around me, fire. My work, in flames. A hand cracking upon my cheek, leaving a mark redder than the burn on Josef's skin. His would fade into nothing. Mine would disappear too, disappear along with three years of careful work, all gone in flames and ash.

And beneath that memory, yet another. And another, and another. Assaults on my tender heart I had suffered until I learned to put my music away in a cage. I had pushed me, the real me, back behind the façade of a good girl, a dutiful daughter. I ceased to be me and became Liesl, the maiden in the shadows. I had been that Liesl for so long, I did not know my way back to the light.

"Because," I choked out, "I need you to break me in order to find me."

I rested my left hand against the klavier. The Goblin King sucked in a sharp breath.

"You do not know what you ask."

I looked into his eyes and pressed a key.

"I do."

The note hung in the air between us as his pupils expanded, then contracted. Those mismatched eyes shifted from frightened to feral and back again as *Der Erlkönig* warred with his better nature.

"You don't."

I pressed another key. "I do."

A long, shuddering sigh escaped him. His hands moved to my shoulders, fingers clenching and unclenching, as though he did not know whether to draw me close or push me away. I pressed yet another key, then another, and then another, calling the wolf from hiding.

"I want you to find me," I whispered. "Every last bit of me."

The Goblin King drew away. Our eyes met, and in that moment I saw not the wolf, but the austere young man.

"Elisabeth," he said. "Have mercy on me."

My eyes were steady upon his face. "I am not afraid of you."

"No?" The Goblin King closed his eyes. "Then you are a fool."

And when he opened his eyes again, the austere young man was gone.

Our lips meet in a clash of teeth and tongue. The retiring room falls away, and we fall together, the Goblin King and I.

We land on a soft bed of leaves that crackle and rustle with every twitch of our limbs, every sigh of our bodies, and the world around us is dark, secret, safe.

His hands hold my face, drawing me in as though he could drink in my breath, my blood, my life. He is certain and sure; I am artless and awkward. My hands clutch at his back, pressing him close, wanting to feel every bit of him against me like a second skin. The diamonds sewn into the bodice of my gown bite into me, and I itch and I sting and I burn.

*You do not know what you ask,* he murmurs over and over again into my mouth. *You cannot know.*

I do not know but I want to learn. I want him to push me to my limits, to find my edges, then call me back. *Find my edges,* I plead, *then obliterate them.*

I tear at the fine lace at his throat, find the buttons and seams of his shirt with my fingers. His skin is cool as I pull at his clothes, and the thrill of this touch, this contact, sends shivers through me. I scrabble and claw at my dress, wanting to shuck my finery the way a snake sheds its old self, leaving behind nothing but the impression of the body that once inhabited it. I want to be naked and new, to experience his touch afresh.

*Stop,* he says, but I don't stop. I don't know how to stop. I'm afraid if I stop, I will never start again. So I keep going, trying to work my arms free of my gown.

*Elisabeth.* The Goblin King pins my wandering hands beneath his forearm, the weight of his body heavy against me. But it's not the feel of him pressing me into the bed that brings my breath short; it's the look in his eyes. I see the austere young man, and suddenly I am embarrassed of my eagerness, my willingness to make myself a fool.

I turn my gaze away, cheeks burning. The hand that reaches up to touch my face is cool, and the Goblin King is gentle.

*Look at me.*

But I can't.

*Elisabeth.*

I look, and the austere young man is still there, waiting for me to follow him into the woods. I am no longer ashamed of my wanting, and I tilt my head to kiss him. He warms to my breath and I follow him as we grow wilder and wilder. We stop for breath and now there is a hint of the devil in his angelic face. The wolf has come out to play.

And then we are grasping at each other, gasping, grabbing. We hold each other close, but it's not close enough, it will never be close enough. Our hands map the hills and valleys of our bodies, exploring, discovering. The fingers of his hand run up my thigh and I gasp, tangling my hands in his thistledown hair.

Time stops. He stops. I stop. We look at each other, a question in his gaze, a reply on my tongue. But we do not speak, and the moment is frozen within my heart—this ask and this answer.

"I wish . . ." I say hoarsely, but I don't know what it is I'm wishing for.

"Your wish is my command," the Goblin King says softly.

I could stop. We could stop. I could fold myself back into the small spaces of my heart, where my music and magic lie hidden, secret and safe.

"You don't . . ." His words trail away, and the rest of his sentence hangs unspoken between us. *You don't have to.*

A choice. He gives a choice, and it is the truest gift he has ever given me.

"Yes." My voice is clear. "My answer is yes."

He presses against me, lost in the wilderness, and the side of his arm catches against my throat. I cough, but the Goblin King does not hear. My gasps are strangled and tears start in my eyes. Fullness. There is fullness.

It hurts. I hurt. *I wish* lingers on the tip of my tongue, but I swallow it back. I don't want him to stop. He's found my edges. I have found my limits. But beyond the border of pain, there is something else.

Freedom.

I start to cry in earnest, a rush, a torrent of emotion, of beauty, of shame. My mind goes blank and I am nothing but my body. Liesl is gone, and I am reduced to my elemental parts: music, magic, imagination, and inspiration. The sensation is frightening in its intensity, and I call out a name, wanting the Goblin King to anchor me back to myself.

His head snaps up and our eyes meet. His eyes, glassy and dark and opaque, grow clear as the wolf retreats and the austere young man returns. But when he does, his gaze falls on the tears staining my cheeks, and he jerks away.

*No, don't go,* I want to say, but I can't speak. *I'm here, I'm here. I'm here at last.*

"Oh no," he says. "Oh no no no." He retreats, hiding his face in his hands.

The Goblin King curls up at the corner of the bed, his back turned to me. As my wits return one by one, I realize we are in the Goblin King's bedchamber. I crawl toward him, heedless of the shredded remains of my dress, and wrap my arms around him.

"I am," he whispers, "the monster I warned you against."

"You are," I say hoarsely, "the monster I claim."

"I don't deserve your mercy, Elisabeth."

We lie there in silence, the rise and fall of our breaths our only movement.

"No," I say at last. "Not my mercy, but my gratitude."

The Goblin King laughs, a choked, almost hopeful sound. He turns to hold me close. "Oh, Elisabeth," he says. "You are a saint."

But I am not a saint. I open my mouth to protest, but the salt of his tears stains my lips, startling me into silence. I listen to the beat of the Goblin King's heart slow and fade into sleep and whisper to myself the truth he does not hear.

I am not a saint; I am a sinner. I want to sin again and again and again.

# ROMANCE IN
# C MAJOR

light shone down upon me. I opened my eyes, and for a moment I was lost, unsure of where I was. I shaded my hand; a mirror—a silver-backed mirror—hung above the Goblin King's bed, showing me a scene of an unfamiliar town.

The town was small, sitting beneath a tall peak I did not recognize. Perched atop the summit was an abbey, the cloisters overlooking the town, a priest looking down his nose at the penitent masses. My mirror showed me the Goblin Grove, my sacred space. I wondered if this was the Goblin King's.

The sun was high overhead in the world above. My husband slept soundly beside me, his breathing soft and even. We had fallen asleep resting against each other, but during the night we had drifted apart, founding our separate kingdoms on opposite sides of his bed. Our borders were delineated by a pile of bedclothes. We had touched each other in the most intimate ways possible, but neither of us could bear the other's closeness. Not yet.

There was nothing visible of the Goblin King but a mess of tangled hair and a bare shoulder peeking out from beneath the blankets. I was naked, I was sore, and between my thighs was a mess of blood. I suddenly wanted nothing more than to be away from here, back in my own chambers, clean and alone. The memory of what we had done the night before returned to me, and a pleasant burn spread through my loins. But with the pleasure came a wash of pain. I needed to be alone, recollect my thoughts, and center myself.

Slowly, carefully, I slid out of bed and began to clean myself up. The Goblin King did not stir, lost to the waking world. He slept blissfully, like a babe after a long night of crying, and I remembered the feel of his tears against my skin. I couldn't face him, not after he had shed those tears and stained my soul. I had touched him, known him, seen every last bit of him, and it was his tears that brought me shame.

"I wish I were back in the retiring room," I said softly to the waiting air.

And there I was, back beside the klavier in the retiring room. My legs wobbled, bringing me crashing to my knees. Distantly, I registered the pain, but everything was muted, muffled.

My wedding night. My true wedding night.

The world was changed somehow. I was changed. The Goblin King had walked into the tidy room of my life and upended its contents. I was left picking up the pieces, struggling to fit them back together into some semblance of what I had known before. My life was divided into two neat and perfect halves: Before and After.

Liesl. Elisabeth. I had been Liesl until the moment we gathered each other in our arms, when I granted the Goblin King mercy as he absolved me of my shame. I had emerged from the other side of our tryst a different woman: no longer Liesl, but Elisabeth. I tested the edges of this new identity, slipping it on, seeing how it fit.

The retiring room looked different by the light of day. The large mirrors hung on one side lent the illusion of enormous windows, sunshine from the world above streaming through them. I saw a fortress on a hill high above a river, a bright red-and-white flag fluttering in the breeze. *Salzburg.* Snow still piled in drifts, but along the Salzach River, the palest hint of green shimmered among the trees. The first hint of spring. I smiled.

I sat at the klavier, hands poised over the keyboard. Then I paused. A great weight had been lifted from me, my soul cleared of a corrupting shame. But the freedom frightened me, and I did not know how to proceed. So I played a few chords, inversions of major C, before expanding them out into arpeggios. Safe. Sure.

From inversions and arpeggios to scales. I ran through every key, falling into the mindless movement like a meditation. Like a prayer. My mind began to reorder itself, to fold its memories and thoughts back into their proper drawers, neat and tidy and clean. Once my fingers were sufficiently limbered up, I took my wedding gown from its rack beside the instrument and laid it across the hood of the klavier. I was ready to move forward at last.

No more halfhearted noodling. No more careless scribbling. I would take my music, rough and unpolished, and turn it into something worthwhile.

I set to composing.

Picking up a quill and dipping it in ink, I marked down the basic melody as swiftly as I could onto a fresh sheet of paper. I also added the notes I had made about ideas for supporting accompaniment, time signatures, et al. Once I was certain I had collected all my thoughts from my wedding gown, I let it fall to the floor. The dress had served its purpose.

I did not know about Haydn or Mozart or Gluck or Handel or any of the other composers whose names I had studied, whose pieces I had played as a child, but music did not flow from my mind like dictation from God. It was said Mozart never made fair copies of his work, that no foul papers existed, for it was all perfect from his mind to the page.

Not so for Maria Elisabeth Ingeborg Vogler. Each note, each phrase, each chord was an agony of labor, to be revised again and again. I relied on the klavier to tell me which note I wanted, to figure out which inversion I needed. I was not Josef, to have this store of knowledge readily accessible; I had to test and sound out everything I heard in my head.

I loved it. This work was mine, and mine alone.

Ink spattered my fingers and the keys of the klavier, but I was oblivious to everything, even the scratch of the quill against paper. I heard only the music in my mind. For once there was nothing of Josef, nothing of Papa, nothing of the sour voice within that sounded like judgment, like fear. There was nothing but this, nothing but music and me, me, me.

There was another presence in the room.

I had been working for nearly an hour or so, but it was

only in the past few minutes that I had noticed another person in the retiring room with me. His presence slowly seeped into my consciousness, emerging from the depths of my thoughts like a dream. I had been unable to untangle my sense of self from my sense of the Goblin King. I lifted my head.

The Goblin King stood on the threshold between his bedchamber and the retiring room. The path between his room and mine was now connected. He was simply dressed, looking less like a sovereign than a shepherd boy. If he had had a hat, he would have wrung it in his fingers sheepishly. He hovered in the in-between spaces, awaiting my permission to enter. I could not make out the expression on his face.

He cleared his throat. "Are you—are you all right, my queen?"

So distant. So formal. He always called me *my dear,* said in that sarcastic tone of his, or else it was Elisabeth, always Elisabeth. He was the only one who called me that, and I wanted to be Elisabeth for him again.

"I am fine, thank you, *mein Herr.*" I matched his distance with my own. The chasm between us grew to twice its size. I ached to bridge it, but did not know how. We had been connected in ways so much more intimate than this. How much more could you bare of yourself when you'd already given everything?

He looked away as soon as my eyes met his. A queer feeling overcame me when I realized I had caught my husband in a moment of unguarded admiration. Admiration. Of me. I felt as though he had walked in on me undressed. Yet he *had* seen me undressed. My mind, tidied into its proper spaces, fell back into disarray.

"How long have you been there?" I asked.

The words came out like an accusation. The Goblin King stiffened.

"Long enough," was all he said. "Do you mind?"

Liesl would have minded.

"No," I said. "I don't mind. Please, sit."

He gave me a grave nod and the slightest sliver of a smile. As ever, the tips of his pointed teeth poked through that smile, but it wasn't as threatening as before. He walked to the chaise longue and sat down, leaning back and closing his eyes as I continued to muddle through the piece.

This was intimacy of an entirely different sort. He was inside me, part of me, in the spirit as well as the flesh. At first I thought I was merely giving him a glimpse into my mind, but before long I realized the Goblin King was already in my head. He offered a suggestion here, a revision there, all so deftly and subtly that his voice became mine. With Josef, composing had been something I gave him, something he took and shaped into the finished product. But with the Goblin King, music was something we molded together, just as we had done when I was a child.

I remembered now. All my memories of him came flooding back, ripped from the tide gates by my release. Sweeping away the cobwebs of shame and disappointment, our friendship shone shiny and new. We had danced together in the Goblin Grove, had sung together, had made music together. After I finished a piece, I would rush into the forest to meet the Goblin King. To share my music with him. As I had until my father told me to grow up.

*I'm so sorry,* I thought. *I'm so sorry I betrayed you.*

My hands shook on the klavier. The Goblin King opened his eyes.

"Is everything all right?"

I smiled at him, really, truly smiled at him. Warmth filled me, a soft, tickling sensation. It was a long moment before I recognized the emotion for what it was: happiness. I was happy. I could not remember the last time I had been *happy*.

"What?" He was suddenly bashful.

"Nothing," I said, but my smile grew broader.

"It's never nothing with you." But he smiled too, and its sweetness hurt. He looked years younger with that smile. He was entirely that soft-eyed young man now, no trace of *Der Erlkönig* in his face.

"Sometimes," I said, shaking my head, "I wish you didn't know me so well."

He laughed. There were no sharp edges to him anymore. The mood changed between us, growing heavier, weightier. We continued working in silence, but thoughts and feelings flowed between us without words, the push and pull, ebb and flow of the music gently rocking us with its sound.

Our conversation wound to a close as I finished working through the theme.

"Beautiful," the Goblin King murmured. "Transcendent. It—it's bigger than Heaven and the world above. Just like you."

Roses bloomed in my cheeks, and I averted my head so he would not see.

"You could change the course of music," he said. "You could change the world above if you—"

He did not finish his sentence. If I—what? Published my music? Managed to get past the barriers of my name, my sex, my death? My final fate hung between us, an invisible but insurmountable obstacle. I would not change the course of music. I would die here, unheard and unremembered. I tasted the unfairness at the back of my throat, bitterness and bile.

"If the world above were ready for me, perhaps," I said lightly. "But I fear I am too much for them—and not enough."

"You, my dear," the Goblin King said, "are more than enough."

The compliment from another's lips would have sounded coy, flirtatious, even arch. A pretty sentiment designed to flatter and then bed me. I had heard such blandishments from guests in our inn, directed even to one as plain as me. Yet I did not think the Goblin King intended to flatter; on his lips, the words sounded like unvarnished truth. I was more than enough. More than my limitations, more than adequate, simply *more*.

"Thank you." If I had been Käthe, I would have deflected the compliment with a coquettish wink or a snide remark. But I was not Käthe; I was plain, blunt, and forthright Liesl. No. Elisabeth. Plain, earnest, straightforward, and talented Elisabeth. I took his words for the gift they were, and for the first time, accepted them without pain.

After a long while—hours? minutes?—the first movement of what I was beginning to call the Wedding Night Sonata was done. Despite the anger and rage in its notes, the key was C major. The shape of the first movement was there now, with most of its supporting structure fleshed out. I played it on the klavier to hear it in full, but I could not adequately convey both the main part and the accompaniment with just two hands.

Instinctively, I reached for Josef. But my brother was not there.

A sharp pain stabbed me in the heart, as though someone had taken a dagger and plunged it into my breast. I gasped and pressed my hand there to stanch the wound. I was certain my hand would come away with blood. But there was nothing there.

"Elisabeth!" The Goblin King rushed to my side.

It was a moment before I could recover enough breath to speak.

"I'm fine," I said. "I'm fine." I shook off his solicitous hands and gave him a wobbly smile. "Just a fit. It will pass."

His face was unreadable, opaque, as inscrutable as any one of his goblin subjects. "Perhaps you should rest."

I shook my head. "No. Not yet. I need to hear this in its entirety. As a whole. It's just," I said with a wry smile, "I lack another pair of hands."

His expression softened. "Perhaps I—perhaps I can assist you. With your music."

I stared at him. The Goblin King turned away.

"Never mind," he said hastily. "Just a thought. Forget it; I didn't mean to offend you—"

"Yes."

He stopped and lifted his head, looking straight into my eyes.

"Yes, you may," I corrected. "Please," I said, when I saw the uncertainty in his face. "I would like to hear this piece played on a violin."

We held each other's gazes for a beat longer. Then he blinked.

"Your wish is my command, Elisabeth." He smiled. "I always did say you had power over me."

Elisabeth. I was Elisabeth again, and the way he said my name sent a throb of longing through me.

"As you wish, Elisabeth," he said again, softer now. "As you wish."

# Part IV

## THE GOBLIN KING

*When all my hopes His promises sufficed,*
*When my Soul watched for Him by day, by night,*
*When my lamp lightened and my robe was white,*
*And all seemed loss, except the Pearl unpriced.*
*Yet, since He calls me still with tender Call,*
*Since He remembers Whom I half forgot,*
*I even will run my race and bear my lot.*

— CHRISTINA ROSSETTI,
*Come Unto Me*

# DEATH AND
# THE MAIDEN

verything was changed. Ever since the night the Goblin King broke me open and laid me bare, the air between us was charged with unspoken emotion. I was a woman remade by his hands; he reached inside me and the music came pouring out.

I understood now what it was like to be struck by divine fire. Our evenings now passed in a fever dream, where we did nothing but make music. I no longer marked the passage of time; yesterday was today was tomorrow, an ouroboros of hours that circled back on themselves. I was burning from within, and I needed no mortal sustenance to nourish me. Sleep, food, drink—all were poor substitutes for the music that sustained me. I lived on music and the Goblin King. The notes were my ambrosia, his kisses my nectar.

"Again," I demanded as we finished playing the first movement of the Wedding Night Sonata for the seventh time. "Again!"

We had been working on the piece for hours, my husband and I. Every time he played it, I heard and understood something different within the movement. Within me. A piece begun in rage and impotence, transformed into inexorable longing, and yet, not a piece without joy.

I had marked its tempo as *allegro*.

To be played *quickly. Swiftly.*

*Joyfully.*

"Again?" the Goblin King asked. "Have you not had enough music, my dear?"

He was tired. I could hear fear in his playing, fear and fatigue. I had worn him down. I had worn myself down. But I did not care; I did not want to stop. The cage about my heart had been opened and I was flying. I was free for the first time in my life, and my soul soared. I could not play, could not compose, could not *think* fast enough; my mind outpaced my fingers, and the errors and wrong notes that ensued caused me as much laughter as tears. More, I wanted more, I needed more. If Lucifer's sin was pride, then mine was covetousness. More and more and more. It wasn't enough. It would never be enough.

"No," I said. "Never."

"Slow down, Elisabeth," he laughed. "I doubt even God Himself could keep up with you."

"Let Him try." The blood fizzed in my veins. "I shall outpace even His angels in a footrace!"

"Darling, darling." The Goblin King lowered his arms to let them rest. "Let it be. The first movement is magnificent."

I smiled. It was magnificent. I was magnificent. No, I was more than magnificent; I was invincible.

"It is," I said. "And it could be even greater." My hands

trembled, fingers twitching. I was nervy, excitable, a hound before the chase. Once more, just once more . . .

The Goblin King saw me shaking and frowned. I snatched my hands from the keyboard and hid them in my skirts.

"Elisabeth, enough."

"But there is still so much work to do," I protested. "The theme is sound but the middle passages are—oh!"

A drop of blood fell on the ivory keys. Puzzled, I wiped it away, when another drop fell on my hand. Then another. And another. The Goblin King rushed forward and pressed a kerchief to my nose. Red stained the snow-white linen, blooming across the fabric at an alarming rate. Suddenly, the world wound down and time slowed to a halt. My thoughts, a fleet-footed hart running through the woods of my mind, stumbled and fell.

Blood?

"Rest." The word was as much a command as a caress. The Goblin King clapped his hands, and Twig and Thistle appeared, one holding a glass tumbler, the other a bottle of a rich amber liquor. He poured me a drink and handed it to me without another word.

"What is this?" I asked.

"Brandy."

"What for?"

"Just drink it."

I wrinkled my nose, but took a sip, feeling the burn of the liquor slide down my throat and warm my heart. He watched me carefully as I finished the drink.

"There," he said. "Feel better?"

I blinked. To my surprise, I did. My hands, which had shaken and twitched with years of pent-up frustration, were finally still. I reached up to touch my face. My nosebleed had stopped, and so had the torrent of song that had flooded from me in the past few days.

"Now." The Goblin King took away the glass and sat beside me on the bench. "We've been playing your music for a long time. Let us pass the time in other ways."

He took my face in his hands and leaned in close, concern in those remarkable eyes. The tenderness there undid me, and a fire of an entirely different sort blossomed within me. The Goblin King gently stroked my cheek and I closed my eyes to breathe him in.

"Have you any suggestions, *mein Herr*?"

His lips brushed against my ear. "I have a few ideas."

I was wound tighter than a violin string, pitched too sharp, and I urged his rough, callused fingertips lower, loosening me, tuning me to the right key.

"We could put down the quill and the bow, and play each other instead," I murmured.

The Goblin King paused and drew back. I opened my eyes to meet his gaze, but instead of desire, I saw something else: worry.

*The longer you burn the candle . . .*

Suddenly, the bloodstained handkerchief seemed like an omen.

But I pushed the foreboding away. I was happy. I was fulfilled. I had music at my fingertips and a willing performer at my beck and call. The Goblin King was a consummate player of violins and of women, and the skill with which he plied both was extraordinary. My arms, my breasts, my stomach, my thighs; he could wring such exquisite emotion from me with just the softest flick of his tongue, the merest touch of his lips. I was in the hands of a virtuoso.

So I kissed him, kissed him with ardor and heat, burning away his worry and my doubt. I felt his concern warm into something altogether more pleasurable beneath my lips, and I traced my hands down his arms, drawing him close.

I let the Goblin King play me the rest of the evening, the sonata, the bloodstained handkerchief, and the candle forgotten for the time being. He was the bow, I the strings, and his fingers brushed my body to make me sing.


The Goblin King was gone when I awoke. At some point during the night he had put me to bed, but had not joined me there. Where my husband went in his private hours, I did not know, but I thought I could hear the distant, dreamy sound of his violin.

The mirror above my mantel showed the Goblin Grove bathed in an eerie half-light, either dawn or dusk, I could not tell. The alders were in full bloom in the world above, awakened to spring before the rest of the forest. I smiled and rose from my bed.

The retiring room was empty.

"He's not here," said a cackle from the shadows. Thistle.

"I know." The Goblin King had not taken his violin from its stand in the retiring room. It rested in the hands of a leering satyr, its clawed fingers running down the curves of the instrument. Yet I could still hear those faint, ghostly strains, familiar yet unrecognizable. "Do you hear that?"

Thistle's bat-wing ears twitched. "Hear what?"

"The music," I said. I ran my fingers over the Goblin King's violin. "I thought it was *Der Erlkönig*."

We listened. The playing was too faint for me to identify

what I was hearing, but Thistle's ears were sharper than mine. After a moment, she shook her head.

"I hear nothing."

Did she lie? It would be like my goblin girl to mislead me, but Thistle watched me with an unreadable expression on her face, neither mocking nor sympathetic. For once, I thought she might be telling the truth.

Perhaps it was all in my mind. I heard music in my mind at all times, but it was never quite this literal. This music wasn't within me; it was beyond me.

Thistle watched me, perched atop the klavier like a cat, her sharp little claws scoring marks into the scattered notes I had made on the Wedding Night Sonata. "What do you want?" she sneered.

If it had been Twig attending, she would have brought me a platter of food, a mug of tea, a new robe, or any other number of small creature comforts without my having to ask. But Thistle chafed at my unspoken wishes, finding ways to fulfill my orders to the letter if not in spirit.

My stomach rumbled. For the first time in ages, I realized I was hungry. More than hungry, I was *starving*. I swayed on my feet, suddenly lightheaded.

"It would be nice," I said mildly, "if you could find me something to eat."

Thistle scowled. I hid a smile; she hated it more when I was nice than when I was demanding. She snapped those spindly-branch fingers and presently, changelings materialized out of the shadows with plates piled high with roasted boar, slices of venison, turnips, and bread. I noted a salver of strawberries in one of the servitors' hands and my mouth watered.

"The food isn't . . . ?" I gave Thistle a questioning glance.

"No glamour," she said. "It doesn't work on the Goblin Queen anyway."

I needed no further encouragement. The changelings disappeared into the shadows again and I tucked in with gusto, devouring the food before me with no thought for the niceties. The juice from the roast filled my mouth, rich and flavorful. I could taste the sweetness of rosemary, sage, and thyme, the smokiness of the roasting fire, the saltiness of the crust.

"You've still got an appetite," Thistle remarked. "Surprising."

I paused mid-bite. "What do you mean?"

She shrugged. "They all stopped eating in the end."

I said nothing and continued eating.

"Are you not curious?" Thistle asked when it became clear I wouldn't rise to her bait. "Curious about your fate?"

I tore off a piece of bread. "What else is there to know? My life is given to the Underground, and I may never again set foot in the land of the living." I thought of the days spent at the klavier, the nights spent in the Goblin King's hands, and my cheeks warmed. "I am dead to the world above."

*The longer you burn the candle . . .*

The food stuck in my throat, but I forced myself to swallow it down.

Thistle brought the salver of strawberries over to me. "You know what your bargain entails, but not what it portends." She grinned, her teeth jagged and sharp.

I sighed. "Out with it, Thistle," I said. "You want to tell me, so go ahead."

She set the salver at my feet. "The first fruits of your sacrifice," she said, picking up a strawberry in her long, many-jointed fingers. "Interesting. Early in the year for straw-berries. Your favorite?"

I thought of the wild strawberry patch in the meadow by the inn. I was born in midsummer, and the patch always bore fruit by my birthday. It would be a race to see who could eat more: me, my sister, or the creatures of the forest. Käthe and I would steal away from our chores as often as we could to fill our bellies, our red-stained mouths always giving us away.

"Yes." I loved strawberries because they tasted of more than sweetness; they tasted of stolen summer afternoons and laughter. "They were always my favorite birthday gift."

Thistle laughed. "First to bloom, first to fade. Enjoy your strawberries while you can, then; the taste will soon fade to ash in your mouth."

"How so?" I picked up the salver and set it on my lap.

"Do know what it means to live, Your Highness?" I rolled my eyes. I was plagued on all sides by philosophers. "Life is more than breath and more than blood. It is"—Thistle ate her strawberry with relish—"taste and touch and sight and sound and smell."

I looked at the salver in my lap. Each berry was at its peak ripeness, its flesh a perfect bright red.

"The price you paid was not the remaining years of your life, you know. Think you the old laws could be bought so cheaply? No. It is not just your heart, but your eyes, your ears, your nose, and your tongue they de-mand." She licked the sticky juice from her fingers. "Little by little, they will take your sight, your smell, your taste, your touch, a slow feast. Your passion, your vivacity, your capacity to feel, all sucked dry. And when you are nothing but a faded shade of your former self, then at last, you will die. Think you your beating heart the greatest gift you could give? No, mortal, your heartbeat is but the least and last."

The ugliness of Thistle's truth left me breathless. I felt sick; I could not stomach another bite.

"Oh yes," she went on, plucking another berry from the tray. "One by one, your senses will leave you. Which of them can you bear to give up first, mortal?"

Which of them? None of them. Could I give up the taste of strawberries? The perfume of a summer's evening, the feel of silk against my skin, the privilege of beholding the Goblin King with my own eyes? The taste of his kisses, the touch of his hands skimming the hills and valleys of my curves, the sound of his violin? And music, oh, God, music, would I ever be able to bear the agony of its loss?

"I don't know," I whispered. "I don't know."

Thistle stole another strawberry from my salver. "Then eat, drink, and be merry while you can, for tomorrow . . ." She did not need to finish her sentence.

For the first time in a long time, I felt the weight, the enormity, of what I had sacrificed. I had spent so long in the world above denying myself that I knew just how well the loss of my senses would devastate and diminish me. Especially now that I understood the fullness of what the body could offer.

"How long?" I asked. "How long before—before it all fades away?"

Thistle shrugged. "You have as long as memory holds, I suppose."

"What does that mean?"

Thistle's eyes glittered. "Do you know what keeps the wheel of life turning, mortal?"

I was taken aback by this sudden turn in the conversation. "No."

My goblin girl grinned, but it was a malicious grin, full of contempt and ridicule. "Love."

I gave a disbelieving laugh. "What?"

"I know, what a foolish notion. But it doesn't make it any less powerful, or true." Thistle leaned forward, breathing deep my sorrow, anger, and confusion. "As long as the world above remembers you, as long as you have a reason to love, your taste and touch and smell and sight and sound shall remain to you."

I frowned. In the distance, I could still hear the violin playing its unidentifiable but familiar song, like a beacon, like a call.

"You mean, as long as someone remembers me, I will live, entire?"

Thistle watched me. "Do they love you?"

I thought of Josef, and of Käthe. "Yes."

"And how long do you think their love will last, when all trace of you that ever was is gone, when their rational, waking minds tell them you don't exist, when it would be easier to forget you in the face of reason?"

I closed my eyes. I remembered the strange half-dream of a life granted to me by *Der Erlkönig* when Käthe had been first taken from me. It had been easy, so easy to slip into that version of reality, a reality where my sister did not exist. But I remembered too the wrongness of it all, that despite all evidence to the contrary, the hole in my heart could only be explained by her absence. I thought of Josef then, and my heart clenched with fear. My baby brother, the other half of my soul, had gone on to bigger and better things. It would be so easy to forget me in the midst of all that fine company. But the piece of a dream returned to me, sheet music open on a stand. *Für meine Lieben, in Lied im stil die Bagatelle, auch Der Erlkönig.*

I opened my eyes. "Their love will last as long as they draw breath," I said fiercely.

Thistle scoffed. "So they all say."

We fell into silence. I could still hear that damnable faraway violin, but Thistle seemed oblivious to its strains. I picked up a strawberry from the salver and brought it to my lips, savoring its scent, the hint of summer sunshine beneath its red sweetness. I took a bite, and its flavor burst over my tongue, flooding me with memories. Me and Mother making strawberry jam as Constanze baked a cake. Käthe's lips pink with contraband sweets. Josef's fingers sticky with sugar, leaving marks across the neck of his violin that took ages to clean off.

And with a start I realized I recognized the music that played in the distance. A queer, haunting little tune, almost like a bagatelle.

It was mine.

And the violin was Josef's.

I cast aside the remnants of my meal and walked to the klavier. Thistle remained with me, a little homunculus hovering over my shoulder, pesky and persistent. I shooed her away, so she sent my papers flying out of spite. I gave her a pointed look, but she stared back mulishly until I mouthed *I wish*. With a harrumph, she snapped her fingers, and my notes and papers immediately arranged themselves into a neat pile beside the klavier.

But instead of continuing work on the Wedding Night

Sonata, I sat down and played the piece I had called *Der Erlkönig*, accompanying my brother from another world, another realm.

*As long as the world above remembers you.*

My music. Of course. All things on this earth and beneath it passed away, but music was immortal. Even if I was dead to the world above, a part of me would live each time my music was heard.

Thistle brought the salver of strawberries and set it atop the klavier, bright, red, and tempting. I ate every last one, grateful for the little sweetnesses that remained to me.

## PERCHANCE
## TO DREAM

When I awoke, it was with Josef.

I stood in an unfamiliar room, beautifully appointed and richly furnished. My brother sat at a writing desk in a nightshirt and cap. The hour was late, and the candles burned low beside him. His fingers, ink-stained and dirty, were wrapped around a quill, laboriously scratching words onto paper.

"Dear Liesl," he said.

A letter. Josef was writing me a letter.

"Six months since I left home, and still no word." He paused, waiting for his hand to catch up to his words. "Where are you, Liesl? Why do you not write?"

*Sepperl, Sepperl,* mein Brüderchen, *I am here,* I said. But I was once again voiceless, mute and silent.

My brother lifted his head, as though he could sense my presence. *Josef!* I cried. *Sepp!* But his eyes went dull a moment later, and he returned to his letter.

"Mother sends letters by the week, and Käthe writes by the hour, but of you, and from you, there is nothing."

I watched my brother struggle with the quill. A bow had always looked so natural in his hand; Josef wielded it with such delicacy, his wrist loose, his movements fluid. But the quill was strangled in his fingertips, the motions of writing and transcription awkward and strange. I wondered then if this was not part of the reason my brother had always preferred that I take dictation in his rare fits of composition— because he could not write.

I staggered back. *My brother could not write.* He had learned his letters at Mother's feet like the rest of us children, and he could certainly read, but Papa—obsessed with the makings of another little Mozart—had taken Josef away, making my brother practice the musical alphabet instead.

Josef dipped his quill in the well and touched the nib to paper—careful, slow, and deliberate. His letters were ill-formed and childish, and I saw that he hadn't even learned to join them properly into up and downstrokes.

"I ponder the reasons why you keep silent, and none of them make sense. It is like you are a ghost, a shade. It is like you don't exist. But how can that be so? How can you be a ghost, when I hold the proof of your existence in my hands?"

He glanced to the side. The piece I'd named *Der Erlkönig* lay open in a portfolio on a low table, my handwriting stark in the flickering candlelight.

"Wherever you are, I hope you knew the moment I released your music into the world, when I played your *Der Erlkönig* piece in public for the first time. I wish you had seen the faces of the audience. They were transported"— he scribbled out the word—"transformed by your music. I wish you had heard their cries of *Encore! Encore!* It wasn't me they were cheering, Liesl; it was you. Your music."

I was crying. I did not know a ghost could cry.

"François insists we try and get the piece published. He thinks it is a work of genius. He is clever and I trust his judgment."

Josef glanced over his shoulder, his eyes turning soft and tender. I followed his gaze. François slept on the couch in the room, his arm thrown over his eyes.

"But I do not want to proceed without your permission. I want to know this is what you want."

*Yes,* I cried. *Yes!*

"François does not understand my delay. He does not seem to understand that it is you who holds the power. So I await your word every day, every hour, proof incontrovertible of my older, more talented sister's existence. My partner-in-arms, my connection to the Underground."

I longed to wrap my arms around him, my Sepperl, my darling baby brother and partner-in-arms. But my hands passed through him and my heart broke. I could never again set foot in the world above, never again embrace my family.

"We are settled in Paris now, so please, please, please write to me, care of Master Antonius." His hand shook, turning Master Antonius's name into an illegible scrawl. Josef swore in French.

"I do not love Paris, although I don't imagine that surprises you. If you've gotten my other letters, you will know how much I miss our little inn and the Goblin Grove, despite all the impressive sights of the great cities of Europe. I keep thinking how much Käthe would love it—it's all fancy balls and dignitaries and people dressed up in frippery and finery. I am ill-suited to this life, Liesl. The travel takes its toll, and I am constantly weak. We scarcely had time to recover from our journeys before it was another concert, another salon."

As Josef wrote that last word, something within him seemed to change. A great sigh left his body, and he seemed to grow smaller, weaker somehow. Travel and time had taken the last of the baby fat from my brother's face, honing his cheekbones, sharpening his chin. It was only then I realized that Josef looked ill. Drained.

"My homesickness affects my playing. I know it, and Master Antonius knows it."

He pressed down harder on the nib of his quill as he wrote Master Antonius's name, much harder than necessary.

"The old violinist is a great performer and I have learned much studying with him. But he isn't patient, not like you or François, and he . . ."

Josef stopped writing, struggling with the words. But I could see what he could not say. The tense set of his shoulders. The way his lower lip and jaw jutted out with stubbornness. The way he kept glancing at François, as though the black boy were both his shield and his refuge. He crossed out the last few words and continued.

"Nobody understands. François does his best, but while he understands my heart, I can't always find the words to tell him what I feel. He's so clever; he can speak French, Italian, and even a little English. But he finds German difficult, and I am a dunce with languages, according to Master Antonius."

My hands tightened into fists. I should have known—I *had* known—on the night of Josef's audition that Master Antonius was not the mentor my brother needed. That vain, selfish man would never raise my brother up; he would only put him down.

"The world outside our little sphere, far from the Goblin Grove, is hopelessly mundane. There is no magic, no enchantment. I feel severed from the land of my birth, and I can feel my talent fade and grow dull. I feel blinded, deafened, muted. The only time I feel connected to the earth again is when I play your music."

Josef paused again, and set his quill down. He stared out the window, a dreamy expression on his face. His left fingers moved up and down an invisible fingerboard, while his right hand moved in smooth, practiced motions. I thought he had finished writing, but Josef picked up the quill and began again.

"I dream of our family often—Käthe and Constanze and Mother and Papa. But never you. You are never there. It's like you don't exist sometimes. Sometimes I fear you are a figment of my imagination, but the music beside me tells me you are real. I fear I am going mad."

His fingers gripped the edge of his writing desk so hard, his knuckles turned white.

"I dream of our family, but at other times, I dream of a tall, elegant stranger." Josef glanced at the slumbering François with a look of guilt on his face. "He says nothing, only stands there, hooded and shadowed. I am filled with both terror and relief at the sight of him. I beg him to reveal his face to me, but whenever he pulls back his hood, he is me. I am the tall, elegant stranger."

If I had breath, it would have been knocked from me. Something terrible was at work here. Something ancient. Something beyond my understanding.

"I wish you would come, Liesl. I wish you would come

and bring the magic and music with you. If you cannot come yourself, then send the next best thing. Send me your music. I am so lost without you, without our connection to the Underground."

I tried to gather my brother in my arms, but like the ghost I was, I only passed through him, nothing more than a breeze in the chamber. Josef looked up again, frowning as the candle flame flickered before him.

"Your ever-loving brother," he finished. "Sepperl."

He lightly sanded the still-wet ink and set the letter out to dry. Then he picked up his candle in its holder and walked over to François. Josef spread a blanket over the sleeping boy's form and stood there a moment, watching him sleep. Tenderness, affection, and anguish, all in one. It was a look of love.

Then the scene broke into pieces, shattering and falling about me like shards of glass. A mirror.

A dream.

There were tears upon my face when I gasped myself awake. My heart raced, and I was both too hot and too cold, my night shift soaked with sweat, my skin clammy. Although it was spring in the world above, down in the Underground it was always cool, as though *Der Erlkönig* carried eternal winter with him wherever he went.

A fire was banked high in my hearth, giving off a comforting heat. But I could not stand to be still, could not bear another moment in my barrow, my prison as well as my home. I pulled out a skirt and blouse from the wardrobe, simple and serviceable. Usually my closet consisted of elaborate gowns, dresses that were more confectionary than necessary. Whenever I opened the wardrobe doors I found something new, and tonight, my wishes yielded something very like what I used to wear in the world above: plain, practical, and warm.

I quickly dressed myself and unlocked my door, emerging into the corridors outside. I was in the mood to wander tonight, and did not care where my feet took me.

I passed the goblin city, glittering in the winking, twinkling fairy lights, passed the enormous ballroom where I had danced with the Goblin King for the first time as husband and wife. But I strode past them all, wanting to go deeper. The paved avenues gave way to narrow passages, rocky and sharp and jagged. Moisture glistened along the walls, the air around me growing damp and dank.

Suddenly, the Underground lake appeared before me.

This was the farthest I could go. My toes touched the edge of the water, sending glowing ripples of light across the surface. The water was cold, colder than an alpine spring, and I minded how these waters flowed into the rivers and pools of the world above.

And then, all around me, the sound of singing. High and clear, the sound of a finger running along the edge of a crystal goblet. The entire grotto rang with its eerie beauty, resounding in my chest and in my bones. The Lorelei.

"Beautiful, isn't it?"

I jumped. A changeling appeared, as suddenly as though he had walked through the rocky walls surrounding the lake.

"Yes," I said cautiously. I had never actually exchanged words with a changeling before. They were the Goblin King's silent servitors, the swoonworthy swains at the Goblin Ball, the lost and hungry children of the world above, the most mysterious and monstrous denizens of the Underground. I knew next to nothing about them, save that they had been "the product of a wish." I thought of the night I had made a wish, when Josef was a baby, dying of scarlet fever.

"They are dangerous, you know, the Lorelei." The changeling sidled closer and I tried not to let my discomfort show. Despite everything, I pitied the creatures, pitied their half-life, their liminal existence. "Beautiful, but dangerous."

"Yes," I said again. "I nearly succumbed to their spell the last time I crossed."

The changeling's flat, black eyes—goblin eyes in that human face—studied me. "What happened?"

I shrugged. "*Der Erlkönig* saved me."

He nodded, as though this explained everything. "Of course. He would not want you to discover their greatest secret."

"And what is that?"

The changeling tilted his head. "That they guard the gateway into the world above."

A cold, ringing sensation numbed me from head to toe. "A gateway? There is . . . a gateway to the world above?"

He nodded. "Yes. It lies on the far side of the lake."

I stared at the lake, at its dark, dark depths, black like obsidian. Like death. Yet on the other side was light. Light and life. If only I could . . .

"It's not safe." The changeling watched me closely. "You cannot cross without a guardian."

Shame lit my face, and I averted my gaze. I had not known my thoughts to be so transparent.

"Here," he said suddenly. "I have a present for you."

Startled, I opened my hand, and he dropped a bundle of wildflowers into my palm. "Thank you," I said in bewilderment. The flowers were nothing more than clover blossoms, prettily tied with a length of ribbon.

The changeling shook his head. "It's not from me. She left it for you in the Goblin Grove."

I went still. "Who?"

"A girl," he said. "A woman in a red cloak with sunshine hair."

*Käthe.*

"How—how—" Goblins could only roam the earth during the uncounted days of winter.

"The grove is one of the few sacred spaces left where the Underground and the world above overlap," the changeling said indifferently. "The girl came by and said your name before dropping the flowers. I took them when she left."

Of course. Now I understood. I understood why it was always to the Goblin Grove Josef and I ran as children, why it was the only place I ever saw the Goblin King, why I had gone there to sacrifice my music and gain entrance to the Underground.

It was a threshold.

The glimmerings of an idea began to form, fragile and fraught. I turned away from it, afraid to look for the hope rising in me. The changeling turned to go.

"Wait," I said. "A moment, please."

The changeling folded his hands and cocked his head to one side. His face was human, but his expression was entirely goblin-like in its inscrutability.

"What—what can you tell me of my brother?"

"Your brother?"

"Yes," I choked out. "Josef."

His black eyes glittered. "All you mortals are so alike,"

he said. "Quick to be born, quick to die. Like mayflies in the night."

"But," I said. "Josef is not dead."

A slow smile spread across his lips. "Are you so certain of that?"

I turned my head away. "What—" I began, my throat hoarse. "What is Josef?"

The changeling did not reply, but I already knew the answer. In some ways, I had always known the answer. My brother died that night I heard him crying, when the fever ravaged his mortal body, leaving nothing but a corpse. Before the scarlatina had taken him, my brother had been rosy-cheeked and hale, a chubby, good-natured baby. The morning after the fever broke, the thing left in his cradle had been sallow and thin, a queer, quiet creature. We all thought it was the fever. But I knew better.

"How can a changeling live in the world above?" I whispered.

He shrugged. "They can't, except by the power of—"

"—a wish," I finished. I wanted to laugh. "I know."

"No." The changeling's voice was amused. "By the power of love."

The bottom dropped out of my stomach, and I was falling. Suddenly it seemed like the rules of the Underground were changing, and I couldn't grasp their meaning.

"Love?"

The changeling shrugged again. "You love him, don't you? Your brother?"

Was he my brother? How could I possibly ask myself that? Josef's nature did not change the fact that he was the other half of my soul, my amanuensis, the gardener of my heart. Of course he was my brother.

"Yes," I said. "I love him."

"Then he stayed for you. None of us have lasted long in the world above, you know. Take us far from the Underground and we wither and fade. You called him by name and loved him entire. That is power."

*I feel severed from the land of my birth, and I can feel my talent fade and grow dull. I feel blinded, deafened, muted.*

"Oh, Josef." I pressed my hand to my anguished heart.

"Do not worry," the changeling said. "He will return to us soon enough. We all come back, in the end."

## UNFINISHED
## SYMPHONY

Of all my mortal emotions, hope was the worst. All the others were easy to carry and easy to put aside: anger flashed then burned out, sorrow gradually lightened, and happiness bubbled then disappeared. But hope . . . hope was stubborn. Like a weed it returned, even after I had plucked it away again and again.

Hope also hurt.

It hurt when, night after night, the Goblin King put me to bed with a chaste kiss upon my brow. It hurt when the clover blossoms from my sister faded, then died. It hurt when I never again heard Josef's violin from the world above, calling my name in A minor.

It also hurt when I thought of the gateway beneath the Underground lake and the threshold beyond.

So I tried my best to stifle hope. Because hope's twin was despair, and despair was infinitely worse. If hope hurt, then despair was the absence of hurt. It was the absence of feeling. It was the absence of caring.

I wanted very much to care.

But it was getting harder to meet each day with purpose. It was hard to find excitement, joy, or anticipation, even in that which had brought me so much happiness before. The Goblin King and I worked the first movement of the Wedding Night Sonata until it was perfect, until there were no mistakes left. I had heard the Allegro more times than I could count, and while I could no longer find anything I wanted to fix, neither could I find anything I liked about it.

*Move on,* the Goblin King had encouraged me. *Write something else. The next movement, perhaps.*

I tried. Or rather, I tried to try. But I couldn't. I stared at the black and white keys of the klavier, but inspiration did not come. I did not know where to begin or how to proceed. And then I realized I did not know how to proceed because I did not know how the story ended.

What was the resolution of a piece begun in rage, impotence, and desire? How did it finish? I knew the rules, how a sonata should be structured. Three movements: fast, slow, fast. A declaration of theme, a deconstruction, a resolution. But there would be no conclusion, not for me; only a slow, sputtering decrescendo.

Those would be the remaining years of my life.

I had thought I knew impotence. I had thought I knew futility. I had been so wrong.

*As long as you have reason to love,* Thistle had said.

I had many reasons to love. I touched the faded clover blossoms on the sheet music beside me.

*As long as the world above remembers you.*

Could I . . . could I send some sort of message? Could I send proof of my love, the way Käthe had, the way Josef had?

*The grove is one of the sacred spaces left where the Underground and the world above overlap.*

And then hope flared again, more painful than before.

There were endless facets to my Goblin King—trickster, musician, philosopher, scholar, gentleman—and I had taken great pleasure in discovering them, one after another. Each new side revealed another dimension, another depth which added to my understanding of my husband.

But there was one facet of him I had uncovered, and it was one I liked not at all: martyr.

It was a while before I understood his curious reticence, his careful distancing. It was even longer before I noticed it, for although my husband was free with his affection— touches upon my face, my hands, my shoulder, my lips—he was a miser in everything else.

*The longer you burn the candle . . .*

There was a hesitation whenever he touched me now, a conscious gentleness that infuriated me. The door had been opened between us, and I wanted him to walk in and treat my body like home. But there was a line he would not cross, for although I felt his ardor in every kiss, every caress, he never entered. If I could still laugh, my laugh would have been heard even in the world above.

It was not my shame that stopped us now; it was his guilt.

"You are not attending," I said one evening after dinner.

"Hmmm?"

We had just finished playing a series of suites in G minor by a composer unknown to me. The Goblin King had an entire repertoire of music, a library of librettos and port-folios stolen from the world above. Many of the composers' names were lost to time, but I wondered if something of their ghosts didn't stir each time their music was played. At first I had thought these compositions the work of the same man, for they were all written in the same hand, until the Goblin King admitted he had copied the notes down himself.

"I was a copyist once," he said. Then he shut his mouth and did not say another word, although I pressed and pestered until his patience snapped.

He was immediately contrite afterward, which only needled me more. In the space between his anger and his apology, I had felt that spark of flame between us, and for the briefest moment, all my senses flared to life, as intense and potent as they had been in the world above.

But his guilt dampened my fire and my hope.

"You are not attending," I repeated. "You were playing by rote; I could hear the emptiness."

The emptiness was not just in his playing. It was in the silences between us. Where the quiet had once been full, full of music and communion, now it was hollow.

The Goblin King's bow, still poised over the strings, trembled in his grip. The horsehair bounced lightly against the bridge, producing a nervous, fidgety sound.

"Forgive me," he said. "I'm tired. I've been up long into the dark hours of the night these past few days."

It wasn't a lie, but it felt like one. I could see the dark smudges of exhaustion beneath his eyes, and had heard from both Twig and Thistle that the Goblin King did not sleep, but spent his time wandering the winding passages of the Underground.

"Then let us rest," I said. I clapped my hands, and Twig and Thistle appeared, one bearing a decanter of brandy and a glass, the other a salver of strawberries. I poured the Goblin King a drink and held it out to him.

He did not miss the significance of the gesture. "I'm fine, Elisabeth."

I shrugged, then took a sip myself. The liquor was weak and watery.

"Well," I said. "How shall we pass the time, then, *mein Herr*?"

"I am at my lady's command," he said. "Your wish is my desire."

"Is it?" I rose from the klavier and took a step forward. "Then I think you know just how I would like to pass the time."

The Goblin King raised his bow like a sword and his violin like a shield between us. "Not tonight, my dear."

Not tonight. Not tomorrow night. Not any nights in the foreseeable future. I would have cried, if I had any sorrow left. I would have shouted, if anger still burned within me. But there was nothing, nothing but hope and despair, and despair was winning.

"Very well." I returned to my seat at the keyboard. I wanted to throw up my hands in defeat, or wrap them around his throat and throttle him. I wanted to pour my frustration out into song. But I did not know how to articulate the swirling maelstrom of confusion within me into words, phrases, sentences, so I twisted my fingers into the keyboard instead. A discordant jangle, a handful of notes that clashed and screeched. "Let us play a game."

Something in the Goblin King loosened, though his wolf's eyes were still wary. "What game, my dear?"

"Truth or Forfeit."

He lifted his brows. "Child's play?"

"The only games I know. Come, *mein Herr,* surely you remember our games in the Goblin Grove."

A smile showed the tips of his teeth. "I do, Elisabeth. With pleasure."

"Good." Hope flickered in my stomach. "I shall start."

I picked up the tray of strawberries and moved from the bench to the floor. I set the berries before me and tucked my legs beneath my skirts, as I had when I was a little girl. The Goblin King made no remark, only set aside his instrument and joined me on the ground. I held forth my hands, palms up. No tricks. The Goblin King took my hands in his own. No traps.

"We'll begin with simple questions," I said. "What is your name?"

He threw back his head and laughed. "Oh no, Elisabeth. That is a question I cannot answer. Pick another."

"Can't? Or won't?"

His eyes were hard. "Can't. Won't. Both. It doesn't matter. Pick another. Or name your forfeit, and I shall pay it."

I hadn't expected the game to start off so poorly, so I hadn't yet gathered any ideas for penalties to dole out. So I asked another question. "Fine. What is your favorite color?"

"Green. What's yours?"

My glance fell on the salver beside me. "Red. Favorite smell?"

"Incense. Favorite animal?"

My eyes lingered on his. "Wolf. Favorite composer?"

"You."

The response was so simple, so sincere, it took my breath

away. "All right," I said, my voice unsteady. "The questions will get harder now. I shall ask you five questions, and you must reply truthfully or pay the forfeit. Then you may ask me five."

The Goblin King nodded his head.

"Where do you go when you wander the Underground at night?"

A flash of pain crossed his face, but he answered without hesitation. "The chapel."

His reply surprised me. "The chapel? Why?"

"Is that your next question?"

I paused. "Yes."

It was a while before he answered. "Solace." I waited for him to continue. "It gives me comfort to offer my prayers to the Lord, even if he never hears them."

"For what do you pray?"

He watched me from beneath those hooded lids, eyes slightly narrowed. "For atonement."

"For what must you atone?"

His eyes glittered. "For selfishness."

I considered pressing him further, but I had one more question and I did not want to waste it. "How did you come to be *Der Erlkönig*?"

The Goblin King's head snapped up and he snatched back his hands. "Don't you dare, Elisabeth."

My hands were still in front of me, palms empty. "You promised to answer truthfully."

His nostrils flared. "There has always been *Der Erlkönig*. There will always be *Der Erlkönig*."

"That is not an answer."

"It is the one you must accept. If you will not, then name your forfeit, and I shall pay it."

I studied him. I remembered the first story he had ever told me. *The king underground knew the cost of sacrifice. He had sold his soul and his name to the goblins.* His soul . . . and his name. But I thought of the gallery of Goblin Kings, an evolving line of different men. My Goblin King was *Der Erlkönig*, but *Der Erlkönig* was not every Goblin King. To whom had my husband given his name? To whom had he given his soul?

"Your name," I whispered. "I claim your name as forfeit."

He stiffened. "No, Elisabeth. I will give you anything but that."

"Is a name so high a price to pay?"

The Goblin King looked at me, and there were a thousand emotions, a thousand years in his eyes. He had the form and figure of a young man, but he was ancient.

"It is," he said quietly, "the highest price I could pay."

"Why?"

He sighed, and it was the wind in the trees. "Who are you, Elisabeth?"

"Am I answering your questions now?" My hands were still empty, empty of his name. "You have not paid your forfeit."

"I am paying it in the only manner I can."

The silence between us began to fill.

"Who are you, Elisabeth? Answer this, and you shall understand."

I frowned. "I am," I began, then stopped. The Goblin King did not press me, but simply waited. His patience was infinite; his patience was immortal.

"I am . . . I am an innkeeper's daughter." It was the answer I would have given when I was Liesl, but it no longer felt true.

The Goblin King shook his head. "That is what you were."

"I am . . . a musician. A composer."

A small smile tilted his lips, but he shook his head again. "That is *what* you are. But *who* are you, Elisabeth?"

"I am . . ."

Who was I? Daughter, sister, wife, queen, composer; these were titles I had been given and claimed, but they were not the whole of me. They were not me, entire. I closed my eyes.

"I am," I said slowly, "a girl with music in her soul. I am a sister, a daughter, a friend, who fiercely protects those dear to her. I am a girl who loves strawberries, chocolate torte, songs in a minor key, moments stolen from chores, and childish games. I am short-tempered yet disciplined. I am self-indulgent, selfish, yet selfless. I am compassion and hatred and contradiction. I am . . . me."

I opened my eyes. The Goblin King gazed upon with me with naked longing. My pulse skipped, tripping over the emotions in my blood. His eyes were as clear as water, and I could see down to the heart of where *he* had been, my austere young man.

"You are Elisabeth," he said. "A name, yes. But a soul as well."

I understood then. He could not give me his name because he was no one; he was *Der Erlkönig*. He was hollowed out, his name and his essence stolen by the old laws. The space within where the austere young man had been was wanting, longing to be filled.

"I am Elisabeth," I said. "But Elisabeth is only a name. An empty word I fill with myself. But you had a word once; I see the echoes of it within you."

I couldn't say why I wanted his name. It didn't matter; he

was *Der Erlkönig*, the Goblin King, *mein Herr*. But these were titles bestowed upon him, not ones he had claimed for himself. I wanted the part of him that did not belong to the Underground, but to the world above. To the mortal man he had been. The mortal man he could have been . . . with me.

"It is gone," he said. "Lost. Forgotten."

We did not speak for a long time. I held his silence close to me. His name might have been forgotten, but it was not lost.

"Well," he said at last. "Do you accept my forfeit?" The Goblin King extended his hands, palms up.

No. I did not accept. It was not what I had asked for, but it was what I would have to take.

"Yes," I said. "Your turn is ended." I placed my hands in his.

"Good." His smile hardened. "Then I shall ask you five questions, Elisabeth, and you must reply truthfully or pay the forfeit."

I nodded.

"Why have you not continued work on the sonata?"

I winced. The Wedding Night—*our* Wedding Night Sonata. The first movement was finished, but I had not taken up the quill to begin work on the second. Our evenings had been filled with music, but not mine.

"I don't know," I said.

"That is not an answer."

"It is the truth."

The Goblin King raised his brows. He did not accept.

"I don't know," I repeated. It wasn't as though I hadn't tried. I wanted to finish it, I wanted to write something wholly and utterly in my own voice, something the world would hear and know as mine. But every time I sat before the klavier, every time I pressed my fingers to the keys, nothing came. "I . . . I can't continue. I don't know how. It's as if . . . it's dead inside."

The Goblin King narrowed his eyes, but I could not give him another answer. He studied me closely, but did not ask me to justify myself, and simply asked the next question.

"What do you miss about the world above?"

I sucked in a sharp breath. The Goblin King's face was carefully neutral, and I could read nothing of his intent. Did he mean to be cruel? Consoling? Or was he merely curious?

"Many things," I said in a faltering voice. "Why do you ask?"

"Your turn for questions is ended, Elisabeth. Answer truthfully or pay a forfeit."

I turned my head. Although I could not say why, I could not look at him while I gave my answer.

"Sunshine. Snow. The sound of branches lashing against a windowpane during a storm. Standing before the hearth in the middle of summer, the feel of sweat trickling down my neck. And then the unexpected sweetness of a cool breeze from an open window." I glanced at the salver of strawberries on the klavier. "I miss the sharp, green taste of lemony grass, the yeastiness of beer."

Tears burned along my lashes, but I did not cry. Could not cry. There were no tears in me, and I felt the stinging of phantom sobs run up and down my throat.

"I even miss the parts I didn't know to miss. The pungent, musky pong of an inn overcrowded with travelers. Leather-clad feet, baby breath, sodden wool. Men, women, children." I laughed. "People. I miss people."

The Goblin King was silent. I still could not bear to look at him, and our only communion was through the meeting of our hands.

"If you could," he said softly, "if it were at all possible, would you leave the Underground?"

This time, it was I who snatched my hands away, to hide their trembling. "No."

"Liar." I could hear the snarl in his voice.

I straightened my shoulders and steeled myself to meet his gaze. The Goblin King's lips were twisted in a sneer, but his eyes were sad.

"Down here," I said, "I have found myself. Down here, I have space to be. It is a gift I never looked for, and I cherish it."

"It wasn't a gift." The Goblin King picked up the salver of strawberries and presented it to me. I picked the biggest, reddest one. "It is merely a consolation prize."

He rose to his feet.

"Where are you going?"

"The game is finished. I'm tired."

"Do you accept my answer, then?"

He looked at the big, red strawberry in my hand. "No."

"Then what is your forfeit?"

The set of his mouth tightened. "Finish your strawberries, Elisabeth. That is what I claim of you."

A strange request, but I did as he asked. I took a bite. And gagged.

I tasted nothing.

I stared at the strawberry in my hand, its flesh still succulent and soft, the juice still running down my fingers. I could still smell its sweet perfume, a promising treat. But without its taste, the berry was nothing but mushy flesh and grainy skin. My stomach turned.

The Goblin King said nothing, only watched as I ate berry after tasteless berry, as I paid my penalty.

# THE THRESHOLD

*i* have a present for you."

It was the changeling again, the one with whom I had spoken on the shores of the Underground lake. I was there again, hiding from my goblin attendants. During my uncounted hours, I often found myself listless; unable to compose, unable to play, and unable to eat. The flesh about my ribs had thinned to reveal a cage of bones, my cheeks sunken to expose a death's-head grin. Food had lost all its savor, a fact Thistle never failed to notice or relish whenever she brought me my dinner tray. I ate to spite her, but it was hard, so much harder when all pleasure was gone from the eating.

The changeling had his hands cupped around an object, offering it to me as though it were a precious thing, a baby bird.

"Another?"

He nodded. His palms opened like a flower, and at their heart, there lay a bloody mass. I gasped.

The changeling tilted his head, his flat, black eyes watching me with no expression. Then I realized that it wasn't a dying creature in his hands; it was a bunch of strawberries, bruised, battered, and bleeding.

"Oh," I said, a bit breathless. "Thank you."

"They're not from me," he said. "They're from the sunshine girl."

Käthe. The sunshine girl. The first smile in an age touched my lips, and my spirits, dead and dull, stirred within me.

"An offering in the grove?"

The changeling nodded again. "I saw her from the shadows. She spoke your name and wished you happy birthday."

Birthday? I had forgotten. I had long ceased to mark the passing of days, weeks, hours. The Underground never changed, never transformed with the seasons, and the years stretched out ahead of me, bland and blank. "Is it midsummer?"

"Yes. Everything is warm and lush and green." The changeling's voice was as flat as his expressionless eyes, yet I thought I could hear a note of longing in it. His longing echoed in me.

It would be my twentieth summer, in the world above.

"I wish I could see it." A useless wish. I had the power to bend the will of the goblins to my desire, but this was not one they could fulfill.

The changeling said nothing, but pushed his hands forward, berries still red in his palms.

When we went strawberry picking, Käthe and I used to argue over which were the best berries to gather. She always went for the biggest, whereas I always picked the reddest. She used to say that it was best to have the biggest, because you got the most strawberry for the littlest effort. I would retort that bigger wasn't always better; the reddest berries, the ones most vibrant and even in color, were always the sweetest.

The berries in the changeling's hands were small, but each was perfect in its red intensity. They shone like jewels in the dark, and I wished I could want them. That I could crave them the way I once had. But the taste of strawberries, of chocolate, of tart mustard on yeasty bread—they were all gone.

I plucked a berry from the changeling's hands anyway.

"Thank you," I said, and took a bite.

Sweetness burst across the tongue. More than sweet; I tasted sunshine in the meadow, lemony greenness, heat. Memories flooded in along with the taste, running down my throat like tears.

I tasted Käthe's love.

"Oh," I breathed. "Oh!"

I devoured the rest, shoving them all into my mouth like a child, as many as I could hold. I should have waited, I should have savored, but I didn't care. Color returned to my world, and I felt my veins run with red.

The changeling was silent as I ate. It wasn't until I had finished that I caught the look of envy on his face. It was the first truly human expression I had ever seen in a changeling and it startled me.

"I'm sorry." I wiped the juice from my lips. "I didn't think to offer you any."

He shrugged. "It would turn to ashes in my mouth anyway."

Sympathy flared through me. We weren't so different, the changeling and I. Neither dead nor truly alive. Along with my sense of taste, all my emotions returned to me with full force. My throat closed with the pity and sorrow I felt for this strange creature. I covered his hands with mine.

Hunger swept over his features, and too late I remembered Thistle's warning. *Careful, they bite.*

But the changeling did not move. Instead, he closed his eyes, and pain thumped my chest. He reminded me so much of Josef, his gentle fragility, his ethereal otherworldliness. This changeling lived a half-life, and suddenly I was glad my brother was far from me, far from the fate from which my love had saved him.

*Stay away, Sepperl,* I thought fiercely. *Stay away, and never come back.*

"They say love can free you," the changeling whispered. "That if one, just one person loved you enough, it could bring you back to the world above." He opened his eyes, those flat, inhuman goblin eyes, and implored me. "Would you love me?"

His words, those little gifts. It was all made clear to me now why this changeling had sought me out. An invisible hand crumpled my heart in my chest. I wanted to gather him in my arms, to soothe him the way I would have soothed my little brother, kissing away the pain from his fingertips after Papa had made him practice his scales so much it tore the calluses. But he was not my brother.

"I'm sorry," I said, as gently as I could.

The changeling did not react to my denial. I searched his face for hurt, for anger, but saw nothing but the inhuman, unfamiliar affect of the other goblins.

"I'll bring more strawberries next time," was all he said. "Is there anything you want me to give the sunshine girl?"

It was as though a thunderclap rang in the grotto. Silence

and shock rang across the lake like a gong, resonating in my bones.

"You . . . you can do that?"

He shrugged. "She doesn't see or hear me standing there. But if I can bring you her gifts, then maybe you can leave something for her."

Hope. Hope so searing it burned me with determination.

"Could you . . . could you bring me with you?"

The changeling studied me. I could read nothing in his goblin gaze.

"All right," he said. "Tomorrow. Meet me here tomorrow."


I returned immediately to the retiring room and gathered the leaves of the Wedding Night Sonata, the beginnings of a fair copy, the foul papers, and all. I folded them together in haste, a jumble of music and half-coherent thoughts, wrapping them with the length of ribbon my sister had tied around the clover blossoms.

"What are you doing?" asked Thistle.

The goblin girls were by my side, though the room had been empty when I arrived. Sometimes I wondered if they were charged with spying on me in addition to attending to me. Then I felt guilty for the thought. There was no reason the Goblin King had to spy on me, no reason for me to hide my actions.

Until now.

"Nothing," I said quickly. "It is none of your business."

"Is there anything with which we can assist you, Your Highness?" Twig asked. Of my two goblin girls, she was the kinder one, the one more inclined to offer deference instead of contempt.

"No, no," I said. "I'm fine. Now shoo, the both of you, and leave me alone."

Thistle crawled atop the klavier and leaned toward me. She breathed in deep.

"Hmmm," she said. "You smell of hope." Her lips split in a jagged grin. "Interesting."

I batted her away. "Get off, you little homunculus."

"Hope, and sunshine," Twig added. I jumped when her branch-laden hair scraped against my side. "Like the world above. Like . . . like her."

I paused in the gathering of my music. "Like whom?"

Twig yelped as Thistle leaped from the klavier and tackled her to the floor.

"Like whom?" I repeated.

"You raging idiot," Thistle snarled, pulling handfuls of tufty cobwebs from Twig's head. "You stupid, sentimental fool."

"Enough!" My goblin girls flew apart, the force of my will sending them crashing into opposite corners of the retiring room. "You"—I pointed at Thistle—"are dismissed. And you"—I pointed at Twig—"are to stay here and explain yourself."

Thistle resisted my command as long as she could, her ugly face twisting and contorting with the effort as her fingers, then her legs, and then her body began to vanish. Her head was the last to disappear, her furious grimace lingering long after the rest of her was gone.

Twig groveled at my feet. Bits of cobweb floated in the air like dust motes as she trembled.

"Twig," I said. "I'm not going to hurt you."

"I know, Your Highness." She lifted her head. "But I am not supposed to tell you."

"Tell me what?"

"About the nameless maiden."

Time ceased. The flames froze in the fireplace, the cobwebs and dust motes hung like stars.

"Do you mean," I said softly, "the first Goblin Queen?" The one who lived.

"Yes, Your Highness."

The nameless, brave maiden. I had forgotten about her, forgotten that she was the first and only one of us to make her sacrifice, and survive.

"How?" I whispered. "How did she escape?"

"She didn't." Twig twisted her spindly fingers into gnarled fists. "He let her go."

Something snapped behind my eyes: pain, explosion, an epiphany. "What?"

She nodded. "*Der Erlkönig* loved her, and he let her go."

For a moment, the sharp stab of jealousy gutted me. *Der Erlkönig* had loved the brave maiden. He had loved her beyond the breaking of the old laws and the end of the world.

"How," I said in a low voice, "is that possible?"

"I don't know," Twig whispered. "But their sacrifices were made in love, a love so vast it spanned both the world above and below. Their love was a bridge, and so they crossed it."

I frowned. *"They?"*

She trembled even harder at my question. Her fingers clenched and unclenched, and the effort of answering—or not answering—was causing her anguish.

"Twig," I said. "Are you saying that . . . that the brave maiden and *Der Erlkönig* walked out of the Underground—*together?*"

blanketing the forest floor. I breathed deep, and the heady scent of the Goblin Grove in high summer filled my nostrils, indulgence and languid possibility.

"Thank you," I said to the changeling. "Thank you."

He did not reply, only watched as I circled the ring of alder trees, so beloved and so familiar to me. I touched every branch and leaf and trunk, reacquainting myself with old friends. When I reached beyond the ring of trees, I felt my fingers brush against something.

I frowned. There was no fence, no curtain, no physical veil, yet there was nevertheless a sense of trespass.

"The barrier between worlds," the changeling said. "Cross, and you stand in the world above."

I gave the changeling a sharp look. The words sounded almost like a taunt. A challenge. But the changeling's face was as unreadable as ever, and he stood patiently in the grove with me, letting me explore the threshold.

Here and there I found traces of Käthe. Bits of ribbon, a scrap of paper with scribbled sketches, and even the beginnings of what looked like a piece of embroidery. I bent down to touch them, and they were real and solid in my hands.

"How is it I can touch and see and smell these things?" I asked, marveling.

"We stand in one of the in-between places," the changeling said. "These objects are both of the world above and the Underground at once. Until you touch them, they belong wholly to the world above. Until the sunshine girl carries your gift back to her home, it remains Underground."

I put my hand in my pocket, where the Wedding Night Sonata rested against my hip. "What if Käthe doesn't see my gift?"

The gallery of Goblin Kings. The changing face of *Der Erlkönig* through the ages. A succession? Sons? Heirs? But Thistle had said no union of mortal or the Underground had ever been fruitful. *There has always been* Der Erlkönig. *There will always be* Der Erlkönig.

Twig wailed, and with horror, I saw a band of granite grow around her chest, a spreading stain of gray. She moved her fingers and they moaned and cracked, like branches caught in a gale. Bark covered her claws, her knuckles, her palms. My kindhearted goblin girl was turning into roots and rock.

"Stop!" I cried. "Enough!"

But I could not stop her transformation, and she stiffened and twisted, turning into a hideous statue of herself.

"I release her!" I shouted. "I release her from my will!"

Time resumed. Once more, the flames danced merrily in the grate. My goblin girl stared at me, all traces of bark and stone gone from her body.

"Is there anything else I can assist you with, Your Highness?" Twig tilted her head, but I could read nothing in her black, expressionless eyes.

I wondered if I had imagined it all. "No," I said, my voice shaking. "You may go."

I half-expected her to vanish the moment I dismissed her, but Twig remained, studying the folded-up Wedding Night Sonata in my hand.

"Whatever you're planning," she said, "don't trust the changelings."

I opened my mouth, then shut it.

"They are not human, despite how they look. Remember what we told you."

I hid the pages of music behind me. "What have you told me?"

"They bite."


Despite Twig's warning, I was back at the Underground lake the following day. The changeling dutifully waited for me by the shore, twisting his fingers and shuffling his feet back and forth with nervousness. He reminded me so much of Josef. It was not just in the tilt of his eyes or the angle of his cheekbones; it was in the set of his shoulders, the biting of his lower lip.

"Are you ready?" the changeling asked.

I nodded.

"Do you have your gift for the sunshine girl?"

I nodded again and brought out the copy of the Wedding Night Sonata.

"Good," the changeling said. "Let us go."

He led me around to a hidden mooring, where a small skiff awaited us. It was not the barge that had borne me to the chapel; we were at another part of the lake altogether. We climbed into the boat, and that beautiful, unearthly singing that had carried me across on the night of my wedding rose up all around us.

The Lorelei.

*They guard the gateway to the world above,* the changeling had said.

The skiff moved swiftly over the black waters. My companion and I said nothing as the Lorelei carried us, and presently, I thought I could hear a faint roaring sound beneath their song.

"What's that sound?" I asked, but I had my a[nswer] moment.

The lake had narrowed into a rushing curren[t] Faster and faster, the roaring growing louder, the going faster, the rapids getting bigger. I clung to the ling's hand, afraid the little skiff we rode would cap[size] it held sturdy.

I don't know how long we rode the currents to th[e] above, but at long last the torrent slowed to a trick[le] we found ourselves approaching a hollowed-out grot[to] light was different here. It was a moment before I re[alized] it was because of the light from the world above.

The changeling got out of the skiff and hauled it to before helping me out of it. Here and there, shafts of brightness cut through the darkness of the grotto, sho[wing] an earthen room with a ceiling buttressed by roots.

"We are beneath the grove," the changeling said pointed above our heads, where a gap between the r[oots] and rocks was just large enough for a small person to c[limb] through.

He helped me make the ascent, although there w[ere] plenty of foot- and handholds to ease the way. At las[t I] emerged.

The light was blinding. I threw up my hands to sha[de] my eyes, but I could see nothing but endless white. Tea[rs] streamed and I pressed the heels of my palms into my eye[s] but nothing could cool their burning.

But little by little, bit by bit, my sight began to return When at last I could bear the light, I removed my hands.

The Goblin Grove. New growth and new life covered branches that I had last seen bare, a lush, verdant green

The changeling shrugged. "Then it never leaves the Underground."

I looked beyond the ring of alder trees. Home was so close, yet so far. If only I could just step outside for a moment, run back home and press my music into my sister's hands.

A perverse thought came to me. What would happen if I should cross? The sun was high in the sky, and the heat of it was fierce upon my skin. It was the middle of summer, and winter had never seemed so far away. I would not be breaking my vows to the Goblin King if I stepped out and then returned . . . right? I had given myself to him, to the Underground, of my own free will. I would return. I would come back. I pressed my fingers against the barrier.

I glanced over my shoulder at the changeling, who continued watching me with neither censure nor encouragement in his eyes.

First my fingers, then my hand, then my wrist, then my arm.

At last I was fully on the other side. I could not pinpoint the exact moment I had crossed from the Underground to the world above, but I knew the instant I had. My vision brightened, my hearing sharpened, and my breathing eased. I was alive.

I was *alive*.

I was alive in ways I had not realized I could be: I felt the thrum of blood pulsing through me, the zinging singing in my veins and beneath my skin. Every particle of dust and dirt, the silky feel of hot *Föhn* winds from the Alps, the faint hint of yeast and rising dough.

The smell of baking bread. The inn. Mother. Käthe. I fell to my knees. I was *here*. I was *alive*. I wanted to tear all the clothes from my body and run naked through the woods. I wanted nothing—*nothing*—between life and my body. All my senses sang, an overwhelming symphony of sensation, and I burst into tears.

Ugly, wrenching sobs tore through the forest. I did not care whether God, the Devil, or the changeling judged me. I cried and I cried and I cried, and even as the sorrow gushed forth in a torrent of grief and homesickness and joy, a part of me relished the pain. I had not known, until I had stepped out into the world above, just how stifled, how buried I had been.

I threw out my arms and closed my eyes, as though I could embrace the whole of creation, feeling the intensity of summer sunshine upon my face.

The light changed.

I opened my eyes to see a cloud pass over the face of the sun. But it wasn't just the veiling of the sun that changed the light around me. It seemed suddenly thinner, weaker, grayer. The hot *Föhn* winds that ordinarily seared the valleys beneath the Alps kissed my cheeks with a cool breath.

I glanced at the changeling in confusion, and recoiled. His lips were pulled back in a feral snarl, and those black goblin eyes glittered with malice.

Chill hollowed out the air around me, and frost began to rim the edges of the branches and leaves, a delicate lace made of ice.

Winter.

I leaped to my feet and ran back into the Goblin Grove. "Why didn't you stop me?" I cried.

The changeling laughed, a sharp and brittle sound that pierced my ears. "Because I didn't want to."

And then, bursting from beneath the roots of the alders,

a myriad of arms and hands. I shrieked and jumped away as they clawed at the earth, a whole host of changelings emerging.

"The Goblin Queen may never again set foot in the world above," the changeling said. "But you have broken the old laws, mortal, and now we are free to roam the earth."

"You tricked me!" I rushed forward to grab him, to wrestle him to the ground and strangle the life he so desperately wanted from his body. But he sidestepped my attack with ease, grabbing my wrists in a superhuman grip.

"Of course," he scoffed. "Of all his wives, you were the easiest to fool. Your soft and tender heart could be shaped and twisted like clay. All it took was a little pity."

His features shifted. The lower lip softened, his shoulders drooped, his lashes lowered decorously. I gasped as the shadow of my little brother emerged.

"I didn't even have to change all the way with you. I can, you know. We all can."

I blinked. I was staring into Josef's face, perfect in every detail, from the tilt of his nose to the freckles that lightly dusted his cheeks. Perfect save for one small thing: his eyes remained the flat, inescapable dark of goblin eyes.

"You monster," I hissed.

The changeling only smiled.

"Take me back," I said. "Take me back!"

"No."

"I wish you would take me back!"

He threw back his head and laughed. "Your power is broken, *Goblin Queen*," he sneered. "You can no longer compel me."

I shook my head. "Then I shall go back without you."

"Too late," he crooned. The others, his brothers and

sisters, took up the chorus. *Too late, too late, too late.* "Once you've crossed the threshold, mortal, there is no returning."

Clouds swirled overhead, dark and ominous. I felt the icy bite of a snowflake land on my cheek before it melted away. A blizzard was coming. I had doomed the world above to eternal winter, all for my selfish desire to *live*.

I collapsed to the forest floor. The weight of my guilt and horror bore down upon me, pressing me into the earth.

*Oh, God,* I prayed. *Oh, God, forgive me. I'm so sorry. Please save us. Please.*

But God did not listen. The snow was flurrying in earnest now, dusting my shoulders, my back, my hands. My glance fell on the wolf's-head ring around my finger, its blue and green eyes twinkling in the light.

*With this ring, I make you my Queen. Sovereignty over my kingdom, over the goblins, and over me.*

"Please," I whispered to the wolf. "Please. Of my own free will, I gave unto you myself, entire. Take me back, *mein Herr.* Take me back."

I would have called his name if I had known it. But he had no name, only a title, and I did not know if he would or could hear me now.

Although ice rimmed the branches of every tree, I was suddenly warm and oh so sleepy. The temptation to lay down my head overpowered me. I could close my eyes and sleep forever, never waking up to the world I had destroyed.

"Elisabeth!"

I knew that voice. I struggled to lift my gaze to meet his, but my lashes had frozen shut. I was blind.

"Elisabeth!"

Arms encircled me, lifting me from the forest floor.

"Hold on, my darling, hold on," the voice murmured in my ear.

"Of my own free will," I croaked. "I gave unto you myself, entire."

"I know, my dear. I know." He held me tight, and warmth—real warmth—flooded through me. Not the false heat of freezing to death.

I opened my eyes to see the Goblin King gazing down upon me.

"Do you accept my pledge?" My throat was hoarse, but my voice was steady.

"I do, Elisabeth, I do." Those mismatched eyes were alight, shimmering with . . . tears? I reached up to brush them away, but my hand fell to my side.

And behind him, the skies cleared, turning blue and cloudless, as the leaves crowning him returned to green. My last thought before unconsciousness claimed me was that I had not known *Der Erlkönig* could cry, and wondered what it betokened.

## ZUGZWANG

I awoke to shouting. I was a child again, back under the covers with Käthe, listening to our parents argue downstairs. Over money, over Josef, over Constanze. When Mother and Papa weren't kissing or cooing at one another, they were screaming.

"How could you let this happen?" The sounds of destruction shattered the room. "I told you not to let her out of your sight!"

More smashing, more breaking. I opened my eyes to see the Goblin King raging at Twig and Thistle, who cringed and cowered at his feet. Their ears were pushed back and they shuffled forward on hands and knees, making obeisance to their king.

"Get out," he snarled. A vase flew from the mantel straight at Twig's head. "Get out!"

"Stop!" The vase halted in midair. The Goblin King whirled around as my goblin girls stared at me, wide-eyed.

"Leave them alone," I said. "They didn't do anything wrong."

The vase crashed to the floor. "You!" His eyes flashed, his nostrils flared, and his hair was wild. Two bright spots of red stained his cheeks, a high, hectic, color. "You— you—"

"Go," I said to my attendants. They did not need to be told twice.

The Goblin King made an inarticulate sound of fury and kicked at a small side table. It went tumbling into the fireplace, sending ash and embers everywhere. The Goblin King hauled the now-smoldering side table out of the hearth and threw it to the ground, stomping it into pieces. He was like a child in a tantrum, fists clenched with anger, face clenched with irritation.

I knew I should be sorry. I knew I should be contrite. But I couldn't help it; I laughed.

The first giggle that escaped me nearly choked me with surprise. I had not laughed in an age, and the muscles of happiness and humor were unused to it. But the more I laughed, the better it felt, and I bathed in my mirth, an endless bubbling fountain.

"And what, my dear," the Goblin King said in acid tones, "is so funny?"

"You," I gasped out between breaths. "You!"

He narrowed his eyes. "Do I amuse you, Elisabeth?"

I collapsed onto my bed, back and stomach spasming with a fit of giggles. Then the storm subsided and my body was no longer wracked with the uncontrollably joyous hiccoughs of laughter. But their aftermath fizzed along my veins, and I felt loose, limber, and languid. My head hung over the edge of my mattress, and I looked up at the Goblin King upside down.

"Yes," I said. "You do."

"I'm glad one of us finds the other amusing," he fumed. "Because I am wroth with you."

"I know, and I am sorry," I said. "But I don't regret it."

The truth dropped between us like a stone, surprising the both of us. The Goblin King went livid, an ashen-gray color. But I . . . I was flush with life and fervor again. I did not need to look at a mirror to know that the pink had returned to my cheeks, or that a sparkle had returned to my eyes. I could feel it in the singing of my blood. I had set foot in the world above . . . and returned.

And the Goblin King was angry. His shoulders were heaving, his eyes alight, his lips tight. I felt his fury roll off him in waves, heating the air between us. He had once said he could no longer feel the intensity of emotion, but I knew that anger boiled his blood, and he held himself tight to contain it. My breath came quicker.

"What, *mein Herr*," I said, "did you think I would say otherwise?"

I watched the pupils of those mismatched eyes contract and dilate. His fingers curled into claws. The wolf inside him was thrashing and shaking to get loose.

*Come,* I thought. *Come and get me.*

"Perhaps I was foolish enough to think that the consequences of your actions would have at least caused you some concern."

I remembered the sky returning to cloudless blue, the leaves greening. I remembered tears in those pale eyes as the world around us returned to summer.

"Have I condemned the world to eternal winter?"

I could see the truth in the Goblin King's mouth. His jaw tightened and his lips thinned with the effort of holding it back.

"No."

"Have I set the denizens of the Underground loose upon the world?"

A furious pause. "No."

"Then there's been no harm done."

Insouciant, impertinent, impudent. A coquette's arsenal of flirtation, and I was reckless with it. He was so close to breaking, so close to grabbing me by the shoulders and punishing me. I wanted it. I wanted the pain and the pleasure, and the reminder that I was still *alive*.

"No harm done!" He grabbed a statue from the mantel and hurled it against the far wall. "What if I hadn't heard you? What if I couldn't bring you back? What if—" He stopped himself, but I heard the rest of that sentence, hanging in the air between us.

*What if you didn't want to come back?*

I got up from the bed. With each step forward, the Goblin King retreated, but when I had his back pressed against the wall, he could run no farther from me. I placed my hands on his chest, a light touch, and rose up onto my toes to whisper in his ear.

"I came back," I murmured. "Of my own free will."

His hands shot out and gripped me about my shoulders, but whether to push me away or pull me close, I wasn't sure. His fingers dug into the flesh about my upper arms.

"Don't you ever, *ever* do that again." Each word was a dart to my heart, deliberate and sure. "*Ever.*"

I felt both his anger and his fear in his grip. Every bit of him was strung with tension, balanced between wanting to put me in my place and wanting to let me go. His trembles traveled all the way down my body, like his passion was the finger that plucked the string connecting us, reverberations and resonance pooling deep within me.

So I kissed him.

The Goblin King was startled, but I grabbed his shirt and pulled him closer. I clung to him like a drowning man clings to a lifeline; he was my lifeline. He returned my kiss with desperation, over and over and over again, each one sloppier and rougher than the last. His arms tightened about me, his hands grasping at the back of my dress, while my own hands found the hem of his shirt and slid them against his bare skin.

It was like coming home.

"Don't," he whispered against my lips, fierce and urgent. "Don't. Don't. Don't."

*Don't touch me. Don't tempt me. Don't ever try to leave the Underground again.* I did not understand what he was protesting, but it did not matter. We were two juggernauts on a collision course, and this joining had been a long time in the making.

"I won't, I won't, I won't," I said, but I did not know what I was promising. I did not care. My flesh leaped at his touch, erasing all conscious thought.

He tangled his fingers in my hair then, yanking me away from his lips. I struggled to kiss him again, but his grip was strong. He grabbed my chin with his other hand, forcing me to meet his gaze.

Those eyes. So pale, so startling, so different. His breath was hot against my face, and we stared at each other. I was stunned to see I was looking into the face of the austere young man, not *Der Erlkönig*, not the wolf, and suddenly I understood what he had been pleading.

*Don't leave me.*

A warmth spread from my center, turning my limbs liquid. But when that warmth reached my heart, it turned into pain.

"Never," I breathed.

At my word, his eyes transformed. Hardening into jewels, the mask of *Der Erlkönig* returned. He lowered his mouth to the column of my neck, a light touch of teeth, his hand moving to rest lightly against my collarbone.

"Good," he growled.

And then with one swift motion, he tore the fabric of my dress from the neck down.


We are rough and reverent. We fall onto my bed together, a twisted, tangled knot of torn clothing and exposed limbs, a pair of wrestling wolves.

Our bodies reacquaint themselves, relearning the other's touch. I hold the Goblin King and he is mine, familiar and new all at once.

"Don't," he says.

*Don't let go.*

"Never," I breathe.

We struggle to find a rhythm, a consensus, a progression, but neither of us give in to the other, both wanting to take and take and take. I deserve it, I deserve this for the ages he starved me of his touch. He deserves it, he deserves it because I nearly abandoned him, abandoned the Underground, abandoned the world. We are angry, but our anger is like play, like hounds practicing for the hunt.

The Goblin King has ever been generous with me in our marriage bed, but it is only now I understand just how much. He presses my shoulders down, legs pinning my torso, and leans over me, his face close. His expression is wild and feral, brows furrowed, mouth curled into a snarl. The austere young man is gone; there will be no one to guide me through the forest now.

He crushes his lips to mine, our tongues dancing, his hands running over my body to rest between my legs. I feel him against me, and tense.

The Goblin King pauses. "Your wish is my command," he murmurs. He waits upon my word.

I hesitate, then nod. "Yes," I whisper. "Yes."

I'm not quite ready for the joining, but I am caught breathless as he pushes close. This is more than fullness, this is fulfillment. I lift my head up to the heavens. Heaven is far away, but the fairy lights twinkle above me, stars in a firmament that will never see the light of day.

And then we play together, our tempos matching, a shared rhythm that grows wilder and wilder. I am not me. I am not Elisabeth. I am not a human girl. I am a wild thing, a creature of the forest and the storm and the night. I run through dreams and fancies, through all the stories of my childhood of the dark and uncanny and strange and weird. I am primordial, I am made of music and magic and *Der Erlkönig*.

I am lost.

Gradually, I return to myself, bit by bit, body part by body part, sense by sense. First my feet. Then my hands. Then my body, draped with the warmth of him. Color returns to the world, the taste of blood where I've inadvertently bitten my lip. Sight and touch and taste and smell.

I wait for sound to join me, but as the moments tick on, I hear nothing but the thudding of my heart.

*Little by little, they will take your sight, your smell, your taste, your touch; a slow feast.*

Fear grips me.

The Goblin King feels me panic, and reaches down to stroke my face. I reach up to touch my nose and my hand comes away with red. A nosebleed.

I feel the horror that runs up and down the length of him a second before he wrenches himself away.

*Elisabeth?* I see the Goblin King's mouth form the syllables of my name, but I cannot hear him.

*Elisabeth!*

He shouts something more, but I can no longer understand him. Words blur into an unintelligible muffled drone, and with a chill, Thistle's words come back to me:

*Think you your beating heart the greatest gift you could give? No, mortal, your heartbeat is but the least and last.*

The Goblin King shouts something again, and within an instant, my goblin girls appear.

No, not this. No. I returned from the world above. My sister still remembered me. My brother still said my name. As Twig and Thistle fuss over me, I hold the Goblin King's gaze, looking for answers, knowing he cannot give me the ones I want to hear, because I can hear nothing at all.

# JUSTICE

Somewhere in the distance, a violin sang a song of sorrow, regret, and apology.

"Josef?" I murmured, stirring from a dream.

But it was not my little brother. I did not hear Josef's characteristic clarity in the music; instead I heard a weighty sort of grief, the notes lacquered with years—centuries, perhaps—of loss.

It was the Goblin King.

I gasped and sat up in my bed. Memories of what had passed between us returned in a flash of heat, mingled with the chilling terror of the consequences. I shuddered and touched my ears, listening, hoping, fearing.

"She's awake."

That was Thistle's voice. I turned to see my goblin girls beside me, watching me with flat, black eyes. I could hear again. Relief flooded me, threatening to submerge me under a wave of tears. I had not lost this. Not yet. I still had sight and smell and sense and *sound*. I threw off my covers and rose from my bed. I wanted to rush to the retiring room, wanted to press my fingers into the klavier, wanted to revel in the music I thought I had lost.

"Wait, Your Highness, wait!" Twig grasped for me, but I hurried out of her reach. "You must rest."

My limbs were still shaky and I trembled as though I were recovering from a bout of illness, but I did not care. Music roiled and churned within me, pushing at my pores, my eyeballs, my fingers, and I needed to get it out, get it out, or explode.

In the retiring room, I saw that Twig and Thistle had taken the Wedding Night Sonata from my apron pocket and set it back on the klavier, but I was in no mood to compose. Everything was an ungovernable, chaotic mess within me, less music than a cacophony of sound. I sat down on the bench, and pushed, pounded, and played the klavier, pouring into the instrument my relief, anger, surprise, and joy. I improvised, I butchered, I wailed. I gave into the tempest of emotions within me until the storm passed.

In the calm that followed, a violin replied.

*I am sorry, Elisabeth.*

I understood the Goblin King's apology as clearly as though he had spoken the words before me. Music had always been the language we shared, a language of love, of laughter, of lamentation. I let him play and play and play until at last I set my hands upon the keyboard and played my mercy.

*I thank you, I forgive you. I thank you, I forgive you.*

But the violin sang over my absolution, an ostinato of guilt and shame. I tried to join him in the music, to find an accompaniment, a *basso continuo,* but the Goblin King kept changing the tempo, the key, the time signature, variation upon variation of remorse.

*I am a monster. I am a monster. I am a monster.*

It went on and on, and I could not get a word in edgewise.

"Fetch him," I commanded Thistle, who was absentmindedly shredding a pile of discarded foul papers. "Fetch *Der Erlkönig.*"

She made a face but did as I asked. But when she returned, she returned alone.

"Where is he?"

For the first time ever, I thought I detected a hint of sheepishness about Thistle's expression. She mumbled an excuse.

"His Majesty will not come," said Thistle.

I knew the Goblin King was not bound to my will as my goblin girls were, but I sent Twig to fetch him, hoping the kinder of my two attendants could convince him. But she, too, returned alone.

"What, is *Der Erlkönig* too ashamed to face me?" I asked. "I would rather he make his apologies to my person than through his violin."

"He is in the chapel, Your Highness," Twig said.

"We do not disturb him when he is in prayer," Thistle added.

I looked at them, astonished. "What? Surely you goblins don't give two figs for his God?"

Thistle crossed her arms. "We don't."

"We do not trespass upon sacred spaces," Twig said. "A courtesy you mortals never gave us. We abide by the old laws, but if nothing else, we respect His Majesty's faith, for who are we to deny the uncanny and unknown?"

This surprised me. In all of Constanze's tales, goblins had no honor or morals, quick to lie and steal and cheat to get their way. But who was I to question the old laws?

"Fine then," I said. "I would deprive him of his voice. Fetch me his violin."

My goblin girls exchanged glances. It would be a useless command.

I made a noise of disgust. "All right. Leave me be, and I shall call him another way."

Twig and Thistle gave each other another glance, then faded away.

I waited.

I waited for the Goblin King to finish, for the guilt to run dry. I waited for the violin to fall silent so I could make my reply.

I organized my papers and began work on the second movement of the Wedding Night Sonata, the adagio.

*You are the monster I claim,* mein Herr.

Through the large mirrors lining the retiring room, I watched the river ripple through Salzburg, letting the mood serve as my inspiration. I heard the delicate pizzicato plinks of a violin, droplets of ice melting into spring and summer. Beneath that, the murmuring susurration of a flowing brook. Arpeggios on the fortepiano. I made notes on the paper in front of me. The key had not yet resolved in my mind, but I thought it might be C minor.

I modulated the arpeggios up and down, not with any purpose, just to play with the sound until I heard something that struck me. Nothing, so I began to expand the arpeggios. Better. Some chromatic color. There was tension building there beneath the notes. I liked it. I recognized it. It was the unbearable weight of desire.

I left no room for the Goblin King to reply.

The first movement had been about anger and impotence. The theme thwarted, the melody reaching and never quite resolving its potential until the end. The second movement would be about loss, and about dreams just out of reach. The world above. My body. His body. The throb of desire beat beneath it all, marrying these two movements together.

I made notes to revise the allegro with these new thoughts.

Softer. Gentler. The slower tempo of the adagio lent itself to a more meditative, melancholy air, but I did not want complacence and resignation. No, I wanted the melody to unsettle and disturb him, even as it beguiled and tempted him. Rising notes, a pause, then resolution. Modulating higher. The same pattern, a pause, then resolution. I thought of the Goblin King's hands, sliding over my skin. A laden pause, then a painful grip. Over and over again. Leaving his mark upon my person. I made my marks on the score.

I leaned into the notes, my body pushing and pulling with the music. I closed my eyes and imagined the Goblin King standing behind me, his hands resting about my shoulders. Sixteenth notes in a chromatic scale. Those same hands, fingers splayed, running down my throat to my collarbone, down my shoulders, down my décolletage. Falling notes, glissando, slower eighths. I let out a sigh.

There was an echo of that sigh in the room.

Let the Goblin King listen to me now. Let him hear my frustration and forgiveness.

As I played, as I composed, I waited. I waited for the soft touch of a hand against my hair, the whisper of a breath upon my neck. I waited for his shadow to fall across the keys, for teardrops to fall on my shoulder. I waited and waited and waited until the sun came up, until the darkness faded to show no trace that the Goblin King had ever been there.

It didn't work. I had been so certain—so sure—that my music, the music he had so desperately wanted of me, would be enough to draw the Goblin King from his guilt. But as the minutes, the hours, the days passed, my husband kept his distance. He had not touched me, not spoken to me, not looked at me since our disastrous encounter after he brought me back from the world above.

I missed him.

I missed our conversations by the fire, when he had read aloud from the writings of Erasmus and Kepler and Copernicus, when I had set aside my self-consciousness and performed for him the works of occasional poetry I had learned. I missed our childish games of Truth or Forfeit, his hand tricks and jests. I missed working with him on our Wedding Night Sonata, but most of all I missed his smile, his mismatched eyes, and those long, elegant fingers of his that worked both music and magic.

Well, if the Goblin King would not come to me, then I would drag him out from hiding myself.

The second movement of the Wedding Night Sonata was nearly finished, and it had nothing of the Goblin King's voice within it. I set down my quill.

"Thistle," I said to the waiting air.

The goblin girl materialized before me.

"What do you want now, Goblin Queen?" she sneered.

"Where is *Der Erlkönig*?" I asked.

"In the chapel. As is his wont these days."

"Lead me to him."

Thistle raised an eyebrow, or she would have, had she had eyebrows at all. "You are braver than I reckoned, mortal, to interrupt His Majesty during his devotions."

I shrugged. "I believe in God's unending forgiveness."

"It's not your God's forgiveness you'd be needing."

Nevertheless, Thistle agreed—after I had wished it—to guide me to the chapel to retrieve the Goblin King's violin. Thistle left me at the entrance and then disappeared as soon as I released her.

The chapel was empty.

I was furious with my goblin girl, berating myself for allowing myself to be swindled by her tricks. I should have asked Twig instead. I turned to leave, but not before a violin before the altar caught my eye.

The Goblin King's violin.

I walked up the aisle to retrieve it, to take his voice and his guilt away. Above, the stained glass windows glowed with an otherworldly light. There were no pews or seats in the space; after all, there was no priest to conduct a service, no parishioners to attend. A plain wooden crucifix hung above the altar, and in the chancel rested the Goblin King's violin in its stand on a small table.

As soon as my hands touched its warm, aged wood, a sigh echoed around me.

I nearly dropped the violin from surprise. I turned around, but there was no one there.

"I don't know if Thou art there, my Lord, but I am here, come once more, kneeling and asking forgiveness. Asking for guidance. I am so far from Thee and Thy grace in the Underground, yet still I yearn for Thy presence."

The voice came from one of the niches lining the aisle,

devotional spaces where one might light a candle for prayer. I tiptoed my way toward the one on my left, from which the voice emanated.

The Goblin King knelt at a small table, head bowed before a small gilt image of Christ. Several candles burned beside him, illuminating the face of Our Lord with a gentle, golden glow.

"As the years pass, one would think the immortal would become accustomed to death. After all, everyone else withers and fades. For one such as me, it is merely a fact of existence. Do mortals wonder at the passing of summer into autumn? Of autumn into winter? No, they trust that the world will turn again, and life and warmth will return. And yet . . ."

The Goblin King lifted his head. I pressed back against the rock wall, hidden from view.

"And yet I keenly feel the bitter chill of each winter. The frostbite of death never lessens its terrible sting. I have watched so many of my brides bloom and fade, but . . ."

His voice faltered.

*I shouldn't be here. I should leave the Goblin King to his private confessions.* I turned to go.

"But Elisabeth . . ."

I stopped.

"Elisabeth is not like the flowers who have come before. Their beauty is fleeting, transient. One learns to admire them while they last, for they will be ashes tomorrow. Once their petals faded to brown, I swept them away."

My ears were not meant to hear his soul poured out before God. Yet I could not move. Did not want to move.

"They would call me cruel, I suppose. *She* would call me cruel. But to be cruel, cold, and distant was the only way I knew how to survive." He laughed, but it was more a scoff than a chuckle. "Why does an immortal need to worry about survival? Oh, my Lord, every day is a struggle to survive."

His voice fell into softer cadences, more reminiscence than supplication.

"My life, my very existence, is a torture unending. I made a bargain with the Devil, and I am in Hell. It's something I never understood, not until I became king of this accursed place. I was so afraid of dying that I took the chance—any chance—to escape its deep darkness. What a fool I was. What a fool I am."

He bowed his head again.

"Anger, heartache, joy, desire, I have not properly felt these emotions in a long time. Especially joy. Of them all, anger was the easiest to feel—bitterness and despair have been my constant companions for centuries. But despite everything, I still yearn for depth. For intensity. Despite the years, I have not forgotten the spark and the burn. I yearn to feel it again, even as time and eternity have inured me to the freshness."

I clutched his violin to my breast, wishing I could go to him, wishing I could take him into my arms and give him comfort.

"I gave up trying a long time ago. Each of my brides had come to me willing to die; their lives in the world above had ended already. They all wanted one last chance to feel again, and I gave them that. I gave them tears, I gave them plea- sure, but most of all, I gave them catharsis. They used me as much as I used them, and once they were gone, I hated them all for leaving me behind. Leaving me to endure alone, until the next one came along. But Elisabeth . . ."

I held my breath.

"She was never a hothouse flower. She is a sturdy oak

tree. If her leaves have fallen, then she will bloom again come spring. She was not ready to die when she gave her life to me. But she did anyway, because she loved, and loved deeply."

Tears scalded my lower lashes.

"I know what Thou wouldst tell me. I should have done the greater thing—the godly thing—and returned her to the world above." A hitch in his throat. "But I was selfish."

Suddenly, the trespass of what I was doing overcame me. I had come to deprive the Goblin King of his voice, only to realize perhaps it was I who should have been listening instead.

"I know what it means to love, my Lord. It was Thee who taught me how. Thou hath shown me through Thy words and Thy death, but I did not understand the meaning of sacrifice until now. To love is to be selfless. Let me be selfless. Lend me strength, my Lord, for I shall need it in the trials to come."

The soft sound of crying, the echoes of which I tried my hardest to suppress.

"In Thy name I pray, amen."

## BE, THOU,
## WITH ME

**b**ack in the retiring room, I studied the violin before me. It was rather plain, devoid of ornamentation, but made of a beautiful, rich wood, stained a dark amber. The instrument was clearly quite old, the belly dinged and scratched with age and wear, although it appeared as though the neck, pegbox, and scroll had been replaced more recently. I thought of the scroll painted with the portrait of the austere young man in the gallery, the woman whose face was contorted in pain or pleasure. It had looked familiar. I wondered what happened to it.

I lifted the violin from the stand. It was an instrument, like countless others I had picked up and played over the years, yet there was a living, breathing quality to it. The wood was warm beneath my hand, and as with the flute the Goblin King gave me oh so long ago, it was a touch that felt back. Like holding someone's hand. Like holding the Goblin King's hand.

I should not have taken it.

*To love is to be selfless.*

I should not have heard those words. It had been neither the time nor the place. The Goblin King and I deserved to face each other when we gave up our most intimate revelations, and I had stolen that from us. Regret roiled through me.

*Mea culpa,* mein Herr. *Mea maxima culpa.*

I tucked the violin beneath my chin, inhaling the faint scent of rosin. Faint traces of an earthier, muskier perfume were ingrained into the wood. The scent of ice curling over pond edges, the woody heart of a bonfire. The scent of the Goblin King.

I tuned the strings first, but the violin had been played recently enough that it needed little adjustment. I practiced a few scales and exercises, running my fingers up and down the neck, acquainting myself with the feel of it. Each violin was different from its brother in the subtlest, smallest of ways, even if the bones were the same. This violin was older than any of the ones we had at the inn—any of the ones we had remaining. The angle of its neck to the body was different, as well as the length of the fingerboard. The sound was fuller and deeper as I ran the bow over its strings.

My hands had not touched a violin since the Goblin Ball, when I joined the musicians playing the minuet, when I had first allowed that seed of music within me to crack and emerge forth. My instrument, by necessity rather than choice, had been the klavier. First because I was needed to accompany Josef, and second because the keyboard was the easiest place I could visualize my music. But the violin was the first instrument I had learned, and therefore the first instrument I had loved. Although it did not sing in my hands the way it did in my brother's, or even the Goblin King's, I knew how to ply its strings.

Vibrations ran along the belly of the violin and along my jaw where it rested against the instrument. I closed my eyes, feeling the resonance sing inside my head. Once I was warmed up, I let my fingers do what they willed—the beginnings of a few chaconnes, phrases from sonatas I had always enjoyed playing, runs of sixteenth notes and trills.

But it had been years since I last played with any serious intent, years since I had practiced. My fingers tangled themselves up, the discipline lazied out of them. I could no longer keep my tempos consistent, nor could I remember an entire piece from beginning to end. But there was no need to prove virtuosity to myself, not anymore. So I picked a simple aria, one Mother used to sing as she worked around the inn.

*Be, thou, with me.*

I heard him breathing.

*Then go I with joy, to Death and to my rest.*

It had been so long since his presence walked in my mind that I knew the instant the Goblin King was near.

*Oh how glad would be my end, if it be your dear hands I see, closing my faithful eyes at last.*

The hitch of a broken breath. I opened my eyes, but there was no one there. But I felt his eyes upon me anyway, feather-light and invisible, gentle fingers tracing the line of my neck and arm as it held the violin. I felt its touch on my bow arm, gently holding my elbow as I moved it back and forth across the strings in a smooth, continuous arc.

"Be, thou, with me," I said, still playing. An invitation.

"I am here, Elisabeth."

The bow faltered, and I dropped my arms. And from the shadows appeared an austere young man.

The Goblin King had appeared before me in many guises before—a tall, elegant stranger, a poor shepherd boy, a peacock-king—but I had never seen the youth in the portrait until now. The black of his tunic set off the pallor of his skin, turning his complexion silver and his hair golden white. There was no ornamentation on his sleeves or collar, save for a small wooden cross at his throat, and there was something of the priest about him: simple, plain, and beautiful.

"You call, and I answer," he said.

I set down the violin and the bow and held out my arms. "You come and I bid you welcome, *mein Herr*."

There was nothing else that needed to be said.

We walked into each other's embrace. We stood like that for a long while, allowing ourselves to adjust to the rhythm of each other's breaths, to relearn each other's shapes and curves. I had not known until that moment how empty my arms had been. He had lived in my mind for so long; now I wanted to hold more than just the idea of him. I wanted to hold *him*.

"Oh, Elisabeth," he said into my hair. "I am afraid."

He was quivering, shaking and trembling like a leaf in a storm.

"What are you afraid of?" I asked.

He laughed, an uncertain waver. "You," he said. "Damnation. My heart."

His heart. It beat beneath my cheek, fast and unsure.

"I know," I murmured into his chest. "I'm afraid too."

A confession, the first admission of weakness I had ever given him. I felt the realization all throughout his body. I had given him my hand, my music, my body, but the one thing I had not given him was my trust. I had trespassed against him in the chapel. Let him trespass against me now.

He kissed me.

It was not like any of the others we had shared. No passion, no frenzy, and I understood then that each time we had kissed before was not a gift; it was theft. We had stolen from each other, demanding something of the other without any thought to giving.

"Elisabeth," he said against my lips. "I have done you great wrong."

"No." I shook my head. "I broke my promise. I gave you my music, but I withheld my trust."

And it was true. I had given him everything but the one thing he truly needed: not my hand in marriage, not my body in his bed, not even my music. I should have trusted the Goblin King back when I was a little girl playing her music for him in the wood. I should have trusted him with the consequences of my choice to become his bride. I should have trusted him when he tried to give me back to myself.

"Oh, Elisabeth," the Goblin King said softly. His eyes were bright, vivid, and intense. "Your trust is a beautiful thing. Let me give you mine in return."

He fell to his knees.

Confused, I tried to bring him back to his feet, but he wrapped his arms about my waist in response.

"*Mein Herr,* what—"

"Be, thou, with me," he murmured. "How glad would be my end"—he lifted his eyes to mine—"if it be your dear hands into which I commend my soul."

Those mismatched eyes were clear as a well, and I could

see down to the boy he had been. The boy he might have been, before he had been transformed and consumed by a wolf in the woods. Before he became *Der Erlkönig*. My hands and limbs were trembling, and I sat down upon the bench.

"Elisabeth," he said. "You gave yourself to me, whole and entire. Let me do the same. Let me give myself back to you."

He lowered his head to place a soft kiss against my knee. And then I began to understand.

"You would . . . you would have me lead you into the dark? Into wildness?"

"Yes," he whispered. I felt every vibration of his voice, every movement of his lips against my leg. "Yes."

I hesitated. "I'm . . . I don't know the way."

I felt the Goblin King smile. "I trust you."

Trust. Did I have the courage to take it? Could I bear its weight? I was the Goblin Queen, but I was also just a girl. Just Elisabeth.

But was I not also a brave maiden?

I swallowed. "All right," I said, stroking his hair and pushing it away from his face. "As you wish."

"As you wish."


The Goblin King bows his head with gratitude, with reverence, with submission. I tangle my fingers in the luxuriant thickness of his thistledown hair, trying to lift his head and meet my eyes. "Look at me," I whisper.

We hold each other's gaze for a long moment. The nakedness in his expression turns me tender and nervous at once, the trust in his face mingling with a waiting apprehension. He has surrendered all power, and it is only now I understand that he had surrendered it to me long ago.

When I offered him my life for my sister's. When I offered him my music. When I offered him myself, entire. He has been in my thrall for longer than I can remember, and the realization of it makes me gasp. I could hurt him; I do not know if I could bear to hurt him.

His heart is in my grasp. It always has been.

His heart and trust are in my hands. I know what I want, but what I want brings a flush to my skin. My heart hammers in my breast, my blood sings in my ears, and my breath comes fast and hard. I strive for control, for an implacable countenance.

"You will . . . you will do everything I ask?" My control over my voice is incomplete. It shakes and trembles and shivers. "Without protest, without question, and . . . without laughing?"

He nods, his smile gentle. "Yes, my queen." His eyes are steady on my face. "Your wish is my command."

A nervous laugh crawls up my throat, but I swallow it, suppress it. The Goblin Queen does not ask for pleasure; she demands it. But I am not just the Goblin Queen. I am also Liesl, Elisabeth, a girl—no, woman—who yearns for nothing more than for the man at her feet to touch her, to take responsibility out of her hands. She does not know what to do with his trust.

Slowly, shyly, I undo the ties of my dressing gown. The Goblin King watches every movement of my hands with intense focus. I cannot control the blush that spreads from my chest through my body, but my hands are steady and sure. His eyes are fixated upon me, and I resist the urge to cover myself.

He waits upon my every word, and a trickle of surety, little by little, begins to fill me like a well.

"Stand," I say.

He complies.

"Undress."

The Goblin King lifts his eyebrows in surprise.

"Please."

Slowly, he raises his hand to undo the buttons of his shirt. He is informally dressed—no waistcoat, no silken breeches, just a simple shirt and trousers. Yet it takes ages for the Goblin King to become revealed to me. I hold my breath; I had not realized how much I'd longed to be able to see him—all of him—unobstructed and uncovered. No furtive glimpses during accidental meetings in his bedchamber, no bits and pieces of flesh between unlaced breeches and unbuttoned blouses, just skin—whole skin—a great, naked expanse of it.

He shrugs off his shirt. Lean muscle covers his torso, and I notice a scar bisecting his left breast. It is small, thin, silver, and glows in the soft firelight of the retiring room. He is slim, much slimmer than the solid working companions of my youth. Unbidden, the memory of Hans returns to me: thick, stocky, and brawny. As a girl I had thought his physique the pinnacle of masculinity. The pinnacle of strength. But the Goblin King belies all of that, nearly feminine in his elegance and grace. But there is nothing delicate about him, no softness about his belly and arms. The shadows play about him, carving the shapes and contours of his body into a work of art.

His eyes meet mine. The austere young man looks at me with a question in his gaze.

"Yes," I say, but I scarcely know for what I am giving him permission. "Yes, you may."

He breathes out in a long sigh. Those eyes, two-toned

and otherworldly, are for once free of the burdens they've carried for so long. The burden of immortality. The burden of unending indifference. He has relinquished them to me. He smiles.

I understand then that the trust he gave me is power. It is not only the Goblin Queen who has the ability to bend the will of those around her; it is me. Elisabeth, entire. "Come here," I say at last, holding out my hand. "Come and follow me into the light."

He takes my hand and I guide him toward my bedchamber. Then I gather him into my arms and we fall together.

We lie like this for a moment. I am no longer his Goblin Queen; I am Elisabeth, mortal, human, warm. He is no longer my Goblin King; he is my husband, the man behind the mask of myth. All pretense fades away and we stare at each other, naked in mind and flesh and soul.

I kiss him. He kisses me back. It is an exploratory dance of lips and tongue, a language we are learning together. There is a hunger within me that still yearns to be fulfilled, to be filled with him, but for now, I revel in the sweetness that is this: this moment, this communion.

And we are met.

This time, I do not leave him. I am fully in my body as my sense of self falls apart. My mind is wiped clean. *Tabula rasa.* He has rewritten who I am down to the core. It is one long revelation where I build myself back together again.

Dimly I become aware of the Goblin King whispering my name over and over, a mantra, rosary, a prayer on his lips.

"Elisabeth," he says. "Elisabeth, Elisabeth, Elisabeth."

"Yes," I answer. I am here. I am here at last.

I am the rhythm, he is the melody. I provide the *basso continuo,* he the improvisation.

"Yes," I whisper in his ear. "Yes."

When he returns to me, we lie there, our chests rising and falling with our breaths, slower and slower as our heartbeats calm, and the tides of our blood retreat. Lassitude overtakes me, a deep restfulness radiating from every part of me. He shifts and I am nestled in the crook of his shoulder, my nose rubbing against the hair of his chest, surprisingly soft.

We don't say anything and I feel myself drifting to sleep, an inevitable, inexorable descent into dreams. But just before I fade from consciousness, I hear four words that are my undoing.

"I love you, Elisabeth."

I hold him tighter to me, even as my heart unravels.

"By God, I love you so."

# THE BRAVE
# MAIDEN'S TALE

**t**ell me a story," I said.

The Goblin King and I lay in each other's arms, nestled against each other's hearts. His fingers lightly stroked the flesh of my upper arm, running them over the hill of my shoulder and down the valley between my breasts.

"Hmm?"

"Tell me a story," I repeated.

"What sort of story?"

"A bedtime story. And let it have a happy ending."

I felt the chuckle roll through him. "Is there one in particular you wish to hear?"

I paused. "Do you know," I said in a small voice, "the true tale of the brave maiden?"

It was a long time before he answered. "Yes," he said. "I know the true tale of the brave maiden. But I only know of it as a fairy tale, the story pieced together from bits of memory, both learned and inherited."

"The story is not yours?"

A beat. "No."

"Does the story not belong to *Der Erlkönig*?"

"The story belongs to *Der Erlkönig*," the Goblin King replied, "but not to me."

*But not to me.* It was the first time he had drawn such a clear delineation between himself and *Der Erlkönig*. Between the man he had been and the myth he had become.

I held him tighter, nuzzling against his heartbeat. I pretended it was mortal, that it pulsed in time with mine. His seconds were my hours, his minutes my years.

"Once upon a time," he began, "there was a great king who lived Underground."

I closed my eyes.

"This king was the ruler of the dead and the living," he continued. "He brought the world above to life every spring, and brought it back to death every autumn.

"As the seasons turned, one after another, the king grew old. Weary. Spring came later and later and autumn earlier and earlier, until one day, there was no spring at all." His voice fell. "The world above had gone quiet, dead, and still, and the people suffered."

I remembered the vivid image of frost tracing the edges of the summer green in the Goblin Grove, and shivered.

"Then, one day, a brave maiden ventured into the Underground," he went on. "To beg the king to return the world above to spring. She offered the king her life in exchange for the land. *My life for my people,* she said."

The burn of tears scalded my lashes. When the Goblin

King first told me this tale, I had thought it beautiful. A noble tale of martyrs and sacrifice. But now that I understood the true cost of my life, I found it painful. I was not noble. I was selfish. I wanted to live.

"*Der Erlkönig* sensed the fire in her," he said. "And desired its warmth. He had been cold for so long that he no longer remembered light or heat or all that was good in the world. She was the sun and he was the earth waking from a thaw. So he accepted her hand in marriage—a hand given as a lifeline is to a drowning man. He clung to that hand with all his strength, and slowly, surely, they woke the world from winter."

The Goblin King paused, as though gathering his next words.

"The role of the king underground is a burden, you know," he said. "Each year, the turning of the seasons becomes harder and harder, for the further away from life and love the years take you, the less human you become. It takes love, you see, to bring the world back to life."

"How so?" I asked.

"You have to love the land, and the people who live in it. Love is the bridge that spans the world above and below, and keeps the wheel of life turning."

I remembered Thistle's words to me. *As long as you have a reason to love.*

"And then what happened?" My fingers traced the scar across the Goblin King's heart, wondering at its history.

"And then *Der Erlkönig* fell in love."

I waited for the rest of the story, for the Goblin King to continue. But the silence between us stretched and grew taut, until I could bear the tension no longer and broke it.

"And?" I whispered.

"It just occurred to me that I cannot in good conscience give this story a happy ending," he said. "After all, do they not all end with *And they all lived happily ever after?*"

A happy ending. Perhaps it was just wishful thinking, but the echo of Twig's voice rang in my heart. *Their love was a bridge, and so they crossed it.* Could not the brave maiden have freed her Goblin King? Was her love not strong enough to span both worlds? *Mein Herr* was not the first; surely he would not be the last.

"Did . . . did not the brave maiden love *Der Erlkönig?*" I asked.

The Goblin King stiffened. "I don't know."

I bit my lip and turned my face away, unable to meet his gaze. "I think she did. She must have done. Otherwise, how else . . . how else could you . . ."

I could not finish.

"Would you like another story, Elisabeth?" The Goblin King's voice was tight.

I swallowed. "Yes."

"It is," he said after a moment, "a story that belongs to me. But I shall leave it up to you to decide whether or not the end is happy."

I nodded.

"Once upon a time, there was a young man."

I turned to give him a sharp glance. The Goblin King merely smiled, but whether sad or sweet, I could not tell.

"An austere young man?"

He laughed softly. "Is that what you call . . . what you call him?"

My cheeks reddened and I was too embarrassed to answer.

"An austere young man," the Goblin King mused. "I suppose so. Austere, pompous, foolish. Yes, foolish," he said decidedly. "Once upon a time, there was a foolish young man, who walked the world above in search of wisdom to make him less foolish. One day, he chanced upon a king in the wood, a king underground, who claimed to hold all the secrets of life, love, and Heaven."

I held my breath. *A story that belongs to me.* A story of how he had come to be *Der Erlkönig.*

"The king offered his knowledge to the foolish young man—for a price. *The price,* said the king underground, *is my crown, for which you must give me your soul and your name.* The young man, being foolish, agreed to the underground king's price."

It was as though all the air had been pulled from my lungs. The austere young man had been tricked—tricked into holding his throne. And that was the truth of the gallery of Goblin Kings. *There has always been* Der Erlkönig. *There always will be* Der Erlkönig. I could not breathe for the pity that wrapped its hand about my throat.

"The foolish young man thought it wasn't much of a sacrifice—after all, a changeling had no soul, and he had never had a name that was truly his own." The Goblin King's laugh was as bitter as anodyne. "But as the years wore on, as the weight of immortality grew heavier and heavier, he realized what a fool he truly had been, to have taken the king underground at his word. For no power in the world above or below was worth the torment he felt."

"Oh, *mein Herr.*" I lifted my hand to push the hair away from his face, but the Goblin King was not finished with his tale.

"Then, one day, he came across a maiden in the wood."

"A brave maiden?" I ventured.

"Brave," he agreed. "And beautiful."

I scoffed. "This is a fairy tale indeed."

"Shush." He touched a finger to my lips. "The maiden was both brave and beautiful, beautiful in ways that she did not see. Could not see, for all her beauty was locked away inside, magic and music, waiting to be set free."

I was brave and beautiful. It was both a pretty lie and an ugly truth.

"They became friends, the beautiful maiden and the foolish young man. They became friends, and the foolish young man began to remember all that was good and wonderful about the world. About humans. Music, faith, folly, passion. But," the Goblin King said, "as they grew older, the beautiful maiden forgot the foolish young man. She forgot him, and the foolish young man forgot why he had wanted to be human."

I cringed.

"So he set out a trap, caught the beautiful maiden, and kept her in a cage. She had a song and he wanted it, so the foolish young man made her sing it again and again until he let her out. But the beautiful maiden dutifully returned to her cage night after night, and for the first time in eternity, the foolish young man thought he could be happy."

"And was he?" I asked in a hoarse voice.

"Yes," he said, barely audible. "Oh, yes. He had never been happier."

My throat closed up.

"But, happy as the foolish young man might have been, the beautiful maiden was not. The cage was killing her, killing her spirit. And gradually, little by little, all that the foolish young man cherished about the beautiful maiden began to disappear. There was nothing he could do but watch her fade into a ghost before his very eyes, nothing unless he ripped out his own heart. Keep her, make himself happy, and watch her die? Or set her free, break his heart, and watch her live?"

He fell silent.

"So how does the story end?"

He met my gaze, and for the briefest moment, I thought those remarkable eyes brightened and deepened in color, just like the portrait of the austere young man, just like the eyes he must have had when he was human.

Then I blinked and they were as they ever had been: pale, faded, and icy.

"You are the one who wanted a happy ending, my dear. So you tell me, how does the story end?"

Tears slipped from my face, and he wiped them away with his thumbs.

"The foolish young man lets the beautiful maiden go."

"Yes." His voice was clotted thick with unshed emotion. "He lets her go."

I burst into sobs then, and the Goblin King gathered me close, rocking me in his arms as I cried. I cried for the breaking of the foolish young man's heart. I cried for the happiness we might have had. I cried for the selfishness I could not overcome. I cried for him, for us, but most of all, for myself. I was going home.

"You must leave, Elisabeth," he said softly.

I nodded my head, unable to speak.

"Choose to live, Elisabeth. There's a fire within you; keep it alight. Feed that flame with music and seasons and chocolate torte and strawberries and your grandmother's *Gugelhopf*. Let it grow with your love for your family. Let it be a beacon to set your heart by, so that you may remain true to yourself." He stroked my cheek. "Do this, so that I may remember you like this: fierce and full of life."

I nodded again.

"Are you ready?"

*No.* "Tomorrow," I said.

He smiled, then kissed me. His lips were gentle, and in them I tasted a farewell.

I kissed him back. Time did not stop for anyone, least of all me, but in that moment of our kiss, I found a little pocket of eternity.

# THE MYSTERY
## SONATAS

f I did not sleep, tomorrow would never come.

I left the Goblin King slumbering in my bed and ran away. Not to the retiring room, where our music waited upon the stand, but to the chapel. It was his sanctuary, his place of refuge, but on this last night before my freedom, I wanted a word with God.

Neither Thistle nor Twig were on hand to guide me, but by now, I had learned that the labyrinth of the Underground unraveled for the Goblin Queen, and the path from my bedroom to God's house was straight and narrow.

I wondered who had built the chapel. High above me, illuminated stained glass windows depicted various scenes, not from the life of Christ or the acts of the Apostles, but of *Der Erlkönig* and his brides. On the right, a series of panels showed a golden-haired woman clothed in white and a dark horned figure. The seasons progressed along with the panels as the maiden in white grew pale and thin. The very last window showed the maiden dying in the horned figure's arms as another woman in blue stood behind them.

The windows lining the left-hand side showed a young man in red, riding a white horse through a forest as little hobgoblins and grotesques cavorted at its feet. As the windows went on, the young man encountered a mysterious horned figure in the woods, a nimbus of darkness surrounding him instead of a halo of light. As the young man knelt at the figure's feet, the dark gloriole enveloped them both, and in the following panel, a shadowy gray man rode away on a white horse, leaving the young man in red with a crown of antlers upon his head.

The answers had always been here. But I had never thought to look for them in the house of God.

I knelt before the altar beneath the crucifix. I was an indifferent believer at best, a possible heathen at worst, having believed in God the way a child believes without question that tomorrow will come. Neither prayer nor catechism were particularly valued in my house, but I bowed my head before the sanctuary.

I did not know how to ask for courage or resolution. I did not know how to ask to stay the march of time, just for a little while. I was not ready to face the world above. Not yet.

There were no mirrors to the outside world in the chapel, but I imagined the Goblin Grove in the predawn lined with dark, with the faintest blush of blue lightening the blackness. *The hour when the kobolds and* Hödekin *come out to play,* Constanze used to say. I imagined the colors of the sky lightening and changing, a change so slight and gradual it might not be happening at all. In the world above, that would be my life, each second of each day passing with so little fanfare that the thought of dying was nothing more than the thought of dawn just beneath the horizon.

I had never given much thought to growing old, and the woman I would be when I was my grandmother's age. Would I be like my grandmother, wizened and crabbed? Or someone more like Mother, whose fine lines and faded hair were graceful touches of wisdom rather than age? I touched my fingers to my cheek, still smooth, still young. As I aged, those cheeks would sink, the skin losing its firmness, its shape.

Käthe would have been horrified at the thought, but the idea of growing old gave me comfort. To grow old was to have lived a full life. Not all of us were so privileged as to have a full life. And now that privilege would once again be mine.

"Elisabeth."

The Goblin King stood at the foot of the aisle, violin in hand.

"I didn't think you were especially devout, my dear," he said, an amused expression on his face.

"I'm not." I got to my feet, dusting the dirt from my knees. "But I came seeking fortitude."

His eyes were soft. "Fortitude for what?"

"To face tomorrow."

The Goblin King smiled, full of compassion and sympathy, striding up the aisle to stand beside me. "And did He answer?"

"No."

He shook his head. "It may be He already gave you the answer, but you have not the understanding to see it," he said softly. He tapped a finger against my heart. "The Lord works in mysterious ways."

"Well, I would appreciate it if the Lord were a little less mysterious and a little more straightforward."

He chuckled. "So say we all."

I rolled my eyes before my gaze fell to the instrument in his hands. "What's that for?"

In answer, he began tuning the violin. *Plink, plink, plink, plink*. Instead of tuning the strings to their standard intervals, the Goblin King tuned them to different pitches. He unstrung the middle D and A strings and crossed them before stringing them back to their pegs, leaving him with a *scordatura* I had never heard used before. *Plink, plink, plink, plink*. G, then another G, D, and another D. His ear was good. The Goblin King ran his bow over each string with a smooth, practiced motion as he fine-tuned their pitches, and I watched how easily his hands and fingers moved across the violin, familiar like old friends who had grown up together.

When he had finished, he turned to me. "Worship," he said simply. "I came here to worship Him in the only way I can. With the only thing remaining to me that is still pure, still . . . mine."

*His.* Despite what the Goblin King said, the austere young man still lived within him. No magic, no spell, no trick had given my Goblin King his extraordinary way with the violin. The power did not belong to *Der Erlkönig*; this gift was his, and his alone.

"I can leave," I offered. "If you would like to worship in private." I thought of the night I had trespassed upon him here, in this very chapel, and felt shame settle over me like a cloak.

He held my gaze for a long moment. "No, stay," he said at last. "Stay, and be with me."

I had demanded every last bit of him last night. His body, his lust, his name, his trust. But there were corners of his soul I dared not ask to reveal; even as I understood the need to hold some things sacred to yourself alone. His piety was one of them. The enormity of what he was granting me whisked my shame from me, replacing it with a sense of awe.

There were no pews in this chapel; there had only ever been one member of the faithful. So I sat down on the steps of the sanctuary, folded my hands, and let myself be with him, to accept this gift.

The Goblin King lifted his bow to the violin and closed his eyes. I watched him take a deep breath and begin the count in his head.

The piece began with a declaration, a proclamation of joy. The phrase repeated itself a few times before it was joined by a chorus of voices. The Goblin King skillfully conveyed them all through various shades of emotion and nuance, one after another, each in turn. All proclaiming *Hallelujah, hallelujah, hallelujah!* beneath his fingers. Then a pause, a breath, before he resumed; a stately sonata, reiterating the glad tidings of the first proclamation.

I had known he played beautifully. Like Josef, the Goblin King played not just with skill and precision, but with *love*. Yet they were as different from each other as night and day. My brother played with purity, but the Goblin King played with *devotion*. Josef's talent with the violin had always been that of ruthless clarity. Nothing of the earth could touch my brother's playing; he trod upon the ether and the air, the notes transcendent and oh so beautiful, so beautiful.

But the Goblin King's playing was weighty; the notes held depth and gravitas. Emotions my brother had not yet learned: grief, tragedy, loss. The Goblin King's virtuosity was *earned*.

The piece came to a close, the last note fading into the silence between us. I hadn't realized I'd been holding my breath.

"It's beautiful," I whispered, not wanting to break the reverent hush in the room. "Did you write it?"

He opened his eyes slowly, emerging from a trance. "Hmmm?"

"Did you write it? It's exquisite."

He smiled. "No. I did not write it. But you could say it wrote me, in a manner of speaking."

"What's the piece called?"

A pause. "The Resurrection. One of the Mystery Sonatas."

"Where did you learn it?"

Another pause. "At the abbey where I was raised."

Such tiny crumbs from his past. I swallowed each morsel like it was my last meal. I hungered for him, for the austere young man, for every bit of him I could not have.

"Which abbey?"

His only response was another smile, with just the tiniest hint of teeth. The Lord and the Goblin King worked in mysterious ways, and I rather wished they didn't.

"Who wrote the piece?" I pressed.

"Are we in another round of Truth or Forfeit?" he teased.

"Only if you wish it."

He paused before giving his answer. "I do not know who originally composed it." His eyes were distant, his fingers absentmindedly thumbing the strings on the violin. "I stole bits and pieces of song from the cloisters whenever I could, listening at corners and fingering the notes with an imaginary violin. I adapted the sonata as best as I could from memory."

I tried to place the sonata in time from my slipshod, piecemeal history lessons. It lacked the melodic musicality to which we'd grown accustomed in the world above, and sounded a bit old-fashioned. But it lacked the structure of a sonata as I knew it, a little wild, a little fluid. We had both skulked in the shadows, the Goblin King and I, eavesdropping on things to which we had no right.

"You could expand upon the themes," I suggested. "The *scordatura* is a little unusual, but it might be interesting to take the melody and play it again in a minor key."

He laughed and shook his head. "You are the genius, Elisabeth, the one who creates. Me? I am a mere interpreter."

The pain that stabbed me was sudden and fierce. I turned my head away so the Goblin King would not see me cry. My little brother had once told me that exact thing, before I came to the Underground, before I understood the difference between genesis and exegesis. I was too full of me, too full of my memories. I was drowning in the mire of my childhood dreams, and the unbearable pleasure of the present.

I felt the comfort of his presence settle down beside me on the steps. The Goblin King rested a gentle kiss on my shoulder blade, but said nothing, waiting for me to pull back my emotions, waiting for me to compose myself.

"Who—who taught you to play the violin?" I managed, clearing my throat of the sadness lodged there.

I felt him smile against my shoulder as he mumbled an answer.

"What?"

He lifted his head. "His name," he said softly, "was Brother Mahieu."

A monk. A monk of no consequence even, one who had

passed from the world above without leaving a mark. Yet the Goblin King remembered him. The Goblin King had clearly loved him, and it was in his love that the beloved old teacher lived on. This was the immortality humans were meant to have: to be remembered by those who loved us long after our bodies had crumbled into dust.

I thought of my brother and sister, those who still loved me, and remembered. They were waiting for me in the world above, and I felt the wings of tomorrow settle over me. Too soon. It was too soon.

"What was he like?" I asked, my back still turned to the Goblin King. "Did he raise you? Who were your parents? How came you to the abbey? What—"

"Elisabeth."

I still did not face him. I was not ready.

"Tomorrow has come."

I shook my head, but we were past the point of no return. I had made my choice. I had chosen myself. I had chosen selfishness.

The Goblin King sensed my hesitation. "Don't regret your decision to live."

"I don't," I whispered. "And I won't." It wasn't a lie, but neither was it entirely the truth.

"Elisabeth."

I tensed.

"Elisabeth, look at me."

Slowly, reluctantly, I turned around. There was a light shining in his eyes, a light that would remember me, long after I had faded from both the Underground and the world above. And those eyes . . . those eyes were brilliant gems. They changed his face utterly. His beauty no longer seemed so unsettling or uncanny, so preternaturally flawless. There was a vividness to his face, and it made him seem young. Vulnerable.

"Who are you?" I asked.

The question fell like a raindrop between us, pinging the glass quiet that enveloped us both.

"I am *Der Erlkönig*, the Lord of Mischief and the King Underground."

I shook my head. "No, that is what you are. *Who* are you?"

"I am the Goblin King, your immortal beloved, your eternal lover."

He was *Der Erlkönig*, and he was *my* Goblin King, but I wanted to know who he was to himself. His name was the last bit of him I could not have.

"No," I said. "I know who you are."

Teeth slipped from his grin. "Who am I?"

"You are a man with music in his soul. You are capricious, contrary, contradictory. You delight in childish games, and delight even more in winning. For a man of such intense piety, you are surprisingly petty. You are a gentleman, a virtuoso, a scholar, and a martyr, and of those masks, I like the martyr least of all. You are austere, you are pompous, you are pretentious, you are foolish."

The Goblin King did not reply.

"Well?" I asked. "Do I have the right of it?"

"Yes," he said thickly. "Yes, you have the very soul of me, Elisabeth."

"Then your name, *mein Herr*."

He laughed softly, but it was a gasp of pain, not of joy. "No."

"Why?"

"So you will forget me," he said simply. "You cannot love a man with no name."

I shook my head. "That's not true."

"A name is something that belongs to a mortal man." There was an expression I couldn't quite decipher in his mismatched eyes. "And the man I was is back there—back in the world above."

He pulled me close to him. I was nestled in his embrace, against the scar that crossed his heart.

"Find me," he said, his voice low. "Find me there, Elisabeth. It's only there, in the world above, that you will find the last bit of me."

He let me go. But he was not just releasing me from his embrace; he was releasing *me*. He was releasing the girl who once played her music for him in the wood, the girl he had broken open to set her soul free, the girl to whom he had given himself, entire.

With a hitching breath, I reached into my pocket and withdrew his wolf's-head ring, the ring he had set upon my finger the night we wed.

The Goblin King shook his head, closing my fingers around the ring. "Keep it."

"But . . . is it not a symbol of your power?"

"It is." He smiled sadly. "But it is only a symbol, Elisabeth. Of my power, yes, but also of my promise to you. Whatever else, I gave that ring to you in earnest, as a husband to a wife."

I wrapped my hand around his ring and pressed it against my heart. "How . . . how is it to be done? How are we to be"—I swallowed—"parted?"

"We made our vows in this room," the Goblin King said. "And so we can unmake them too."

A chalice of wine appeared on the altar. He reached for the goblet, then hesitated.

"I cannot . . . I cannot help you. Once we break our troth, your power as the Goblin Queen, *Der Erlkönig's* protection . . . it will all be gone. Have you the courage to make the way on your own?"

I did not. But I nodded just the same.

"The . . . the others will not make it easy. But I have faith, Elisabeth. Faith in you."

I had no faith of my own, but the Goblin King had his, and it was his faith in me that would be my courage. *The Lord works in mysterious ways.*

He took my hands in his. "Rejoice, for you shall live," he said softly, "and I shall rejoice with you."

I kissed his hands. His eyes were worried, but his mien was calm. He was being strong for me.

"I do solemnly swear," he said, "that I return the gift of your life, selflessly and selfishly given."

It was hard to speak through my tears. "And I do solemnly swear," I said, "that I accept my life, taken from your hands of my own free will."

The Goblin King retrieved the chalice from the altar and offered the goblet to me.

"Let us drink," he said. "And break our troth."

## THE RETURN

**m**y reign as Goblin Queen was ended.

I knew the moment my power had broken, for the passages around me had rearranged themselves. The chapel and the Goblin King had vanished, and I was on my own. No more would my path through the Underground be straight and clear. I had no map, no compass to guide me, but I knew where I had to go. To the shores of the Underground lake, to find the skiff the changeling had moored in its secret dock, and row and ride my way to the world above.

The Underground was far less civilized without the grace and protection of my power as Queen. Goblins scuttled underfoot, their long, multi-jointed fingers click-clacking over stone, beetles skittering in the dark. Their beady eyes shone down on me, the watchful touch of a thousand inhuman eyes at my back. The eerie, watchful, waiting silence had a shape and texture to it. It brushed over me like dark, musty cobwebs, which clung to me no matter how much I tried to shake them off. The silence raised all the hairs along my arms, sending prickles of ice and needles up my spine, and with each step I took, fear and dread increased a hundredfold.

*They will not make it easy. But I have faith, Elisabeth, faith in you.*

I was careful of my step, but the malice of the Underground was deviously clever. A crevice suddenly opened up beneath my feet, and I tripped and wrenched my ankle. Wincing with pain, I trod on the hem of my skirt, tumbling head over heels. I wiped at my stinging chin.

Blood.

The instant a drop of my blood hit the earth, a storm of hissing arose. This was the opportunity the goblins had been waiting for.

The clacking cacophony grew and swelled, like waves approaching some distant shore. Hands burst from beneath my feet—hands like gnarled and twisted branches, growing from the earth like brambles or vines. They grabbed at my ankles, my hair, my dress, my shoes, any part of me they could reach.

"Stop!" I shouted. "Stop!"

The corridors echoed with the sounds of their hands coming free, rattling off like gunshots. I covered my head and my ears as hands burst forth from the walls and the ceiling overhead, reaching, reaching, reaching. The hallways echoed with my screams.

"Stop! Please! I wish you would stop!"

But my wishes no longer had any power here. Crawling hands, myriad eyes, pointed teeth, all reaching to devour me, tear me apart limb from limb. Fingers twined about my feet brought me crashing down onto their waiting hands, a creature felled by a snare. I shrieked, struggling to break their grip, but their knobby fingers were strong. The hands bore me down into darkness, musty and rank with the sour scent of my panic.

*Oh, God, oh, God*, I thought. *I will be buried alive.*

Buried alive; what an ignominious end. Sacrificing my life for spring had been noble, but this? This was a terrible way to die. Not with a bang, but a whimper. I thought of the trees in the Goblin Grove, their uncomfortably human branches, and wondered if that was to be my fate, my limbs and shape immortalized by dead wood.

"What do you want from me?" I cried.

*You, you, you*, their hissing voices returned. *We want you. You cannot leave the Underground, mortal, not without paying the price.*

"What price?" Goblin hands crawled over my mouth and neck, as though to strangle the sounds coming from me. "Tell me and I shall pay it!"

The scuttling hands stopped. A few of them broke away to join together, their curled fingers and thumbs forming two eyes, a nose, a mouth. I was staring into a face.

There were only holes where the eyes should have been, only darkness inside its maw of a mouth. Yet I sensed a presence there, many goblins joined into a singular entity. I stared into the abyss, and found it staring back.

"What is it that you want?" I asked.

It was a while before those fingers could work together to form lips, a tongue, words.

*You have something that belongs to us, mortal.* Myriad voices joined together as one, a dissonant mass of pitches.

"What—"

*It lives in the world above.* More hands had come together to make a more complete face. High cheekbones. A pointed chin. Curls. The features were familiar. *Free from our reach. Our influence.*

Cold fear trickled into my veins, slowly turning me to ice. "No."

*Yes,* they hissed. *You know of whom we speak.*

I shook my head. I did know of whom they spoke; they spoke of Josef. But I wasn't going to give my brother up to the goblins.

*The changeling, mortal,* they said. *The one you freed with the power of a wish. We want it back. It has no place among you humans; it belongs down here. With us. With its kin, here in the Underground.*

"No."

*Yes,* they repeated.

"No!"

The hands tightened about me.

*We want it,* they said again. *It is rightfully ours. Bring it back, maiden. Bring it back.*

*It.* As though my baby brother were an animal. As though he didn't have a name, a life, a personhood. Josef might have been a changeling, but he was no less human than me, than Käthe, than all those who loved him.

"No," I choked out. "He does not belong to you."

*Nor does he belong to you.*

"No," I gasped. "Josef belongs to himself."

Those goblin hands squeezed tighter, and a sparkling blackness began to fill the corners of my vision. *Your love is a cage, mortal. Set him free.*

I laughed. It was lost amidst choking coughs as twining hands strangled the life from me, but I laughed nonetheless. I could no more stop loving Sepperl than I could stop the sun from rising each dawn.

*Your love is killing him.*

My laughs turned to sobs. Tears leaked from my eyes, scalding hot and salty. They tasted of my reluctance, my despair, but most of all, my love for the little changeling boy who stayed in the world above because he wanted to play music. Josef had died all those years ago, but my true brother, the brother of my heart, still lived. My tears dripped onto goblin hands, staining them with love.

A hiss of pain rose from them all, a collective susurrus like the sighing of branches in the wood. Multi-jointed fingers uncurled from my wrists, my arms, my waist, dropping me to the ground.

*It burns!* they cried. *It burns!*

Once released, I coughed and gulped down great gasps of air as all around me, echoes of *It burns! It burns!* blended with warnings of *Your love is killing him* into a symphony of discord.

I lay on my side, there on the floor of the dirty corridor, long after the goblin hands had disappeared. For although their voices had faded away, the damning words remained.

*Your love is killing him.*


I don't know how long I lay there, crushed beneath the crippling weight of my doubt.

*As long as you have a reason to love,* Thistle had said. Love kept the wheel of life turning. Love created bridges between worlds. If there was nothing else I had learned, I had learned that love was greater than the old laws.

But uncertainty crept over me on silent wings, whispering

in the changeling's voice: *None of us have lasted long in the world above.*

I might have lain there in the dust and dirt, save for my promise to the Goblin King. *There's a fire within you; keep it alight.* Move or die. If I could not walk, I would crawl. If I did not know the answers now, I would discover them later. While there was breath, there was time. I got to my feet.

And then, faintly, a violin began to play.

I closed my eyes. I had expected obstacles, physical trials to overcome, but the Underground knew to attack me where I was the most vulnerable: my heart.

*It's not Josef. It's not the Goblin King. It is a trick,* I chanted to myself. The mantra had saved me before, when Käthe and I trod these paths to fight our way back to the surface. But the words no longer possessed the power they once had and, almost against my will, my feet followed the sounds to a large cavern.

It was the ballroom. The ballroom that held the Goblin Ball, where the Goblin King and I had danced together for the first time. It was also the room where we had greeted our subjects as husband and wife. But it was empty now, no beautiful or otherworldly decorations, no banquet tables laid with bloody feasts. Yet in the center sat a quartet of musicians: a violinist, a keyboardist, a violoncellist, and a flautist.

The violoncellist and flautist held their instruments in their laps, their hands still. The other two were playing a slow, mournful piece, which I immediately recognized as the adagio from the Wedding Night Sonata. The violinist wore Josef's face, but no glamour could fool me; the changeling could imitate my brother's golden curls and delicate features, but he could never, ever recreate Josef's skill.

In the changeling's hands, my music was flat and uninspired. The notes thunked and thudded to the floor, carrying no emotion, no weight, no meaning. I had put so much of my frustration into this movement; the desire to go *faster*, go *further*, only to be met with denial at every turn. I had wanted the music to unsettle and agitate; instead it merely bored.

I ran forward to snatch my music off the stands, to take it back, when the violoncellist spoke.

"You waste your talent on this drivel."

I startled. *Papa.*

"I hear no genius in the notes, no inspiration in their arrangement. This should all be burned in the rubbish heap." He turned to me. "Ah, Liesl. Do you not agree?"

I closed my eyes. Papa was by turns autocratic and convivial, depending on how many drinks were in him. I could never guess which version of my father I would be facing, so I took care never to face him at all.

"Well?"

I tried to cling to those moments with the Goblin King when we had been both lost and found in my music. When we had both been transported by sound and rapture, when nothing else had existed outside the time we played together. But I could not hold them, as Papa and my doubt wrenched them from my fingers.

"No," I whispered. "No, I do not agree."

I could hear the scrape of the chair push back as the violoncellist stood to his feet. *A changeling,* I told myself. *It is a changeling. Not Papa. It can't be Papa.*

"No?" Papa's voice was closer now, and the stink of stale beer overwhelmed me. "What have I told you, Liesl?"

If I opened my eyes, if I looked my father in the eyes,

the illusion would be broken. I would see black goblin eyes in a human face, and *know* him for a changeling. But I couldn't open my eyes, couldn't face the possibility that it might not be true.

"You will never amount to anything."

I flinched, expecting the blow of a violin bow like a rod upon my skin. He had broken several bows that way, bent against our backs as punishment.

"You overreach yourself. Grow up and stop indulging in these romantic flights of fancy."

His voice seemed to come from the cracks, the nooks and crannies through which the wind from the world above whistled and wuthered. I tried to stand my ground, tried to push against the cruelty he wielded like a scythe, but I was shriveling, curling, drying up inside.

"Stand in the world above as you are, Elisabeth Vogler, and be judged as your father judged you: talentless, forgettable, worthless."

Elisabeth.

Papa never called me Elisabeth. Within our family I was always Liesl, occasionally Lisette, and sometimes even Bettina. But my father never called me by my full name; it was a name reserved for friends, acquaintances, and the Goblin King. It was a name for the woman I had claimed myself to be, not the girl I had been.

"Then let the world judge me as I am."

I opened my eyes. The changeling who wore Papa's face had done a good job of it; the ruddy cheeks, the sunken eyes, the patchy skin. But his face held a malice that my father never had, an intentional cruelty that could be wielded with precision. Papa was a blunt instrument, his blows made indiscriminate by drink.

"Stand aside," I said, "and let me pass."

The changeling smiled, and his features shifted. "As you wish, mortal," he said, giving me a sweeping bow. Then he snatched the Wedding Night Sonata from the stand, the sheets of paper written all in my own hand, and began to rip them apart.

"No!" I cried, but the flautist came to hold me, while the others joined the first in shredding my music to pieces. The changelings savaged my work, bits of paper floating and falling in the air like snow, settling in my hair, my eyes, my mouth, tasting of bitterness and betrayal.

So much lost. So much effort, all to ash. Those early works Papa had burned in retribution for burning Josef's face. The pieces I had written in secret, all sacrificed to gain entrance to the Underground and save my sister. And now this, my latest and possibly greatest, all gone, gone, gone.

I screamed and sobbed, but it was only after the last few notes had fallen to the floor that the changelings released me.

"No matter," said one cheerfully. "I'm sure you can re-create it, if you've the talent you claim."

Then they abandoned me in the empty cavernous ball-room, the echoes of their spiteful laughter ringing in my ears.


I arrived at the shores of the Underground lake.

I had been stripped of everything—my confidence, my esteem, my music—but still I forced myself onward. They could take everything else away from me, but I had myself, entire. Elisabeth was more than the woman who bore the name, more than the notes she produced, more than the people who defined her. I was filled with myself, for they could not take my soul.

I glanced about. I had come to an unfamiliar shore, and could see no barge or skiff to bear me across. I stared across the great black expanse. Its glassy surface seemed deceptively calm, but beneath those obsidian depths, danger lurked.

The Lorelei.

As though called by my thoughts, glistening shapes rippled beneath the water. I squared my shoulders. I had come this far. I had faced the goblins. I had faced the changelings. I would face the Lorelei. If I could not row across, then I would swim.

There was no way through but down.

I took a step into the lake and gasped when the water touched my skin. It was cold; colder than ice, colder than winter, colder than despair.

The Lorelei swam closer, drawn to my presence like pikes scenting blood. One by one, they emerged, breaking free of the glassy black in a shower of glowing droplets.

They were so, so beautiful. Beautiful in the way the Goblin King was beautiful, a relentless symmetry to their features that was both alluring and terrifying. They were as naked as newborn babes, but their voluptuous, feminine shapes seemed molded by a hand that did not understand their function. So perfect, so flawless, nary a dimple or nipple or hair to betray any hint of humanity. Their flat black eyes focused on me, and they moved toward me with sinuous, flowing grace.

I was up to my waist in the water now. The closest Lorelei reached out with her hands, and my arms lifted of their own volition to meet hers. She smiled, row upon row of prickly teeth, and moved in to press that jagged grin against my skin.

The others swam close, fanning out around me, encircling me, entrapping me. Their hands stroked my face, my hair, my limbs, my waist. I was numb but I felt their fluttering touches slide up between the valley of my thighs, the ridge of my spine where it met the curve of my backside, the underside of my breasts. My body, so like theirs and not. One tangled her fingers in my hair, undoing the plaits I habitually wore in a coronet about my head, letting the dark locks fall into the water. The weight of my hair dragged me down like an anchor.

I don't know when it happened, but suddenly, it was no longer my feet taking me farther and farther into oblivion. I was being pulled, dragged, coerced, caught in an undertow I had not sensed. I stopped, but the current around me was irresistible, and I began to struggle.

The Lorelei hissed, and the serenity surrounding us was shattered. They grabbed at whatever part of me they could reach, my chemise, my belly, my toes, my hair. They grabbed, and dragged.

I was submerged in darkness, broken only by wavering ripples of light as we disturbed the surface of the lake. I fought and kicked and clawed, but the Lorelei only bore down harder. The gleaming, glowing surface of the lake was growing farther and farther from reach. My aching lungs hitched, screaming for air they did not have.

But no. If I were to drown, then I would take as many as I could with me. I would not go quietly into the long darkness. I had not come so far to give up. I would go with fire and fanfare and a fight.

I grabbed at the Lorelei whose arms were locked about

my waist. Her head was the closest to mine, and I wrapped my fingers in her hair, jerking her face hard toward mine. I did not know what I intended—to bite, to tear—but my lips found hers and I opened my mouth to the end.

A breath passed from her to me, and my lungs seized upon the air. Hot, humid, and moist, but air nonetheless.

And then it wasn't the Lorelei with her arms about me, it was me clinging to her. She thrashed in my embrace, but I held on, Menelaus against Proteus, and I was the King of Sparta. With every kiss I stole, I drew another bit of breath, until at last the Lorelei returned me to the surface.

I broke through the water with a choking gasp, and I broke through alone. The Lorelei had vanished, but I was now caught in the grip of something just as terrifying: the rushing current.

"Help!" I called, but my cry was lost in the watery, gurgling rattle of my chest. "Help!"

But no one came.

I was tired, so tired, I could scarce keep my head above the water. But I would not succumb to fatigue. I had escaped near drowning by the Lorelei. I would escape this. The water battered and bashed me against hidden rocks, but despite the growing darkness in my head, despite the utter exhaustion in my body, I kept swimming. I kept breathing.

At last, the river slowed to a gentle crawl, a burbling brook that gave way to a still pond. The water pushed me against a rocky shore, and with a herculean effort, I managed to clamber out of the river, heedless of the cuts and scrapes and bruises on my body. I collapsed, coughing and retching, water running from my nose and mouth, still shimmering, still glowing, but tinged red with blood.

When I had coughed up the last of the water, I sat up.

The world reeled, turning both black and sparkling at the edges.

*Stay awake,* I ordered myself. *Stay alive.*

I took a shuffling step forward, but if the mind was willing, the flesh was still weak. Darkness crashed down on me, and I remembered no more.

# IMMORTAL
# BELOVED

lisabeth."

A gentle hand shook me awake. I stirred and groaned, retching up the last bits of lake water from my lungs. In the blurry darkness, I could make out a long, lanky figure, with a shock of silver-white hair around his head like a mane.

My lips shaped a name before I remembered I did not know it.

*"Mein—mein Herr?"*

"Yes," the Goblin King said softly. "I am here."

"H—how?" I croaked.

"You may not have had *Der Erlkönig's* protection as you walked the Underground," he said, a smile in his voice. "But you always had mine."

He held out his hand and I took it. Slowly, painfully, I got to my feet. I was aching all over, bruised and battered in more than just my body.

Above us, the same gap in the earth and tree I had crawled through to break the old laws the last time I came here. I was tired, so tired, but I forced myself to climb the ladder of roots and rock to the surface. The Goblin King supported me, encouraged me, helped me, until at last, I tumbled onto the forest floor of the threshold.

The world above was blue, the deep indigo of predawn. The starry veil of the night sky still held reign, but soon it would be gone, hidden by the rising sun. Already the darkness was lightening to purple, and the shadows were beginning to retreat.

I turned to face the Goblin King. He wore a soft expression and held a leather portfolio in his hands. Without another word, he took two steps forward and gave it to me.

"What is this?"

His only response was a smile. With shaking hands, I undid the ties that held it shut and opened it to find scores upon scores of music. I did not recognize the hand, but I recognized the composer. Me. It was my music, copied out in his hand. All of my music, the unfinished Wedding Night Sonata as well as the pieces I had sacrificed to gain entrance to the Underground.

"They're all there," he said softly. "All your compositions."

"But," I choked out. "They were destroyed."

"Oh, Elisabeth," he said. "Did you truly think they had been lost? I treasured your music as much as you. I kept it safe. I remembered each and every little thing you ever wrote; after all, had you not played them for me your entire life?" He chuckled. "Did I not say that I was a copyist once?"

Tears fell from my face to stain the paper in my hands. I closed the portfolio to save me from ruining his labor of love.

"You played them for me; now you should go play them for the rest of the world. Finish the Wedding Night Sonata, Elisabeth. Finish it for us."

"I will write it for you," I whispered. "For my immortal beloved."

It was close, so close to what I wanted to tell him. *I love you,* I insisted, but my lips would not comply.

"Play it for me," he said. "Play for me, my dear, and I will hear it. No matter where you go. No matter where I am. I swear it. I swear it, Elisabeth."

A name came to my lips. I tried to lift my hand, to hold it against his cheek, to tell him I loved him.

"Will I see you again?" I whispered.

"No," he said. "I think—I think it is better that way."

Even though I had expected it, his refusal still struck me like a blow. But perhaps he was being cruel to be kind. We would never again truly *be* together, would never again feel the touch of each other's hands upon our bodies. Not even in the thresholds of the world, where the Underground bled into the world above. I had had all of him. I had tasted all of him. To see but to never touch . . . I would be a woman in the desert, forever thirsting for water she could see but never reach.

"Are you ready?" he asked.

No. But I would never be ready. This day and the day after next and the day after that would be full of unknowns, full of uncertainty. And I would face each one as I was, Elisabeth, entire.

"Yes."

He gave me a nod, more a gesture of respect than agreement. "Then," he said. "The whole wide world awaits you."

I walked to the edge of the Goblin Grove. I placed my hands against the barrier, invisible yet tangible. Taking a deep breath, I steeled myself to push through. I stepped past the barrier, and into the forest beyond.

For a moment, I stood there, beyond the edge of the Goblin Grove. The air, warm and mild, did not change, did not grow cold. I had crossed the threshold, and there was no going back. And yet, still I lingered, unwilling to go, unable to stay.

"If—if I could find a way to free you," I whispered, "would you walk the world above with me?"

My back was to the Goblin King; I could not face him. It was a long time before he answered.

"Oh, Elisabeth," he said. "I would go anywhere with you."

I turned around. His eyes deepened in color and for a moment, just for the merest glimpse, I could see what he would have been like as a mortal man. If he had been allowed to live the course of his life, from the child he had been to the man he would have become. A musician—a violinist. I ran back into the circle of alder trees, wanting the circle of his arms around me. I reached out my hands, and his fingers brushed mine, but we passed through each other like water, like a mirage. We were each nothing but a shimmering illusion, a candle flame we could not hold.

And yet, the Goblin King was still here, in the Goblin Grove, with me. He stood in the Underground while I stood in the world above, but our hearts beat within the same space.

"Don't look back," he said.

I nodded. *I love you,* I wanted to say. But I knew those words would break me.

"Elisabeth."

The Goblin King was smiling. Not the pointed smile of the Lord of Mischief or *Der Erlkönig,* but a crooked one. Twisted to one side, lopsided and goofy, it cracked my heart open and I bled inside.

He mouthed a word at me. A name. "You've always had it, Elisabeth," he said softly. "For it is to you I gave my soul."

His soul. I held my music—our music—to my heart. We were sundered forever, never to be with the other again. The grief shattered me, broke me into sharp, jagged pieces. I wanted the touch of his hand, for my austere young man to put me back together, scarred but whole.

But I was already whole. I was Elisabeth, entire, even if I was Elisabeth, alone. The knowledge of it gave me strength.

I straightened my shoulders. The Goblin King and I held each other's gazes for the last time. I would not look back. I would not regret. He smiled at me and pressed his fingers to his lips in farewell.

Then I turned and walked away, into the world above, and into the dawn.

*Ever Thine,*
*Ever Mine,*
*Ever Ours.*

—LUDWIG VAN BEETHOVEN,
the *Immortal Beloved Letters*

To Franz Josef Johannes Gottlieb Vogler,
care of Master Antonius
Paris

My dearest Sepperl,

My heart, my love, my right hand, I have not abandoned
you. It is true your letters did not reach me, but it is not
because you've offended or because I've left you. No, mein
Brüderchen, your letters did not reach me because I was
unreachable, because I was gone.

You have undertaken a journey, and so have I: a journey
far beyond and just beneath the Goblin Grove. It is a tale
full of magic and enchantment, such as Constanze might have
told us when we were children, only it is true. Only it is real.
Do my stories have a happy ending? You must tell me, for I
cannot decide.

I thank you for the news of your gala performance of my
little bagatelle and its reception. I pray you do not reveal
its true authorship quite yet, despite how popular you claim
it's become. Strange to think of elegant, sophisticated Paris
enamored with the works of a queer, unlovely little girl, and
I can't imagine what they would say when the composer of
<u>Der Erlkönig</u> revealed herself as Maria Elisabeth Vogler, the
daughter of innkeepers.

I would rather not imagine. I would rather see it for myself.

Käthe talks of nothing but publication now, especially after seeing the fee you sent her after selling the print rights to <u>Der Erlkönig</u>. She has taken it upon herself to meet with Herr Klopstock, the traveling impresario, to learn all she can about managing musicians, but I think it is Herr Klopstock's brown eyes that intrigue our sister more than the details of the work. She misses you. We all miss you.

As for your other request . . . stay, Sepp. Stay in Paris with Master Antonius, with François. There is no need to come home, no need, for I shall send you a piece of it.

Enclosed are some pages from a sonata I have written, although the last movement is still unfinished. I send it to you with my love, and a leaf from the Goblin Grove. Tell me what you think, and then tell me what the world thinks, for I think it is my best yet, my most honest and my most true.

Yours always,
Composer of <u>Der Erlkönig</u>

# A GUIDE TO
# NAMES AND TITLES

CONSTANZE—*Kohn-STANTS-eh*

DER ERLKÖNIG—*Dere ERRL-keu-nikh*

ELISABETH—*Eh-LEE-za-bet*

JOSEF—*YO-sef*

KÄTHE—*KEI-teh*

LIESL—*LEE-sul*

MAHIEU—*MAY-yew*

MEIN HERR—*mine Hehrr*

SEPPERL—*SEPP-url*

# A GUIDE TO
# GERMAN PHRASES

AUF WIEDERSEHEN—*owf VEE-der-zayn*—Until we meet again

DANKE—*DAHN-keh*—Thank you

FRÄULEIN—*FROI-line*—Miss, maiden, a form of address

GROSCHEN—*GROH-shen*—A unit of currency

HÖDEKIN—*HU-deh-kin*—A sort of sprite, similar to the British brownie or pixie

KAPELLMEISTER—*Kah-PELL-mai-ster*—The highest position in a nobleman's orchestra, the person responsible for finding and producing new music and directing productions, as well as conducting and playing

LÄNDLER—*LEND-ler*—A folk dance

**MEIN BRÜDERCHEN**—*mine BREW-der-khen*—My little brother

**VIEL GLÜCK**—*VEEL GLYOOK*—Good luck

**ZWEIFACHER**—*ZVAI-fahkh-er*—A folk dance

# A GUIDE TO
# MUSICAL TERMS

ADAGIO—A tempo marking meaning a piece should be played slowly

BASSO CONTINUO—The bass line or accompaniment to the melody in a piece

CHACONNE—A short composition, often with a repetitive bass line, used as a vehicle for variation; can also be a sort of warm-up or exercise for a musician

CONCERTO—A piece of music written for a solo instrument to be accompanied by an orchestra

DESCRESCENDO—A musical term indicating that the phrase should be played with increasing softness

ÉCOSSAISE—Originally a Scottish dance, a short, lively piece that accompanies a social dance (like a waltz)

ÉTUDE—A short musical composition written for a solo instrument, usually of considerable difficulty in order to practice various technical skills

FERMATA—A musical notation indicating a note should be held longer than its usual duration

F-HOLES—The holes on the body of a violin, shaped like the letter *f*

FORTEPIANO—A precursor to the modern piano

GLISSANDO—A musical notation indicating that there should be a glide from one note to another

KLAVIER—A general term for an instrument with a keyboard

LARGO—A tempo marking indicating a piece should be played very slowly

OSTINATO—A repeating musical phrase

PIZZICATO—A playing style that involves plucking the strings with fingers instead of bowing

PRESTO—A tempo marking indicating a piece should be played very quickly

RITARDANDO—A change in tempo indicating a gradual slowing down

SCORDATURA—The tuning of a stringed instrument differently from its standard tuning, e.g., a violin is tuned to G-D-A-E; the scordatura referenced in *Wintersong* is the retuning of the strings to G-G-D-D

SONATA—A musical composition written to be played (as opposed to sung), the definition and form of which has changed over the years

SONATINEN—The plural of sonatina, or "little (short)" sonatas

SOTTO VOCE—Not actually a musical term, but it means the dropping of one's voice for emphasis

VIOLONCELLO—The precursor to the cello

S. Jae-Jones (called JJ) is an artist, an adrenaline junkie, and erstwhile editrix. When not obsessing over books, she can be found jumping out of perfectly good airplanes, cohosting the *Pub(lishing) Crawl* podcast, or playing dress-up. Born and raised in Los Angeles, she now lives in North Carolina, as well as many other places on the internet, including Twitter, Tumblr, Facebook, Instagram, and her blog

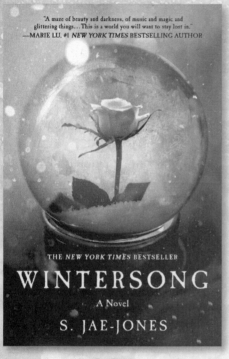